When
Women
Were
Warriors

The strong, supple prose on display in all three novels, the intelligence of the plotting, and the skillfully varied pacing make this a standout trilogy — highly recommended.

— from a review by The Historical Novel Society

★ ★ ★ ★ ★   In Book II, Tamras moved from her home into the lands beyond its border. In Book three, the stage widens further: she deals with the struggles of whole peoples. Caught up in intrigues that would once have been far above her, the heroine risks everything unless she can not only learn to swim in treacherous waters, but to master them. The heroine's inner journey continues to match her outer one. She must confront the meaning not only of personal love, but the love that extends beyond oneself and those we hold dear. Catherine Wilson's skill at tackling the big issues of love, meaning, and humanity is so deft that it all seemed, to me at least, to flow naturally from her narrative in a way I found technically quite breathtaking....

—from a review by Charles Ferguson, *Goodreads*

★ ★ ★ ★ ★   Being the third and last volume in a series I enjoyed immensely, I knew that I could expect this last book to deliver a happy and satisfying ending. What I didn't expect was the intricate and daring storyline of this last volume. It is bigger and broader than what has come before, and it is spectacular. This book takes up where the last left off but instead of merely working out the story conflicts already apparent, this time the story unfolds on to a whole new level. More characters, more intrigue, greater losses, wonderful reunions.... There's no taking the easy road here—the story opened up into unimagined dimensions to tell a tale that really is that of a hero.

An incredibly captivating story, *When Women Were Warriors* manages to blend mythic storytelling with characters who feel so real you could imagine stepping into the pages and having a conversation with them. *A Hero's Tale* skilfully weaves the questions of love, faith and fairness into a dramatic story; not only of a relationship between the main characters, but of a quest so much bigger it takes the breath away. There is everything you could wish for here — power struggles, forces for good and evil, dramatic tests of faith, daring rescues, fatal rivalry, but it is managed with such a deft hand that in the end it is all one beautiful story.

What else is there to say? This is not just lesbian fiction, but a story about being human.

—from a review by Kate Genet, *Kissed By Venus*

ALSO BY CATHERINE M. WILSON

WHEN WOMEN WERE WARRIORS
BOOK I
THE WARRIOR'S PATH

WHEN WOMEN WERE WARRIORS
BOOK II
A JOURNEY OF THE HEART

WHEN WOMEN WERE WARRIORS

BOOK III
A HERO'S TALE

CATHERINE M. WILSON

SHIELD MAIDEN PRESS
BOULDER CREEK, CALIFORNIA

Publisher's Cataloging-in-Publication
(Provided by Quality Books, Inc.)

    Wilson, Catherine M., 1944-
      When women were warriors / Catherine M. Wilson.
      v. cm.
      CONTENTS: bk. 1. The warrior's path -- bk. 2. A
    journey of the heart -- bk. 3. A hero's tale.
      LCCN 2008901689
      ISBN-13: 978-0-9815636-1-9 (bk. 1)
      ISBN-10: 0-9815636-1-9 (bk. 1)
      ISBN-13: 978-0-9815636-2-6 (bk. 2)
      ISBN-10: 0-9815636-2-7 (bk. 2)
      ISBN-13: 978-0-9815636-3-3 (bk. 3)
      ISBN-10: 0-9815636-3-5 (bk. 3)

      1. Women heroes--Fiction. 2. Lesbians--Fiction.
    3. British Isles--Antiquities--Fiction. 4. Feminist
    fiction. I. Title. II. Title: Warrior's path.
    III. Title: Journey of the heart. IV. Title: Hero's tale.

    PS3623.I57785W44 2008   813'.6
        QBI08-600093

Library of Congress Control Number: 2008901689
ISBN-10: 0-9815636-3-5
ISBN-13: 978-0-9815636-3-3

Cover photo by Donna Trifilo

Published by Shield Maiden Press
P. O. Box 963
Boulder Creek, CA 95006-0963
www.shieldmaidenpress.com

For my mother

Acknowledgements

Many people offered advice, support, and encouragement during the "quite some time" it took to finish this project.

It is an extraordinary piece of luck for a writer to find someone who is willing to discuss a work in progress, someone who can enter the world of the story and gossip about the characters as if they were real people, who will question their motivations, scrutinize their actions, complain when they step out of character, and cast a light on a side of them their creator may have missed — someone who will take the work as seriously as the author does. For me that person is my friend and editor, Donna Trifilo, who, in addition to all of the above, pushed me through the hard times.

To everyone who was willing to read a work in progress, sometimes more than once, I offer my gratitude and the assurance that everything they had to say about it mattered.

Susan Strouse helped me overcome a major stumbling block at a crucial turning point. Lisa Liel, whose enthusiasm for the story rekindled my own enthusiasm, showed me how I could take a good idea and make it better. Ann Thryft's considerable knowledge of the time, place, and culture deepened my own understanding of the story and its characters. Jo Trifilo's insightful comments and careful critique gave me a new perspective on the story.

In ways too numerous to mention, significant contributions were also made by Jen Davis-Kay, Katherine Gilmartin, Rebecca Hall, Rob Field, Carmen Carter, Kate Maynard, the late Dr. Susan Barnes, Judi Miller, Jack Contento, Ru Emerson, the members of my first writers' group— Morgan Van Dyke, Barbara Murray, Cooper Gallegos, Sandralee Watters, Marlene Michaelson, Rebecca Morn, and Eileen Thompson—who suffered through my early attempts to get my story started, and Heather Rose Jones, who helped me find my characters' names.

And many thanks to George Derby and Marissa Holm for keeping me well fed.

CONTENTS

CONTENTS

A Visit

Maara's voice intruded on my dreams. I heard her mumble something about visitors.

"Wake up," she whispered into my ear. "Don't show surprise or fear. Treat them as you would treat a guest at home."

I opened my eyes and looked up at her. While she waited for me to understand, she held me firmly against her side, to keep me still. When she saw that I was awake and in control of myself, she let go of me and sat up.

By the pale light that sifted in through the cracks in the tree trunk, I made out the figures of half a dozen people sitting only a few feet away from us across the fire. They were dressed in furs from head to foot and were so small I thought they must be children until I saw their faces.

"Don't stare," said Maara.

She uncovered a few coals that still glowed under the ashes and fed them twigs and kindling. Soon she had a bright fire burning.

All the while our visitors watched us in silence. I couldn't keep from glancing at them out of the corner of my eye.

At last I whispered to Maara, "Who are they?"

"The forest people," she said.

"The old ones?"

She nodded. "Hand me the water skin."

When I sat up, I was aware of my nakedness. After I handed Maara the water skin, I looked around for my shirt, only to discover that several of the forest people were sitting on our clothing. Maara was naked too and didn't seem concerned about it, so I resisted the urge to cover myself. Maara filled our copper pot with water and set it to boil.

One of the forest people spoke. Her words were incomprehensible to me, but her voice was lovely, melodious and sweet. She spoke only a few words, then gazed at Maara, as if she expected an answer. Maara stared back at the woman, on her face an expression of delight. I was about to ask her if she had understood, when she spoke two or three words in the same incomprehensible tongue.

There was a moment of silence. Then all the forest people spoke at once, until the woman who had spoken first made them be quiet. She turned back to Maara and began to speak again. This time she made quite a long speech, and I took the opportunity to observe her more closely. She appeared to be the oldest person there. Her wrinkled face was dark. Wisps of black hair streaked with grey escaped from under a white fur hood that covered her head and shoulders. She wore fur leggings under a long skirt of deerskin and a cape of rabbit fur around her shoulders.

When she finished speaking, I whispered to Maara, "Did you understand what she said?"

"Some of it," she replied.

Maara thought for a little while before making her reply. Although she spoke awkwardly, the woman nodded that she understood.

Steam began to rise from the pot of water. I assumed that Maara had intended to make some tea. While I rummaged through our things looking for my package of herbs, I listened to the halting conversation. When I heard Maara speak her name, then my own, I looked up.

"Aamah," the woman said, and pointed to herself. She named the others too, but I couldn't keep the strange sounds in my head.

I took the pot of water from the fire and crumbled into it some chamomile. The fragrance of the flowers rose into the air. The forest people seemed to find it pleasant. When the tea had steeped for a few minutes, Maara offered it, first to Aamah, then to the others.

"Hand me the oat flour," said Maara.

"How much?" I asked her. We had very little left.

"All of it," she said.

With the last of our oat flour, Maara made oat cakes. While we ate, the forest people spoke softly among themselves. All of them were beardless, and I listened closely, trying to discover which were women and which were men, but they all had the same high, sweet voices. Soon my curiosity was satisfied. The heat of the fire and the crowd of people inside the tree made it uncomfortably warm, and the forest people threw off some of their clothing. Only Aamah wore a garment I would have called a shirt, although it was made, not of cloth, but of deerskin. The rest were naked under their fur tunics. Two of them were men. One sat beside Aamah and appeared to be advising her. The other was no more than a boy. All of the forest people were thin, light-boned, with their ribs showing.

Their clothing was cleverly made. They didn't have the ragged look of the men who had been prisoners in Merin's house. I saw no weapons among them other than the knives at their belts. Some wore carved tokens of wood or bone. At first their faces all looked much the same to me, but as I looked longer I began to see how each one was unique.

When I compared them to Maara, I saw both similarities and differences. Maara was bigger than the forest people, taller and more strongly built. Their skin was darker than hers, and there was a difference around the eyes, but I saw in them the people she had come from.

There were enough oat cakes for everyone to eat their fill and still leave a few left over. Maara wrapped them in a cloth and handed them to Aamah, who fingered the cloth and smiled. I believe she valued the cloth more highly than the oat cakes.

The others were becoming restless, but Aamah gave no sign that she was ready to leave us. She reached across the fire and touched Maara's cheek, turning Maara's face first to one side, then the other. Then she coiled a lock of Maara's hair around her finger. Maara submitted patiently to Aamah's curiosity. When Aamah spoke to her again, it was both a question and a command.

Maara settled herself and took a deep breath before she began to speak. Her speech seemed a bit more fluent than before, though she often groped for words and made up for the ones she didn't know with gestures. She spoke my name several times and pointed toward the south and east, where we had come from. Aamah asked an occasional question, but most of the time she was content to listen.

Something Maara said made the forest people giggle and whisper among themselves. Aamah hushed them with a sharp rebuke.

I couldn't contain my curiosity.

"Why are they laughing?" I whispered.

"They say I speak as a child speaks," Maara said.

"You were a child, when you spoke as they do."

"Oh," said Maara.

Again she spoke to Aamah, and I had an idea that she was telling her what I had said. Aamah nodded solemnly. Then she turned and spoke to the man who sat next to her. They conversed for several minutes, loudly enough for Maara to hear, although she pretended not to listen. At last they seemed to come to a decision. Aamah took a token, a piece of carved bone, from a pouch she carried on her belt and handed it to Maara. Then, as silently as they had come, the forest people left us. I turned to Maara, eager to learn what she and Aamah had talked about.

"She made us welcome," Maara said.

"Then we can stay?"

She nodded.

"What did she say?" I asked her. "What did you say?"

"She told me a little about her people, and she asked me about mine, as if she might have known the people I came from. What concerned her most of all, though, was why we're here."

"What did you tell her?"

"I told her the truth."

"You told her we were outlaws?"

"No," she said. "I told her that you are heir to a powerful house and that your enemies tried to kill you."

I would never have thought to put it like that. "That makes me sound like the hero of a story," I said.

"You are."

An icy finger touched the back of my neck. I was afraid to ask her what she meant. I thought about all the tales I'd heard of heroes. Were they once just ordinary people? Were they once just like me?

"Aamah agrees with me that no one from Elen's house is likely to come here in wintertime," Maara said. "Sometimes hunters will come, but the people of Elen's house stay away from the forest this time of year."

Again the icy finger touched me. "Why?"

"The forest frightens them. Old memories grow strong in wintertime."

As soon as she put it into words, I recognized my own feeling about the forest. This place that had at first felt so unfamiliar, now seemed more like a forgotten memory of childhood. Fragments of old stories hung in the branches overhead and told themselves in the sound of rustling leaves. Echoes of ancient songs murmured in the music of falling water. Childhood fears haunted my dreams.

"In a day or two, we'll return their visit," said Maara.

I brought myself back into the present moment. "Where do they live?"

"Their winter camp isn't far from where we were yesterday."

"Is that how they knew we were here?"

Maara chuckled. "They knew we were here from the moment we set foot in the forest."

"How many of them are there?"

"I have no idea."

"Is Aamah their leader?"

"She's their mother," Maara said. "Aamah means mother."

I took it to be a symbolic title rather than a literal one. Surely Aamah hadn't given birth to all of them.

Maara gazed at the carved bone, Aamah's gift, turning it over and over in her fingers. She frowned, as she watched the pieces of a puzzle fall together in her mind.

"I once thought Aamah was my mother's name," she said.

I wondered then if childhood memories were haunting Maara too.

"Was your mother one of the forest people?"

Maara shook her head. "We lived in a village. We were farmers."

"You speak the same language."

"Similar, but not the same."

"But you understood Aamah, and you made yourself understood."

"Yes." She smiled. "I don't know how I remembered so much of the old speech. I haven't spoken it or heard it spoken since I was a child."

"You speak it to me sometimes," I told her.

"I do?"

I nodded.

"I don't remember."

"You speak it when you're troubled," I said. "And when we make love."

The memory struck us both at once. When our eyes met, I forgot all about the forest people. My body longed for her so intensely that I feared I might burst out of my own skin without her arms around me.

I held out my hand to her. "Come lie with me," I said.

She didn't hesitate. We lay down and let our bodies entwine themselves together. I closed my eyes and felt myself slip back into the darkness where I had found her the night before. Now if I opened my eyes there would be daylight and firelight. I had seen her so clearly in the dark. Would the light reveal or hide her? I opened my eyes.

I had forgotten how beautiful she was. My gaze fell first on her cheek, covered with the softest down. Her lips were slightly parted, as if they were waiting for a kiss. At the base of her throat, the blood beat beneath the tender skin.

The curve of her breast seduced my eyes. I laid my cheek against it. Its roundness fit perfectly against the palm of my hand. To my tongue her skin tasted sweet and salt together. I heard my kiss release her breath.

"Show me what pleases you," I whispered.

"Your touch pleases me," she said.

It was sweet to hear.

I leaned up on one elbow and smiled down at her. I couldn't resist teasing her a little. "You leave me no choice but to discover the answer for myself."

Maara tried not to smile. "Do you intend to spend all day in bed?"

"Is there anything we need to do today?"

"I suppose not," she said. "Nothing that won't wait."

"Is there something else you would prefer to do?"

A little color came into her cheek. "No," she said.

I could have spent half the day just looking at her. I was not unfamiliar with her body. I had so often bathed her, dressed her and undressed her. We had swum together in the river and sunbathed on the riverbank. While I had always thought her beautiful, I had never seen her quite like this. Before we were intimate with each other, her nakedness had been clothed in a veil of courtesy. Now my eyes had permission to enjoy her beauty. Not my eyes only, but my hands and my mouth admired her.

Her body was no longer shy with me. She welcomed each new touch. When her muscles tightened, they did so, not to protect her, but to express her pleasure. I still found a few tender places. I didn't avoid them. I touched them with tenderness and with great care, to teach them not to be afraid.

I took my time with her, both for her pleasure and for my own. I delighted in discovering how best to please her. Sometimes I caught her watching me, smiling a mysterious smile, as if she had a secret she was about to share.

As her desire grew, she closed her eyes. When she raised one knee, I took it as a sign that she wanted a more intimate touch, but when my fingers lightly brushed the curls between her legs and caressed the inside of her thigh, I felt the first hint of resistance in her.

"What shall I do?" I whispered.

With a touch of her fingertips, she turned my face to hers. Her mouth invited my kiss. We kissed until my own desire almost overcame my resolve to wait for her. At last she turned me so that I lay beside her.

"Touch me," she said.

As our knowledge of the world comes through the body, so too does the evidence of love. My heart's longing flowed from my lips in words and kisses, flowed through my body as I held her and through my fingers as they caressed her. Her body accepted the pleasure I gave her, and it was pleasure that opened the way for love to enter.

She put her hand over mine, to hold me still.

"I don't want this to end," she said.

"It never will," I told her.

And she slipped easily over the edge.

I woke late in the afternoon. Maara lay beside me sound asleep, one arm across my body, her breath warming my shoulder. The fire was almost out. Even under my heavy cloak, I was not quite warm enough, but I didn't feel like moving. My body was peaceful with satisfied desire, and the gentle glow of joy filled my heart.

Twilight drifted in through the smoky air. While I waited for Maara to wake, I amused myself by looking for meaning in the patterns of light and shadow overhead, as one might look for meaning in the shapes of clouds. Fantastic figures emerged from the texture of the wood—here a goblin face, there the furry body of an animal.

The more I looked, the more I saw, and as I watched, the figures seemed to move, tumbling over and around each other, until they became one living tapestry. I saw, not whole figures, but bits and pieces, resolve themselves, then disappear—the clawed foot of a hunting cat, a fin, a fish's scales, leaf shapes and flowers, a bird's wing, squirrels' tails. The tree itself was telling me a story, was telling me that everything that lives arises only for a moment out of a great sea of life before falling back into it again.

"Hush," said Maara.

I opened my eyes.

Maara brushed the tears from my cheeks. "You were dreaming."

The memory of my dream was still vivid, and as I told it to her, Maara grew thoughtful.

"Did the dream frighten you?" she asked.

"No," I told her. "It was beautiful."

She smiled at me. "I think you must be one of us at heart."

Before I could ask her what she meant, she looked up at the fading light and said, "We need to collect firewood before night falls."

When I got up, I saw a large bundle, tied with a rope of twisted vines, set just inside the fissure in the tree trunk. The knot looked so complicated that I would have cut it, but Maara pulled at one loose strand and it came undone. She unfolded the entire hide of an elk, with the elk's thick winter coat still on it. It was lined with soft deerskin, and another deerskin fell out of the bundle.

"The forest people have given us a proper bed," said Maara.

She handed me our cloaks, laid the deerskin down in place of them, and spread the elk hide over it. Then I noticed a covered basket in the shadows by the doorway. When I took the cover off, I saw that it was filled with something that resembled coarsely ground grain. I handed it to Maara, and she tasted it.

"Acorn meal," she said.

She held the basket out to me. I took a pinch of the meal and tried it. It was bland, with a faint nutty aftertaste.

"It makes a good mush," said Maara. "Bread too. My mother used to make a dough of it, roll it into balls, and bake them in the ashes of the fire."

"The forest people brought us gifts?"

Maara nodded. "When we make our visit, we'll take them something."

We had so little, I couldn't think of anything we had that we could spare, but Maara seemed confident that we would find something worthy of the wealth they'd given us.

❧❧

By the time we had gathered enough firewood for the night, it was almost dark. For supper we made a stew of venison and wild onions. Maara tried her hand at making acorn bread. She kneaded the dough and shaped the loaves as if she had done it all her life, and the bread turned out very well. We dipped it into the broth of the stew to soften the crust. It was delicious.

After supper Maara set me the task of braiding creepers into a stout cord for making snares, while she wove a fish trap out of hazel wands. As we worked, I thought about the forest people and wondered what they thought of us inhabiting their sacred tree. I hoped they didn't see us as intruders.

"Do you think we're really welcome here?" I asked Maara.

"Yes," she replied. "I didn't expect we would ever see the forest people. That they have befriended us is more than I could have hoped for."

I remembered my anxiety for Maara and my fear that we would be discovered, and I surprised myself by questioning the forest people's good intentions. Although I didn't like to doubt them, I had to ask, "They won't betray us, will they?"

"Betray us?"

"To Elen's house."

Maara shook her head. "The people of Elen's house see the forest people so seldom that many doubt their existence, and Elen's house has nothing they want. The forest people want only to be left alone, and the less Elen's people are aware of them, the better."

I was reassured, but her reply piqued my curiosity. "If they wouldn't show themselves to Elen's people, why did they show themselves to us?"

Maara gazed at me as if I should have understood.

"They showed themselves to you," I said, "because you're like them."

With a slight nod of her head, she agreed with me. She continued to gaze at me in a way that made me uncomfortable. As I looked at her, her face changed, just a little, but enough to make me feel that I was looking at a stranger. For the first time she was not just Maara, not the unique person I knew, the person who was like no one else. She was of another tribe, another people, whose ways I didn't know, who spoke a tongue I didn't understand. I was the stranger here.

"What if they don't accept me?"

"They will."

Suddenly I felt very much alone, and my imagination began to run away with me. Was there a Vintel among the forest people?

Maara took my hand. "They will accept you now because you belong to me," she said, "and soon enough they'll accept you for yourself."

Because we had slept so long that day, we sat up late. When we tired of our chores, we huddled close to the fire and talked a little. For Maara the smell of acorn bread must have opened a door into memory, because she began to tell me little things about her childhood home—about round houses with the fire in the center, bitter berries that left an aftertaste of honey, a man who used to play with her by hiding so that she could find him.

As I listened, I found it impossible to shake off the lonely feeling that came over me when I realized Maara had people here, while I had none. When there were just the two of us, I hadn't felt lonely at all. Now, for no reason I understood, the presence of other people had put a distance between me and Maara. Maara felt it too.

"What's wrong?" she asked me.

I shook my head. I couldn't put my feelings into words.

"Are you afraid?"

"A little," I admitted.

"Of the forest people?"

In a way I was, but not in the way she was thinking of. "I'm afraid you'll belong more to them than to me."

Maara smiled. "Don't be silly."

Her teasing only made me feel worse. A tear trickled down my cheek.

"You're homesick," she said.

She offered me no easy promises that I would see my home again or that I would someday feel at home in this strange place. She put her arms around me and let me weep against her shoulder for a while. Then, with a mother's tenderness, she undressed me and put me into bed, where we lay awake for hours, sharing our memories of childhood.

THE FOREST PEOPLE

T he next day we returned the visit of the forest people. We had stayed up so late the night before that we overslept a bit. While I made breakfast, Maara washed our dirty shirts, then hung them near the fire to dry. I knew without her saying so that they would be our gift to Aamah.

We followed the brook to the bathing rock and continued up the steep hillside. The forest canopy was thinner here, and a dense growth of holly and brambles grew beneath it. The only way through the tangle was a deer path that wound around the hilltop.

Maara, who was always so quiet, now began to make a great deal of noise. She scuffed her way through piles of brittle leaves and spoke to me out loud, careless of being overheard. Suddenly she stopped and spoke a word of greeting in the language of the forest people. I couldn't imagine who she was speaking to. The woman's clothing blended so perfectly into the colors of the forest that I didn't see her until she moved. When she approached us, I recognized her as one of the women who had been our guest the day before.

The woman smiled and spoke a few words of welcome, then led us up the path a short distance before ducking through a curtain of vines into what appeared to be an impenetrable thicket. We would never have found our way through it without a guide. The faintest of paths led us over obstacles of deadfall and through briars that tugged at our clothing, until we arrived at a bramble wall so tangled that we could go no farther. Our guide grasped one of the stout canes and pulled, and the bramble wall began to move. The gate had been so cleverly concealed that I thought for a moment I was a witness to magic. We stepped through the gate into the winter encampment of the forest people.

The camp lay inside a large enclosure. On three sides we were surrounded by the bramble wall. On the fourth, the rocky hillside loomed over us, too steep to climb. All around us was evidence of much activity. A deer carcass hung from a scaffold, ready for butchering. Inside a long shed, built against the bramble wall and open on three sides, people were busy at their chores. In the center of the enclosure, several people were gathered around a fire pit. No one seemed surprised to see us.

Our guide led us to the fire and invited us to sit down. Someone offered Maara a tightly woven basket, black with soot. Maara dipped her fingers into it and drew out a sticky glob of porridge, which she ate with appropriate noises of appreciation. When they offered the basket to me, I did likewise.

We began to draw a crowd. Soon a score of women and men had joined us around the fire. Half a dozen children peered out at us from behind their elders, who were just as curious but less inclined to show it, although their quick glances took us in from head to toe. Maara greeted the forest people in their own language and repeated our names several times. Hers gave them no trouble, but their tongues tripped over mine until they settled on something that sounded like Tamara.

After a while, Maara asked for Aamah, and the forest people escorted us to the shed. Its roof was made of skins stretched over a pole framework and was so low that I could barely stand upright under it. Maara had to stoop to enter. The children laughed at her, and she laughed with them.

In a cozy corner, behind a wattle screen, a small fire was burning. Aamah sat beside it. Next to her sat the man who had been with her the day before. Aamah made us welcome at her fire, and the rest of the forest people settled themselves nearby. Again words of greeting were exchanged and food was offered. Aamah handed each of us a spit with strips of roasted meat skewered on it.

We were both full of porridge, but we ate enough to be polite. Then Maara offered our gift to Aamah, who accepted our woolen shirts with unconcealed delight, unfolding and admiring them before passing them along for the others to admire. The children touched them cautiously, as if they found the shirts mysterious and a little frightening. Their elders must have seen woven cloth before, although they seemed to have no means of making it themselves.

Maara spoke with Aamah for a little while, repeating enough of their conversation to me so that I could follow it. They spoke at length about the coming of winter. Over the last few days the weather had warmed a bit, but Aamah seemed to think that more snow was on the way. She also gave Maara some advice on where to set out our snares and fish traps.

When others joined in the conversation, Maara grew quiet, content to listen. I lost interest in listening to talk I couldn't understand, and my eyes began to wander. There was a lot to look at. This was where the work of the community was done, where meat was smoked and hides were cured, where acorns were husked and soaked and ground into meal. Here reeds were woven into baskets and stone was worked for tools and weapons, but it was clear that no one slept here, nor would they find the open shed comfortable in bad weather. I saw no other shelter within the enclosure. Perhaps their sleeping quarters were as hidden as the village itself.

The man sitting beside Aamah began to speak. From the way he first settled himself and from his tone of voice, I knew he was about to tell a story. The children, who had been playing nearby, sat down to listen. Maara smiled in anticipation. Then, to my surprise, she moved behind me and pulled me back against her. The storyteller paused often to make noises and gestures to illustrate his tale, and Maara took each opportunity to whisper the story in my ear.

Honey Paw is very thin. Sleepy and bad-tempered, he blinks at the sun. The bees are hard at work among the flowers. Honey Paw follows them home. He satisfies his hunger, and the bees begin again.

Four Legs walks a great distance. Berries grow where only he can find them. Long Claw digs out the rotten hearts of trees and eats the grubs he finds there. Yellow Tooth gnaws on bones of elk and deer.

Fur Man is fat. His winter coat is thick. His great head grows heavy. He shelters in his cave and sleeps.

While I was trying to understand the meaning of the story, the children all began to shout at once, "Urti. Urti."

"Bear," Maara whispered in my ear.

"Oh," I said. "It's a riddle."
But the storyteller hadn't finished.

She-bear has lost her cub.
"He left the den too soon," she says. "He wandered too far."
Beside her hearth fire, she waits through the night for his return.
In the morning, she-bear goes out to find him. She looks in the forests, in the meadows, in the streams. She looks everywhere. She searches drifts of fallen leaves. She searches every cave and hollow tree. She searches everywhere.
She asks the squirrel, the beaver, the hunting cat, "Have you seen him?"
She asks the fish, the bird, the grasshopper, "Have you seen him?"
She asks everyone she meets. No one has seen him.
Night falls. In the branches of a tree, old mother Owl unfolds her wings.
"Old mother owl," says she-bear, "where is my son?"
Old mother Owl takes wing. Silently she ascends into the sky, high over she-bear's head. She-bear follows her with her eyes.
There in the sky, she-bear sees her son, on his back, lying in a field of stars. Then she knows that her son has met his death, and in her sorrow, she seeks her den and falls into the long sleep of grief.
Old mother Owl is sorry for she-bear's sorrow. Old mother Owl flies to the body of she-bear's son and plucks his spirit from his mouth. Old mother Owl flies to she-bear's den and sends his spirit into his mother's heart.
In the spring, she-bear wakes with her cub beside her.

The story filled me with sadness. A tear trickled down my cheek and drew Aamah's eye. Aamah spoke to Maara, and Maara said, "She wants to know what made you cry."
I had no ready answer. I shook my head. Maara answered for me.
"What did you say?" I asked her.
"I told her that your mother too has lost her cub," she said.
Aamah smiled at me and spoke to me directly.
"She will send old mother Owl to your mother's heart," said Maara.

We left the village of the forest people so late in the afternoon that we didn't arrive home until after dark. Neither of us was hungry. The forest people had fed us until we couldn't take another bite. We huddled under our cloaks while we waited for our fire to warm the hollow tree.

Although my body was tired, my mind was wide awake, full of all the things I had seen and heard that day. I had spent the homeward journey thinking about the story of she-bear and her cub. I understood its meaning. It was a tale for teaching children about the bear stars.

As everyone knows, the bear travels in a circle in the northern sky, completing one circle in the course of the year. At summer's end, the bear lies on his back, a sign that winter is coming. The story also taught something of the ways of bears.

When I was small, my mother told me animal stories to teach me about the world. Each story was the answer to a question. How did the bobcat lose her tail? How did the hare get his white winter coat?

I was a little disappointed.

"Is the story of she-bear only a tale for teaching children?" I asked Maara.

"If it were," she said, "would it have made you cry?"

Then I remembered her reply to Aamah. The story of she-bear was also a story about motherhood.

"Are our mothers searching for us, do you think?"

"I hope not," said Maara. "I hope they're both safe at home, but I think their hearts must be searching for some news of us."

As I drifted into sleep that night, I dreamed of old mother Owl. She flew into the heavens and touched the stars. She flew all night on silent wings. She heard the prayers of she-bear and answered them. She heard Aamah's prayers and answered them. She heard the love in every mother's heart and brought their children home to them.

The next day was cold and dark, and we had work to do before bad weather kept us at home. In the morning we followed the brook downstream, looking for a place to put our fish trap. On the way back, we set our snares. We spent all afternoon collecting firewood. It was fortunate we did, because that night, as Aamah had predicted, snow fell.

For the next few days we stayed snug and safe in our hollow tree. To pass the time, Maara repeated the story of she-bear, a few words at a time, first in the language of the forest people, then in my own tongue. I learned the strange words more easily than I thought I would. At least I learned to recognize the sound of them. Making many of those sounds myself was more than I could do. Maara tried not to laugh at me.

After our visit to their village, I had no more anxiety about the forest people. My experience there convinced me that they had kind hearts. None of them seemed to doubt our good intentions. I felt that they accepted us, not just as neighbors, but as friends. Even the children lost their fear of us. One little girl laid her head in my lap and fell asleep and neither knew nor cared that a few hours before I had been a stranger. Now I was ashamed that I'd had doubts about them, because most often it is the trusting who are trustworthy.

After the snowfall, the forest people came to visit us again. Nearly a dozen of them crowded into our hollow tree. I was disappointed to see that Aamah wasn't with them. This time the man who usually stayed by Aamah's side, the storyteller, whose name was Sett, appeared to be their leader. They had brought us a shoulder of venison, which we cooked and shared with them. While we waited for the meat, we offered our guests some tea and acorn bread.

Once we had eaten everyone relaxed and a general conversation began. I didn't understand a word of it, but I found it soothing. It reminded me of when I was a child, listening to the grown-ups talk. Although I couldn't always follow what they were saying, the threads of their conversation wove themselves together into a tight fabric around me, and if the sharp words of some tore it a little here and there, the mending threads of others drew us all together again. So the forest people's talk surrounded me, until at last I drifted off to sleep leaning against Maara's shoulder.

For several weeks, weather permitting, we exchanged visits with the forest people, and when we could, Maara and I returned their generosity. Even the gift of a few fish pleased them, although they could easily have caught all the fish they needed for themselves. While fish seemed to me a more practical gift, they greatly prized our woolen shirts, not for their usefulness, but for their novelty. Aamah had shared them out by tearing them to pieces, so that everyone could have a few strips of cloth. Some wore the strips tied around their wrists or ankles or as headbands, while others braided them into their hair.

I soon discovered why the forest people had no use for woolen clothing. Whenever we traveled to their village, brambles would tug my cloak from around my shoulders and tear holes in my heavy woolen trousers, scratching the skin underneath, while the forest people, in their fur tunics and deerskin trousers, glided through the thickets unhindered and unscathed.

I envied the forest people their sturdy clothing for its warmth as well. In stormy weather and at night, they retreated into a cave in the rocky hillside behind their camp, but they preferred living in the open. As long as daylight lasted, they sat around the central fire in the enclosure or, if snow was falling, around Aamah's fire in the covered shed. While Maara and I were seldom warm enough, even wrapped up in our cloaks, they didn't seem to mind the cold at all.

The forest people always had work of some kind to do, but they were never too busy to spend an afternoon with us sitting around the fire. They were fond of conversation and could spend hour after hour talking and telling stories. Although they never seemed to tire of hearing tales they must have heard a hundred times before, they took even more delight in hearing something new. They asked Maara endless questions about who we were and where we'd come from. Maara did her best to answer them. Her once halting speech became more fluent every day. Her tongue had not forgotten how to make the sounds of its first language, and what she didn't know, the forest people were glad to teach her.

While they always treated me with courtesy and kindness, the forest people seldom spoke to me directly. If I failed to understand their gestures, they might speak to me through Maara, but for the most part they ignored me. In general conversation Maara tried to make me feel included by repeating some of what was said so that I could understand it, and she continued teaching me in private, as she had taught me the story of she-bear.

I began to listen closely to the forest people's talk. As the days went by, I caught more and more words I understood. Sometimes I could put together for myself a little of their meaning. My ear was learning to attune itself to the strange sounds the forest people made, but my ear proved more clever than my tongue. Their simplest words felt awkward in my mouth, and I was too shy to try speaking to them.

Then one day Maara taught me to say a simple greeting. She made me repeat it endlessly, until my tongue had grown accustomed to it. When they heard me try to speak as they did, the forest people were delighted. They responded by telling me the names of everything they could find to point to and waiting for me to repeat the words after them. They were relentless. Maara finally had to rescue me. Later that afternoon, as we sat around their fire, I heard one of the women whisper something to Maara while tapping the side of her head in a gesture I understood. I didn't need Maara to tell me that the forest people had thought me feeble-minded.

Because their lives were so different from my own, I listened fascinated to everything the forest people talked about. Most of all I loved their stories. Almost all of them started with a riddle. It was a clever way to capture the attention of the children, who were delighted with themselves when they shouted out the answer, although they must have heard each riddle many times. The stories themselves were simple. Each one taught a lesson about the world, about the ways of animals, about which plants were good to eat, which bore fruit, when and where to find them, and what could be learned about the weather and the seasons from the lives of plants and animals, and from the night sky.

As simple as they were, I found the stories strangely moving. Beneath the surface lay a meaning that touched my heart, although it took my head a while to find it. Almost without exception, the heroes of the stories were animals, yet all the strengths and foibles of humankind were there, in the fierceness of the badger and the wild pig's stubborn pride, in the suspicious nature of the hunting cat and the mother-love of bears. All their favorite story characters wore a human face, like the squirrel whose scolding chatter brought back the memory of an ill-tempered woman who used to frighten me when I was small. It gave me a sense of satisfaction to laugh at the memory of that old woman's silly squirrelish face, and I enjoyed even my own rueful laughter when a story showed me an unflattering image of myself.

One day when we were visiting the forest people, we overstayed our time. It had been a gloomy day, and before we knew it, dusk had fallen. Aamah insisted that we stay the night.

As the darkness grew, all the fires in the enclosure were put out. The forest people were careful to keep their presence hidden, even when no stranger could be near enough to see their firelight reflected off the cloudy sky.

For the first time, Maara and I entered the cave where the forest people slept. The cave mouth was well hidden. A fracture in the rock, so low and so narrow that we had to slip through it on our hands and knees, opened into a large cavern. Far above our heads I heard a distant moaning sound that might have been the wind echoing in the cavern's rocky vault.

Inside the cave the air was still and smelled of damp. Someone made a fire, which drew in a draft of clean, cold air. A sudden gust sent showers of sparks upward into the dark. Around the fire pit, skins and furs covered the earthen floor. When we sat down, the forest people gave us robes to put around our shoulders while we waited for the fire's warmth to take the chill out of the air.

No one spoke until Aamah crumbled a handful of dry leaves into the flames, making a thick smoke that smelled of cedar, and murmured words that ascended with the smoke to the ears of gods I didn't know. Then, in voices soft enough not to echo, the forest people resumed their conversation.

After the children had been put to bed, the grown-ups sat around the fire for several hours more. For a time their talk was light-hearted. Then someone told a story, a tale darker than I'd heard from them before, about a hunter lost in a land of dreams. The story put them in a somber mood. After the story ended, there was an uneasy silence, as if the forest people knew that the time had come to speak of something disturbing.

Sett began by saying, "Where were they today?"

One of the men answered him, and others added to his story.

Although I caught a few words and phrases, I couldn't quite follow their meaning, but their furrowed brows and worried voices told me that this conversation wasn't for the ears of children.

"Is there trouble of some kind?" I whispered to Maara.

"There are strangers in the forest," she replied.

"People from Elen's house?"

"Perhaps." She touched a finger to my lips to keep me quiet, so that she could listen.

Unlike Merin's council of old women, who could spend all day talking about nothing, the forest people seemed to want to have their serious discussion over with as quickly as possible. Sett listened to what everyone had to say, then thought for a little while before speaking a few words to each one. Then the forest people rose and went to bed.

Maara and I followed their example and crept naked into the bed they offered us. The news of strangers worried me. I was full of questions, but before I could whisper even one of them, Maara put her arms around me. For a long time, being close to her was all I could think about. The love I felt for her made me feel strong, while her love for me made me feel safe. Soon I slept.

The children woke us. They must have been up long enough to grow impatient with waiting for their elders to wake up. I was reminded of the many mornings of my own childhood when I would play almost quietly enough not to wake the sleeping household.

The fire was out. The only light inside the cave came from a little daylight that found its way through fissures in the rock. Two ghostly figures all in white cavorted by the cave entrance. I rubbed my eyes. Then I saw that they were children. Each was wearing one of our shirts. I glanced around me, looking for the rest of our clothing. Every stitch was gone. One boy wore my trousers wrapped around his shoulders, while another wore Maara's on his head, with the legs trailing along behind him like a train. Our tunics were nowhere to be seen.

We still had our cloaks. We had spread them out under us, to keep us from the cold floor. Our fur leggings lay where we had left them, and Maara found our boots, which the children had used to scoop cold ashes from the fire pit. We shook the ashes out and put them on, and wrapped our cloaks around our naked bodies. Then we joined the others, who were gathering around the fire.

No one scolded the children for taking our clothing or tried to take it from them to give back to us. One of the women found a couple of fur tunics for us to put on. Mine covered me fairly well, but Maara's ended above her waist, so that she had to wear her cloak wrapped around her like a skirt.

We breakfasted inside the cave. When I went outdoors to relieve myself, I saw why the forest people hadn't yet gone outside. A heavy snow was falling. The wind drove it under the hood of my cloak and down my neck, and it lay in drifts so deep that my knees above my leggings were soon blue with cold.

When I went back inside, Maara was standing naked, surrounded by the women, while the men watched and gave advice. Beside her lay a pile of furs and deerskins. One woman held a deerskin up to Maara's waist, while another wrapped it around her thigh and marked it with a bit of charcoal.

All afternoon we stayed inside, while the women made Maara a complete suit of clothing. In only a few hours they had made her a pair of deerskin trousers, decorated with clay beads colored blue and black and baked hard in the fire. By the end of the day, they had made her a tunic of rabbit fur, greyish-brown in color, with bits of red squirrel worked in for decoration. I thought she looked quite splendid.

We stayed with the forest people for several days. By the time we left for home, both of us had new clothes—trousers of soft deerskin, leggings that covered our legs to above the knee, long-sleeved fur tunics, and fur caps with flaps that turned down over our ears. To replace our heavy boots they made us moccasins of elk hide lined with fur. We would have been satisfied with our own cloaks, but the forest people insisted on making us capes of deerskin, tanned with the hair on it to repel the rain and snow.

My new clothes felt strange to me at first. Instead of the scratchy wool that I was used to, the forest people's clothing felt like a second skin, so much so that I could almost believe I wasn't wearing clothes at all, except that I was warm. No cold air leaked in, even at the seams, and they were a delight to travel in. Bramble thickets let me pass. Falling snow caught in the fur of my cap as in an animal's pelt and was easily shaken out before it melted and trickled down my neck. I felt like a creature of the forest as we made our way home, silent and invisible in animal guise.

65

The Hunt

As much as I enjoyed the company of the forest people, I was glad to come home again to our hollow tree. I missed spending time alone with Maara, and for a week, while snow continued to fall, I had her undivided attention. Her conversations with the forest people had awakened memory, and she told me more stories of her childhood. She even spoke a little of her time in Elen's house, although those memories were more painful. When we ran out of things to talk about, we lay in each other's arms and let our bodies speak of love.

Sometimes I felt her thoughts stray from me, and I knew what she was thinking.

"You miss them," I said to her one day, when I caught her gazing at the entrance of our hollow tree as if she awaited visitors.

She admitted that she did.

I surprised myself by saying, "I miss them too."

Not only did I miss the forest people. I missed what I saw in Maara when we were with them. When she was the center of their attention, she seemed half pleased and half shy, as if having the attention of others was something new to her, which I suppose it was. I missed watching her in conversation and in banter too quick for me to follow. I missed seeing her unguarded, as I had never seen her in company before. I surprised myself again by suggesting that perhaps we should spend the winter in the village of the forest people.

Maara nodded, as if she had already thought of it.

"Would we be welcome?"

"Aamah has dropped a hint or two," said Maara. "I think it would be wise. We endanger them whenever we travel back and forth."

It was true. We risked being seen by strangers, and we had begun to wear a path between our home and theirs. Maara's other reasons I let her keep to herself.

⟨⟩

The next morning we took up our packs and left our hollow tree. I felt a bit nostalgic about leaving our cozy home. On an impulse, without Maara knowing, I left something of myself behind. I slipped one of my arrowheads from my pouch and left it in the crevice where I had found the offering of the forest people.

Not far from the forest people's village we came upon the fresh tracks of a family of deer. Beside them were the pawprints of a wolf. Maara knelt to examine the tracks. At the same time, out of the corner of my eye, I caught a glimpse of something moving through the trees. When I turned my head to see what it was, there was nothing there. I felt the hair rise on the back of my neck.

Slowly, careful not to make a sound, Maara slipped her pack from her shoulders and set it down. Then she relieved me of mine. She made a sign to me to take out my bow and string it.

Another movement caught my eye. This time I thought I knew what it was, and all my childhood fears blew like a cold wind through my heart.

"Wolves," I whispered to Maara.

"No," she whispered back. "Men."

My fear of wolves yielded to a fear of something yet more dangerous.

"Strangers?"

"No."

Before I could say more, she put her finger to her lips and drew an arrow from my quiver. When I offered her the bow, she shook her head. She handed me the arrow, then fastened the quiver to my belt.

Maara gestured to me to stay close behind her, as she followed the tracks into the forest, moving with a stealthy gait that was faster than a walk, yet not quite a run. I imitated her as best I could, and for once I moved as quietly as she did. The moccasins cushioned my step. In my new clothing, I was as silent as an animal in its skin.

As we traveled farther from the brook, the trees closed in around us. The shade was so deep that even the snow-covered ground failed to lighten the gloom. What little light entered here hung in mist that baffled the eye.

On either side of us, others were moving through the trees. Their ghostly figures drifted at the edges of my vision. Whether they were wolves or men, I couldn't tell. In the snow and mist, their coats of silver-grey disguised their form, but more than once I imagined I caught sight of a pricked ear, a snarl of teeth, a gleaming eye.

Maara stopped and crouched down beside a tree. Against the trunk, in her cap and tunic of mottled greys and browns, she was almost invisible. She motioned me down beside her.

Some distance ahead of us I heard the sounds of the hunt, of the pursued and the pursuers, running through the forest. Too late now for the deer, in peril of their lives, to stand silent in a thicket while the hunters passed them by. Too late now for the hunters to stalk their prey in silence, to take them unawares. Some of the hunters must have lain in ambush, because the deer had been turned back and now ran toward us.

Closer they came, and closer still. The sounds of their flight, muffled by the snow and mist, deceived my ears, making me believe they were farther from us than they were. A doe flew by us, so swiftly that I had no time to nock an arrow. Next, the stag rushed past, and this time I was ready. I loosed my arrow. At the same moment two more arrows flew. Mine sailed over the stag's back, but the others found their mark. One struck the stag's flank. The other found its way between the ribs, behind the shoulder.

The stag ran a few steps, then stopped and stood, stiff-legged, his tongue protruding from his mouth, his hot breath white as the mist, then red with his heart's blood. Still he stood, defiant.

A grey shape sprang up from the snowy ground. Its jaws closed on the stag's throat and dragged him to his knees. Another wolf sprang out of the mist and took hold of the stag's hind leg. Together the two wolves brought him down.

Another form leaped up, a wolf that ran on its hind legs for several steps before it transformed itself into a man. He ran to where the wolves held the stag, still living, and cut its throat. Blood spilled into the snow, and the man scooped up a handful and tasted it. Two more men emerged from their hiding places and ran to join him.

Now I could make some sense of what I'd seen. Each man wore, over his ordinary clothing, the entire pelt of a wolf. The head, complete with ears and eyes and teeth, covered their heads like a cap, while the forelegs dangled down over their shoulders and the long tails trailed behind them in the snow.

The men paid no attention to the wolves, who had dropped to their bellies and slunk away when the men approached. Wielding knives and axes, the hunters went to work on the carcass, while the wolves waited, watching the men through narrowed eyes. More wolves, still panting from the chase, joined their fellows, until I had counted eight of them.

I stared at the scene before me, hardly able to believe my eyes. The men opened the stag's belly and spilled its organs out, and the wolves rushed in and tore the mess to pieces. The men dragged the carcass a little distance away and began to butcher it.

While the wolves fed, the wolf-clad men skinned and dismembered the stag. One man took up the skin and antlered head. Another motioned to Maara and me to come and help carry the meat. We took with us both hindquarters, the ribs of one side, and a shoulder. We could have carried more, but we left a generous portion for the wolves.

Maara and I had to take the long way home, so that we could fetch our packs. When we arrived at the village, everyone was waiting for us. Women relieved us of the meat we carried. The hunters, still wolf-clad, motioned us to join them where they were resting by the central fire.

Sett came to greet us and handed me the arrow that had missed its mark. One of the hunters must have found it and brought it back. I should have looked for it myself, but in the excitement of the hunt, I had forgotten all about it.

"What is this?" Sett asked me. "A hunter wishing?"

I turned to Maara for an explanation.

Maara answered for me. "A hunter," she said.

Sett smiled. "She needs to wish."

Before I could ask him what he meant, he turned away and went to sit with the three hunters by the fire.

"Even when I understand the words, I don't know what they mean," I mumbled to myself in my own language.

Maara laughed. "I think he means you need more practice."

As we settled ourselves by the fire, I whispered to Maara, "Ask them about the wolves."

Before she could speak, one of the hunters said, "My brother called me in a dream. He called me to the hunt. I woke my brothers, and we went together."

Soon the other two joined in telling the story of the hunt. They all spoke at once, so quickly and with such enthusiasm that I had trouble following what they were saying. Since I had witnessed the hunt myself, I had more success reading their gestures. Little by little the story came together in my mind. I had thought at first that when the hunter spoke of his brothers he meant the men who had hunted with him, but I came to understand that at least some of the time he was speaking of the wolves. It was the wolves who had trailed the deer by following their scent, who had run ahead and turned them back. The hunters had only to follow the chase and wait. Then the wolves had waited for the hunters to wound the stag, so that they could bring it down with little to fear from the stag's hooves and antlers.

"Do you always hunt with wolves?" I asked, when I could get a word in edgewise.

"Not always," said one of the hunters. "Sometimes they call us."

"Or sometimes we call them," said another.

"Why do you speak of the wolves as your brothers?"

"They are our brothers," said the first man, as if that explained everything.

"Did you kill your brother, you who wear his skin?" said Maara.

The hunter laughed. "Sometimes brothers fight," he said.

I had been nodding for some time, leaning against Maara's shoulder and listening with half an ear to the conversation and storytelling that went on in the evenings inside the cave. Usually, after one last story, everyone got up and went to bed, but this night only the women left the fire, while the men stayed where they were. When Maara and I started to get up, Sett motioned to us to stay.

"Let's talk together," was all he said.

I thought they might be having second thoughts about our staying in the village, but we were there at Aamah's invitation, and Aamah had gone with the other women to her bed. Whatever Sett wished to talk about, it was something that concerned the men alone. He talked with the others for a little while, in low tones that Maara pretended not to hear. Then he turned to me and spoke. I understood the words for brother and for hunting and that he was asking me a question, but I couldn't put it all together.

"Sett asks if you wish to learn the hunting magic of the forest people," said Maara.

"Hunting magic?"

"I don't know how else to say it," she said. "All the hunters here are men, but it may sometimes happen that a woman who has not yet borne a child will ask them for their secrets. They have seen for themselves that you are skilled with the bow. They will teach you, if you ask."

The idea of learning the forest people's secret lore filled me with excitement, but before I gave my answer, I wanted the blessing of my first teacher.

"What shall I do?" I asked her.

Maara saw my eagerness and smiled at me. "Never miss an opportunity to learn something new."

I turned to Sett and said in my own language, "I would be honored to learn the hunting magic of the forest people."

"She said yes," said Maara.

When I was to learn to hunt was a mystery. Once I had given my consent, everyone rose and went to bed, and nothing more was said about it. It was three days later, at the first glimpse of the new moon, when they surprised me.

The men came for me in the middle of the night. They took me naked from my bed, from the warmth of Maara's arms, and carried me outdoors. They set me down by the cold ashes of the central fire and wrapped me in a robe. Still I shivered, more from excitement and from fear than from the cold.

I looked for Maara, but she hadn't followed me. Already I missed her reassuring presence. And how would I understand the men without her to explain the meaning of their words? Even as my mind was considering the question, I knew the answer. There would be no words spoken to me this night. This was a thing beyond words, a teaching and a testing, all at once.

Above me the sky was clear, alive with stars. Like distant fires, they winked and twinkled in the winter sky. They cast an eerie light on the frosty ground and on a dozen men clad in wolfskins. They were the color of frost, of winter mist, of snow and ice. They were the wolves in their winter coats, and then I understood that this kind of hunting, this brotherhood of wolves and men, was something that happens only in the dark time of the year, the starving time.

One of the hunters put into my hands a wooden bowl, a steaming bowl of tea. I huddled over it to warm myself. The man lifted it to my lips, and I drank. The tea was so bitter I almost spit it out. Once I had swallowed a few sips of it, the drink warmed me from within.

The men in their wolfskins sat down around the central fire pit. The air was freezing, but no one lit a fire. Wolves fear fire.

A noise began, a low, murmuring noise, a humming, growling noise. Although it seemed to come from nowhere, or from everywhere at once, it had to be coming from the men. They were sitting cross-legged around the circle. The forelegs of their wolfskins fell over their shoulders. The men leaned forward, until the wolves' paws touched the ground. The men bowed their heads, so that I couldn't see their faces. They showed me instead the faces of the wolves.

The wolves' black eyes twinkled with starlight. Their ears pricked forward, as they listened to the chant. The wolves had called a council, and I was sitting there among them. I blinked and saw that they were men, but a moment later they were wolves again.

One of them stood up and began to move around the circle. He stood on two legs like a man, but bent over, so that the shape of his body took on the likeness of a wolf. He was a wolf too in the way he moved, as he stalked, low to the ground, freezing in mid-step when his quarry raised its head to look for danger. Twice around the circle went the stalking wolf before he stopped and glanced around. He looked with curiosity at the other wolves, as if something had changed and he couldn't discover what it was.

Then he saw me. He approached me, doing a stiff-legged dance, as if inviting me to play or perhaps to fight. He stopped in front of me and gazed into my eyes. He raised his muzzle to the night sky, and I expected to hear him howl, but from under the wolf's face, Sett's face appeared. Sett the storyteller, who could speak with the voices of the animals, who could transform himself into each animal as he told its story, Sett grinned at me with a wolf's grin. He crouched down before me on all fours, then leaped up and bounded over my head and ran away into the shadows.

Another man stood up and moved around the circle, as he too transformed himself into the animal whose skin he wore. Another followed him, and then another, until all of them had joined the dance. I watched them stalk each other, now crouching, now leaping, as they ran and fought and played together, and after a time I could not have said if they were wolves or men.

Suddenly the wolves stopped where they were, and their heads all turned together. I turned my head in time to see a stag step out of the shadows. Holding his proud antlers high, he came toward us, one step at a time, cautious and courageous. The wolves began to stalk him. From time to time the stag stopped and sniffed the air, and the wolves crouched down and watched him. When he dropped his head as if to graze, the wolves crept closer, until he caught a glimpse of them and leaped away.

The wolves pursued him, but the stag was unafraid. The closer they came, the less he minded them. Among the wolves he danced, and no wolf touched him. Like children who play at life before they have to live it, the hunters and the hunted played at life and death. They made life and death into a dance.

Without knowing I had done it, I stood up. Wearing only my own skin, I joined the dance. As the fish who swims in icy water doesn't feel the cold, as the bird perched on an icy bough doesn't feel the cold, no more did I feel the cold, I who was only life in a different form.

It seemed that the dance went on forever, yet I was sorry when it ended. The stag lifted his antlered head from his shoulders and set it down, and Sett emerged from his disguise. The wolves stood up like men, although they kept their wolfskins on. I stood among them, not knowing which form I took, though I was neither man nor wolf, not yet.

Sett led us out of the enclosure and into the wild wood. Unseen creatures watched us pass. I felt their eyes. Sett led us around the hilltop and up a narrow path that ended at a pile of tumbled rock. With the help of two others, he moved one of the rocks aside to reveal among the shadows a deeper shadow. One by one the hunters vanished into it. I was the last to enter. The passage was so narrow that I could feel the rock on either side, and in places the rock above me was so low I could barely raise my head. Sometimes on our bellies, sometimes on hands and knees, we crawled and crept into the mountain's heart. There was no light at all.

The men pulled me from the passage into a larger chamber and helped me to sit up. My eyes were blind. By the sound of their breathing and the warmth of their bodies on my naked skin, my mind formed a picture of them sitting in a circle all around me. I waited for what would happen next, but no one moved or spoke. I heard only a roaring in my ears, as may happen in small spaces where no sound is.

After a timeless time, someone struck a spark. It fell into dry tinder and smoldered there, sending up a curl of sweet-smelling smoke. The man breathed on it until it grew into a flame. With it he lit the wick of a stone lamp.

As my eyes became accustomed to the light, I looked around me. The passage we had come through may have been made by human hands, but the cavern where we sat was not. The rock beneath us was smooth, as if water had once flowed over it, but the rock above was rough and craggy. I felt its great weight, not many feet above my head.

I looked up. Swirls and patterns, patches of color, red and brown, streaks and smears of charcoal, covered the rock. I leaned back to get a better look, and what I saw so astonished me that I lost my balance and toppled over backward. Someone's hands broke my fall and laid me gently down.

I gazed up at the animals. Red cattle with long, sharp horns ran across the cave roof from end to end. Among them ran antelope and deer. They ran, not as if they fled from danger, but for the simple joy of running. I saw stags with branched antlers, goat-like animals with long horns that curved over their backs, as well as animals so strange they could never have existed, the kinds of animals we see in dreams. One had the body of a boar, his tail like a boar's tail waving in the air, but he had two horns on his face, one between his eyes and the other on the end of his nose. Another resembled a cow, but was bearded like a goat, with tiny horns, and a great hump on his back covered with curly hair. Most beautiful were the horses. Although I had never seen one, my people remembered them in stories, and they looked much as I'd imagined them, with their long curving necks, rounded bellies and rounded rumps, black legs, black noses, and tails of long black hair, their bodies multicolored, red and brown and dappled yellow.

The painted rock brought to mind the wall of painted shields in Merin's great hall. By firelight their animal devices seemed to come alive, as if by invoking their courage and their strength, we had invited the spirits of the animals to join us by our hearth fire. The shields became, not instruments of war, but relics of our past, and now above me I saw the world they came from.

Around me the men began to chant, not the wolf chant this time, but the steady rhythm of running animals. Several of them tapped on the rock with sticks, making a sound like running hooves. Although I knew it was impossible, the animals began to move. On my bare skin I felt the wind of their passing. They ran and ran until I became so dizzy I had to close my eyes. Then I felt them all around me. They teased my spirit from my body, making me run with them, until I was as fleet of foot as they, as stout of body, as strong of limb, and as wild as they were wild.

I woke with only Sett beside me. He helped me to sit up and said, "Tamara, he is a brother of the animals, the same."

I understood.

66

Men and Women

When I emerged from the narrow passage, a faint light shone in the eastern sky. Sett wrapped me in a robe, and together we returned to the village. It was too early for anyone to be up, but when we entered the cave where the people slept, the fire was already lit. Three women sat beside it.

My eyes met Maara's first. I smiled when I saw her pride in me. Aamah sat beside her. Next to Aamah was a young woman whose name was Daani. She stood up and came to meet me. She had a bundle in her hands. As she approached me, she shook it out. It was a wolfskin.

"Mine," she said. "Now yours."

I hesitated, not knowing how to accept such a valuable gift or if to refuse it would be impolite. She thrust it toward me again, insisting that I take it.

"Why?" I asked her.

In answer she smiled and rubbed her belly, which had begun to swell with her first child.

Although I was neither cold nor hungry, Maara made me sit close to the fire while she fed me venison and acorn mush. Then she put me to bed. Even as I protested that I wasn't sleepy, I fell into the land of dreams.

A fortnight passed, and I had not yet been called to the hunt. I looked forward to it with both eagerness and apprehension.

I knew Maara would not go with me. When I had once suggested that she too might ask to learn the hunting magic of the forest people, she shook her head.

"This is for you," she said.

I couldn't persuade her to make more clear to me what she meant. Nor would she allow me to share with her what the men had shown me. Whenever I tried to speak to her about it, she put her finger on my lips and refused to hear me.

I didn't speak the forest people's language well enough to talk to the men about it. Even if I could have made them understand my questions, I doubt they would have satisfied my curiosity, but they seemed to know what I was feeling, and they would smile at me as if to say, "Be patient."

One thing Maara did try to explain to me. I thought at first it was my own ignorance of their language, but it seemed that sometimes the forest people spoke of me as he and at other times as she.

"Hunters are men," said Maara.

"If I'm a hunter, am I no longer a woman?"

"A woman is always a woman."

"How can I be both?"

Maara sighed. "Tamara, he is a hunter. Tamras, she is a woman."

I didn't find this explanation very helpful.

"Men and women are different," said Aamah, when I asked her the same question. She spoke to me as patiently as she would have spoken to a child, and with so much kindness that I could not take offense.

All the same, I didn't want her to think that I was ignorant of something so obvious.

"I know there are differences," I told her. "My people tell lots of stories about the differences between men and women." I smiled, remembering a few of them. "Some of them are quite funny."

Aamah smiled back at me. "We tell those stories too."

Someone called me out of a sound sleep. It was almost morning, but still too dark to go outside and much too cold to get out of bed until someone else had made a fire. The hunter who came for me saw that I was awake and waiting.

"Good," he said. "You hear."

When I left Maara's arms, she didn't wake, or perhaps she was pretending. She turned over and pulled the elk robe over her head. Four men, wolf-clad, waited by the cave entrance. The man who had come to wake me joined them. They talked quietly together while I hurried into my clothing. When I picked up my wolfskin, one of them gestured to me to come to him, and he helped me put it on. It fit as snug as a cap over my head, with straps concealed by the wolf's forelegs that went over my shoulders and a belt that tied around my waist. I fastened my quiver to the belt and strung my bow.

The men took up their weapons. Two of them had bows, but I was surprised to see that the other three carried spears. I had seen hunting spears in the armory in Merin's house, although few there hunted anymore. They were lighter than the spears used in war, light enough for throwing. The spears the forest people carried were short, but their thick shafts and long stone blades made them look heavy, too clumsy to throw. None of the men who had hunted the stag had carried spears. I wondered if this hunt would be different.

The men seemed to know where they were going. We followed no trail that I could see, and no wolves traveled with us.

All morning no one said a word. The hunters spoke to each other only with their hands. Many of their gestures I understood. Someone would point to us to go this way or that, or hold up a hand to make us stop, or cup his ear to tell us to listen. Other signs were not so obvious. Their hands seemed to speak a language of their own. At first I tried to pay attention, but while my mind was distracted, puzzling out their meaning, my feet would trip over a root or step on the heel of the man in front of me. At last I gave up trying to understand. I did what seemed reasonable to me and relied on the others to let me know if they wanted me to do something else.

About midday we entered a thicket. Here the hunters walked more cautiously, and our leader knelt often to examine the ground. We'd had a thaw, and much of the snow had melted, but the ground had frozen again. I could see neither hoofprint nor pawprint on the frozen ground. Nevertheless it was clear that the men had found the trail of something, and their hands had a great deal to say about it.

Not long afterward we came upon a sign that even I understood. A pile of fresh dung lay in the trail. Its strong odor, both sour and bitter, was the odor of the pigpen. At once the hunters grew still, while their excitement hummed in the air around me. Two of the men with spears slipped silently into the thicket. The third led the rest of us farther along the trail.

We traveled slowly, stopping many times to listen. We walked for perhaps as long as half an hour, but I hardly noticed the time passing. I needed no one to explain to me that the men who had gone ahead through the thicket were our wolves, and they would drive the game back toward us. The deer had surprised me. This time I would not be unprepared. I forgot to be afraid that I might fail. Something was about to happen. It might come at any moment, and every moment I was ready for it.

At last we heard shouts in the distance. We stopped when we heard them coming toward us. As wolves lie in wait, the two archers knelt beside the trail, while the man with the spear blocked the trail itself. All three crouched down and lowered their heads, peering out from under their wolf's-head caps, showing more of the wolf's face than their own.

Although no one had told me what to do, I saw what was going to happen as clearly as if I could glimpse the future through the veil of time. Whatever came toward us down that trail would see three wolves waiting there and stop. It would pause only for a moment while it decided what to do. I would have that moment to send an arrow through its heart.

I hid myself beside the trail where I thought the pig would stop. One thing I did not foresee. He was immense and very fast, and he had little to fear from wolves. He paused only for the briefest moment and my arrow was too late. It struck him in the belly, not a killing wound, but a painful one. He whirled to face me.

I nocked another arrow and drew the bow, knowing that even if my arrow struck his bony head, it wouldn't stop him. Without taking time to aim, I loosed the arrow. Then I fled. I would have climbed a tree if there had been one handy, but in the thicket I found only shrubs and saplings. Too late I remembered my disguise, although I doubt I would have had the courage to stand my ground and hope to convince the boar that I was a hungry wolf, not the frail child of humankind.

Behind me I heard a shout of triumph. I turned to see our spearman standing not three paces from the boar, who tottered, then sank to the ground. The shaft of a spear protruded from his body. The blade had pierced his heart.

When I approached, I saw that the boar also had several more arrows in him. My second arrow had missed his head and lodged in the fat of his shoulder. Four more arrows had pierced his side. Another had gone through his neck, so that he would soon have choked on his own blood. Even so, I admired the courage of the spearman who had struck the killing blow.

Before I could praise his courage, he spoke to me.

"A good shot," he said.

He must have meant my first shot, not the second, which had done more to anger the boar than do him harm.

I gestured at the spear. "A brave blow," I replied.

The hunter smiled.

The two archers joined us. Each admired the shots the other had made, and mine as well. When the men who had gone ahead to intercept the boar appeared, they too joined in the general exchange of praise, of which I received an equal share. I hardly felt as if I had done enough to merit their compliments. Nonetheless they pleased me very much.

Then the hunters turned their attention to the boar. One of the archers praised his courage, and the other men agreed with him. The archer used his bow to measure the boar's length, while the others had a lively argument, most of which I couldn't follow, that seemed to have something to do with whether or not this boar was bigger than another that had been killed by someone else. I began to think that when we returned home, the size of this boar would have grown by at least half a bow-length.

As they had done with the stag, the hunters butchered the boar on the spot, all the while exchanging stories of the hunt. The men who had been so silent all morning now spoke as if the killing of the boar had released their tongues from an enchantment. The hunters who had gone ahead told how difficult it was to discover where the boar was feeding and how clever they had been to slip past without alarming him. Then, when they showed themselves, as a boar will often do, he chose to fight before he chose to run. Both men had bloodied their spears in their attempt to change his mind.

Next it was the archers' turn to tell the story of the kill. They didn't seem to mind that I had missed my shot. Of course they knew that I had meant to send my arrow into the boar's heart, but they spoke as if I had inflicted the belly wound on purpose, to turn the boar so that they would have a better shot. The way they spoke let me know that they approved of what I had done.

Just as I was about to think very well of myself, one of the archers said, "And Tamara, how fast he is!"

The other archer chuckled. The two spearmen who hadn't witnessed for themselves my headlong flight from the tusks of the angry boar understood perfectly what had happened.

"Did he climb a tree?" said one.

The other made a show of looking around him, as if assessing which slender sapling might have served as a place of refuge.

Now all the men were laughing. I blushed to the tips of my ears. Then I too began to laugh. I didn't know that the feelings of the hunt still remained so strong within me until my laughter started to release them. The anxiety, the excitement and the fear, dissolved into our laughter. Perhaps this was how the warriors of Merin's house had felt when they returned from their pursuit of the northerners after the battle on Taia's day. They were full of an energy that the fighting failed to dissipate. Maara once called it "the wildness." Now I felt the wildness in myself.

We returned to butchering the boar, still full of talk about the hunt. We calmed ourselves with talk and laughter, until the butchering was done and it was time to start for home. Each man took his share. My burden was as heavy as the others, and it pleased me that they expected no less of me than they expected of one another.

The hunt had taken us far from home. Darkness fell before we reached the village. Although we had eaten nothing all day, I wasn't hungry. I was so tired that I would have liked to go straight to bed. The others were just as tired, but when we entered the enclosure, we were immediately surrounded. The women took the meat from us, while the men questioned us about the hunt, and the hunters began again to tell the tale. I looked for Maara, but didn't find her.

The night air was bitter cold. As soon as I stopped moving, I began to shiver. We all went inside the cave, where the fire had been burning for some time. Maara sat beside it. When her eyes met mine, something in them stopped me for a moment. Pride was there, a pride I had seen many times before, and as it always did, it filled my heart with pride in myself. But there was more than pride in Maara's eyes. In them I saw both admiration and respect. This was not the look that a mother gives her child nor the look a warrior gives her apprentice. This was the look that passes between equals.

The hunters asserted their right to the best places by the fire. I would have sat next to Maara, but she moved away to give the hunters room, and they insisted that I stay with them. Twice more the men told the story of the hunt, first for the ears of the other men alone, as the women kept themselves busy somewhere else, and then a second time after the women joined us.

The story the hunters told the men was mostly an imparting of information. They told of where we had found the boar and of other signs they had seen along the way. There was some boasting too, and the squabble I'd foreseen over the boar's size. The story they told for the women's benefit was completely different. It was intended to impress, to show off the hunters' skill and courage. They boasted of me too, and no one said a word about how fast I was.

By the time the meat was done, the smell had made me ravenous. The hunters ate first, while the children watched us with envy in their eyes. At any other time I would have felt too guilty to eat while a child went hungry, but this was the custom among the forest people, and I knew why. As the warriors of Merin's house took as theirs by right the spoils of war, the hunters of the forest people took what was their due, and the children's envy was not just for the meat, but for the glory.

After everyone had eaten, there was a little of the usual talk and storytelling, but it was late, and the women soon left the fire and went to bed. Maara went with them. When I would have followed her, the hunter sitting next to me took hold of my arm and held me there.

"Let the women go," he said. "Tonight, Tamara he is a man among men."

A Hunter of the Forest People

Warmed by the fire, with a belly full of meat, I had dozed through much of the storytelling. Now I was wide awake, and I didn't mind sitting up a while. The hunters too seemed to want to talk some more, as if they felt they had to say it all, to quiet their minds enough to sleep.

The boasting and the praise were over now. The hunters spoke of the day's hunt in a simple and straightforward way. When they had said all there was to say about it, they told tales of other hunts, and the men who had stayed home that day told stories of their own. The hunters spoke of going to the hunt as Merin's warriors spoke of going to war, with excitement and anticipation, and enough bravado to conceal their knowledge that they would soon be in harm's way. To them each hunt was a contest, which might be won or lost, in which the prize was life itself.

They told more than one tale that night of hunters killed or maimed by wounded boars. They told them for my benefit, so that I would understand, while the wildness still sounded through my blood and bones, what I had accomplished, what I had overcome. Their stories taught me how the world felt to them, and how they understood it and their own place in it.

They told tales of times of plenty, when the gods had all but laid the game at their feet, and they told tales of hungry times, when they had fought with their wolf brethren for what little game there was. They told tales of great hunters and legendary hunts, remembered from a distant time. Beneath the surface of their stories ran a thread of meaning that eluded me until I noticed that they never spoke the words for killing or for death. Instead of saying that an animal had died, they said, "he gave himself" or "he gave up," as if his death were a surrender, or an offering. And if a hunter lost his life, they spoke of his death in the same terms. In their eyes, the hunter and the hunted shared a common fate, the hunt itself a ritual in which one or the other would become the sacrifice.

When at last I lay in Maara's arms that night, I was more than ready to retreat into my woman self. My glimpse into the world of men had frightened me a little. Though I felt no less the privilege of having been included in the day's adventure, their nighttime tales created in my mind a vision of the hunters of the forest people standing on the edge of an abyss into which someday each of them would fall. I too had once stood on the edge of an abyss, before I fell into the Mother's arms, but it seemed that these men would fall into a cold and lonely place. If they knew or thought they knew what fate awaited them, they never said so.

I slept until midmorning, and I might have slept the day away if Maara hadn't brought me breakfast.

"We should check our snares today," she said.

I smiled. Checking our snares was our excuse to spend time together, just the two of us. We did set a few snares, so that we could make a contribution to the village of meat and furs, but oftener than not, we had more than half the day to spend in our hollow tree. There we could speak our own language without being rude and talk of private things. In the village of the forest people, we did as they did and made love at night, hidden by the dark, and they pretended not to hear us, as we pretended not to hear them. In the hollow tree we could make love in the open, in the light.

That day I was glad to find all our snares empty. We arrived at the hollow tree before midday. Maara had brought a thick elk robe for us to lie on. She lit a fire, and while we waited for it to drive off the chill, we huddled close to it and to each other.

"What do they do in Merin's house when an apprentice becomes a warrior?" asked Maara.

I was surprised to discover that I didn't know. There was no public ceremony. One day an apprentice would appear in the great hall with a sword hanging from her belt, carrying a shield that bore her own device.

"I think her warrior presents her with a shield," I said.

"So it's a private thing between warrior and apprentice?"

"I suppose so."

"I believe your shield hangs now in Merin's hall," said Maara. "Unless Vintel took it down."

"You mean the wolf shield?"

She nodded. "Wolf shield, wolf skin. If Tamara he is a hunter of the forest people, then Tamras she must be no less than a warrior in Merin's house." Maara turned to me and gazed into my eyes. "I have no other token to give you, Tamras, Tamnet's daughter."

"Your regard means more to me than any token," I told her.

She smiled. "Then from this day let us be comrades in arms. Your apprenticeship is over."

I nodded, but I accepted her decision with mixed feelings.

Maara touched the frown lines on my brow. "Why does that make you unhappy?"

"My apprenticeship bound us together," I said. "What binds us now?"

With her fingertips she lifted my face to hers and kissed me.

The desire of the body we satisfied too quickly. I wanted to stay longer in that place where I felt our bodies mingle with each other until I knew what she was feeling as intimately as she did herself. Afterwards, as I lay exhausted in her arms, I let my mind ponder the meaning of desire and its fulfillment, as if it were possible to comprehend a mystery.

With pleasure come the things that matter. Could I name them? Trust, of course. Without trust, how could we so entirely unclothe ourselves? Sometimes, as I made love to her, I felt her rise up into me, felt my spirit welcome hers, make room for hers, let her come in where anyone else would have felt to me like an intruder. In my spirit's house, she was welcome everywhere.

I trusted her not to be careless with my heart or with my feelings. I trusted her to understand and to accept what might be broken or imperfect. In some dusty corner there may be things I tossed away, forgotten, things that might once have shamed me. I trusted her with those things too. I trusted her to accept me as she found me and to love me as I was, as I loved her.

Of course I accepted her completely, and everything about her. Her virtues I found admirable and her faults endearing. More than endearing. They filled me with compassion, because I knew their source. And for all these years she'd had so much patience with my faults. She must have loved me for a long time.

That thought startled me and made me wonder.

"When did you begin to love me?" I asked her.

She yawned. "I don't remember."

"When I revealed my love to you, you loved me then."

"Mmmm," she said.

"How long before that?"

"I don't know."

"A long time?"

"Yes," she whispered. "A long time."

"All summer?"

"Longer than that."

"All year?"

"Longer."

I leaned up on one elbow and looked down at her. "Why didn't you tell me?"

"What could I have said?"

"You could have told me about your feelings for me."

"I didn't know if they'd be welcome."

I was beginning to be impatient with her. How could her love for me ever have been unwelcome? "Why would you think that?"

"Because you had a lover."

"No I didn't." Then I remembered. "Oh," I said, and at once I understood what I had done. Without meaning to, I had allowed her to believe that for the second time she loved someone who loved someone else.

"I'm so sorry," I whispered.

"Hush," she said. "It doesn't matter."

"I should have told you about Sparrow long ago."

"It doesn't matter," she said again.

The thought that I had caused her pain was at that moment a cause of great pain to me.

"Of course it matters," I insisted.

"Why?"

"Because I hurt you."

She laughed at that. Then she slipped her arm around my waist and rolled me over onto my back. Her eyes sent a wave of desire through my body and at the same time kept me still, so that I could hear what she was about to tell me.

"Today," she said.

"What?"

"We have today."

"And tomorrow."

"Perhaps."

I opened my mouth to protest that of course we would have tomorrow and many more tomorrows after that, but she kissed me lightly on the lips, then laid her cheek against my cheek and whispered, "Be careful what you say. The gods may hear you."

Something kept me quiet. Instead of brushing her words aside, as I would have liked to do, I let their meaning settle around my heart, until I saw more clearly a side of her that she kept turned away from me. This was how she saw the world. It could take from her in a moment everything she loved. It could deny her anything she wanted. The world had granted almost my every wish, and none more precious to me than this one. The world had granted her only this.

"If I saw the world as you do," I said, "I don't know if I would have the courage to risk my heart."

"Do you doubt that your heart is at risk?"

"I don't think about it," I told her.

"Ah," she sighed against my ear. "It's just as well."

Our conversation ensured that I would think about it. I thought about it as I lay in her arms that afternoon, as I walked home with her that evening, as I sat beside her by the fire, as I held her in my arms that night. In the morning I remembered to be grateful that we would have another day together.

What I could not face was the thought of life without her. Nothing else the world might offer me could ease the pain of it. I understood now why Sparrow had almost followed Eramet and why only my mother's presence in the world kept Merin in it.

Before I loved Maara, life seemed filled with endless possibility, yet I knew even then what I was waiting for. Love was only an idea to me then, something to hope for, a promise of happiness, insubstantial and immortal, until it found the one to settle on. Now love and Maara were one and the same, and love had become as mortal as she was.

⌒⌒⌒

As the days went by, I lived more and more in the present moment, not only because of the fear of loss that Maara's words awakened in me, but because that was how the forest people lived. They spent little time looking forward, either in anticipation of some good thing that might happen or in dread of some trouble that might come. Present pleasures were enough for them, and while they did attempt to foresee trouble and forestall it, they considered worry a waste of time.

They spent even less time looking back. They learned from their remembered past, but they never allowed it to intrude upon the present. They refused to regret what was past changing or carry with them the useless burden of things best left behind. They teased their children out of pouts and grudges. Aamah would sometimes remind them that the story of an old dispute should be retold only when no aftertaste of bitterness remains upon the tongue. I admired Aamah's wisdom. Too many of my people retold the stories of their grievances with the intention of fanning into flame the hot coals of their resentment.

One afternoon I spoke these thoughts to Maara.

To my surprise, she said, "Don't live so much in the present moment that you forget your home and those who love you."

She had anticipated me. More than once I had entertained the thought that I would be content to spend my life among the forest people. Here Maara belonged as she would belong nowhere else. Here no great responsibility would fall upon my shoulders. I would be the heir to no great house. I would never have to face Vintel, to challenge her, to take by force the inheritance I didn't want. Here Maara would be safe, and together we could live out our lives in peace.

"We've been happy here," I said. "We could be happy here all our lives."

"Don't you care for the happiness of others?"

"I care for your happiness."

In spite of herself, Maara smiled, but I felt she was about to scold me.

"I care for my mother's happiness too," I said. "And for Namet's, who must miss you terribly. And Merin's. And all the others."

Before I could say their names, the faces of my friends came back to me, and I was a little ashamed of myself, that I had forgotten my love for them, and theirs for me.

That night, while I was drifting into sleep, I heard the echo of my own words, spoken to Maara not long before we met the forest people. *The fairy folk live in the hollow hills, in vast caverns lit by a thousand lamps, where feasting and merrymaking go on for days on end.* I remembered stories of people who had been invited to a fairy banquet, who had tasted of the fairies' meat and drink and listened to songs and stories that told of a world older than the world they knew. Charmed by all these things, they fell into forgetfulness, until one morning they awoke back in the world above, and although it seemed to them that they had been only a short time among the fairies, they found that in their own world a hundred years had passed. Were we now among the fairy folk? I dreamed that night of going home and finding Merin's house full of strangers who knew my name only from stories of a girl who disappeared a hundred years ago.

At the time I didn't see that Maara was preparing me for my return. The end of my apprenticeship was more than a recognition of my ability or the change in our relationship. In her cunning way, Maara had made a connection in my mind between the wolfskin I wore as a hunter of the forest people and the wolf shield I had won in battle and hung in Merin's hall. I could not go wolf-clad to the hunt without remembering that my shield awaited me. Maara had given it to me as a token that I was now a warrior, but it was not a gift. I would have to win it for myself.

The end of my apprenticeship was also a recognition of my independence. I had been in the habit of looking to Maara for direction. Now she often left it up to me to decide how we would spend the day. Sometimes, if I said I wanted to go out, she would make up her mind to stay at home, and I would have to go alone. I knew better than to change my mind. It was almost worth missing her all day to come home to her at night. She let me know she'd missed me too.

68

THE FOREST AT MIDWINTER

The brook had frozen, the snow lay deep, the days were short and dark. Even in deepest winter, men went to the hunt. When there was moon enough to see by, we left long before the sun came up. Game was scarce, and too often we returned home empty-handed.

Although I had been called to nearly every hunt, I had not yet hunted with the wolves. Then one early morning I awoke with a wolf's cry in my ears. None of the hunters had come to wake me. When I got up, I saw that they too had only just got out of bed.

We walked for several hours, into a part of the forest where I had never been. I had almost forgotten about the wolves when I caught sight of one. Soon I saw that there were at least three traveling with us.

One of them, bolder than the others, stayed in plain sight. He was the largest wolf I'd ever seen, and though his winter coat was silver-tipped like the others, his undercoat was black. In the changing light he appeared at times as dark as a shadow, at other times as faint as a ghost. He was their leader, and he assumed the leadership of us as well. He kept ahead of us, so sure we would follow that he never bothered glancing back.

The wolves took us into hilly country where the snow had piled up in deep drifts. On their great paws they glided easily over the surface of the snow. The hunters of the forest people had learned from their wolf brethren to make big feet of their own. They bent supple branches into hoops and laced them with a webbing of leather strips, with wide straps to fasten them to their feet.

Worr, the leader of the hunt, had made a pair for me. It took me several days of practice before I learned to walk in them. They kept us from sinking into the snow, but the wolves had four feet to hold them up while we had only two, and I felt their impatience with our clumsiness.

A shiver of fear ran down my spine when I remembered the hunting stories of the forest people. What would happen if we found no game? Would the hunters turn upon each other?

As the day wore on, I began to tire. A cloudy sky hid the pale winter sun. I didn't know how late it was until the light was almost gone. Whether we found game or not, we would have to camp out for the night. Then I wondered if the wolves were leading us through this rough country to wear us out, so that they could make a meal of us.

What if it was so? Only our weapons made us a match for them. No, we still had fire. That thought made me feel a little better. We had fire, and there were enough of us to keep a good watch. With fire we could hold our own against many wolves.

None of my fears came true. At last we wounded a young doe, who bounded away while we floundered after her through drifted snow. By the time we reached her, the wolves had brought her down and begun their feast. This time, when we approached, the wolves refused to yield, although there were only three of them and we were half a dozen. Fierce with hunger, they stood their ground, warning us away with flattened ears and snarling lips and growls that would haunt my nightmares.

"Let them take the edge off their appetite," said Worr, and we settled down to wait.

Beneath their heavy fur, the wolves were gaunt. All the same, hunger gnawed at my own belly, and I worried that when the wolves had fed there would be nothing left for us. Hunger made the other men impatient too.

Once I had been foolish enough to ask why we never brought food with us. "To show the forest we are confident," was Worr's reply.

For a while we watched the wolves as the wolves had once watched us. Then we began to glance at Worr, looking for a sign that it was time to take our share. Suddenly he gave a shout that rang through the cold air. Startled, the wolves leaped up and turned to face us. Worr ran directly at them. Brandishing his bow, he made them scatter and knelt by the kill just long enough to cut himself a piece of meat. The black wolf quickly recovered from his fright and started to give chase, nipping at Worr's heels as he fled. I thought for a moment that the wolf would catch him, but even on his clumsy feet, Worr stayed a step or two ahead.

When he reached us, Worr was laughing. Safe now among his friends, he turned and waved the chunk of meat in triumph at the wolf, who had stopped a mere ten paces from us. The wolf laughed back. His bloody jaws gaped open, pulling the edges of his mouth up into a grin. I never thought that wolves could laugh, but there was something in his eyes that made me think he had enjoyed the game. That didn't make me fear him less. I feared him more, because I saw how intelligent he was, and how well he understood the ways of humankind.

The wolf turned and trotted back to join his fellows, and Worr squatted down in the snow and took a bite of the raw meat. I thought that now we would all rush the wolves at once, to drive them from the kill, but only one man started toward them, while the others leaned on their bows to watch.

Surprise was lost. The wolves still fed, but with one eye on the hunter who approached them, slow and deliberate, his bow unstrung, the better to strike with. The wolves stayed just out of reach. They retreated toward the head of the carcass while the hunter took his share of meat from a hind leg. Just as he was turning to come back to us, the black wolf stood up and challenged him. The hunter backed away. With the wolf so close he dared not turn and run.

Urtik, younger than the rest of us and still as playful as a boy, bent and scooped up a handful of snow. He formed it into a tight ball and threw it hard. It shattered against the big wolf's ear. With a yelp that deepened to a growl, the wolf snarled his anger at us. In reply, the men began to chant. It was the same sound they had made for the wolf dance, but louder and more menacing. Two men ran at the wolves together, and in confusion the wolves gave way. One at a time, each man drove them from the kill just long enough to take his share.

The black wolf paid no attention to them. Now he bore a grudge. He kept his eyes on Urtik, waiting for his chance to take revenge. Only Urtik and I had not yet taken our share of meat. We went together. I tried to distract the wolf while Urtik approached the kill, but he refused to be distracted until I scooped up a handful of snow. I held it ready while Urtik cut a piece of meat. Then it was my turn.

By now the other wolves, too full to fight, had abandoned the carcass. One moved off a little distance, dragging a foreleg with him. Soon I heard him crunch the bones. The other was rolling in the snow, to clean the gore from his winter coat.

The black wolf stood motionless a few paces from the kill. He watched me, but he made no move as I approached. Without taking my eyes from his, I cut a piece of meat and began to back away. I had not practiced walking backwards. My feet in their webbed hoops tangled with each other. My arms flailed at the air, my bow went flying. Before I hit the ground, the wolf had leapt. We landed at the same moment, he on his feet, I helpless on my back. He was so close I could have touched him.

I had never been more frightened in my life. The wolf was savoring the moment. His shining amber eyes held mine, as he wrinkled his lip at me in a half-snarl, half-smile.

I had forgotten my companions. Face to face with my own death, I was alone. If I was going to die, it didn't matter what I did, so there was nothing left to fear. As helpless as I was, I prepared myself to make the wolf's victory as difficult as possible. Then I thought of Maara.

Something new came into those amber eyes, a hint of doubt, a question. They saw that something new had come into my heart. After fear had come a burning anger, not that my life would be cut short, but that Maara's fears were coming true, as if this wolf were the embodiment of the doom that haunted Maara's life. My own death was bad enough, but Maara's grief outweighed it. Even knowing death was unavoidable, I would have fought it. For Maara's sake, I would refuse it. I would refuse to die.

Against his will, the wolf looked away. Twice he tried and failed to meet my eyes. Ears flattened in submission, he dropped his head and slunk away.

Urtik came and helped me to my feet. I had dropped the piece of meat that I had almost paid for with my life. I went to the carcass and cut another. The wolves were gone.

The hunters came to butcher what was left of the doe. I would have helped them, but Worr saw my hand tremble that held the knife and told me first to eat my share. The raw meat filled my mouth with sweetness. It was as sweet as life itself.

We kept our fire small. The six of us huddled close around it. While we cooked some of the venison, we talked together in soft voices, as if we feared to be overheard. Perhaps the wolves were listening. The forest certainly was. Its dark spirit, awakened from its winter sleep by our brawling with the wolves, hovered just beyond the reach of firelight.

No one spoke of my encounter with my death, just as no one spoke of his own encounter. Each of us had faced his death that day. I saw in their eyes what they must have seen in mine, a thoughtfulness, a turning inward, to guard and tend the little flame of life that might have flickered out. No one boasted of his courage or gloried in our victory. When death comes so close, there is no making light of it.

That day I had watched each man approach the wolves alone. At the time I didn't understand why we wouldn't use our strength in numbers. At first it had seemed like a game, one of those reckless, foolish games men play that make their women frown and shake their heads, murmuring their disapproval. Now I saw that it was more than just a game. It was a dance.

When I first envisioned the hunters of the forest people standing on the edge of the abyss, I wondered what they saw when they gazed down into it. Each man seemed so alone and so defiant. They would not fall, as I had, into the arms of love. I could have no idea what they saw there until I had danced with them along the precipice, until I had peered over the edge. Not love, but power dwelt there, and these men drew power from it. I had drawn power from it. Daani too had once drawn power from it, and that was why she had given up the wolfskin. She who carried life within her could no longer dance with death.

We kept our fire small.

In the stillness of the forest, at the darkest time of year, a band of hunters sat around their fire, while all around them in the dark the wolf clan gathered.

I woke with a start and saw, across the circle, a wolf sitting among us. I was about to cry out a warning when I realized that it was a man asleep, his chin resting on his chest, so that the shining eyes of his wolf's head cap seemed to gaze directly at me. I peered out into the darkness. I saw no wolves, but I felt their presence, more than the three we had hunted with.

Two of the men were dozing, as I had been. The others kept the watch. One of them saw that I was awake and caught my eye. He nodded, to pass his watch to me, then tucked his chin against his chest and closed his eyes.

When I was a child, I used to lie awake at night in my familiar room, where even in the dark I could picture everything around me, the image in my mind's eye as faithful as that of ordinary sight. As I kept the watch that night, I beheld a picture in my mind of the forest all around me. It was not a picture left in memory or conjured by imagination, but a knowledge that came less through the senses than through the heart. I saw squirrels asleep in hollow trees, rabbits in their burrows and hunting cats in their dens, weasels and badgers curled up tight against the cold. A tawny owl drifted in the sparkling air, listening for the scurrying feet of mice and voles in their runways beneath the snow. While furred and feathered creatures stirred with life, the slumbering trees reached deep into the earth in search of dreams, their roots descending, deep into the dark.

At the time I didn't think it strange that I should be aware of all these things. Even as it slept, the forest was aware of me, as it was aware of all the animals that sheltered there. It was the forest that had dreamed us into life, and I shared the forest's dream.

In the morning the wolves were gone. Their pawprints in the snow showed us how close they had come. The day before, this evidence of danger all around us would have terrified me. Now, while I still had great respect for the power of the wolves, I no longer feared them.

The journey home seemed endless. I think I must have slept through part of it. I fell into that strange waking sleep in which the body does what it must do while the mind steps through a veil into the land of dreams. I lost awareness of my body, as my dreaming self rose into the air and looked down on a band of hunters trudging homeward through the snow. Then I lost sight of them, as my dreaming self rose above the treetops into a dark winter sky. Below me I heard the forest sighing, as a woman sighs in sleep, while above me grumbling clouds blew by. This was the time for sleep, while darkness gathered.

Through the dark of early evening, our feet guided us along the familiar path. It drew us on, as more and more we felt the pull of home, where we would be warm and welcome.

Maara took me to bed right after supper, while the men were still telling the story of the hunt. I listened, half-asleep, to a tale so full of whimsy that if I had not lived it myself, I would have considered it no more than a dreamer's wild imaginings. The telling of the story mingled in my mind with my own dreams.

I heard Worr say, "We had a good laugh over it," and knew he was speaking of the big wolf who had chased him, but he told the story in such a way that I saw him and the wolf sitting side by side at our hearth fire, as fond as brothers, sharing a joint of meat and an amusing tale.

When I heard someone speak my name, my curiosity struggled against sleep.

"And Tamara the Fast—"

"No, Tamara Clumsy Feet."

"Yes, he fell."

Someone made a whirring sound that brought into my mind an image of myself, arms waving wildly as I tried to keep my balance.

"And the wolf—" A whooshing sound and the shadow on the cave wall of a hunter's upraised arms. "Such a leap!"

Maara's arms tightened around me. I tried to tell her that the story ended happily, but I found I couldn't speak.

It was dark when I awoke. I was too warm. I tried to throw off the elk robe, but it had grown too heavy. At last I freed one arm, and I was enjoying the touch of cold air on my fevered body when someone wrapped me up again.

"Too hot," I said.

My voice sounded strange to me, as if it came from far away.

Someone brought me water. It stung my lips. Although I was thirsty, my throat was so sore and swollen that I found it difficult to swallow. A part of my mind knew that I was ill, while another part seemed not to care. It let my painful body drift away and lost itself in pictures like those we see in dreams. Green hills and blue skies reminded me of home, where in my memory it was always summertime. I drifted there, dreaming of a life I might once have lived, but when the sky began to darken, I looked for the way home in vain. There was no path to guide me. This place was strange to me that had put on for a little while the guise of home. Soon the light was gone.

I floated weightless in the dark. I drifted, light as thistledown, carrying a tiny seed of life that might fall either on good earth or barren ground. I neither hoped for one nor feared the other. I lay upon the air and let it carry me, until a breath of wind wafted me over the abyss, where in the depths there stirred some nameless thing, an ancient power that knew me not at all.

As I drifted over the abyss, too light to fall, I felt it reach for me. I was not afraid, just curious, and my mind filled up with wordless questions. The nameless thing that dwelt there in the dark had questions it would ask of me, and promised, if I answered them, to whisper me its secrets.

Above me a bird of prey glided through the sky and cast the shadow of its outstretched wings over the abyss. The power, like a hunted thing, withdrew. The hawk's soft-feathered wings embraced me. Sharp pains pierced my shoulders where its talons gripped me, as it flew with me, up into the light.

I woke to the touch of feathers on my naked skin. Smoke tickled my nose and made me sneeze. With a fan made from a raven's wing, Sett wafted more of the sweet-smelling smoke over me, until I had sneezed twice more. Then he leaned close to me and looked into my eyes, looked past my eyes, and his were cold, as sharp as flint. Hawk's eyes.

69

A Bargain

As I grew strong again, my journey over the abyss seemed more and more unreal, but as we dream of places that we recognize, I knew I had dreamed of someplace so familiar that for days my waking mind wandered in the dark, searching for a landmark that would help me find my way through this forgotten landscape.

Sett came to see me often. He never spoke about my journey, though I knew that he had shared it, and I knew better than to speak to him of things that can't be spoken of. Instead he told me winter stories. He mimed the sleeping animals and made me see their dreams, as each created for himself the world that he would live in, a world of warmth and light. Squirrels in the treetops, rocked by winter winds, might dream of soaring leaps from tree to tree. Did they ever dream of falling?

Worr came to see me too. He seemed to think it was my battle with the wolf that made me ill. Perhaps it was. I didn't think too much about it. Winter sickness can come to anyone. Then I thought of Merin, whose illness had almost let her fall into the soft dark of midwinter's night, and I knew why I remembered the abyss.

Throughout my illness, Maara stayed beside me. When dreams troubled me, she held me fast. When I woke she fed me, bathed me, carried me outdoors, well wrapped up in furs, to use the privy. She cared for me with a tenderness that told me of her love more than there are words for. In fact she spoke very little. At first I didn't notice. While I was ill, I slept. When I was stronger, she made me sit up with the others around the fire. During the day we were seldom alone, and when I lay in her arms at night, she soothed me to sleep with her caress, though she refused my touch with the excuse that I was not yet strong enough.

As the days went by, her excuse wore thin. At last, careless of who might overhear, I said, "If you don't want me to touch you anymore, then say so."

"It isn't that," she whispered.

"What then?"

She didn't speak, so I went searching for the answer. My lips questioned her as they caressed her face and found another question in her tears. My hands too questioned her and found her closed against me. This was nothing new, and I was patient. When I finally unclosed her, it was her anger that leapt out at me. She pushed me away, only to grapple me closer, and when her anger burnt itself to ashes, I felt her grief, as if she had already lost me.

The next morning, for the first time in many days, the sun was shining. Still too weak to warm the wintry air, its pale light made the world feel a little warmer. Maara shaded her eyes against it as she measured the height of its arc through the treetops.

"Midwinter is past," she said.

"How long past?"

"It's hard to guess. A month perhaps."

While the promise of spring lifted my spirits, at the same time I felt a touch of melancholy. I wanted to ask her how long it would be before we would have to leave the forest people, but I hadn't the heart to mention it. To speak of leaving would make it real. I made up my mind to remain in the present moment for as long as possible.

For some days I had been well enough to go outdoors. When the weather was mild, Maara took me out walking, a little longer every day, to help me regain my strength. We had not yet gone as far as the hollow tree. On this first sunny day, I asked her to take me there.

She smiled at me, a shy smile. "Was last night not enough for you?"

"Last night we didn't talk," I said.

She nodded, but when we were sitting beside our fire in the hollow tree, I couldn't think of anything to say. She too was silent. While I tried to think of how to question her, she gazed into the fire, her thoughts so far away from me that I watched her for a long time before she felt my eyes.

"What?" she said.

I couldn't put my question into words. I didn't try. My heart knew the answer. What more could she have told me than her body had already told me in the dark? Weren't her tears eloquent enough? Could I have misunderstood her anger? Or her grief?

"It didn't happen," I said.

"What didn't happen?"

"Whatever you're so afraid of."

"You know what I'm afraid of."

I took both her hands in mine. "Someday we will lose each other. I fear that too, but I refuse to let it spoil the time we have together."

Maara wasn't listening. "I wish I could persuade the gods that if some dreadful thing must fall upon us, to let it fall on me."

Hadn't we settled that between us long ago? Could she doubt that whatever fell on her would fall on me too?

Before I could protest, she gave me an unexpected smile. "Of course if I could persuade the gods of that, I might do better to persuade them to leave us alone altogether."

I took her words more seriously than she had intended them.

"What gods do you believe in?" I asked her. "The way you speak of them frightens me. They frighten me."

Maara shrugged. "I don't know whether I believe in them or not. I think I speak of them as I do just to have someone to blame. Better to blame the gods than blame myself."

"Perhaps no one is to blame," I said. "I don't know why the world is as it is, but I doubt that it's my fault. Or yours. Neither one of us is as powerful as that."

Her eyes smiled at me. "No?"

"No."

Her skin looked very soft. I touched her cheek. She took me into her arms and rocked me.

"Why the world is as it is," she whispered.

When I heard my own words echoed back to me, I wondered who on earth could answer such a question. Could Sett or Aamah? Could Namet answer it? Could Gnith? I had never heard any of the wise ones attempt to answer it. I had never heard it asked.

As we walked home that evening, I tried to feel the way I should have felt after we had spent an afternoon together, but that night, when I lay beside her in the dark, I had to look at something that disturbed me, knowing I would not be left in peace until I faced it. That afternoon, when I made love to Maara, there was a part of her I couldn't reach. I felt that she had hidden something from me, just a small thing, as tiny as a grain of sand and as worrying as a pebble in my shoe.

I went over in my mind the talk we'd had that day. Short as it was, much had been said, and now I saw what I had missed. I had thought that her fears were the same as mine—that we would lose each other, that something would come between us, either time or distance or the abyss of death. Although she told me that wasn't what she feared, it had taken me all day to understand her. More than losing me, she feared what might befall me, leaving her to bear, not just the grief, but the guilt of somehow having caused it.

A new fear ran through my blood like ice. Had Maara struck a bargain with her gods? It was clear that she had no faith in their benevolence. Simply asking wouldn't be enough for them. There would have to be a sacrifice.

I felt more hopeful in the morning. More than she herself, I knew the wounds in Maara's heart. Grief uncomforted, hopes unfulfilled, unanswered dreams—I had stumbled over almost all of them at one time or another. I dared to hope that with love I had begun to help her heal them. Perhaps foolishly, I believed that the darkness that yesterday resisted me would yield to me tomorrow. In the meantime, I decided not to talk to her about it. Sometimes to speak of such things makes them come true.

Soon I was quite well and strong enough to hunt. As the weather grew warmer, game became more plentiful. The snow melted in all but the most sheltered places, and the deer came out of their snug nests to feed on the tender new leaves. Whenever we hunted, I kept an eye out for the wolves, fearful they would join us, yet disappointed when they didn't. One day I asked Worr why we had seen no sign of them.

"Our brothers have gone ahead of us, up into the mountains," said Worr. "We will follow in a little while. We may see them there, but we won't hunt with them again until the snow falls."

It was the first I'd heard that the forest people would soon be leaving their winter encampment, but Maara already knew.

"They're waiting for the new moon," she said.

"Will we go too?"

Maara only looked at me.

"Oh," I said. "We're going home."

"Isn't that what you want?"

I nodded, knowing that what I wanted was impossible. I wanted home to be all in one place.

As the time of the new moon drew near, I tried to cling to every moment. I wasn't ready to accept the loss of these people I had grown to love. Whenever Sett told a story, I wondered if this might be the last tale of his I'd ever hear, and I wished the telling could go on forever. When I sent an arrow into a boar's heart, I took into my own heart the hunters' praise, knowing that no one would ever again see me with their eyes. When a child fell asleep in my lap, I thought it must be true that the last time for anything is the sweetest.

The forest people too were sad at the thought of our parting, though they had something to look forward to. They lived all winter in small bands of a few dozen people, but in summertime the clans would come together, and they had begun to speak the names of friends they hoped to see. I wished I could look forward with as much pleasure to seeing my own friends again. Instead fear cast its shadow over the thought of our reunion. What would I find on my return to Merin's house? What had become of those I loved? Would I find them well? Would I find them all still living?

On the last day, late in the afternoon, Aamah sent for us. We found her sitting by her fire in the covered shed. She gestured to Maara and patted the ground beside her. Maara sat down there, and I sat across the fire from them, so that I could see their faces.

Aamah took Maara's hand in hers. "I will be sad tomorrow," she said.

Maara glanced away, to hide the look of pain that crossed her face. My own loss seemed small when I compared it to what Maara would be losing. This might have been the home she wanted when she left Merin's house the first time. Perhaps, if not for me, she would have found it. I had never thought of that before. And now, despite the dangers I would face there, I was going home, while she would have to leave a place where she belonged for a place where she would always be a stranger.

Thinking of Maara's loss made me so sad that I missed much of their conversation. When I heard Aamah ask Maara which way we planned to go, I began to pay attention. I had assumed that we would go back the way we came, but Maara said, "Through the forest is, I think, the safest way. If we can reach the river, it will take us where we're going."

"The forest may be safer," Aamah replied, "but it's easier to lose the way. Do you know how to find the river?"

Maara shook her head, and Aamah drew with her finger on the ground between them.

"This is the brook," she said. "It joins a wider stream here, but don't follow it. If there are strangers in the forest, they too will stay close to the brook, to keep from getting lost. Go this way." And she drew a path that crossed several ridges before descending to the stream that would lead us to the river.

"Do you know where the stream and the river flow together?" asked Maara.

Aamah nodded and traced a twisting way that followed what appeared to be a tangle of streams that flowed together until they became the river. She marked places that were impassable and places where we might encounter strangers, tracing paths that would let us go around them, until she had shown us as much as she remembered. Much of it came from her own experience, but some also came from others who had wandered farther or from stories that had been passed down through the generations. I hoped her people had remembered well, or we might find ourselves wandering forever.

"Why not go back the way we came?" I asked.

Maara was patient with me. "What will we find there, this time of year?"

I knew the answer well enough. "Cattle raiders," I said. "And the warriors of Merin's house, who are now just as much our enemies as the warriors of the northern tribes."

Maara nodded.

"Or we might not encounter anyone at all."

"But if we do, where can we hide in the wilderness?"

She was right. No matter how difficult the journey through the forest and down the river, it was less dangerous than the swords of our enemies.

In the evening, when everyone had gathered around the fire, Sett told a story I hadn't heard before.

The world was a vast and empty place, until the spirit of the moon came down. Drawn by curiosity, she set her small, silver foot on the bare earth and felt something move beneath it. Where she had stepped, a fissure opened in the earth, and a tiny animal sprang out of it, a creature no bigger than a thumbnail. With skin of shining green, enormous eyes, long fingers, longer toes, he hopped here and there over the surface of the ground.

"Who are you?" asked the spirit of the moon.

"My name is Frog," the creature said.

"Are you alone here?" asked the spirit of the moon.

"We are many, who have lived within the earth since time began," said Frog.

"Are the others as beautiful as you?" asked the spirit of the moon.

"They are," said Frog. "All different, and all beautiful."

The spirit of the moon took another step. Beneath her foot, the earth opened, and a tiny animal flew out. Clad in feathers of the deepest blue, she soared into the air, then came back down again.

"Who are you?" asked the spirit of the moon.

"My name is Bird," the creature said.

The spirit of the moon took another step. This time the earth released a seedling that thrust its green stem toward the sky, unfolded branches, clothed them in leaves, caught the wind, and yet remained deep-rooted in the earth.

"Who are you?" asked the spirit of the moon.

"My name is Tree," it said.

The spirit of the moon traveled far and wide, and everywhere she went, her step released new life. Everything now living on the earth she set free that night.

When dawn came, the spirit of the moon faded from sight, and all earth's living things had to learn to live in sunlight. The day was long and hot. Some creatures slipped back underground, awaiting the return of night. Others loved the daylight and learned to fear the dark. Soon all forgot that they had once been brothers in the belly of the world.

70

Going Home

O n our last morning I awoke alone. My heart was heavy, and I was
in no hurry to get out of bed. I hoped Maara would forgive me
for not helping her prepare for our departure. There was little
left to do. We had made up our packs the day before, so that we could see
the forest people on their way. Neither Maara nor I could bear the thought
of staying on in the encampment once they had left it.

We shared a silent breakfast with the forest people. Afterwards, as is the
custom everywhere, we exchanged gifts with them. Although I had little
skill with the needle, I had made a few small things — dolls for the children, cut from scraps of Maara's woolen tunic and stuffed with moss, and
for Worr a beaded quiver. To Sett I gave what remained of the healing herbs
I had brought from Merin's house.

Each of the hunters gave me an arrow that bore his own distinctive
markings, so that the sight of the arrow would bring to mind an image of
its maker. When I understood the purpose of the gift, I gave each man an
arrow of mine.

Aamah handed Maara the women's gift, a bundle wrapped in deerskin.
Maara seemed to know what it contained. She thanked Aamah and the
women sincerely, but she set it aside without opening it. Then she offered
Aamah the gift she'd made, a carrying bag much like the one she gave to
Breda, but made of half a dozen white weasel skins, the best of what we'd
trapped all winter.

We accompanied the forest people as far as the brook, where they turned north, to follow it to its source, while we would go the other way. Our parting was even more painful than I feared. The children cried and clung to us, until their elders coaxed them away with the promise of a new adventure. By evening I hoped the children would be cheerful again with the anticipation of seeing other friends, but it would be a long time before I got over missing them. The women embraced us, and each one whispered a word or two — wishes for a safe journey and fine weather, curses on our enemies and blessings on all who would befriend us. The men had Sett say their farewells for them, which consisted mostly of good, though obvious, advice. No fires at night. Keep a watch. Beware of strangers.

When there was nothing more to say, the forest people turned and left us. After we watched them out of sight, we stood where we were for a long time gazing after them, too sad to take another step.

"This is not the way we should begin," said Maara. "Let's camp somewhere for a day or two, until our hearts have had their fill of looking back."

We followed the familiar path as far as the hollow tree, but we didn't enter it. Maara made our camp out in the open. We were both reluctant to carry sorrow into a place that had held so much joy.

Maara spent the afternoon using a charred twig to draw Aamah's map from memory onto a bit of deerskin. She had me watch her, so that I could learn it.

"How do you know that the river Aamah remembers is the same one that flows through Merin's land?" I asked her.

"I don't," she said, "but south is the direction we must go, and this is the only way."

The sound of birdsong made us both look up. It was so like the sound the forest people made to let the village know of their arrival that my heart lifted in anticipation. I saw on Maara's face the same hope I felt, followed by disappointment when we realized it was just a songbird.

"We'll never see them again, will we?" I asked her.

"No," she said.

The next day Maara tried to turn my thoughts to the task ahead of us. She had me draw Aamah's map on the ground, first from the one she'd made, then several times more from memory. Aamah had told us of landmarks we would pass—a tree split by lightning, with half its trunk rotting on the ground and the other half still green and growing, a rock shaped like an antlered elk, a stone cairn left by travelers, and many more. Maara had me memorize them all.

"What will we do once we reach the river?" I asked her. "Assuming that it's the right river, we can't just walk down the river road to Merin's house."

"We're not going to Merin's house," said Maara.

"Where are we going?"

"I'm not sure yet. Perhaps to Laris. Perhaps to your mother's house. We'll have to see how things are."

"Laris is far to the south of Merin's house," I said. "And to get to my mother's house we'll have to cross the heart of Merin's land. Someone will surely see us."

"No one will see us if we go up the ravine."

It was a clever thought. Something I very much admired about Maara was her ability to send her mind far ahead, following many paths at once, so that she could foresee where each might lead and choose the best. I had not the gift of foresight. I tended to take the obvious path unless something deflected me, and then I would react by instinct. So far my instincts had served me well enough, but it would be wise of me to learn Maara's way.

The next morning, though I missed the forest people no less than I had the day before, I was impatient to begin our journey. Maara agreed with me that it was time we were on our way. She opened our packs and laid everything out on the ground so that we could take stock of what we had.

With any luck we wouldn't starve to death. We had plenty of acorn flour and smoked venison, and we were sure to find fresh food along the way. The packs also held our fur tunics. We had exchanged them for shirts of deerskin as the weather grew mild, but on chilly evenings, their warmth would still be welcome. We had our cloaks too, to use for bedding and to turn aside the spring rains. In Maara's pack, half hidden in the folds of her tunic, I saw the sword she took from Vintel's warriors. I'd forgotten that she had it.

Although the thought of parting with my wolfskin was more than I could bear, it was so bulky and impractical that I doubted the wisdom of bringing it along, but Maara insisted, and she took most of our supplies into her own pack to make room for it in mine.

Before she did up our packs again, Maara opened the mysterious bundle Aamah had given her. In it were a few pieces of our woolen clothing, a shirt and a pair of trousers for each of us, stained and threadbare, but still usable, and the bedraggled shreds of what had once been my tunic. These she added to our packs.

"Are they worth carrying?" I asked her.

"They may come in handy if we should need a disguise."

"A disguise? Will we disguise ourselves in our own clothing?"

"We'll wear whatever will allow us to blend in."

Her words sent a prickle of apprehension up the back of my neck. Blend in? With whom would we have to blend in?

"If someone should see us at a distance," she said, "we want them to see what they expect to see. We're dressed now as people of the forest dress. We could be hunters, or we could be outlaws. Either way, anyone who catches sight of us will be content to keep their distance and let us continue on our way. But once we leave the forest, we will look out of place. In our woolen clothing, we can pass for country people."

We followed the brook south for a little distance until we reached the place where Aamah had told us to take a different way. The landmark she described was obvious. The trail was not. Hunting with the forest people had made me adept at seeing the almost imperceptible trails they used, and I spotted this one before Maara did. It led us over the crests of several hills, where the forest was so dense that we had hardly a glimpse of the sky. When several trails came together in a tangle, Maara kept our direction true. Between the two of us, we found the stream that would lead us to the river.

It was now late afternoon, too early to stop, I thought, with over an hour of daylight remaining, but Maara left me to make camp while she scouted both sides of the stream for half a mile in each direction, looking for signs that others had been there. She found only an old hearth from the year before and a tangled fishing net, torn beyond repair, that could have washed down the stream from anywhere.

I made a lean-to of fallen branches next to a pile of deadfall. Once we crept into it, we would be invisible. A little distance away I made a small fire and put acorn bread to bake in the ashes. By the time Maara returned, supper was ready.

While we feasted on acorn bread and venison, I took the opportunity to look around me. The forest here was different, its trees less ancient, its canopy more open. Alders grew in marshy places near the stream, and on its banks were meadows, with wildflowers in colors I hadn't seen all winter—red and orange, yellows bright and pale, cornflower blue—scattered among the bracken. For the first time since we met the forest people I was homesick.

"Will we be home in time to see the wildflowers?" I asked Maara.

She gave me a puzzled look.

"The flowers here reminded me," I said. "I can't imagine spring without the sight of a carpet of wildflowers covering the—" I groped for the word, only to realize that I was still speaking in the language of the forest people. "—pastures," I said in my own tongue. The forest people had no word for pastures.

Maara knit her brows. "You just gave me an idea. If we should meet others, speak to me only in the language of the forest people, and if someone speaks to you in your own language, don't let them see that you understand it."

"Why?"

"So that I can be our tongue, and you can be our ears. People may speak carelessly among themselves in your hearing, and what you hear could prove useful."

"I thought we were going to avoid meeting anyone."

"That may not be possible." She turned to face me. "This land belongs to no one, but many travel here, some to hunt and some to trade, some as ambassadors of goodwill to their neighbors, and some because they are unwelcome elsewhere. If we should encounter any of them, we must be whatever they will find least threatening and least profitable."

"Least profitable?"

"As hostages," she said. "Or as slaves."

"Oh," I whispered.

Maara saw that she had frightened me. "Better to talk now about what may happen before the need arises."

I nodded. "What else?"

"If it should happen that we are separated, you must find your own way home."

"I will do no such thing."

Maara scowled at me. "Don't be stubborn and don't be stupid. Find your own way home, and I will do the same. We have no time to waste wandering around looking for each other. Go to your mother, if you can, or go to Laris. If I had to guess what may be happening now in Merin's land, I would say that your friends are gathering together, perhaps to search for you, perhaps to take revenge on the one who betrayed you. If any of Merin's warriors are still loyal to her, they will be making their own plans, to rescue Merin if Vintel has kept her in Merin's house, or to restore her to her place if she has left it."

I put all these things away in the back of my mind to consider later. First I had to make Maara understand.

"Stubborn I am," I said, "and stupid I may be, but I won't go home without you."

Maara's scowl deepened.

"We may argue all night about it," I said. "I won't change my mind."

"The world may change it for you."

"No."

"Do you imagine that you are stronger than the world?"

"Not at all," I said, "but I will always have the power of refusal, and leaving you behind is one thing I will not do."

Maara knew me well enough to stop. She wouldn't argue with me, but I felt within her a determination to have her own way, whether I agreed with her or not. I saw one thing clearly, and I held my tongue about it. She had no intention of making her own way back to Merin's land alone. She would no more leave me than I would leave her.

For several days we made good progress. We didn't stop to hunt. A few snares and a fish trap, set out at night, provided us with almost more than we could eat. Although we saw no sign of strangers, we were careful to follow Aamah's advice and take the long way around places where we might encounter them, places where one stream joined another or where several trails came together.

The long way round was difficult. We climbed steep ridges, clambered over piles of boulders, threaded our way through dense thickets. It was no wonder that no one ever saw the forest people if they kept to trails like these.

A week after we set out, we smelled the smoke of a campfire. We skirted around it undetected, but the knowledge that there were others nearby made us more cautious.

The next morning we were following a trail that ran close by the stream when we heard voices on the water. We watched from a thicket as three boats made of hollowed logs approached. Four men in each boat paddled them upstream. They were all dressed in woolen clothing. They looked so out of place that I had to remind myself that I too had once dressed as they did.

Late that afternoon we found the place they came from. It could be called a village, though a temporary one, with only tents and huts made of mud and sticks for shelter, but there were dozens of them, enough to house a hundred people.

Here three streams flowed into one. I recognized the place from Aamah's map, but not the village.

"Aamah said nothing about this," I whispered to Maara.

"No," she said. "This is something new."

We withdrew into the forest until we had put a good distance between the strangers and ourselves.

"This is something we may not be able to go around," said Maara.

"Why not?"

"This place casts a wide net. Not just the streams, but many trails must come together here. It will take us far too long to go around it."

"What else can we do?"

"We can do as they do. We can go down the river."

"But they'll see us."

Maara smiled. "There is more than one way to hide. Sometimes by trying to hide one only makes oneself more conspicuous. Now I think we must try hiding in plain sight."

After considering every course of action we could think of, we decided that going down the river was worth the risk. It would be much faster than walking, especially if we had to take the arduous trails used by the forest people, and I believed Maara was right, that if we were caught trying to avoid detection, people would suspect our good intentions.

The only problem with our plan was that we had no boat.

"We dare not steal one," I said.

"Of course not," said Maara, "but we can trade for one."

I couldn't think of anything we had that was worth a boat.

"We have the sword," said Maara.

"We may need the sword."

"What for?"

"Without it, you'll be defenseless."

"Don't deceive yourself," she said. "We are defenseless. Our best defense is to be not worth killing."

In the morning we walked in plain sight down the trail beside the stream and into the village. Maara reassured me that we would be in no danger there. Where so many strangers came together, anyone who broke the implied truce that governed such places would become the enemy of all. The dangers we might face in the days ahead would come upon us when we were once again alone, and our main concern while we were in the village was to arouse no one's suspicion and no one's enmity.

To my surprise no one gave us more than a brief glance. We were just two more travelers among a crowd of people who were all intent upon their own pursuits. There were both men and women here, dressed for the most part in woolen clothing, although some, like us, were clad in deerskin. I caught fragments of their speech and couldn't understand a word of it. Each person seemed to be speaking a language of his own. Then bit by bit my ears became attuned to a tongue that, as I listened, transformed itself from something utterly incomprehensible into a speech I recognized. It was my own language, the language of Merin's house, but spoken very badly, full of mispronunciations and misuse of common words, as well as words I had never heard before, whose meaning I couldn't guess.

Maara moved through the village like one who belonged there. I tried to look as relaxed and unconcerned as she did, but it had been a long time since I had been around so many people, and I began to feel hemmed in. All around us men and women shoved their way through knots of people gathered around those with goods to trade. Men dressed as we were stood surrounded by piles of skins and furs. Women traded woven cloth, and a few had metal goods — cooking pots and knives and axes.

At last we left the marketplace behind for a place where there were fewer tents and fewer people. Some were deep in serious conversation and paid us no attention. Others glanced at us with undisguised curiosity.

The path ran along the riverbank, where dozens of boats were pulled up onto the shore. Most were made of hollowed logs, some big enough to carry half a dozen men and a cargo of their goods, some just big enough for one. Other boats were flimsy things made of hides stretched over frames of wickerwork. A few of the larger boats were made of hewn planks. Too heavy to pull up on shore, they were tied to pilings driven into the mud.

When Maara stopped to examine a log boat that looked big enough to carry the two of us, a man approached her. His smile was friendly, while his eyes took us in from head to foot.

"A fine little boat," he said, in the inharmonious tongue that offended my ears.

Maara prodded the boat with her toe. "A good size, but waterlogged."

Although she knew better, she spoke as badly as he did.

I feared the man might be insulted. Instead he laughed.

"Floats well enough," he said, and gave it a little push away from the shore, so that it bobbed in the shallow water, still tethered with a bit of rope fastened around an anchor stone.

Maara shook her head and gestured at another boat that was a little bigger than the first and appeared to be in better shape.

"Whose boat is this?"

The man resigned himself to keeping his waterlogged craft and led us to a nearby hut made of sticks and twigs daubed with river mud. He told us to wait and went inside. We heard the sound of voices, the man's voice and a woman's, as he negotiated a finder's fee. When he came out again, he gestured to us to go inside.

The hut was dark and full of smoke. Before my eyes could see much more than shadows, the woman asked us to sit down. By the time we settled ourselves by a fire that gave off more smoke than light, I could see a little better.

The woman was the only person there. Her careworn face made her appear to be past her middle age, but there was no grey in her dark hair, and she still had all her teeth. She looked us over with a critical eye.

"My friend tells me you want a boat," she said, "yet you come empty-handed."

It was true we had no goods to trade, but she mistook our lack of goods for poverty, and I resented it. Maara shrugged out of her pack, laid it on the ground, and opened it. She pulled aside our bits of ragged clothing to reveal the sword.

The woman stared at it for a moment, then gave Maara a shrewd look.

"How did you come by this?" she asked.

"I didn't steal it."

"I meant no insult," the woman said. "I only wonder if you are more than you appear to be."

"I appear to be a traveler with a sword to trade for a boat," said Maara.

"If you are skilled in its use, you may regret letting go of it."

"Why is that?"

"Do you intend to go downriver?"

Maara hesitated. Then she said, "Is it the custom now to pry into the business of travelers?"

The woman made a gesture of impatience. "You mistake me," she said. "Like everyone else, I have my own interests at heart, but I doubt they conflict with yours. You may serve my interests, and your own as well."

Maara waited for her to go on.

"If you're bound downriver," the woman said, "you may run into trouble. Traveling alone is dangerous, and as it happens I have goods to send downriver. Why not keep your sword and buy your passage with your service?"

Once Maara had given her consent, the woman offered us her hospitality, which consisted of a bowl of barley soup and a place to sleep beside her fire. The soup we accepted gratefully, but we preferred to sleep outside, out of the smoky air.

All evening, as we sat by our fire, people joined us to chat, some who wanted only a pleasant way to pass the time and some who tried in subtle ways to learn more about us — where we came from, where we were going, and the nature of our business. Maara evaded their questions skillfully, and without giving offense. She even lured them into revealing more about themselves than they intended. How foolish were the people of Elen's house, I thought, who had not used Maara's skill with language and diplomacy to their advantage. They should have made her an ambassador.

I listened to the conversation as if I understood not a word of it, and when anyone spoke to me, I smiled and nodded, to be polite, then looked to Maara to tell me, in the language of the forest people, what they had said. They spoke my language so dreadfully that I often did have need of her assistance.

To my ears the language of the forest people sounded lovely, soft and melodious, so I was very much offended when one woman said, on hearing Maara speak to me, "Stars! What a barbarous tongue!"

Maara quickly drew attention to herself, before the woman could see that I had understood her.

"I imagine that to her ears ours sounds just as barbarous," she said.

In the morning, Maara, who had no scabbard for her sword, fashioned a makeshift sling for it out of deerskin and fastened it to her belt. I would have taken my bow from its case and strung it, but Maara stopped me.

"Best not," she said.

Before she could offer me an explanation, a boy came to tell us that the boats were leaving. Half a dozen were to go together. Maara sat at the front of the first boat, and I sat right behind her. Our companions in the boat were three men who had shared our fire for a while the night before. They were traveling together, to look for wives, they said.

After an hour in the boat, I decided I would have preferred to walk. My legs were cramped and stiff, and the boats, heavy with goods and people, rode so low in the water that, although we were bailing constantly, my deer-skin trousers were soon soaked through.

It was a long day. At twilight we beached the boats and made camp on the riverbank. The next day was like the first. I tried to occupy my mind with studying the country we passed through. We were now beyond the boundaries of Aamah's map, and the countryside began to feel familiar. Though we still had forest on both sides of us and there was no feature of the landscape that I recognized, the quality of light, the fragrance of the air, and the shape of the hills I caught a glimpse of in the distance all felt like home.

⚬⁄⚬

The next morning, not half an hour after we set out, boats filled with warriors blocked our passage. By the style of their clothing and the devices on their shields, I knew them for warriors of the northern tribes. As soon as we spotted them, we beached our boats and stood together, prepared to defend ourselves. I had little confidence in our companions, for they seemed to have little confidence either in each other or in themselves.

Once again Maara prevented me from readying my bow.

The northerners were no more eager for a fight than we were. They sent their leader to speak with us. The man who had assumed the leadership of our ragged band of mercenaries went to meet him and talked with him for several minutes. When he returned to us, he pointed to the boat that Maara and I had ridden in and said, "Leave them this one."

At once our companions began to slide the other boats back into the water. The men who had shared our boat left it and ran in a mad rush to find places in the others. Maara understood what they were doing before I did. She took hold of me and pushed me into one of the boats just as it left the shore, but when she tried to board it, a woman cried out, "She'll sink us," and struck Maara with her paddle.

My mind could not comprehend such a betrayal. I thought at first the blow must have been an accident, that in her hurry to get away the woman had been careless. Accident or not, when I saw Maara fall, I went into the water after her.

No one helped us. No one waited for us. Our fellow travelers paddled for their lives downriver, while I lifted Maara's head out of the water and dragged her onto the shore, where the northerners surrounded us.

71

Turning Point

The northerners bound Maara's hands. They had no need to. Her sword was gone, lost in the river. She was still dazed from the blow of the paddle, and blood ran down her face from a cut on her forehead. They left my hands unbound. They seemed to think me insignificant, perhaps because I bore no arms. My bow lay unnoticed with my pack, hidden among the cargo in the boat our companions had left behind.

The northerners waited while I tended Maara's wound. After I stopped the bleeding, they ordered us into our boat and took us a short distance downstream, where they beached the boats and hid them. Their encampment lay a short walk from the river. There they unbound Maara's hands and let us dry our clothing by their fire. In fact they were not at all unkind. When Maara began to feel a little better, they fed us, and one of them gave me a scrap of cloth to bandage her head.

At midday another band of warriors arrived at the encampment. Their leader came to speak with us. A tall woman with flaming hair, she reminded me of Taia. I knew that Maara spoke a little of their language, but it surprised me when I found I understood a word or two. I heard Maara speak the word for travelers, which was the same in many tongues, and I heard other words with a familiar sound. Although I couldn't follow their conversation very well, by her face and by her gestures I knew what the red-haired woman wanted. She was trying to discover how to make best use of us.

"Do they have any idea who we are?" I asked Maara after the woman left us.

Maara shook her head. "They believe we came from the north, like the others."

"What will they do with us?"

"We'll have to wait and see," she said.

All afternoon we stayed where the northerners had left us, by the fire at the center of their camp. They left us unbound, but there were so many of them all around us that it was no use trying to escape.

Maara pretended to be unwell. She lay down and shielded her face with her arm, as if the light hurt her eyes. All the while she was listening to the conversations of our captors. I tried to listen too, though I learned nothing of value. It was an odd tongue they spoke, the sound familiar but with an unfamiliar cadence. Unlike the language of the trading village, which was my own tongue spoken badly, this was another language altogether, yet sometimes I felt that I caught a thread of meaning, even if I didn't understand the words.

I tried to take in everything that was going on around me without being obvious about it. From what I could see, at least half a hundred warriors were encamped there. The camp seemed well established. No attempt had been made to hide it, as if no one would challenge their right to be there. I didn't know how far we were from Merin's land or if the warriors guarding our frontier would come this far. Clearly the northerners did not expect them to.

Late in the afternoon they fed us again. After we had eaten, I looked again at Maara's wound. Anger burned in my belly when I thought about the woman who had dealt that treacherous blow. In my mind I judged her, and if it had been possible, I would have punished her myself.

I wondered if we might be able to make our escape at night, while the northerners were sleeping, but when darkness fell, they bound our hands and feet and set a watch, and the watchman kept an eye on us.

For a long time I was wakeful. I worried about Maara's injury and about the northerners' intentions. By now I knew the world well enough to understand how serious was our predicament. Captives were either held as hostages or sold as slaves. Hostages might hope to be treated well, but the value of a hostage was in her ransom, and who would ransom us? We were so close to Merin's house, so close to home, yet the only price Vintel would pay would be the blood price on my head.

In the night she touched me. Because of our situation, we had not gone to sleep in our usual embrace. We lay side by side, with a little distance between us. Her fingertips brushed the bare skin of my forearm. When she saw that I was awake, she took my hand.

"Do you trust me?" she whispered.

"Of course," I said.

"Will you do what I tell you?"

"Yes."

"Good," she said.

I waited for her to tell me what she wanted me to do, but she didn't speak again.

"Do you have a plan?" I asked her.

"Hush," she said. "Hush, before they hear us, and go to sleep."

I hushed, but I didn't sleep. Nor did she. The backs of her fingers rested against my bound hands. From time to time they moved a little in a soft caress. Her touch was a comfort, and I thought I understood it. I thought she meant to reassure me. I should have listened more closely. If I had, I might have heard the good-bye in it.

In the morning two of the northerners unbound us and took us to relieve ourselves. Then they made us welcome to the remains of their break-fast. While we ate, the northerners broke camp. Some were forming into raiding parties. They had seen to their weapons the night before, and their packs held supplies for just a day or two. Others were preparing for a longer journey, their packs heavy with food and supplies. I recognized them as the warriors who followed the woman with red hair.

Maara seemed on edge. No doubt her wound bothered her, but I felt more at work in her than pain. I knew her moods so well. This one was new. Her restless eyes went from one thing to another, like the eyes of an animal brought to bay. They frightened me.

The red-haired woman appeared among her warriors and spoke impa-tiently to those who were still fumbling with their packs. When all were ready, she beckoned to an older man and gave an order. At once he turned and approached me, while she strode away, to speak to someone else.

The man said a few words to me and saw that I didn't understand them, so he gestured to me to follow him. When I stood up, Maara rose too. The man spoke to her, short and sharp. He must have expected her to sit back down, because when she didn't, he gave her a shove and repeated his order. Maara stumbled back a few steps, but she stayed on her feet. The man went after her.

Before he reached her, she spoke to him. Her voice betrayed her fear. It was not fear of what the man would do to her. It was fear of something that was about to happen, something she was helpless to prevent.

Then I realized that they were going to separate us. The red-haired woman's band intended to take me with them on their journey and leave Maara behind.

The man took hold of Maara and tried to force her to sit down. Her knees refused to bend. The man grew angry. He shouted at her, and she spoke again. They were respectful words. Nothing in her tone justified what he did then. He drew his sword and held the blade against her throat.

I cried out and took a step toward her. Before I could take another step, someone grabbed my arm and held me.

Two warriors took hold of Maara's arms and held her still, waiting to see what the man would do. I was terrified, but she had mastered her fear. She didn't struggle. She paid no attention to the sword. She raised her voice and called out several words in that strange tongue, and the red-haired woman came to see what the trouble was.

At first, when Maara tried to speak to her, she refused to listen. She gave an order, and three of her warriors forced Maara to her knees and prepared to bind her hands. The red-haired woman turned away, and Maara called to her again. The woman turned back, about to lose her patience.

Maara said something else, and the woman's face changed. She listened as Maara spoke a few words more. The woman weighed Maara's words, careful of being taken in, yet curious to hear what Maara had to say. Then she spoke to her warriors, who pulled Maara to her feet and stepped away.

The woman approached Maara and began to question her. Maara gave short answers, and the woman's curiosity grew. Maara drew her in. With a guile I never knew she had, she led the red-haired woman down the path she had prepared for her.

I heard every word without understanding what was being said. Maara stood a little turned away from me, so that I had to try to learn her meaning from her tone of voice and from the red-haired woman's face. For every question Maara had a ready answer, but something more was happening. This was a negotiation.

Though the red-haired woman held the power here, Maara had something to counter it. They soon reached an agreement. Maara made the woman swear an oath. Not with blood. That would have been too much to ask. A blood oath is sworn only between equals. Because we were her prisoners, it astonished me that the red-haired woman would consent to bind herself by any oath at all. Maara made her swear on her sword. The two of them swore together. The red-haired woman grasped the hilt, and Maara, in an act of trust, grasped the blade. Then it was done.

What Maara had to bargain with, what she had sworn to do, I could not imagine. Too confused even to frame a question, I waited for her to tell me what was going to happen.

"You're going home," she said.

Were they going to let us go?

"I'll follow you," she said.

There was nothing in her words to frighten me, nothing in her voice, soft as it was, or in the way she moved, slow and careful, as she took my hands in hers and gazed into my eyes.

"I'm going with them, just for a little while," she said. "I have something to offer them. In exchange they're going to let you go. Take one of their boats and go down the river. In a day or two you'll reach Merin's house. Do what I told you. Go to your mother, or to your friends."

At last I found my voice. "I won't go home without you."

"You mustn't follow me."

"I will. You can't prevent me."

"If you follow me, you will break my oath."

"I never swore an oath."

The northerners were all around us. The red-haired woman was impatient to be gone. They took hold of us and broke us apart.

"Don't leave me," I said.

They were pulling her away from me. When I tried to follow, others held me back. Relying on her oath, they didn't bind her hands. They took her by both arms, a warrior on either side, and led her away. She gave me a last look over her shoulder.

"Don't do something foolish," she said.

I wished I could have seen her face, but I was blinded by my tears.

"Make them take me too," I shouted after her.

"Go home," she said. "Don't let it all have been for nothing."

⟳

The red-haired woman's band went east, away from the river. The raiding parties went south and west, all but one. Half a dozen warriors stayed to guard me, to prevent me from following Maara. They made me sit still, but they didn't bind my hands or hobble my feet. I was not a hostage any longer. My ransom was agreed on, and Maara's oath was given. Now all I had to do was wait for my captors to release me.

I did what they wanted. I sat still. What else could I do?

Over my mind a cloud of doubt descended. This must be some dreadful dream, and soon I would awaken to the teasing laughter of the children, who had heard the murmurs of my nightmares.

But of course we had left the forest people. We were going home. How had it come about that I sat now in this pleasant place, in the midst of strangers and alone?

I didn't want to think. Once I began to think, I would know that this nightmare world was real.

How had it come about? A woman had struck Maara with her paddle. If she had not, Maara would still be with me. We might be home by now. That woman, by her act of cowardice, had changed the world.

For a time I entertained myself with visions of what I would do to her when next we met. I would strike off the hand that dealt the blow. I would do to her what she had done to me. I would take from her what she loved. I would reach into her breast and break her heart.

For a time my anger shielded me. Then I began to cry. They say revenge is sweet. Revenge is not as sweet as love.

An hour passed. I kept myself distracted by watching a patch of sunlight move across the ground. Another hour passed, and at last my courage found me. Maara would have used this time. She would have tried to understand her situation. She would have thought things through. When the time came for her to act, she would be ready.

I spent the rest of that day trying to make sense of what had happened. Maara said she would follow me, but how could that be so? What did she have to offer the northerners? What thing of value could she deliver that was enough to buy both my freedom and her own? When they discovered she had nothing, they would accuse her of swearing an empty oath and forego her price for the pleasure of taking a savage revenge for their disappointment.

Did she think she could escape? These people were not fools. They would guard her more closely now that she was worth two lives.

Maara could send her mind down many paths at once. That was more than I could do. I would have to take each path in turn, one path at a time. I started with the one I knew I would not take. What if I did what Maara wanted and went home? There I would find my family and my friends and they would join with me against Vintel. Vintel's power would be broken, and the Lady Merin would once again preside over her own house, a house that would in time belong to me.

It was the path that, should I choose it, fate would roll out before my feet. As I sent my mind down the path of my destiny, I saw all the good things the world would give me—praise and power, peace and plenty, and all the souls I loved but one.

One thing my heart knew. If I went home, Maara's path and mine would never cross again. If she had bought my freedom with empty promises, she would pay the penalty. Even if they let her live, they would salvage what they could. She might live out a short and painful life mining salt or tin, or she might become again what she had been in Elen's house, a warrior slave, whose purpose is to take the blows meant for those whose lives have value. Warrior slaves do not live long.

The thought of Elen's house disturbed me. I made myself think of something else.

A new thought tempted me. What if I was wrong? Maara was wise and clever, no one more fit to find a way to live than she. The life she'd led had made her so, had taught her to use whatever strengths she had against the weaknesses of others, had given her a power greater than the force of arms. She said she would come back to me. Why didn't I believe her?

I heard once more the sound of her voice as she spoke to me that morning. She spoke to me the way one speaks to a child, to soften a blow or to conceal a bitter truth the child is not prepared to hear. I am not a child. What truth could be too bitter for me to bear?

I thought again of Elen's house, and then I knew. Maara owed the people there a debt of blood. They would pay the northerners well for the opportunity to take revenge. Having nothing else to offer, Maara had offered them herself. She had bought my life with hers.

In my mind, things that had puzzled me fell into place. I saw how Maara had prepared herself for this, as she had tried to prepare me to go home without her. Maara had indeed struck a bargain with her gods. She wasn't coming back. She wouldn't try. She hadn't sworn an empty oath, but it was not her word given to the red-haired woman that bound her. She had been bound already, by a promise made to gods I didn't know.

✐

My captors brought me meat. Porridge had been good enough for us when we were prisoners. Now I was their guest. I wasn't hungry, but I knew better than to turn away their hospitality. I tried to remember that this was not their fault.

When I had eaten all I could, my eyes began to close. A warm fire, a full belly, and my sleeplessness the night before made me helpless to resist the dark. That was my excuse, though my desire to escape my own dark thoughts would have been enough.

I took the coward's way and closed my eyes. I had forgotten that nightmares pursue the cowardly. Cruel dreams came, in which Maara lay beside me, her breath warm against my cheek, her arms around me. I woke in the dark, alone.

Darker than the moonless night, an abyss of darkness opened in my heart, and into it fell all my hopes and dreams. The promise of a life lived with love beside me vanished, leaving in its place a wasteland. There I would live out a life that was not a living life, but a living death, in which I would simply pass the time until my final death released me. For a long time that path was the only path I saw, and the only power I had left was to choose to take that path or to take no path at all.

My anger rescued me. Silently I cursed the gods who had demanded Maara's life. It was at their feet that I laid the blame. As much as I hated the woman in the boat, she was just an instrument. Fear, not malice, caused her to strike out. Through her the gods had granted Maara's wish, and they would demand their payment.

What right had they to demand anything of Maara? Their power over her was without compassion, without love. They had no right to her compared with mine. My right was absolute, because I did love her, because I would have given her the world.

Yet who was I to challenge the power of the gods? What merely human power is a match for theirs? We were at their mercy, and merciful the gods are not. I remembered my own brave words to Maara, that I would always have the power of refusal. That seemed such a small thing now. What had I the power to refuse?

Then I remembered Maara's words to me, words spoken long ago. *She could have forced your body, but your spirit would never have submitted to her.* Maara had been speaking of Vintel, when she tried to take my brooch. As powerful as Vintel seemed to me then, there was a limit to her power. So too must there be a limit to the power of the gods. Though they might change the world around me, they had no power to change my heart. It was a sanctuary whose threshold they could not cross, and within it, love was safe. Not even the gods could take it from me.

And they couldn't make me stop. I would follow her. I would search the world for her, and if she were to leave this world for another, I would follow her there too. I would love my life for as long as Maara lived. More than that no one could demand of me, not even my own gods.

I began to make my plans. How long had it been since Maara left me? Little more than half a day? How long would it take them to reach Elen's house? It might take many days, more than a week perhaps. And once she reached it, what would happen then? They wouldn't kill her right away. They would send word to all those to whom she owed a debt of blood. It would be the ones she'd injured who would decide her fate.

Perhaps someone would speak for her. Perhaps Elen would speak for her. It was Elen who had helped her get away. If Elen had found compassion in her heart for Maara, in spite of her loss, might not others also feel compassion, whose injury was less than hers? Time had passed. Tempers had cooled. Grief may have faded. I began to hope.

Soon there would be moonlight. Around me I heard only the sounds of sleep. The fire was out. If the northerners had set a watch, the watchman too was sleeping.

I felt my way over to the fire pit, where there were still some bits of spitted meat. I ate a little of it and used one of my shirt laces to bind the rest into a bundle. There would be enough for several days.

It was still too dark to travel. I waited for the moon to rise.

SACRIFICE

When I could see well enough to find the trail, I slipped away from the northerners' camp and went back to the river. Our boat with all its cargo still lay hidden there, and my pack was in it. I had no time to search for Maara's pack. There was nothing I needed in it anyway.

I opened my pack and took out everything I could do without. All my extra clothing, even my cloak, I left behind. For warmth the wolfskin would be enough. Hidden in its folds I found my knife, Maara's gift. Before we entered the trading village, she had me take it from my belt and pack it away. At the time I thought she was being overcautious, but whatever her reasons, she had been wise. If I had been wearing it, the northerners would have it now.

The boat's cargo included several sacks of barley. I cut one open and made a smaller bag from one end of the sack, keeping as much of the grain as I thought I could carry. I did my pack up again. Then I took my bow from its case and strung it, and fastened my quiver to my belt.

Maara had told me to take one of the boats and go down the river. That's what the northerners would be expecting. I picked out a small log boat, just big enough for one. Into it I put the things I had taken from my pack and slid it into the water. With my bow I pushed it out into the stream, until the current caught it and carried it away. I backed away from the river's edge, careful to step in the footprints I'd just made. A child could have read the signs.

The first light of dawn glowed in the mist that hung in the branches of the trees. I returned to the northerners' camp and hid myself where I could watch them, to see what they were going to do. They were awake now and cooking breakfast. They seemed unconcerned about my disappearance. After they had eaten, they sent one man down the trail to the river, while the others made ready to travel. When the man returned, he told them what he'd seen. The northerners were satisfied.

I hoped they would go south, as the other raiding parties had done, but they started down the trail taken by the red-haired woman's band. I gave them half an hour's start, so as not to risk running into them again. I had no fear of losing the red-haired woman's trail. With the hunters of the forest people I had followed the faintest trails left by elk and boar. I would have no trouble following a trail made by a band of warriors.

In a few hours I came to a crossroads. There the warriors of the raiding party had at last turned south onto a trail that would take them into Merin's land. The red-haired woman's warriors had gone the other way. With the raiding party no longer in front of me, I began to close the distance.

The trail took me north and east. Before long I reached the forest's edge, and by early afternoon I was traveling through hill country that was almost barren of trees. There I was more exposed than in the forest, but unless I was unlucky, the hills themselves would hide me.

It was only midafternoon when I reached the place where the red-haired woman's band had spent the previous night. They wouldn't have stopped this early, which meant that I was catching up to them. I kept on until it was so dark that I was afraid I would miss the trail. Before the first light of dawn I took advantage of the moonlight to get an early start. At midday I found their next campsite. I was less than half a day behind them.

Now I took more care to read the signs that told me how long it had been since they passed by, so that I wouldn't suddenly stumble into their midst or run across a straggler. When I was no more than half an hour behind, I stopped. Soon it would be dark. Once the northerners made camp, it would be both easier to find them and safer to approach them.

I hid in a gully between two hills and risked a fire to make myself a proper meal of meat and porridge. For whatever happened next, I would need all my strength. While I ate, I thought about what I was going to do. In the dark the advantage would be mine. I could be among them before they knew it. Perhaps they had grown careless enough that I could succeed in setting Maara free, but even if they caught me, she and I would be together. That was as much as I could think about.

I dared to doze a little. It had been several days since I'd had a whole night's sleep, and I woke later than I intended. Still it was not yet midnight. There would be time enough to do whatever could be done.

Now that I was no longer in the forest, the stars gave enough light to travel by. I started down the trail. It narrowed as it wound between the hills, and I grew cautious, in case the northerners' camp might lie just around the next bend.

Then I saw in the distance the flickering light of a campfire. It seemed too far away to be the camp I was looking for. A few minutes later I saw another fire, and then another. Before me lay a narrow valley, where fires burned on every hillside as far as I could see.

The familiar sight made me long for Merin's land. It must be the night of the spring festival, and bonfires like these would be burning there too. The pain of loss wrung my heart, that I was not with Maara on this night. Then I began to wonder. What people lived here? There were no farms, no cottages, only the open fires. Not bonfires. Campfires. The campfires of an army.

I lost all hope of overtaking the red-haired woman's band. They would have kept on until they reached the encampment. All I could do now was wait for daylight, to see if what I feared was true. Just before dawn I climbed to the top of the nearest hill and hid myself in the tall grass. The growing light confirmed my fears. In the valley below me, warriors of the northern tribes were gathered, many more than anyone could count, hundreds upon hundreds.

I set my plans aside. I had no hope now of freeing Maara from the red-haired woman's band. Finding them among so many people would be impossible. I would be captured before I came close enough to find them, and there my hope would end.

I tried to think of something else, of some way to follow Maara through that maze of people. Even if I could pass unseen through the camp, even if I could go around it, the trail of the red-haired woman's band was lost, trampled into dust. I couldn't send my mind any farther down that path. No matter how many twists and turns I took, it always ended in defeat.

I still had one hope left. I knew where she was going. I knew it with a certainty that conquered all my doubts. The red-haired woman would take Maara north into the wilderness. It was the quickest way to Elen's house. I had taken that same way with Maara half a year before. I might not find the red-haired woman's trail, but I could find the forest, and once in it, I could find the bathing rock, and from there, with any luck at all, I could find Elen's house.

As Maara had reminded me, there were no hiding places in the wilderness, but if I traveled at night, the dark might hide me. What other path could I take? Only the way I had just come, back to the river and through the forest. It had taken us a fortnight to come this far. The journey back would take at least as long. The journey through the wilderness would take no more than a few days.

I heard voices and the tramp of feet on the trail behind me. I made myself small in my hiding place and turned toward the sound. A band of warriors came in sight, and a chill went down my backbone. While I had been following the red-haired woman's band, I hadn't thought that others might be following me. I hadn't taken any care to hide the signs I made when I left the trail to climb the hill, but they passed by the place without taking any notice of it. That band of warriors made my decision for me. It was as dangerous to go back as it was to keep going forward.

From my vantage point I studied the valley and the hills that surrounded it until I saw a trail that bypassed the encampment, winding through the hills to the northwest. Unlike the well-traveled trails used by the northerners, this one was faint and overgrown, a game trail that would take me unseen into the wilderness.

As I sent my mind down that trail and through the wilderness to Elen's house, I began to feel uneasy. Was there something I was missing? This plan was no more hopeless than the others I had made. There was indeed uncertainty at the end of it, but not hopelessness, not until I could see farther.

Movement below me drew my eye. I turned my attention to the encampment, where the warriors of the northern tribes were living one of the uneventful days so typical of camp life. For a while I tried to convince myself that this might be a base camp from which to launch their raids, but in my heart I knew that there was only one reason to gather so many warriors together in one place. They could have only one purpose, and only one destination.

The weight of obligation settled upon my shoulders. Soon on Merin's people the might of all the northern tribes would fall. Who would warn them if I did not? Yet I could not, unless I turned my back on Maara. At the thought my heart cried out, knowing it would be torn apart.

I might have time. That was my first thought. I might have time to find Maara and free her, and still bring back a warning. At once I saw it was a foolish hope. There was a good chance I would be captured too, or worse.

My next thought was that the warriors of Merin's house must already know of the gathering of this army. How could they not? They must have some idea of the northerners' plans. Surely they understood they were at war. And if Vintel had not foreseen that this could happen, were there not wise ones still in Merin's house?

These thoughts and many more ran through my head, and all the while I knew what I was doing. Maara had taught me the danger of self-deception.

I didn't care. Why should I care for those who had betrayed me. Whatever befell them now, it was no more than justice. As Vintel had stolen my inheritance, now the northern tribes would steal from her, not only what she took from Merin and from me, but all she had, and perhaps her life as well. I didn't care.

And Vintel's warriors had seen injustice done and done nothing to prevent it. Those who owed their loyalty to Merin, what had they done? Their fear, their cowardice, had increased Vintel's power, until they had no power to resist it. They had earned whatever fate awaited them. Why should I care?

Yet I did care. Though I tried to feed it, my anger faded, until I had to tell myself the truth. No matter what they'd done, I still belonged to them, as they belonged to me.

And what of those I loved, who might still be in Merin's house? Merin herself might be there. My mother too. And Tamar. Sparrow. Namet. Gnith. The loss of any one of them would break my heart. And even if they had left Merin's house, even if they had escaped Vintel's power, how would they escape the power of the northern tribes if Merin's house should fall?

I laid my cheek against the warm earth under me and closed my eyes.

Around me stood the council stones. They held me captive in the circle. The wisdom of the ancients lay beneath them, entangled in their roots, beyond my reach. Stone is one of the oldest things on earth, so my mother told me. Water is the other. One always still, one always moving, opposites, they worked upon each other, until between them they made the world. The stone circle held me still, while within my heart the tides of love flowed back and forth, awaiting my decision.

Had I, in my anger, invoked justice? How would justice weigh the claims of love? On one hand rested the lives of many, on the other, only one. Though all the world believes that the good of many souls must tip the balance, there is a flaw in their reckoning, for the value of the soul cannot be weighed or measured but by love. If my heart held the scales, I knew which side would fall.

I wondered at my willingness to sacrifice the lives of those I loved, until I saw that my own life too lay in the balance. Their lives and mine, for Maara. Why? To keep her with me? If I lost my life, I couldn't keep her with me. For her own sake? Perhaps. Yet hadn't she exchanged her life for mine? There was a certain symmetry about it, and an irony as well.

My mind had wandered far beyond the boundaries of understanding, until it stumbled into mystery. The more my reason tried to penetrate the labyrinth, the more I understood that love is not moved by reason. I had no power to abandon Maara. I couldn't shame myself or argue myself into it. I couldn't force myself to do it. Nor could I convince myself that I was doing the right thing. I might try to find excuses or to justify my heart's decision, but there was no excuse, and what I was about to do was impossible to justify.

I lay on the warm earth, half asleep, remembering. Another time, another place, a picnic, Namet's voice telling us a story. I wished then for Namet's innocent heart. The question life had never asked her, it was now asking me, and there was treachery in every answer. I consoled myself with this—that I would be a traitor to my people, but not to my own heart.

73

The Mist

My hiding place in the tall grass was as good as any other. I let myself drift into sleep, to seek wise counsel in my dreams. When I awoke late in the afternoon, I had no memory of having dreamt at all.

After dark I found the game trail I had spotted from the hilltop. Before dawn I was in the wilderness. I saw no sign of anyone, but that meant little. In the wilderness travelers could be seen from a great distance. If there were people about, I would see them at the same moment they saw me. I dared not risk traveling in daylight. I found a thorn bush, its low and spreading branches thick enough to hide me. There I slept the day away.

Two more nights of travel passed without my seeing anyone. Then on the third day voices woke me. There were no bushes here. I had made a nest of bracken barely thick enough to cover me. From a distance I would be invisible, but if anyone were to stumble across my hiding place, they couldn't fail to see me. Still I felt safe enough. The ground here was uneven, and low hills made up for the lack of cover. I lay some distance from the trail and out of sight of it.

I waited for the voices to pass by. Instead they grew louder, until through a flimsy wall of fern I saw two children crest the nearest hill. What children might be doing in the wilderness I could not imagine. They wouldn't be there alone. Their elders would be nearby, and if they had children with them, they were not warriors. They might be herding people in search of pasture or folk for whom traveling is a way of life.

I would have been safe from a band of warriors. Warriors would have stayed on the trail, but children seldom keep to trails. Their longing for adventure leads them into places where they believe no one else has been. These two were exploring. I watched them as they wandered over the hillside, coming ever closer to my hiding place.

My pack lay next to me, half undone. I slipped my wolfskin out of it and put it on, pulling the wolf's head cap well down, to cover my face. I waited motionless as they drew near. When they were close enough, I moved, just a little, just enough to draw the eye.

I couldn't see them very well through the wolf's head cap, but the voices stopped, and there was silence for a moment, then a small cry and the sound of running feet. I peered out from under my mask and watched them, until they vanished behind the hill.

Perhaps none of their elders would believe the children's story of a lone wolf prowling the wilderness, but if they were shepherds, they would come anyway, to ensure the safety of their flocks. I had no time to lose. Still clad in my wolfskin, I did up my pack as quickly as I could and ran the other way.

It was only midafternoon, and I was debating with myself which was the safer course, to find a new hiding place or to keep moving, when I caught my first glimpse of the forest. Even if I were spotted and pursued, once within it I would become as invisible as the forest people. In another hour I was safe among the trees.

Though the forest felt like home to me, I saw nothing that I recognized. I must have been some distance to the south of the place where Maara and I had first entered it. I started north, trying not to stray too far from the forest's edge. I could find hidden trails without Maara's help, but I had less faith in my ability to judge direction. Nevertheless, despite my best intentions, the forest drew me deeper into it, until I had no choice but to trust where it was leading me.

It was safer now to travel in daylight than in darkness. Here no one could see me from a distance or approach me unawares, and in daylight I could read more easily the signs left by other travelers. There weren't many. Sometimes I ran across the trail of two or three traveling together, people more likely to be hunters than warriors.

I spent my first evening in the forest listening to the sounds it made. At midwinter I had listened to the forest's dreaming. Now the forest was awake, and the ancient trees were listening too. They were aware of the animals scurrying around their feet, of the birds and squirrels nesting in their arms. They were aware of me. At midwinter they had let me share their dreams. Now they were curious and questioning, as if I were telling them a story, as if I were the dreamer.

Late the next day I found myself in a familiar place. With the hunters of the forest people I had tracked a boar and killed it there. Now green with spring, it had been snow-covered then. I knew it only by a tree that I remembered, an ancient yew growing out of solid rock. How it had begun to grow there, I could not imagine. Now it held the rock captive in the tangle of its roots.

I kept on for another hour, until the light was gone. By then I was sure of where I was. If I got an early start, a day's travel would bring me to the bathing rock.

In the morning I took the hidden and more difficult way used by the forest people, the way Maara and I had taken when we started home. It was longer than I remembered. By the time I reached the hollow tree, darkness had fallen. That may have been what I intended all along. For a time I stood outside the entrance before I found the courage to step inside.

I thought at first that it would hurt, that being there alone would make the loss of Maara yet more painful. Instead I found it comforting. We were there still. What we had shared there the tree remembered. I remembered. I sat within the living tree, within its open heart, and closed my eyes, until I brought her back to me.

What surprised me was how much of her I still had with me. I could bring her image into my mind's eye, could see again the smile she kept just for me and feel her fingertips across my cheek. More than that, I could live again in memory the moments after we made love, when we lay heart to heart, open to each other, unafraid, when we would speak endearments that knit our hearts together and tell each other stories we feared to tell ourselves.

A little of the mystery unraveled. That I would risk my life to regain what we had shared, that much I already understood. Now I began to understand the sacrifice. I had seen the world the way it should be, and I would accept nothing less. Not only for myself. For Maara.

∽

When I reached the bathing rock early the next morning, there were no signs that anyone had been there. Leaves covered the rock itself, some still bright with autumn color, though they had lain all winter under snow. This was not what I expected. I thought that a few of Elen's people might have visited the rock, leaving a trail for me to follow back to Elen's house.

Maara told me that Elen came there with her companions only in summer. At the time I thought she said it just to reassure me, but now I saw that it was no more than common sense. It was too early in the year for farming people to seek shelter from the heat in the coolness of the forest. Elen's house must be close by, but in which direction? I knew only that it lay on the far side of the brook, because the forest people seldom went there. They would travel a great distance to the north and south and east, but they treated the brook as a boundary. They seldom crossed it, and when they did, they grew more cautious.

That knowledge didn't help me much. I could follow the brook either north or south, or I could travel west, which meant that I would have to climb the ridge that blocked my way and hope to find some sign of cleared land on the other side of it. Which direction should I go? I searched my memory for clues. Had Maara given it away? Had she revealed it in a glance or gesture?

I couldn't remember. I hadn't been thinking of Elen then. I had been thinking about Maara, and I had put Elen out of my mind for reasons I was just beginning to understand. One of them was jealousy. If I had asked Maara to tell me about Elen's house, she would have. I didn't ask. I didn't want to know.

Had my jealousy kept from me the knowledge I would need to save her life? It seemed too great a punishment for such a small crime. Jealousy is just a part of human nature. I wanted Maara's heart. I wanted all of it, as she had all of mine.

I crossed the brook and spent all morning and half the afternoon searching upstream and down for any remnants of a trail. I found no sign of one. At last I decided to climb the ridge. From there I might see something to guide me.

The way up was difficult. By the time I reached the top, the sun was setting, and I could see nothing for the trees. I followed the ridge north for a little distance before I found a tall pine that I could climb. From its branches I had a clear view over the treetops. I saw just what I feared to see—another wooded valley and another range of hills. The forest stretched into the distance in all directions, until it vanished in the mist.

I camped that night where I was. Going down the hill in darkness would be dangerous, and I hoped that in the morning the mist would burn away, so that I could see farther. The damp made the night feel colder, but I dared not indulge in the comfort of a fire. I rolled myself up in my wolfskin. While it kept me almost warm enough, my sleep was troubled, by the cold and by my dreams. Once I awoke from a dream in which I was trapped inside a maze. I understood its meaning well enough. I did feel trapped in this maze of hills, where every step might be taking me farther from my destination.

I had counted on finding a trail from the bathing rock to Elen's house, but I realized I had been too optimistic. I had trusted that the way would open up before me. Now I had lost my way. I began to question my decision. Perhaps I had done wrong, and now I would be punished for my treachery. Perhaps the way home was the only way that had been open to me after all, and now it was too late. That way had closed behind me. It was too late for anything but regret.

The morning mist covered the forest. Above my head the treetops vanished into a shroud of white. Foggy tendrils hung like ghosts above the forest floor. Drops of water beaded on the leaves and slithered down the branches of the trees. Silence swallowed every sound. I never heard them fall.

I would see nothing from the ridge today. Should I wait where I was, hoping the mist would lift, if not today, perhaps tomorrow? I had no time to waste, and I had wasted an entire day, with nothing to show for my fruitless climb but aching legs and troubling doubts.

I usually felt more hopeful in the morning. Not today. Today I was truly lost, in a world that made no sense to me. Once all I had needed was the courage to take the next step on the path before me. Now every path was closed against me, or perhaps I had blundered off the path, to wander forever in the mist.

If this was punishment, I must be guilty, though I hardly knew what I was guilty of. I had made a choice of evils. And of course it was not I who made the choice. It was my heart that made it. I had learned to trust my heart. When had it misled me?

That thought gave me a little hope. One thing was certain. If I stayed where I was, I would never reach my destination. I might as well go back to the brook and follow it, in one direction or the other. I started down the hill.

I could see little through the mist. That didn't matter. There was no way to go but down, though the hillside was steeper here. I hadn't bothered going back to the trail I made climbing up, and I was beginning to think that was a mistake, when suddenly my feet slid out from under me. As I fell, I caught hold of a shrub that held me for a moment before its roots let go of the hillside. I slid down a steep embankment and landed in a heap on a rocky ledge.

It was a hard fall, but I didn't think I'd broken anything. The embankment was too steep to climb back up, so I slipped off the ledge and slid the rest of the way to the bottom. I made a softer landing this time in a pile of leaves.

I tried to discover where I was. The hillside looked nothing like it had the day before. Not only was it steeper here, but the soil was thin, and the mountain's bones protruded everywhere. Loose stones and slippery leaves made the footing treacherous. I would have to be more cautious. Another fall could cripple me.

The mist was so thick that it was impossible to see how far down the hill I'd come, but I didn't think I had come farther than halfway. My fall convinced me to find an easier way down. If I worked my way south along the hillside, I would eventually run across the trail I had made the day before.

As I traveled, the hillside grew less steep. I went quite a distance without seeing anything familiar. In a moment of inattention I could have crossed my own trail without seeing it. I gave up looking for it, and when I came to a gentle slope, I started downhill. At the bottom of the hill there was no brook, nor anything I recognized.

Then I understood what must have happened. The mist had baffled me. Somehow I had gotten turned around and started down the far side of the ridge. I had followed it north, not south, and instead of going toward the brook, I had been traveling away from it.

There was nothing else to do but climb back up the hill. When I reached the top, I grew even more confused. This ridge seemed to run the wrong direction, more east to west than north to south. I walked along the crest, trying to find my way back to where I had been that morning, but everything I did was wrong. The mist declared itself my adversary. With insubstantial fingers it blocked my way, deceived my senses, sent me in the wrong direction, stole my sense of time.

At last I had to stop. I was exhausted. I lay down on the forest floor and closed my eyes. This time I didn't try to soothe my fears with the hope that soon the mist would lift. Even if it did, I had wandered so far into this maze of hills that I would be lost for days.

When I awoke, I didn't know if it was day or night. It could have been either sun or moon glowing through the mist. I forgot my destination and my plans. All I wanted was to escape this murky half-light and find a clear view of the sky.

And I was thirsty. I had a gourd of water with me, but it was almost empty. I found a gentle slope and started down it. When I reached the bottom, a thicket barred my way. There was no water here, and the thicket was so dense and full of brambles that I dared not try to fight my way through it. To go around it, once again I would have to climb the hill.

I fell to my knees as if I had been dealt a blow, and I had no strength to get up again. The heart went out of me. Under a thin scattering of leaves the ground was covered with sharp stones. I lay down there anyway, on that damp and rocky ground, curled myself into a ball, and pulled my wolfskin close around me.

I was alone. There was no path for me to follow, nothing to guide me, no one to help me. The world had turned against me. The sun refused its warmth and light. The trees offended me with their indifference. The earth denied me comfort. I felt her waiting for my bones. If there was no way forward and no way back, then let the abyss open at my feet, and I would throw myself into it. I let go the last slender thread of hope.

74

The House of Kindness

A hunter found me. I heard him draw his bow. I heard the sound it made, the groaning in the wood as it took the hunter's strength into itself. There was no game here, no sound of hooves picking their way over stones, no rustling of fallen leaves, no birdsong. What could be his quarry?

I opened my eyes. From under the edge of the wolfskin I saw his feet and legs. He stood a little distance from me, but within bowshot, and by his stance I knew that if he was holding a drawn bow, he was aiming it at me. I waited for the singing of the bowstring. I waited for my misery to end.

Into a corner of my mind came a flicker of curiosity so faint that I almost disregarded it. Why would a hunter send an arrow through me without knowing who I was? Was every stranger here an enemy? Then I saw myself through the hunter's eyes. Wrapped in my wolfskin, to him I was a wolf, curled up asleep at the edge of the thicket.

If I was going to die, a wolf's death was not the death I wanted. I was a hunter of the forest people, and I would die standing on my own two legs. And if this hunter was about to kill me, let him know that he was killing one of his own kind.

Because I too was a hunter, I knew what he would do. He was making certain of his aim, taking care that he had a clear shot, with no leaves or twigs between that might deflect his arrow, but at the slightest movement of his quarry, he would let the arrow fly.

I rolled quickly to one side. The moment I began to move, I heard the bowstring and then the arrow as it struck the ground beside me. While the hunter nocked another arrow, I threw off the wolfskin and sprang to my feet. I had nowhere to run with the thicket at my back. I stood facing him and watched his eyes. He had drawn his bow and was staring at me over the arrow's tip.

At that moment I was as ready to meet my death as I would ever be. When he lowered his bow, I was both relieved and a little disappointed. Then I stepped back into the flow of time.

I made a sign to him with my open hand, the sign the forest people made when they greeted one another. He approached me, his bow lowered but with the arrow nocked, ready to draw again if need be, and stopped a dozen feet away.

He wrinkled his brow at me. "Who are you?" he said.

At least I think that's what he said. I recognized the word for "you." It was the same word used by the forest people.

"A traveler," I replied, using the word everyone understood.

He gazed at me, undecided.

"No harm," I said, in my own tongue.

He shook his head. When I repeated it in the language of the forest people, he looked puzzled, but I believe he understood.

"Lost," I said, in the language of the forest people. "I'm lost."

The hunter debated with himself.

"Come," he said at last, and took his arrow from the bowstring.

I didn't take time to open my pack, to put my wolfskin into it. I bound it to the outside of the pack as quickly as I could, before the hunter changed his mind. Then I looked around for my bow. At first I didn't see it. Lying on the forest floor, it looked like a fallen branch among the leaves. I did see the hunter's arrow, and when I bent to pick it up, I saw my bow beside it. At the same moment, the hunter saw it too. His shout of warning stopped me from reaching for it. I had the arrow in my hand. Slowly I straightened up and held it out to him. Still untrusting, he approached me and took the arrow before he bent and picked up my bow. He didn't offer it to me. Carrying both my bow and his own, he turned and started up the hill.

I had been wondering how the hunter found me, but when I saw the trail I made as I blundered about, lost in the mist, that puzzle solved itself. A wounded boar running from his pain and terror could not have left a clearer sign of his passing. I knew better than to leave a trail like that, and though it seemed that all was now well, my encounter with the hunter might have ended in disaster. While I berated myself for my carelessness, at the same time I was encouraged. I'd had a bit of luck. Perhaps the world hadn't turned against me after all.

When we crossed a stream, the hunter waited while I satisfied my thirst and filled my water gourd. Although I was still very hungry, I felt much better, and a little of my hope returned.

The hunter seemed to know where he was going. I followed him blindly. I had become so lost that all directions were the same to me. Whether we were going north or south, east or west, it made no difference. The hunter knew the way, and I did not. I decided to trust my luck a little longer.

We had been walking for several hours when we came to a bit of cleared land. I wasn't surprised that I hadn't seen the clearing from the ridgetop. Though it was quite large, several acres altogether, it was patchy and irregular, as it followed the contours of the hillside.

At one end of the clearing stood a round house made of wattle and roofed with a thatch of reeds. Before we reached it, the hunter called out a greeting, and a woman appeared in the doorway. A child came running out the door but stopped when he saw me and hid himself behind his mother's skirts. The hunter gestured to the woman to take the child inside. He made a sign to me to stay where I was and followed them.

The thought came to me that I now had an opportunity to run away. Then I thought again. The hunter had my bow, and I was more lost now than I had been before. If that were not enough, the smell of cooking would have held me there.

A few minutes later the woman came to the doorway and invited me inside. She offered me a place beside the hearth and handed me a bowl of soup. I was so hungry that I forgot my manners. I swallowed the soup down almost at a gulp and didn't make even a polite gesture of refusal at the offer of more. When I finished the second bowl, I found the courtesy to apologize for my greediness and thank the woman for her hospitality.

She seemed to understand me better than her husband did. She spoke a few common words of welcome and saw that my needs were met, for food and drink, for warmth and rest, before she let her husband question me.

He started by pointing at me. "Home," he said, and looked around at the four directions. "Where?"

I would have gestured to the south if I had known which way it was. The forest people had no word for south or any of the four directions. With no clear view of the sky, they didn't orient themselves by the sun or moon or by the stars. Instead they used features of the landscape. "The way the water runs," I said, and hoped that here the streams also ran from north to south.

Then the man said something I didn't understand about the common speech. I knew the phrase because I had learned from Maara, as well as from my own experience, that the common speech was whatever people around one spoke, while other ways of speaking were outlandish.

I shrugged and shook my head, to let him know I didn't understand what he was asking me.

He pointed toward the direction we had just come from and said, "The way the water runs speaks not."

I thought he was asking me why I spoke as I did, since I came from a place where nothing resembling his common speech was spoken. Whether or not he knew of the existence of the forest people, he would learn no more of them from me.

"A traveler," I said, pointing to myself. "A traveler speaks outlandish."

For the first time, the hunter smiled. His wife interrupted our conversation to offer me a bowl of tea. We sat in silence for a while, sipping our tea and enjoying the fire's warmth on this damp and chilly day. Then the hunter spoke again.

"Your bow," he said. "Is from?"

At the time it didn't seem like an odd question. I was trying to think of a way to explain its origin to him when I didn't know myself.

"A gift," I said. I hoped it was a word he understood. The forest people had no word for gift, not the way my people understood it. Among the forest people, no one owned anything. Whatever they had belonged to all, so a gift to them was just something held in common, and the act of giving consisted of someone who had a thing offering it to someone else who needed it.

The hunter thought that over for a while. Then he said, "Gift from who?"

I first thought of Maara, who had given me the bow, before I remembered what she told me. "Someone has left a gift for you," she said, and I knew now who it was she meant.

"The world," I said.

The hunter asked me no more questions. He sat still and silent for a long time. I woke many hours later, lying under my wolfskin with no memory of having gone to bed. Around me in the dark I heard the sounds of sleeping people. Feeling as safe as if I were at home, I closed my eyes.

When I woke in the morning, the hunter was gone. His wife offered me breakfast, and in the guise of idle conversation, she soon had out of me the whole story of my travels from the time I entered the forest until her husband found me. I also told her my destination. I didn't tell her why I was going to Elen's house, but I wanted to know if she had heard of it and if she knew where it was. Though she knew Elen's name, she told me she had never been there. When I asked her if her husband had, she shrugged and shook her head.

I was waiting for the hunter to come home before I took leave of them, partly out of politeness, but also because he hadn't returned my bow. It was nowhere to be seen within the house. When I went out to relieve myself, I looked around for it. I didn't see it anywhere.

It was growing late, and I was losing precious time. When I asked the woman when she expected her husband to return, she smiled and offered me more tea. At last, late in the afternoon, we heard him shout a greeting. We both went out to meet him. With him was a stranger, and the stranger held my bow. When he saw me, he stopped and stared.

"She is!" he said.

I had to wait while the hunter's wife performed the rituals of hospitality before I learned what he meant. I used the time to study him. He looked familiar. He must remind me of someone, I thought, because surely I've never encountered him before.

After all were greeted, warmed, and fed, the hunter's wife sat down with us beside the fire and drew her child into her lap. Holding him firmly between her knees, she began to finger-comb his hair.

I felt the stranger's eyes on me. I met his gaze. The warmth of his regard surprised me. He looked at me as he would have looked at a dear friend he thought he would never see again. He picked up my bow from where it lay beside him and with some ceremony offered it to me.

"I return to you my brother's bow," he said.

He took me so aback I hardly knew that my hands had accepted it. I had no words to make an appropriate reply. I stared at him, and began to see the man as I had seen him years before, a gaunt man in ragged clothing made of skins and furs, sitting on the floor of the men's house beside his wounded friend, the man whose pain had filled me with compassion, though he was my enemy.

Then I thought of that man's fate.

"I'm sorry he was lost," I said.

Although it took us a little time to become accustomed to each other's speech, by the end of the day, with the aid of signs and gestures I had learned from the forest people, we understood each other very well. The stranger, whose name was Finn, recognized me as the one who came with the healer to care for his brother. He remembered it was I who brought the medicine that eased his brother's pain. The hunter too had been among our prisoners, although he didn't recall seeing me.

Despite what Vintel had done, they and all who had been with them remembered with gratitude the treatment they received in Merin's house. They called it the house of kindness. They called Merin's people the kindly ones, and they judged us all, not by the vengeful act of one, but by the compassion of the many.

Of course they didn't know that it was I who interceded with Merin on their behalf. I said nothing to them about it. As it was, their warmth of feeling for me as one of Merin's people was more than I deserved. We too had reaped the benefit of what we did for them. They never returned to trouble us, they formed no alliance with our enemies to seek revenge against us, and they thrived on our gifts of grain and cattle, the loss of which we never felt at all.

Now I too had been nourished by the gift, and more precious than the gift of food, they offered me their friendship. I didn't tell them why I left Merin's house. It would have taken me forever to explain how I became an exile, even if I could have found the words. That didn't matter anyway. There was a much simpler explanation. I told them that someone I cared for had been captured by the northerners and that they were taking her to Elen's house.

The hunter nodded. "Our faithless friends," he said, and told me about their last dealings with their treacherous allies.

They had crossed the river into Merin's land at the urging of a chieftain of the northern tribes, with assurances that the northerners would divide Merin's forces by attacking from the north. A shiver went down my spine when I realized how close we had come to disaster. The northerners waited for news of the success of the river crossing. When it didn't come, they left their allies to their fate and went back home.

"You come to trade?" asked Finn.

He was asking me if I had come to negotiate Maara's ransom.

I shook my head. "I come to steal," I said. "To take her back."

The two men exchanged a look. Now they understood things that had puzzled them. If I had come to negotiate a ransom, I would have come with a guide, under safe conduct. I wouldn't have been wandering, lost in the mist, with no idea where I was going. The time had come to tell them the whole truth.

"My friend owes the people of Elen's house a blood debt," I said, "but she is innocent of the crime they accuse her of."

The two men stared at me and said nothing.

"Do you know Elen's house?" I asked them.

They nodded.

"Will you take me there?"

"Not alone," said Finn, and the two men put their heads together. They spoke for several minutes, loud enough for me to hear, but so rapidly that I could hardly understand a word. Then the hunter got up and left the house.

"He brings your friends," said Finn.

Before nightfall the hunter returned with three other men, and in the morning more arrived, until there were two dozen altogether, armed with swords and bows. All of them had once been prisoners in Merin's house.

ELEN'S HOUSE

B y midmorning we were ready to travel. When I took leave of the
hunter's wife, I thanked her for her hospitality and tried to reassure
her that I wouldn't lead her husband and his friends into danger. I
told her that, while I was grateful for their escort, I didn't intend to draw
them into battles that were mine to fight.

She smiled at me and rolled her eyes. "Try and stop them," she said, and
kissed me on both cheeks.

Then I understood that I had with me more than an escort, and although
they had pledged themselves to help me, they were not mine to command.
As we traveled I watched to see who the others looked to for direction. Finn
was one. The other was a man they called Bru, which seemed to be, not
a name, but a title of respect. He stood half a head above the others, and
his mane of dark hair and bristling beard would have made him look quite
fierce if he hadn't smiled so much.

That evening I invited both Finn and Bru to take counsel with me. In full
hearing of the others as we sat around the fire, we made our plans.

"How soon can we expect to be there?" I asked.

"By the day after tomorrow," said Bru. "If all goes well."

"What is the country like?"

"Beautiful," Finn said. "A valley. Not like yours, not so big, but flat land
between hills so steep that water falls in places almost straight down from
top to bottom."

"And Elen's house?"

"A fortress within a fortress," said Bru. "First the hills, then the walls."

They told me that while Merin's house stood on a hilltop ringed by earthworks, Elen's house stood on flat land, ringed only by a palisade, but well guarded nonetheless by the steep hills all around.

"How will we get in?" I asked.

"We'll go in through the gate," said Finn. He tried not to smile at my look of surprise. "A friend of mine is a craftsman there. We'll go in on the pretext of paying him a visit."

"All of us?"

Two dozen armed men traveling together were seldom on the business of paying a friend a visit.

"I think not," said Bru. "Let Finn and one other man go first, to see if there is any news of your friend."

"I'll go with Finn," I said.

Bru shook his head. "They will suspect a woman."

When he saw that his objection made no sense to me, he said, "Our people are so few, and the world we live in is so dangerous, that we cannot risk our women. They stay at home, and even if we had brought a woman with us, she would not dress or conduct herself as you do."

I was determined not to stay behind while others risked themselves on my behalf.

"Then I'll go in alone," I said.

There was a moment's silence, while Bru tried to think of something else.

"They won't suspect my son," said Finn, and gave me a hearty thump on my shoulder. "Dirty his face a little and no one will know the difference."

I had to acknowledge the resemblance. Finn's hair was no more than a shade or two darker than mine. He too was small and slightly built. Even our deerskin clothing looked similar enough, and our weapons were almost identical.

"Are your people on good terms with the people of Elen's house?" I asked Bru.

"We are on no terms with them," he replied. "We leave them in peace. They leave us in peace."

"They need us now," said Finn. "We dread the day that is no longer so."

A somber mood descended over all of them, as Finn explained their situation. The people of Elen's house lived both by farming and by trade, but their wealth came from goods made by their craftsmen.

Finn's people kept animals and grew much of their own food. They also trapped and hunted, and traded game and furs for what they couldn't provide themselves. They traded both with the northern tribes and with the people of Elen's house, but they had entered into an alliance only once, and the failure of that alliance convinced them that the dangers far outweighed the benefits. Yet because they were so few in number, both their neighbors were encroaching on the forest they regarded as their own. It seemed to them inevitable that someday they would be forced to ally themselves with one against the other.

"It is a delicate balance," said Bru.

"Then we must not disturb it," I replied. "I would be a false friend to you if I put you in open conflict with either side."

Bru knit his brow. Though he knew that what I said was both true and wise, he would feel bound by honor as well as by obligation to help me in any way he could, regardless of the consequences.

Before he could protest, I said, "In any case we are too few for open conflict. We will achieve more and at less cost by stealth."

Bru laughed. "Finn's son is still a woman at heart. A woman counsels caution, while a man's heart burns to see justice done."

"Justice will be done," I told him, "as justice was done to you."

The countryside surrounding Elen's house was as beautiful as Finn had said. We traveled through a forest of young pines, following a stream that tumbled down the wild hillside. On the day when we expected to reach Elen's house, around midafternoon, I heard a roaring in the distance.

"The falls," said Bru.

Soon the roar grew so loud that we had to shout to make ourselves heard. At the forest's edge we stepped out from under the trees onto solid rock. The stream flowed gently by, then vanished into mist, as it fell from the rock into the abyss. I approached the edge and looked over. I must have wobbled a little. Finn took hold of my arm to steady me.

When I lifted my eyes from the dizzying drop, I saw mountains in the distance. All stone and ice, their cold breath made me shiver, and the mist that overhung the waterfall beaded in my hair. Below me lay a narrow valley. Sunlight sparkled on the waters of the stream that, after its violent fall, grew calm again as it meandered through fields and pastures. Green and golden, abloom with spring, the valley seemed as pleasant a place as any I had ever seen. Only a few farmsteads were visible from where we stood. No fortress was in sight.

"Where is Elen's house?" I asked Finn. I had to raise my voice and speak close to his ear to make myself heard above the thunder of the falls.

Finn gestured downstream. "Just around the bend," he shouted back. "We'll see it from trail."

Set between high cliffs of stone, frighteningly steep, the valley floor appeared unreachable by any creature that had not the power of flight.

"Where is the trail?" I asked.

Finn pointed to a place not far away, where I could just make out a faint path that zigzagged back and forth down the cliff face. I would have descended into the valley that afternoon, but Bru feared the dark would overtake us before we reached the valley floor.

"A little patience," he said, "or we may take you to your friend in pieces."

We withdrew into the forest until we were far enough from the falls to be able to carry on a conversation. There we made our camp. I thought about the bands of warriors who guarded the borders of Merin's land, and I worried that a band of Elen's warriors might find us there.

"They already know we're here," said Bru, when I spoke my fears aloud, "but they won't challenge us. Tomorrow, when you and Finn go down into the valley, they'll keep an eye on you until you walk openly through the gates of the fortress. The rest of us will travel south, as if we're bound for somewhere else. We'll wait for you below the Giant's Maw."

"What place is that, to have such a dreadful name?" I asked.

"Where the stream flows out of the valley," said Finn, "there is another waterfall, less than half as high as the one that flows into it, but much more terrifying. Rocks like sharp and broken teeth thrust up through the water everywhere. A few careless boatmen have gone over the high falls and lived, but anything that falls into the Giant's Maw is dashed to pieces."

"It seems that it's easier to get into the valley than to get out of it," I said. "Once I find my friend, how will we get safely away?"

"There's no getting out by the same way you go in," said Bru. "If you go by light of sun or moon, they'll see you on the trail, and if you try to go by dark of night, one misstep will be your death."

That much I had seen for myself.

"We know a thing or two about this place," Bru said, smiling a mysterious smile. "Luckily for you."

"Our fathers lived here once, many ages past," said Finn. "They left us their lore in grandfathers' tales."

Of times long unremembered, old stories long forgotten old men tell.

Totha, king in his great hall, welcomed his brothers and his mother's brothers, his sisters and his sisters' sons, to hear him name his heir. One of them it must be, as the custom always was, while Totha's wife made her own plans.

"Husband," she said, as she lay on his breast at night, caressing him with her long hair. "Husband," she said, "you have the son I bore you. Name him."

Every night she asked, and every night he answered, "I will do as the custom always was."

Until one night his wife withdrew herself from his embrace and said, "Make me understand. Why is the custom as it is?"

So he said, unthinking, "To be certain of the blood."

Totha's wife knew well the meaning of his words, but she pretended innocence. "Explain this to me," she said.

"From the mother's body comes the proof of kinship," said Totha, still unaware of his wife's design, while she laid the coils of her trap around his feet.

"Do you accuse me?" she said to him. "Do you doubt that your son is as much from your body as from mine?"

As every father takes pride to see in his son his own reflection, so Totha took great pride in the son his wife had borne him. "I claim him," he told his wife, "and every hair on his head. It is no doubt of mine that must be overcome, but the doubt of others."

Then Totha's wife had the way open to her.

"Where a great king leads," she said, "his people follow. What you believe, they will believe."

So she persuaded him, and before all his mother's kin, he named his own son his heir. At first no one dared to speak against him, for they were guests in his house, but the dispossessed seldom go quietly away. They met in secret, and among themselves they came to an agreement.

First they tried to persuade Totha of his foolishness. His mother's brother said to him, "From my mother came many sons. Where will your son find so many of his kin to fight for him?"

As a king must stand by his word, so Totha stood by his decision.

Next they tried to shame him. His brother said to him, "Does Totha leave men's counsels to counsel with his women?"

As a king must not be goaded, so Totha told his brother that his decision was his own.

Next they tried to threaten him. His sister's son said to him, "I have the loyalty of many. Name your heir as the custom always was."

As a king must draw his sword against a challenge, so Totha drew his sword against his sister's son. Then all his mother's kin, who had been waiting outside the door, rushed in and overcame him. They bound him and set him in a boat, giving him into the hands of fate, whose judgments are swift and just.

Down the stream went Totha in his little boat, down the stream and through the mist, over the falls into the Giant's Maw, where the boat struck a rock and burst apart. From above the falls his treacherous kin watched Totha disappear into a whirlpool, while below the falls others waited to take possession of his body. Though they kept a careful watch, none of them set eyes again on the body of the king.

Where he journeyed after the Giant's Maw devoured him not even Totha knew. In later years he sometimes dreamt of caverns in the rock, lit by the eyes of beasts glowing in the dark or by the fiery breath of a serpent who slept under the mountain. All he knew was that while his foes still celebrated his defeat, he woke on a ledge behind the falls.

There the story ended, though this must have been only the first of many tales of Totha the king, who I guessed to be the father many generations back of the men with whom I traveled. Before I could ask my questions about Totha's fate, the men began to speak together, reciting a verse each knew by heart.

Three sisters stir the cauldron,
Below the eagle's beak.
Stand by the eagle's eye and leap.

Three times they recited it. Then they let silence fall, while the power of their chant reverberated in the air and its meaning breathed fear into my heart. To leave the valley, would we have to leap into the Giant's Maw?

The men seemed to be waiting for me to speak. It crossed my mind that they might be having a joke at my expense. Surely there was another way to reach the ledge behind the falls. Or perhaps they meant to test my courage, as the men of the forest people would sometimes test each other. Before a hunt, no hunter of the forest people admits his fear. Fear feeds on fear, until it devours a hunter's heart. When they were afraid, the forest people found ways to make fear grow small again. As if I thought nothing of leaping into the abyss, I made my face grow thoughtful.

"What happened next?" I asked. "Did Totha escape the ledge behind the falls?"

"He must have done," said Finn, "or none of us would be here."

"Did he regain his throne?"

"If he had, we would not have lived all these years in exile."

"What became of Totha's wife?"

Finn shrugged. "I never heard," he said.

That evening my thoughts returned often to the story of Totha the king. It seemed to me a wicked tale, to blame a woman for men's folly. In other circumstances I would have debated its meaning with my companions. Instead I was content to accept the gift in it, the knowledge of a secret way by which we might escape from Elen's house.

76

THE ARMORER

In the morning Bru and his men made a show of preparing for a journey. Bru added the contents of my pack to his own, so that I could enter Elen's house unencumbered. Finn carried only what one would bring along when he expected to enjoy a friend's hospitality at journey's end. Finn and I took leave of the others by clasping each man's arm in turn, as if this were a true parting.

Both Finn and I kept our bows, though we carried them unstrung to show our good intentions. They came in handy as we picked our way down the trail into the valley. Finn had me take hold of the end of his bow over the steepest places, where more than once loose rock almost took my feet out from under me.

When we had descended halfway, Finn stopped and pointed.

"Look," he said.

Only when I had made certain that my feet were securely planted did I dare lift my eyes from the narrow trail to gaze for the first time on Elen's house. It was not what I expected. Less a fortress than a village, it covered several acres of flat land beside the stream that flowed through the valley. Within a palisade breached by many gates, most of which stood open, at least three score cottages surrounded a timber building twice the size of Merin's house.

It was after midday when we reached the valley floor, and we were still an hour's walk from the village. I was impatient to reach our destination, but Finn insisted that we sit for a while by the stream, to rest and bathe our feet.

"It's what travelers do," he said.

Aside from the obvious reason that after such an arduous descent a little rest was welcome, the custom served another purpose. With our bare feet dangling in the water, we were unthreatening enough to be approachable. Several passers-by paused to look us over before a man of middle age, clad in warrior garb, stopped to speak to us. I let Finn do the talking, while I held my tongue and tried to look respectful, as a youngster should.

The warrior spoke Finn's language, though not well enough to convince me that it was his own. He asked Finn what our business was.

"I've come to see the armorer," said Finn.

The man's eyes narrowed with suspicion. "You have business with the armorer?"

"Just a visit," Finn replied. "He is my long-ago friend."

"I'm on my way to see the armorer myself," the warrior said. "Shall we keep each other company on the road?"

It was a polite way of saying that he intended to see us to our destination, in case we were not what we claimed to be. We had no choice but to accept his invitation.

The path was only wide enough for two, which allowed me to tag along behind. As we walked, Finn chatted with the warrior, keeping the man's attention on himself. He made casual mention of 'my son and I' without causing him to do more than glance at me over his shoulder once or twice. He spoke at length about the armorer, until he had convinced our escort that he knew the man.

As youngsters do, I gawked at everything, all the while fixing in my mind an image of the place. The valley couldn't have been more than a mile across at the widest point, and in several places it narrowed to a quarter of a mile. It would be so easy to defend that I was hardly surprised to see the condition of the palisade surrounding the village. Half-rotted palings barely held each other up, leaving gaps big enough for a child to wriggle through. We entered the village through a sagging gate that looked as if it hadn't been closed in years.

Just inside the palisade we turned into a narrow lane that led to the workshops of the craftsmen. The forge and the tanning shed stood side by side. Finn went to the doorway of the tanning shed and called to a man who was stirring something in a vat. When he saw Finn, he came outside, and the two men greeted each other like the friends they truly were. Our escort, who had no business there, continued on his way.

A few of the armorer's neighbors glanced at us with curiosity, and Finn suggested to his friend that we go indoors. The smell inside the tanning shed unsettled my stomach. The tanning of hides creates a number of unpleasant smells, among them the odor of a badly kept privy and the stench of rotting meat. I was relieved when the armorer led us out the back of the shed, across a courtyard, and into a tiny cottage.

The disorder in the house told me that no woman lived there, nor did the armorer take the trouble to perform the rituals of hospitality. I hadn't eaten anything since breakfast, but there was no stew, no soup, not even porridge warming over a fire that had all but gone out. The armorer cleared off a bench for Finn and me to sit on. Then he settled himself on the hearthstone and regarded me with frank curiosity.

"Who's this?" he asked.

"A friend," said Finn. "A friend who needs our help."

Finn explained my situation, and as I listened, I grew more and more convinced that he must be speaking of someone else. He told a tale I barely recognized. From the point of view of one of Elen's people, it could be said that my people had unknowingly taken in a murderer and for three years shielded her from justice. Now that she would be made to pay her debt, I had come to frustrate their revenge. I saw in the armorer's eyes his opinion of my quest.

"My friend did not do murder," I told the armorer, when Finn had done.

The armorer shrugged. "The innocent don't run away."

"She was a slave. Who would have believed her?"

"She was a slave?"

I nodded.

"No one mentions that," he said. "I wasn't here when the king was murdered in his bed. I knew nothing about it until they began to tell it all again, when a band of strangers brought her here."

My heart took its first full breath in days.

"When was that?" Finn asked him.

The armorer counted on his fingers. "Five days ago."

"Are we too late?" asked Finn.

I hadn't thought that far ahead. My heart waited for the answer before it dared to beat again.

"No blood has yet been spilled that I know of," the armorer replied. "I hear little of the doings of the mighty, but that much we would have heard."

"Where is she now?" I asked.

"She must be in Elen's house," he said. "I saw her taken in with my own eyes, and no one has seen her brought out again."

"Where is Elen's house? Will you take me there?"

The armorer pointed in the direction of the center of the village, where I had already seen for myself the imposing timber building that served as the seat of power.

"You can find it easily enough," he said, "but it's no simple thing for common folk to enter the king's great hall."

"The king's great hall? Is there a king?"

The armorer shook his head and spoke past me to Finn. "That woman still refuses."

"What woman?" I asked. "Refuses what?"

"The wife of the dead king."

"Who? Elen?"

The armorer spat into the dying fire. "She won't take another husband, claiming she still grieves the one who died. Some have begun to hope that revenge will assuage her grief, while others believe it isn't grief, but love of power, that keeps her from marrying again. In either case, once justice has been done, she'll have to put the past behind her. Then they can demand that she provide them with a king."

That the people here had good reason to insist on taking their revenge frightened me so badly that it took a few moments for me to see the implications of what the armorer was saying — that Elen's power here might not be absolute.

"Why would she be made to marry?" I asked.

The armorer looked at me as if I had asked him why water flows downhill. "Because it's time we had a king," he said, and seeing that I still didn't understand, he added, "It is the king who rules."

"Where I come from, a woman rules."

The armorer frowned and scratched his chin. I don't think he believed me, though he was too polite to say so.

"It's true," said Finn. "I've been there."

Then Finn went on to tell the tale of his captivity in Merin's house. It was a tale the armorer had heard before, but he seemed to take pleasure in hearing it again. Afterwards he told me that several of his friends had been among our prisoners. For their sake he was disposed to think well of anyone who belonged to the house of kindness, and he began to regard me with more warmth and less suspicion.

"What do you intend to do?" he asked me. "Will you bargain for your friend's life?"

I shook my head. "I have nothing to bargain with."

"No, I thought not." He gave me a shrewd look. "Did you intend to beg?"

"Will begging do me any good?"

"None whatsoever."

"No, I thought not," I said.

The armorer and I stared at each other. I knew what he was thinking, just as he knew what I intended. For a long moment I waited, while he considered what to do. Then he said, "I've overstayed my time here anyway."

"I don't mean to draw either of you into danger," I told him.

As soon as the words were out of my mouth, I saw how worthless were my good intentions. I knew what would happen to them both if I were caught trying to set Maara free.

"If you can tell me how to find a way into the great hall," I said, "that's all I'll ask of you."

"I ought to drag you into the great hall by force and tell them about your plans. That would get you inside at no risk to me."

Finn opened his mouth to object, but I made a sign to him to hold his tongue.

"If that's what you must do," I told the armorer, "I'll go with you willingly."

The armorer laughed. "Brave little thing," he said to Finn. Then he turned back to me. "I owe no one here my loyalty. They make use of my skill, and in exchange they provide me with what I need to live and little more. As you can see, I have no one to keep my house or cook for me, so the mighty allow me to beg for scraps at their kitchen door. At suppertime I'll take you there, and we'll see what can be done."

The three of us approached the kitchen by a narrow lane that ran along the back of Elen's house. Though the building was large enough to be seen from everywhere in the village, I never did get a good look at the front of it. Only those who enjoyed the freedom of the house approached its front door. It was they whom the armorer referred to as the mighty, the warriors of the household and those who commanded them — Elen, of course, and her counselors.

In Elen's house the common folk were unwelcome among the mighty. They were given grudging admittance only at the back door, where they were allowed no farther than the yard behind the kitchens. Many of the common folk depended on Elen's generosity. At least half a hundred joined us at the kitchen door. The yard was filthy, and there were neither benches nor tables where we could sit and eat like persons of dignity. With our plates balanced on our knees, we had to sit cross-legged on the ground, which was strewn with kitchen garbage and animal droppings.

All around me the only tongue I heard was the language spoken by Finn's people. Knowing a little of the history of the place, I believed it to be the language of Elen's people too, until I heard someone say, "We need a dozen more. See that their hands are clean," spoken in something resembling my own tongue.

I had no time to ask my companions for an explanation. A woman wearing a cook's apron approached and rapped me on the shoulder with a wooden spoon.

"Get along inside, then," she said, and when I made no move to get up, she added, "Meat from the king's table for your friends. Hurry up."

"Go on, boy," said Finn. "Isn't this what you wanted?"

I stared at him, not knowing what he meant.

"Forgive the lad," Finn said to the cook. "He was just telling me how he longed to see the grandeur of the king's great hall." He elbowed me. "Go make yourself useful among your betters."

I set my half-eaten supper aside and, along with several others, followed the cook into the kitchen. Someone tossed me a basket filled with loaves of bread and gave me a shove in the direction of an inner doorway, where I joined a stream of servants carrying an assortment of baskets, platters, bowls, and tankards into the great hall.

Inside the hall the noise made my ears ache. Hands reached out and snatched the loaves from my basket as I passed. When it was empty, I started back to the kitchen for more. While I waited by the kitchen doorway as another group of servants brought in their trays and tankards, I took the opportunity to look around me.

Elen's great hall was large enough for Merin's to fit within it twice over, and if Merin's hall held a hundred warriors and their companions, Elen's must hold three times as many. The tables stood so close together that it was difficult to thread one's way between them, and the servants carrying tankards of ale were so jostled that as much ale ended on the floor as in the warriors' cups.

I stood there a little longer than I should have, until a serving boy took my wrist and pulled me with him back into the kitchen. I made several trips more before I discovered, in the midst of the commotion, the high table where Elen herself presided. While Merin's table stood at one end of her great hall and a little apart from the others, so that she could see and be seen by everyone, Elen's table was at the center of the hall surrounded by tables packed with warriors in full armor, as if even here she needed their protection.

I knew Elen by the chair in which she sat, elaborately carved as a queen's chair should be, and with a high back of solid wood, strong against both drafts and treachery. I knew her too by the empty chair beside it, the king's chair, larger and more grand. That it stood empty told me much. While Elen's power depended on the absence of the king, the presence of his chair betrayed its limits. If I had been Elen, I would have sat in the king's chair myself.

At first I couldn't see her face. She wore a heavy robe, deep red in color, with a hood that covered her hair, and she was speaking with someone at the far end of the table, so that her face was turned away from me. I was about to try to work my way over to a place where I could see her better, when a servant beside me dropped a platter that shattered on the stone floor. The noise made me jump, but no one else paid much attention. Perhaps dropped platters were a common occurrence here, or perhaps few had heard it over the din.

Elen had heard it. When I glanced back at the high table, her eyes met mine and lingered for a moment before they went on to search for the source of the disturbance. How can I describe her? It would not be enough to call her merely beautiful. Wide-open eyes of startling blue gazed at me from a face whose every feature was at the same time both delicate and strong. Under her dark hood lay a crown of golden hair, gleaming in the lamplight. No crown of gold could have become her more.

Two adversaries contended with each other in my heart—admiration and despair. It was impossible not to admire her. Her delicate beauty and the strength it could not conceal, the intelligence in her bright eyes, her calm demeanor, the charm of her attention, would have appeased a demon bent on her destruction. Her brief gaze worked its charm on me. Her smile of forgiveness to the servant who dropped the platter made me long to have been the one who'd dropped it. The despair I didn't understand until I faced my growing fear that this woman was worth loving, so that love once given could not easily be taken back. Maara must love her still.

A sharp rap on the back of my head sent my thoughts flying.

"Impudent boy!"

A stout servant took me by the collar and pushed me before him out of the great hall. When we were back in the kitchen, he turned me around, took me by the shoulders, and gave me a shake that made me bite my tongue.

"I catch you more look that way," he said, in a strange combination of Finn's language and my own, and drew his finger across his throat in a gesture universally understood. Then he dragged me to the back door and with his boot shoved me out of it.

When I sat down again beside my companions, Finn handed me what was left of my supper.

"I see you made a good impression," he said.

"Did you misbehave yourself?" asked the armorer.

As I gathered up the shards of my dignity, I tried to think of a reply that would conceal my wounded pride. Nothing occurred to me. I only shrugged, to show how little I cared for the opinion of the servants of the mighty.

"Did you see your friend?"

I shook my head. "I saw nothing but warriors, hundreds there must be, and Elen in the midst of them."

"You saw the queen herself?"

"I did."

"How did you know her?"

"By her chair," I said, "and by her face."

The armorer nodded solemnly, then glanced around to see if anyone was listening before he leaned toward me and whispered, "She is a beauty, isn't she?"

I couldn't disagree.

"While you were inside disgracing yourself," said Finn, "we've been keeping an ear out for news of your friend."

"Maara," I whispered. "Her name is Maara."

As if it were a word of power, Maara's name on my tongue broke the spell that bound me. I had left the great hall enveloped in a cloak of shame and rapture, enthralled by Elen's beauty, ashamed of having been caught gaping at it. Now I shrugged that cloak from my shoulders and remembered why I had come to Elen's house.

"What have you heard?" I asked. "Has anyone spoken of her?"

"They speak of nothing else," said Finn, "though no one speaks her name. They seem to care nothing for her fate, one way or the other. They're thinking of themselves. They speak of what will happen next. The mighty have sent for the kinsmen of the murdered king. Many have arrived already, and his brother is expected in the morning. How many more will come, they wonder? Will more help be needed? Will the mighty be in want of game? Will there be profit in it? Will they be entertained?"

A servant carrying a platter was going from group to group, offering to those who lingered in the yard what looked like plate scrapings from the tables of the mighty. The platter also held a joint of mutton with some meat left on it. I was still hungry, and rather than take the leftover pieces, which were mostly gristle, I took my knife from my belt and cut a bit of meat from the bone.

For a time nothing happened. The servant returned to the kitchen, and I gave my attention to finishing my supper while I tried to think of a way to get back inside.

"There!" someone said, quite loudly. It was a voice I recognized, the voice of the man who had scolded me for staring at the queen.

Someone took hold of me from behind, took hold of the back of my shirt so forcefully that if it had been cloth he would have torn it, and dragged me to my feet. I dropped my plate. My knife fell with it. The stout servant snatched it up.

"Did you pilfer this, eh boy?"

Finn was on his feet. The armorer stepped between him and the man who held me.

"No harm done," he said. "Just a boy. He meant no harm."

The armorer stood between Finn and me. People surrounded us, then came between and parted us, and the man who had kicked me out of Elen's house dragged me back into it again.

77

THIEF!

P retending a fear I didn't feel, I stood dumb before my accuser. I knew better than to speak until I understood what was happening. The man still held my knife. He shook it in my face and shouted questions at me. From whom did I steal it? One of the warriors of the household? One of their guests? Easy enough to do, he said. Someone jostles you, you fall against someone, you beg his pardon while you filch his knife.

He didn't wait for a reply to any of his accusations. He gave me time to think, time to remember. How Maara got the knife I never thought to ask, but where else could it have come from? Once I understood, I knew why the man accused me. As everyone in Merin's house knows the work of Merin's armorer, so anyone in Elen's house would know a knife made there. How would a serving boy, one of the common folk, come honestly by such a fine bronze knife? I must have stolen it. There was no other explanation.

The servant dragged me down the passageway that led to the great hall. I stumbled along behind him, trying to keep my balance and resisting just a little, while I wondered how to turn the situation to my advantage. First I had to convince them of my innocence. I had just come from the armorer's house. I could say I had brought the knife from there. Surely no one would claim it. No person of honor would claim what wasn't theirs. If there was no victim of the theft I was accused of, I must be innocent.

Perhaps I could gain their sympathy as the victim of an unjust accusation. I might even ask a boon to soothe my wounded pride. They would expect a request for some thing of value. Sometimes it's best to do the unexpected. I would ask to serve the queen's household for as long as help was needed. Such a request would flatter them, these mighty folk who thought themselves deserving of my envy. They would believe they understood my desire to remain among them, that I would consider it an honor to be allowed to serve them. But nothing happened the way I thought it would.

The noise of the great hall drowned out the servant's accusations. Still he kept shouting, "Thief! Thief!" until we stood before the high table.

"He stole this!" said the man, with such self-satisfaction in his voice and such an air of expectation that I thought he must be anticipating a reward. He held up the knife and turned to the assembled company. "This pretty knife. Who belongs?"

We stood not twenty paces from Elen's chair. When she rose, everyone fell silent.

"Let me see it," she said.

The stout servant had to let go of me while he approached her and handed her the knife. I stood where he left me, hemmed in by the warriors of the household, but held there by Elen's eyes. Instead of examining the knife, she kept her gaze on me.

"Who is this?" she asked.

I would have blurted out my name if my accuser hadn't answered for me.

"Him? No one," the man said. "No name. Thief! Nobody."

Elen looked long at me, until it seemed that all my thoughts must have revealed themselves to her inner eye.

"Is he a servant here?" she asked.

The man turned to look at me, as if seeing me for the first time. "Maybe so. Don't know it. Silly face."

He was speaking with great difficulty a language not his own. To me he had spoken mostly the language of Finn's people. Now he spoke, barely well enough to be understood, the tongue spoken by the mighty.

"What is your name?" Elen asked me.

I had the good sense this time not to answer truthfully, but I could think of no other name to give her. She must have thought I hadn't understood her. She repeated the question in the language of Finn's people, speaking it as easily as she spoke her own.

I remembered that the forest people would sometimes call a child Little So-and-so, using his father's name until he earned a name for himself.

"You may call me Little Finn," I said.

"Well, Little Finn, how do you answer your accuser?"

"If I stole this knife, then someone must be missing it. If no one claims it, it must be mine."

"Proof of nothing," said the servant. "Man drunk maybe. Or gone pissing."

"Perhaps," said Elen. "Keep this boy in the kitchen until supper is over. Then bring him to my chamber."

The stout servant, disappointed in his hope for a reward, shoved me ahead of him back into the kitchen. There he made me sit down on the floor in an out-of-the-way corner. To keep me there he tied a piece of strong twine around my ankle and fastened the other end to a table leg. After a quarter of an hour he had forgotten me.

More than once a careless cook left a knife within my reach, so that I could have quickly cut the cord and run away. In fact the cooks and kitchen servants paid so little attention to me that I could have worked openly to untie the knot. I had no intention of trying to free myself. I would never have a better opportunity to discover what Elen meant to do with Maara and perhaps to find out where she was keeping her.

I learned nothing from the kitchen talk, which consisted mostly of shouted orders and shrill scoldings. With so many guests to see to, there was no time for gossip in the kitchen.

Instead of eavesdropping I made my plans.

It occurred to me that if I admitted to the theft, they might lock me up in whatever place they had put Maara, but I quickly abandoned that idea. If we were both locked up, how would we escape? I would do better to convince Elen of my harmlessness. Then she might allow me to remain within the household.

First I had to refute the accusation made against me. As I was innocent, the truth would be my best defense, if the truth were not so complicated. A partial truth might do. If I claimed to have brought the knife from the armorer's house, well, so I had. I need say no more than that. With such a simple explanation and without an injured party, how could she convict me?

Next, in order to stay within the house, I would have to ingratiate myself with Elen. Although she must be accustomed to adoration, even jaded by it, a young boy smitten by her beauty might slip past her defenses. Flattery she would recognize at once, but my admiration was genuine enough.

I had already, without guile, given a false impression that would work to my advantage. Elen had spoken to me first in her own tongue and thought I hadn't understood it. I had said very little to anyone in the household, and to my best recollection I had spoken not a word in the language of the mighty. People of importance speak carelessly before those they consider beneath their notice, before children, before servants, both of which they thought I was. How much more freely would they speak if they believed me ignorant of their language.

When careful thought gave way to useless worry, I allowed myself to fall asleep. It must have been past midnight when the stout servant woke me. He turned me over to a warrior of the household, who took me to the queen by a back way that I would have mistaken for a passage to the servants' quarters. It wound through a maze of narrow corridors and up several flights of stairs until we reached a tower room. A guard posted by the door rapped on it with the hilt of his sword. I heard the bar slide back. The door swung open. A woman in a plain apron stood back to let me enter. Then she went out the door and pulled it shut behind her.

It was a spacious room. Unshuttered windows on every side would in daylight reveal a view of the entire village, as well as much of the countryside beyond the palisade. There was no fire, only the light of one small lamp.

At first I didn't see her. When I shielded my eyes from the lamplight, I could just make her out, standing by a window, a dark form against a deeper darkness.

"Come here," she said, in her own tongue.

I was glad I couldn't see her eyes. They had a charm in them that might have robbed me of my self-possession. I think that by speaking from the darkness she meant to confuse me or take me by surprise, to spy first upon her adversary before she set her strategy and deployed her strongest weapon, but by doing so she allowed me to collect myself and prepare my own defenses.

"Please," I said, in the language of Finn's people. "Please, ma'am, I've done nothing wrong."

Slowly she approached me. Her back was to the lamp, her face in shadow. The lamplight was shining in my eyes.

"Did you fool them all?" she said.

It was fortunate for me that she had spoken in the language of Finn's people, because I could not have hidden my surprise.

She reached out her hand and with her fingertips lightly brushed my cheek. "No beardless boy, I think."

Weak-kneed with relief that she had discovered only my sex, not my intentions, I didn't try to conceal the blush that warmed my face. With so much else to hide, I gave her the satisfaction of believing she had found me out. Denial was pointless. Small-breasted as I was, I would not have put it past her to touch me there too or to strip away my clothing until no denial was possible.

"You see, I am frank with you," she said. "Will you not be open with me? Why do you pretend to be what you are not?"

It was a question I had not prepared an answer for. Unpracticed in deceit, I could do no less than tell the truth.

"I am told," I said, "that in Elen's house a woman of the common folk cannot go about as freely as a man."

"And are you not a woman of the common folk?"

"I am not."

"Who are your people, then?"

I almost said I had none, but I couldn't deny those I still felt a part of, though so many of them had denied me.

"Lady," I said, "I am an exile."

"You would have done better to admit the theft of the knife," she said. A chill had crept into her voice. "For that we might have given you a sound thrashing and sent you home. Now you must convince me that you haven't come to do me harm."

It seemed an odd conclusion for her to leap to until I remembered her precautions—the warriors surrounding her in the great hall, the tower room, the barred door, the guard outside. With good reason or without, she must always feel herself in peril.

So I touched the only place in her where I had seen a sign of weakness.

"What cause have I given you to doubt my good will?" I asked her. "I find it strange that someone so powerful should be so fearful. Am I so threatening?"

I gestured to my small and humble self. "Is this enough to make the mighty tremble?"

I caught a flash of anger in her eyes before her smile masked it.

"Threats come in many guises," she said. "What you see is not fear but prudence. Power comes from understanding, and I understand the world. It is full of ill will, while all good will has self-interest behind it. Shall I tell you what I see?"

I waited.

"I see someone who has proven her own guilt already. At the very least, you are guilty of deception, and for what harmless purpose would you come into my house wearing a false face?"

"Indeed, ma'am," I said, "this is my true face. I have only the one."

Elen laughed, a kinder sound than any I had heard since I first entered her house.

"All right," she said. "If you've come with good intentions, then tell me, what is your purpose here?"

Nothing occurred to me to say. Nothing I had planned would be of any use. She had seen through my disguise, and she seemed to have no interest in asking me about the knife.

Elen made an impatient gesture. "Speak," she said, "and speak quickly, before you can perfect a lie."

Indignant at her accusation, I almost spat back at her that I was not a liar, until I saw the reason for my indignation. Was I not at that moment trying to deceive her? And of course a lie was just what she expected.

"Lady," I said. "I would not insult you with a lie. My business here is my own concern, and I will keep it to myself, but I mean you no harm."

Elen was silent for a moment. Then she turned toward the light. "You must forgive me if I cannot simply take you at your word. Come sit with me a while and tell me of your misfortunes. Perhaps that will help me to form an opinion of your character."

She seated herself on a chair beside the table that held the lamp, so that I could see her very well, and gestured to me to sit down on a stool opposite her.

"First," she said, "tell me where you've come from."

In her eyes I saw nothing to alarm me. It seemed a harmless question, yet I was cautious.

"I doubt you've heard of the place," I said. "Where I come from no one has heard of Elen's house."

"A careful answer," she said. "You will not quiet my suspicions with such careful answers. Tell me at least in which direction your home lies."

I saw no harm in saying, "My home lies south of here."

"Is it far?"

"Yes, very far."

"Is it a lovely place?"

"It is," I said, and blinked back sudden tears as my mind filled with images of Merin's land.

"I understand," she said. "It is a longing mixed with regret. One does not value something justly until it is lost beyond recall."

She did understand, and my heart began to warm toward her.

"I too have lost things I should have valued more highly," she said.

The sorrow in her voice evoked my pity. Perhaps she was thinking of her husband. Though I was not aware of it, her charm had begun its work. She was not forming an opinion of my character. She was forming my opinion of hers.

"Sometimes, though, we are given a second opportunity," she said. "You may yet find your way home again."

I nodded. "I have not lost hope."

"You may find some means of making restitution, and so heal the breach caused by your misdeeds. Tell me, what wrong have you done, that your people made you a stranger?"

Her eyes searched mine, as if to find the flaw in me that had created all my troubles. Now, instead of understanding and compassion, in her eyes I saw pity mixed with scorn. For a moment I resented her willingness to believe I was at fault, but my resentment soon gave way to a desire to gain her good opinion.

"I've done nothing wrong," I told her. "I said I was an exile, not an outlaw."

"Much the same thing, I think."

"Not at all. What I did wasn't wrong, only unwise."

"What did you do?"

"I made an enemy of someone stronger than myself."

Elen nodded. "That was most unwise."

She leaned back in her chair and regarded me with amusement, as if I were, not Merin's rightful heir betrayed by a usurper, but just a child who, because of some imagined slight, has run away from home.

"So," she said, "you are a stranger to your people because you made enemies among them, and you have come into my house disguised as something you are not for a purpose you won't reveal. Am I wrong not to be reassured?"

What more could I tell her? I believed then that I had calmed her fears, but I didn't know how to win her confidence.

"Lady," I said, "how can I reassure you?"

"Tell me about the knife."

I had forgotten all about the knife. Before I could reply, she leaned forward and placed an icy finger against my lips, so cold it burned, yet I couldn't draw away.

"Take great care," she whispered. "One false step will be your doom. If you are a thief, say so, and leave this house unpunished. On that you have my word."

She unsealed my lips and leaned back in her chair to await my answer.

"I am not a thief," I said.

She smiled, but all warmth had left her eyes. "Then someone has lied to me," she said. From a hidden pocket in her skirt she drew the knife. Its blade shone in the lamplight. "Now I must have the whole truth out of you. This was my husband's knife, and if you didn't steal it, you had it from the hand of someone in whom I once placed all my trust."

How cleverly she had tricked me. Admitting to the theft would have proved me innocent of a much more serious offense. If I could have named the man I took it from, he would soon have been standing in my place, accused of treachery. Now the knife connected me to Maara, and I knew without her saying so that Elen recognized it, not only as her husband's knife, but as the knife she last saw in Maara's hand, the knife that killed him.

Elen caressed the blade. "Beautiful, is it not?"

Beautiful as it was, I didn't understand why Maara would have kept it. It was a reminder of the harm she'd done. Perhaps that was why.

"I think it's no coincidence," said Elen, "that this knife returns to me so soon after the one who wielded it."

I had to ask, "Where is she? Is she safe?"

"Before I tell you that, will you now tell me your business here?"

"Please, Lady, I beg you. Let her go."

Elen sighed, and a look of sympathy came into her eyes. "You've come a long way for nothing."

"Is she not still living?" I whispered.

"Oh, she is very much alive," said Elen, "but what you ask is not within my power to do."

I had to find a way to persuade her. Elen had saved Maara's life before. She might again, if I could give her a way to justify it. I spoke the first thing that came into my head.

"I believe your self-interest coincides with mine," I said.

"What do you mean?"

"Had you not considered that by freeing Maara you will also free yourself?"

"Free myself? From what?"

"Why is the king's chair empty?"

"Because the king is dead."

"So the king is still the power here."

"I am the power here."

"Yet you leave the seat of power empty. And now will you throw away the last thing that keeps power in your hands?"

"What is that?"

"Revenge."

She waited to hear more.

"Among the common folk, they say that once your loss has been avenged, your grief must end, and you will have to provide them with a king."

It was the best I could do, and for a moment I thought I had persuaded her.

Then she smiled, a sad smile. "You misunderstand," she said.

Elen rose from her chair and picked up the lamp. Holding it before her, she took a few steps toward a dark corner of the room, then turned and gestured for me to follow.

"Don't," came a voice from the shadows. It was a voice I knew.

A few steps more and Elen stood by a bed draped all around with tapestry. She pulled aside the veil, and there, unfettered and unclothed, was Maara, sitting up against the headboard. The light fell on her face. She raised one hand to shield her eyes. Not from the light. From me. And in a gesture of modesty that denied what we had once been to each other, she took up the bedclothes, to cover herself. She could not have made it clearer if she had told me in so many words. She was no longer mine.

Elen let the curtain fall. "Maara is free," she said.

78

LOVE

The world had changed so suddenly that my mind let slip the thread of reason. One thing followed another without my comprehension. While I struggled to pull air into my chest against the weight that pressed upon my heart, I heard as if from a distance Elen's words. At the time they made no sense to me. They came back to me in pieces, while I lay under the table I had been tied to only an hour before, when the world was something that could be understood.

I knew she would return to me one day. I hoped it would be sooner. She has yet to tell me what kept her from me for so many years.

So many years. How many years had Maara stayed in Merin's house? Then I remembered, a hurt so old the scar had faded until I never noticed it anymore. Maara never intended to stay at all. She had abandoned me, after she had been in Merin's house less than a year. But she came back. Why? Maara's own words told me, in the answer she gave Fodla. Obligation. A debt unpaid. Not love.

I knew I could persuade my husband's brother to forego his vengeance after time had eased his grief a little. Though I too felt the injury, the assassin was one of my own household, and I took upon myself the debt. I paid him well in gold, not a king's price, but the hint of a promise went with it, that one day I might ally my house to his. Now I intend to keep my promise. Maara's life is bought already, but as a wedding gift I will ask him to forgive, so that I can welcome my faithful servant home.

She meant to marry him. That much I understood. Why he would allow his wife to keep an assassin in the bosom of his household, I didn't understand at all. But that was no concern of mine. I had so much else to worry the fragments of my heart.

I remembered Elen's hands. They were smooth and soft, but very cold, as they led me from the bedside. They drew me down beside her on a bench where we sat close together. She smelled of roses. I began to breathe a little easier.

I want you to know that she did not betray you. Even when I questioned her more closely, once I had seen the knife. Had anyone come with her? Could someone have followed her? I had to show the knife to her, to persuade her that you were here. Even then she withheld the truth from me, but I felt it in the trembling of her hands. So she must bear you some affection. I wish she had trusted me to deal kindly with you.

Elen gazed back at the bed, now hidden by the dark. Even so, I dared not look again.

She knows my jealousy, and I am a little jealous, but I'm also grateful, that she had someone who would care for her, while she couldn't shelter under my care.

Elen put her arm around my shoulders.

I'm sorry to have hurt you, but I had to show her to you. Now you can go home, knowing that she is well and safe.

Home? Elen knew I had none.

Well, if not home, you may find another household that will welcome you. I will not offer you a place with me.

She drew away from me a little.

Oh, I'm not afraid of you. Not at all. I'm thinking of your pain. I don't doubt Maara's heart. That she came here willingly was proof enough, and she has since given me many more proofs of love.

The image of Maara's nakedness in Elen's bed came again before my eyes. I washed it away with tears.

A kitchen servant woke me, then held a plate under my nose.

"Here, have a bite of breakfast," she said.

The smell of food made me feel sick.

"I wouldn't stick my nose up at good food if I was you," she said.

I sat up and took the plate, and she left me alone. I crept back into my out-of-the-way corner and set the plate down beside me.

After my grandmother died, I woke every morning innocent and free for just a moment before the memory of loss fell upon me like a blow, and I remembered that death had stolen someone from me. Weeks it was before I could accept it, and that sudden blow softened into a thing more like regret.

That morning death of a different kind fell upon me.

At first I thought I must have dreamt it all. None of it could be true. And yet my eyes had seen the proof, my ears had heard the story.

How had I been so deceived? I saw a new vision of events that once I had seen so differently. Maara had intended to return to Elen years before, but obligation kept her tied to me, and when at last she had the opportunity, she led me here. Why here, when we could have gone anywhere?

And when we began our journey home, she intended all along to leave me. She made me memorize the map, told me, if we were parted, to go on alone, while she returned to one whose love she still desired.

If we had not been captured, would she have left me in the middle of the night? Would she have told me what she meant to do, or would she have let me go on believing that she loved me, so that my heart would have been hers for years to come, for all the years to come. Could she have been as cruel as that? Would she have kept my heart from loving someone else?

How had I so deceived myself? I never doubted that she loved me. Now memories I once cherished filled me with shame. Had I misunderstood the barriers between us? I had thought she wanted me to breach them, to free her from the fortress that held her heart fast. The thought that I had forced from her an intimacy she didn't want made me ashamed of the love that I had once been proud to offer her.

So intent was I upon my own misery that I was unaware of the activity around me, until I opened my eyes to see several pairs of boots, all pointing at me. I was surrounded.

Someone picked up my plate. "Waste of good food," she mumbled. Then a woman said, "He's taken ill, poor lad." A cool hand felt my brow. "She can't send him off like this. Tell the captain he can go. We'll find another escort in a day or two, when he's feeling better."

A woman gathered me into her arms, carried me into another room, and laid me on a cot. When she settled a blanket around my shoulders, I pulled it over my head, and she left me alone.

Escort. Elen had said something to me about an escort. I didn't take it in. She could have been offering to provide me with an escort from her lands or with an escort to the graveyard. It would have been the same to me. I was dead already. Only my body had not noticed it. If it wouldn't follow my heart into the oblivion of death, perhaps it would fall into sleep, and for a time release me from my pain.

But pain followed me into sleep and haunted my dreams. Wolves in their many guises, some on two legs, some on four, danced with me along the edge of the abyss. And when I fell, they looked down at me and laughed. The fall woke me. It was dark.

Hunger made me forget my mortal wound. As Maara once said, the body keeps us living, even against our will. I sat up and saw all around me the sleeping forms of the household servants, lying on cots like mine or on pallets on the floor. I got up as quietly as I could and crept into the kitchen, where I made myself a meal of meat scraps and heels of bread that I found in a basket beside the door that led out into the yard. Then I retreated again to my out-of-the-way corner.

Once I had eaten, I felt a little better, but I didn't feel like myself at all. I no longer cared for anything or anyone. Where not long before a searing pain had been, now there was no feeling, none at all. Can a body go on living whose heart lies dead within? Perhaps it can, but to what purpose? Injury provokes a desire for revenge, but who had injured me? I could only turn my sword against myself.

Who else could I accuse? Not Elen. Hers was a prior claim. If I accused her of the theft of Maara's heart, I would make of myself a thief. A would-be thief, I reminded myself. And how could I blame Maara? Of what could I accuse her? Only that she had lied to me, not once, but many times. Why? To shield me from a painful truth or to keep me from keeping her from Elen? Either way, how could a lie have killed me?

Then I saw in my mind's eye, as if I were a witness, a battleground where the dead, the truly dead, would lie, and I remembered the northern army, at that very moment gathering its strength, intending to lay waste to Merin's land.

Because I had believed in Maara's love, I had left to their fate all those who truly loved me. I had betrayed them because Maara had betrayed me.

Where love had fled my heart, now hatred hastened to rush in. Never before did hatred find more than the briefest welcome there. Even my hatred for Vintel was a little tempered with pity and understanding. Now my hatred for one I had so loved raged like a storm within me, though my body still sat slumped against the kitchen wall between a table and a rubbish bin.

And I did indulge it. I used it, to push my love away from me, to reclaim myself a little. Hatred lit the spark, and anger fueled it, until it burst into a flame that revealed to me the darkest places in my heart, where I would fight for what I wanted, where I would murder any who opposed me. That fell knife that had betrayed me, I held to Elen's throat. I could not bring myself to imagine taking Maara's life, but to take love from her as she had taken love from me seemed only justice.

I'll never understand how love can turn so quickly into something else.

Merin's words. They echoed in my head as if her voice had spoken them aloud beside my ear. At last I understood. I set my heart in Merin's place and watched my mother, her beloved, turn her back and walk away. At last I understood.

Merin's voice spoke to me again. The rest of it. Her sorrow, her regret. And the very thing that had kept the two apart, whose hearts still yearned toward one another.

It was bad enough to call her love for me a lie. It was unforgivable that I denied my love for her, even to myself.

I refused to see her meaning. Her words did not apply to me. Maara's love was a lie, and Maara's lie released me. I could deny anything I liked. If I did not deny it, how could I bear the humiliation of giving her a love that was unwanted. She had made a fool of me.

How could loving someone ever be a foolish thing? This was a side of love I had never seen before. Isn't love always about the other person?

And that thought stopped me.

What I had just been calling love was something else. If my love for Maara depended on her love for me, it was not love, but a bargain. I thought of the night we spent together in a shelter in the wilderness, when I first told Maara that I loved her. I never asked her if she loved me back. I only asked her if she wanted what I had to give her. My heart. Myself. And she had accepted.

Maara hadn't taken love from me. I had it still.

But now Maara didn't want it. Of what use was my love if Maara didn't want it? What could love do for her? What could love offer her?

Once I asked the question, I knew the answer. I could let her have her heart's desire, even if it wasn't me. I could wish her well and let her go.

Still I resisted. It can't be done, I thought. Not by the human heart. Perhaps the hearts of gods can grow as great as that. Not mine.

Yet what choice was there? What else could I do?

I blew upon the embers of my anger, envisioned myself at the head of a great army, breaking down the walls of Elen's house, bludgeoning the tower door to splinters, finding Maara there and taking her by force, to carry her away with me. Yes, if I had the power, I could force her body. No power in the world could force her heart. Nor, if I imprisoned her, could I ever hope to win it.

The last little flame of anger flickered out. The ashes began to cool. I wish I could say I felt a little better. In fact I felt a good deal worse. Now there was nothing I could do but reconcile myself to the greatest loss of all. Greater than the loss of life itself, I thought it was, because death brings forgetfulness. While I lived, I would remember.

My mind reached the end of thinking, and I sat quietly for a little while without a thought left in my head. The ravaged place within my breast began to knit itself together. The raw pain had subsided, though it was still tender to the touch. Like all pain, it would someday fade to just an ache that I would grow accustomed to.

Then it occurred to me that I couldn't pass the rest of my life sitting under a table in Elen's kitchen. What should I do now? Wait for Elen's escort? Where would they take me? I had friends to meet. Finn and the armorer. Bru's band of warriors. I should release them from their obligation to me and send them home. And it might not be too late to take a warning back to Merin's house.

I stood up.

79

THE ABYSS

The first glimmer of dawn had begun to light the yard. The shuttered windows let in feeble rays that tangled in the smoke of the banked fires. On one of the kitchen hearths I saw a suckling pig still on its spit, well roasted and keeping warm beside the coals, ready for the warriors' breakfast. Loaves baked the night before filled the kitchen with their fragrance. I began to step back into the world. It was a world both familiar and strange.

I would need food for my journey, and I would have no time to hunt or set snares. I took the piglet from its spit and put it into an empty grain sack, along with several of the loaves.

I opened the kitchen door a crack and peered out, to see if the yard was empty. I didn't notice anyone. A moment more and I would have been gone.

"Stop! Thief!"

The two guards posted in the yard had been asleep. Once out the door I would have seen them and could have easily slipped past them, but the shout awakened them, and they sprang to their feet, confused, until they saw me. While I was trying to decide whether I should dodge between them or around them, and so make my escape, someone dragged me by the collar back into the kitchen and tore the sack from my hands.

"You! Thief!"

It was the stout servant who had accused me of stealing the knife.

"No," I said. "It's all right. The Lady let me go."

He didn't seem to understand a word I said. While he continued to berate me, he dumped the contents of the sack out onto a table.

The two guards had come into the kitchen and now stood one on either side of me. The man turned to them and repeated his accusations. I caught the word for pig.

"I have to go home," I said. "You can keep your pig."

When I turned to leave, the guards took hold me of me.

"You have no right to keep me," I said. "The Lady let me go."

The stout servant shook the empty grain sack in my face and called me names I didn't know the meaning of, though it was quite clear what he meant. I appealed to the two guards. They pretended not to understand me.

The woman who had cared for me the day before came into the kitchen in her nightshirt and demanded to know the cause of the commotion.

"Please," I said. "Tell them the Lady has granted me safe conduct."

She shook her head at me and shrugged.

I tried to recall the word she had used the day before. "An escort," I said. "The Lady promised me an escort. The Lady let me go."

The stout servant held up the sack and babbled something to the woman I couldn't understand at all, but I knew what he accused me of.

"Do you not practice hospitality here?" I asked her. "I took a little something. Food for my journey. I don't need an escort. I have no time to wait for another escort. I know the way. I must go home. I must leave now, today."

The woman regarded me with suspicion. "Time enough to wait," she said.

I think she meant that I would have to wait for an escort, whether I wanted one or not. This was beginning to be tiresome. Why could they not just let me go about my business? I had only one thing left to do that was of any importance. Lives hung in the balance.

"You don't understand," I said. "I have to go right away. It's a matter of life and death."

My weary voice did not convince them. Nor would it have convinced me. I tried to awaken in myself a sense of urgency. I brought before my mind's eye the images of those I cared for—of Merin and my mother, of my sister Tamar, of Namet, and of Sparrow, whose love I counted on—and it seemed as if their ghosts were standing there beside me, watching me, to see if I had the will to save them.

"My people are in danger," I said. "I must take back a warning. It may already be too late. Even now the northern tribes are gathering an army."

One of the guards who held me made a noise like, "Urr?"

"Army? Where?" said the other. He was not so ignorant of the language of the common folk after all, but only reluctant to be drawn into their altercations.

"To the east, in the hill country beyond the wilderness."

"How far?"

I had to count the days. It had taken me almost a fortnight to reach Elen's house from the northerners' encampment, but I had taken the long way round. When I realized how much time had passed, I grew more fearful that I would be too late. It takes time to gather up an army, and an army moves more slowly than a person traveling alone. Still, I would have to hurry.

"How far?" the guard asked again.

"Four days, maybe five."

Before I could say or do anything to stop them, my captors dragged me between them through the great hall and up a wide staircase, to the rooms where the warriors slept. The stout servant followed after us, hoping perhaps to see me punished for my crimes.

One of the guards held me, while the other awakened one of their war leaders. I knew him for a chieftain by the device upon his shield, which hung beside the doorway of his room. It was a black bear, standing up on its hind legs, drawn so that when the warrior held his shield in battle, the bear would face his sword arm, looking as fierce as he, all raking claws and gleaming teeth.

From the hallway I heard the conversation, the man's complaints on having been awakened, then his alarm when he was told of the presence of the northern army. I heard him get up and dress himself. I heard the creaking of the leather, the clicking of the buckles, as he fastened on his armor. I heard the clank of metal as he took up his sword.

The bear shield chieftain emerged from his room like a bear emerging from his den. He had to stoop and turn a little sideways to fit through the narrow doorway. His uncombed hair, as black as soot, stood up all over his head. A little grey had begun to lighten his beard. When he saw me, he knelt down on one knee, so that he could look me in the eye.

"Hey now, small little wee lad," he said, in the strangest version I had ever heard of the language of Finn's people. "What's this? Comes your army to lay siege to us?"

"Your men misunderstood me," I told him. "The army I saw threatens my people, not yours."

"You saw this?" he asked. "These eyes," and he held two fingers up to my face, as if to touch them, "these eyes saw this?"

I nodded.

"How long?"

I counted on my fingers up to ten. It was close enough.

"Army so far off, ten days?" he asked, then glanced at the guard who had awakened him. Perhaps he would be reassured and go back to bed.

"He said four or five," the guard replied.

"I got lost," I said.

"You got five days lost?"

"Yes," I told him. "I got lost in the forest."

"Ah," he said. "Army close. Four days. Five days."

"Yes."

Even so, the northern army was far from being encamped on Elen's doorstep.

"Speak everything you saw, those eyes," he said. "Speak where are they."

Though his speech sounded awkward to my ears, the man was fluent, not searching for a word here, a phrase there, not making me repeat myself. He could almost have been a native speaker of the language of the common folk.

"I saw them in the hills east of the wilderness," I said.

"Armsmen, they prepare a march?"

"No," I said. "They are encamped."

While he thought that over, I opened my mouth to tell him again that they were coming after my people, not his, but I changed my mind and held my tongue. I wanted to see what would happen.

"They are many?" he asked.

I nodded.

"How many?"

"Their campfires on the hills I took for the bonfires of springtime."

I didn't know his word for the spring festival, but he knew what I meant.

"They are encamped," he said.

"Yes."

"Better to speak, encamped they were, ten days past."

"That's true," I said.

"And if they have unencamped, which way their intention is?"

I kept my mouth shut. I was beginning to have an idea.

He took me by the arm and gave me a gentle shake. "Your people. Which way?"

I pointed to the south.

"Armsmen, their intention is to south?"

I shrugged. "Where else?"

I saw the answer in his eyes. He thought they were coming here.

The bear shield chieftain suddenly stood up and gestured to me to follow him. The two guards came too, one still keeping a firm grip on my arm, and the stout servant trailed along behind. We took another way to find it, but I knew where we were going. They took me to the tower room.

Again the guard rapped on the door with the hilt of his sword, but for a long time no one answered it. As he raised the sword to knock again, it opened, and the servant I had seen before peered out. When she saw the bear shield chieftain, she hastened to pull the door wide open and let us in.

The sun had just risen, and its light spilled in through the unshuttered windows. Elen was sitting up in bed, a shawl around her shoulders against the morning chill, sipping a warm drink from a silver cup. She was alone.

She smiled when she saw the chieftain, but when her eyes fell on me, she frowned, and anger reddened her cheeks. She was about to say something to me when the rest of them trooped in.

"What's this?" she asked.

Once they were in her private chamber, the guards and the stout servant looked as if they felt very out of place. They blushed, to find the Lady in her bed, and looked everywhere but there. The chieftain turned and saw them.

"Out," he said, in the language of the mighty. "I think I can master one small boy."

When the bear shield chieftain and I were alone in the tower room with Elen, she didn't question either of us. She gazed at us, waiting for one of us to speak. For the first time I saw her unprepared. She had no idea what was about to happen. She was at a disadvantage.

"Disturbing news, my Lady," said the chieftain. "This boy has seen an army gathering in the eastern hills."

I had kept my wits about me. I pretended not to understand a word, as he repeated to Elen what he had just learned from me.

"How did you come to hear of this?" she asked him.

"Our guards caught the lad as he tried to leave the house. He gave as his excuse that he had to take a warning to his people. Warning of what, they asked him, and then he told them of the army."

"He could have made it up, to convince the guards to let him go."

"If he did, he was a fool. It was that news that caused the guards to bring him to me."

"You questioned him yourself?"

"I did."

"And you believe him?"

He nodded.

"What do you suggest we do?"

"It's too late to send out scouts," the chieftain said. "Our enemies may be already in the forest. We must meet them in strength, and we have barely time to gather our strength together."

Elen's attention was all on her chieftain now. "How many are they? Have we strength enough to turn them back?"

"They will count on our being unprepared," he said. "Those that brought the assassin back, they will have told the rest that we are occupied with celebration, that they will find us drunk and staggering, like witless fools."

"Will our guests join us, do you think?"

The chieftain nodded. "If their lord aspires to be your king, must he not show himself a man? He dare not cower here while you go out to meet the enemy."

"Make ready then," said Elen. "Go now and give the order. Then return to me and let us make our plans."

The chieftain took me by the collar, to escort me out, but Elen said, "Leave the boy with me."

"Is this how you repay my kindness?" Elen said.

She spoke in the language of the mighty, I think to test my understanding. I blinked at her and kept my silence.

"Why did you withhold this news from me?" she said in the language of the common folk.

I saw no need to lie to her about it. "Lady," I replied, "I did not withhold it. It never occurred to me to mention it."

"You didn't think the presence of an army on my borders worthy of mention?"

"No, Lady."

"Whyever not?"

"I doubt they're coming here."

This much she knew from what the bear shield chieftain told her.

"Where else?" said Elen.

"They have been my people's foes for generations. They fight with us every year."

"Do they bring with them an army every year?"

"No, Lady."

"Can you give me proof of their intentions?"

I shook my head and tried to look more doubtful than I was. My plan was beginning to take shape. If Elen believed the northern army was a threat to her, if she gathered an army of her own and marched on their encampment, their attack on Merin's land would be turned aside. And if the northern army had marched south already, the news of Elen's army at their back would stop them.

I was certain they would hear the news. I understood the ways of armies from the stories told around the hearth in Merin's great hall. Some of the northerners would remain in their encampment, to guard their supplies and to keep secure a place to which their warriors could retreat with their wounded. Their scouts would warn them of the approach of Elen's army, and they would send messengers to call their army back. Better than taking a warning to my people, I might succeed in sending out an army against the enemies of Merin's house.

Through the window I saw the perilous cliffs, stronger than any palisade. With defenses like these, why would Elen send out an army?

"Would the northerners be so foolish as to attack this place?" I asked her. "I have never seen a fortress more well guarded."

"Northerners?"

"The northern tribes. They live to the north of us, so that's how we have always called them. I don't know what they call themselves."

Elen smiled. "We call them the mountain folk," she said. "They call themselves so many names no one but they could sort them out."

I wondered if she would answer my question. Instead she said, "Is not your home a fortress as strong as this?"

"It is a mighty fortress," I replied, "but it has no cliffs like these."

"Ah," said Elen. "These cliffs guard us, but they also hem us in. We can well withstand a siege, but sieges may be costly. We will not have help enough to bring the harvest in, and there will be no trade. Even one summer's siege could impoverish us. We would have to come to terms."

I was beginning to understand Elen's situation. In order to prevent a siege, her warriors must stop the northerners before they reached the cliffs. If it was too late to stop them in the wilderness, where one army could meet another on an even footing, they would have to stop them in the forest, and if they allowed themselves to be pushed back, they would soon have their backs against the cliffs, where they could be easily outmaneuvered. Fighting in the forest would be difficult, but if they split their army into smaller bands, they could harry the northern army's flanks and threaten to close off their escape. The northerners would have to stand and fight, or they might find themselves between Elen's army and the cliffs, and then they would be the ones outmaneuvered.

I remembered that I was supposed to be ignorant of Elen's plans.

"What will you do, Lady?" I asked her.

"We will go out to meet them," she replied. "Unless you can assure me that we are not their intended victims."

Her eyes seemed to encourage me to convince her of her safety, not because she would be reassured, but because she expected to be lied to. I knew how she would hear the truth.

"When I first saw them, Lady, I believed they intended to make war against my people. I have no reason to think otherwise."

"When did you first see them?"

"Ten days ago," I said.

"And you saw no indication they intended to come here?"

"No, Lady."

"And nothing you've learned since has changed your mind?"

I shook my head.

"Not even knowing they are also foes of ours?"

"Have you done something to provoke them?"

"Not that I'm aware of."

"My people have," I told her. "Vintel, our war leader, the one I made my enemy, Vintel provokes them constantly. When I saw their army, I knew their intentions, and I was not surprised."

I saw the doubt in Elen's eyes. The more I tried to convince her, the more doubtful she became.

"So you would ignore this threat?"

"If I were you, yes, I would ignore it. For myself, I cannot ignore it. I meant to leave your house this morning, to take a warning to my people, but your servants prevented me."

"Ah," said Elen, "I am reminded to ask why you are still here. Did I not send someone to see you on your way?"

"I fell ill yesterday," I replied. "A kitchen servant took pity on me and put me to bed, and your captain left without me."

"I will have a word with him," she said, more to herself than to me. "He should have taken my request to heart."

"Lady," I said. "I need no escort. I will go willingly from your lands, and as soon as possible. I may yet have time to warn my people. Will you not instruct your servants to let me go?"

"You must think me very foolish," Elen said.

I could find no words to answer her. I did not think her wise, as Merin was wise, but to think her foolish would be dangerous.

"You are a skillful liar," she said. "Your words ring with truth. Yet one mistake unmasks a lie. If you were so concerned about your people, why did you not take them a warning when you first saw this army gathering?"

Elen did not expect an answer, nor did I give her one. Her gaze wandered out the window. "I knew they were up to something when they brought Maara here."

Maara's name on Elen's tongue woke the place where I thought my love for her had died. It hurt. I closed my heart against it.

Elen shrugged off her shawl, threw back the covers, and arose from her bed. Like a fairy queen she was, draped all in white. Her crown of golden hair lay loose around her shoulders. When she passed before the window, the sunlight pouring in revealed her form, as perfect as I had imagined it.

She went to the door and pulled it open. The guard stood ready. She spoke a few words to him I couldn't hear. Then she closed the door and turned back to me.

"You must accept my hospitality a little longer," she said. "I think your people will be safe enough. And of course, if you truly are a stranger to them, why would they believe your warning?" She smiled, a smile of victory. "You see, the fabric falls apart. You find the lie, you pull its thread, and the whole unravels."

The guard pounded on the door. Elen opened it, and the bear shield chieftain came into the room.

"Lock him up," she said, in the language of the mighty.

This time no one tied me to a table. This time they put me in a tiny room and barred the door. It was smaller than Merin's armory, windowless and dark, without even a pile of rags to lie on. I didn't care. I lay down on the floor. Whatever plans they had for me, it didn't matter. There was nothing more for me to do.

Once I would have thought myself clever for deceiving Elen with the truth. Once I would have been amazed at what I had set in motion. Now I felt only relief, that my part in it was over.

Elen wasted not a moment. She called her warriors to battle. I heard them making ready. I knew the sounds. I had heard them all before, in Merin's house. Armored warriors clattered up and down the stairs and shouted orders to their companions. Servants rushed about, packing up supplies. I heard the sound of weapons taken from the wall. Swords clanged against their scabbard pieces, shields thudded to the floor. For half the day I listened to the din. Then silence fell.

I lay there in the dark and dozed a little. No dreams troubled me. I had passed beyond the land of dreams.

When I woke, I sat up and listened to the silence, wondering at what I had set in motion. Two armies would meet, and when armies meet, they must do battle. Blood would flow and men would die. And they would die for nothing. All because a fat servant had caught me stealing a roasted pig.

How the gods must laugh at us. How easily the courses of our lives are turned aside. This time the fates had given me an opportunity. I'd had a bit of luck, and I had made good use of it. For the present Merin's land was safe. At what cost I could not imagine, but the safety of my people would be dearly bought.

Once I would have cared for those whose lives would soon be sacrificed, as once I had cared for Merin's prisoners. They too had been the enemies of Merin's house. Where was the girl who spoke for them? I could not find that girl within me. She was an innocent. I was not.

I felt no pity for the dead, not because I loved my friends so much, but because I cared for life so little. Their safety was my doing, but even now it seemed a futile gesture. Though their lives were saved today, tomorrow death would come for them again. Did not death visit someone every day?

I knew the lessons of the forest. Life and death do battle there. Every day the fight begins anew. The fallen fall by chance, and those who win their lives today will fall tomorrow. Some may pity them, a few may mourn them, but should we not instead pity those who mourn? Those who will soon lie down upon the field of battle, they will face their death for just an instant. Then they will forget it all. Those who survive will feel as I feel now. It will not be the dead, but the living who will feel the absence, as death takes hold of them, bit by bit, its grip growing stronger with each loss.

Why do we bother living? I could not now imagine how I had once found life so sweet. I could not find that girl at all. I tried to remember her, and knew that she'd had something I did not. The self that once I was would have asked the Mother to keep my loved ones safe. I could not ask. No words of mine would reach the ears of Love. I had fallen into the abyss, where love is not.

Now I understood what lay in the depths of the abyss. The hunters of the forest people had found power there. They had drawn it up, as they danced along the edge. I too had drawn it up. But now I wasn't dancing. I had fallen. Death had already come for me, though in my living body I still walked among the living.

Now I knew the truth that lay behind the shields the living fashion for themselves. Death is our destiny, and nothing matters. In the depths of the abyss the end of all things lies. Death is too small a word. It is annihilation, not of my life alone, but of everything that lives and of the world itself. In the end the whole world will fall.

I felt grow strong within me a power that filled up the void where once my heart had been. If nothing matters, nothing is forbidden. All things are permitted to the dead.

80

FREEDOM

I must have slept for hours. There was nothing else to do. At last I heard footsteps in the hall. They stopped outside my door. The bolt slid back, the door opened, and a young woman came in. I thought of pushing past her and making my escape, until I saw the guard, who had followed her and now stood blocking up the doorway. In one hand he held a lamp. Its light revealed the woman's face. I remembered having seen her in the kitchen.

She was carrying a tankard and a plate. "I've brought you some breakfast," she said.

My hands reached out for the tankard before I was aware of being thirsty. I took a long drink. It was not ale, but water, cold and sparkling.

"I'm sorry," she said. "You must be starving." She set the plate down beside me. "In all the confusion no one remembered."

It was a feast of bread and cheese. I fell upon it as if it had been days since I'd had a bite to eat.

The woman turned to the guard and said, "I'll wait until he's done."

The guard handed her the lamp, and without a word he shut and barred the door. I heard his footsteps echo down the hallway.

The woman sat down beside me on the floor.

"Did you really steal it?" she whispered, as if we might still be overheard.

"What?"

"The knife."

She sounded like she thought the theft was something to be admired.

"No," I said between bites. "I didn't."

"You don't have to lie to me," she said. "That was just the bravest thing!"

"It was?"

"I thought I'd never seen any folk as arrogant as the mighty, but these so-called guests of theirs are worse!"

Clearly she expected my sympathy. I had to nod my understanding, because my mouth was busy eating.

"You're new here, aren't you?"

I nodded again.

"Are you a slave?"

I shook my head.

"You took an awful chance. What are they going to do with you?"

I shrugged my shoulders.

"Oh," she said, "I wish I could let you out of here. The last boy they caught stealing, they beat the daylights out of him." She gazed at me with sympathy. "I'd hate to see them hurt you. Maybe with the war and all, they'll forget."

She spoke of the war as if it were no concern of hers.

"Aren't you afraid of what may happen?" I asked her.

She didn't understand me.

"What if the mighty lose? What if the enemy wins?"

"Oh, nobody ever wins or loses," she said. "Nothing changes here. I wish it would."

While I ate, she chattered on, about the mighty and their doings, which seemed to have little to do with the life of the common folk other than to provide them with work to do and something to gossip about. It was almost as if the two peoples dwelt in different worlds, though they shared the place they lived in.

When my plate was empty, she took it from me and set it aside.

"Are you feeling better?" she asked.

I nodded and remembered to thank her for thinking of me.

"I have been thinking of you," she said. She sidled closer. "If you like, I could think of you a little longer."

She was flirting with me. She was more than flirting. She was offering herself. Then I remembered. It was springtime.

I was tempted. The touch of someone who cared for me, if only for the moment, was not a thing I would lightly turn aside. Yet how could I share with this young girl what I had so entirely given to someone else.

"What if the guard comes back?" I whispered.

"What if he does?" she whispered back.

"Won't they punish you?"

"What for?"

The answer had seemed obvious, until I thought about it.

"They don't care what we do," she said, "as long as we keep them warm and fed and don't cause any trouble."

"He may think you'll help me to escape."

"He thinks that already. That's why he came with me. That's why he barred the door."

Knowing as I did the pain of unwanted love, I tried to be kind to her. I took her hand. "You're lovely," I said, "but I can't."

"Oh," she said. "I don't mind if you're an innocent." She pouted at me. "Or do you have a sweetheart?"

She must have seen the answer in my face. Still she was undaunted. She leaned against my shoulder. "If you don't tell her, I won't."

"I had a sweetheart," I replied.

Speaking the word aloud brought tears to my eyes.

"Oh, dear," she said. "You've lost your sweetheart."

She put her arms around me, and from her body I took only comfort. I found no seduction there. A moment earlier she would have cheated another woman of my affection, but the loss of love was something she respected.

"There, there," she said. She held me for a moment more, then kissed my cheek before she let me go.

"My name is Lily, like the flower," she said. "What's yours?"

"Tamras," I whispered.

"So, Tamras," she said. "Tell me all about it."

"There's nothing to tell," I said. "I thought she loved me. For a while I believe she did. But she doesn't anymore."

"How do you know?"

"Because she loves someone else."

"Maybe she loves you both."

"It's not the same," I said.

"No, I suppose not. Some things can't be shared."

I remembered that I had recently had a few revelations about love, but now I couldn't think what they were.

"Love can be shared," I said, "but not hearts. No one wants a love that is half-hearted."

Lily laughed. "Aren't you clever!" She took my hand and squeezed it. "When your heart is whole again, pay me a visit."

The guard came to let her out. Before she got up to leave, she leaned toward me and again kissed me on the cheek. When I turned my face to hers, she kissed my lips.

"There," she said. "I think your heart has begun to mend already."

The door closed, but the light remained. Lily had left the lamp.

I looked around my prison but could see no point of weakness in it. Three walls of hewn planks, joined by stout pegs to the beams that supported the floor and ceiling, would resist all but the ax. The fourth wall, of mortared stone, was warm to the touch. One of the kitchen fires must be on the other side of it. The door was set so tightly in its frame that I couldn't see the bar that held it shut, much less slip something through the crack to coax it open. I resigned myself to staying where I was until someone decided what to do with me.

I still felt the touch of Lily's lips on mine. How sweet it was to find in this treacherous place a little unexpected kindness. Perhaps, as she had said, my heart would be whole again someday, though I could not now imagine it. I tried to conjure an image of myself loving someone else. I couldn't do it. Maara was too much a part of me. Like a forest tree that has grown up entwined with another may keep its shape long after its companion has been taken down, my spirit had bent to the shape of her and now could neither straighten itself nor accommodate to the shape of someone else.

Lily had reminded me of what was now beyond my reach. For me life's sweetness lay in loving and in being loved. That was all I'd ever wanted. I never coveted my place as Merin's heir. That was only something I was willing to accept because I did have what I wanted.

The voice of duty chided me. My destiny awaited me. There was still a place the world would make for me. I had no doubt of it.

I could defeat Vintel. Of that much I was certain. I never considered that I might die in the attempt. Death would be too easy. Death would be a gift.

From the abyss I had drawn the power to achieve my victory, and if I was wrong, what did it matter? But even if I found the will do to it, would I have the wisdom to wield the power I had won, or would I become another Merin, wise in many things, yet in the end defeated by the breaking of her heart.

I saw the irony. By losing what I valued most, I had gained the power to defeat my enemies. Yet I had a greater power, and I had had it all along. I had the power of refusal. Whatever power had anointed me, be it god or demon, I could cheat it of its victory.

I spoke aloud. "Not without love," I said.

After a few hours passed, the lamp went out. I slept the afternoon away. A woman brought me bread and meat for supper. It wasn't Lily. The air that came into the room with her chilled me. Though the kitchen fires would have long since burned down, the stone wall held their heat, and I sat with my back against it. I wasn't sleepy, but I lay down anyway.

A breath of cold air touched my face. It must be a draft from under the door, I thought, but what had drawn it in? When I sat up, I couldn't feel it. It only blew across the floor.

I lay down again and turned to face the wall. I saw a glow, so faint that I thought my eyes, deprived of light, had kindled it out of wishful thinking, but it shone just in one spot, and when my fingers explored there between the stones, the mortar crumbled and the stone wiggled a little, as if someone had been working at it.

I had no implement, so I used my hands, wearing my fingernails ragged, until I broke a bit of stone away. Then I used it to chip away at the mortar. When I stopped to listen, I heard snatches of conversation from the kitchen. I worked as quietly as I could, and at last an entire stone came loose, but no matter which way I turned it, I couldn't pull it into the room with me, so I gave it a push. Although it was level with the wooden floor I was lying on, it must have been at least a foot above the kitchen hearth, because it landed with a loud crack of stone on stone.

The sound stopped the kitchen talk for hardly a moment. I was glad that Elen's was such a noisy household.

When I peered through the hole I'd made, I could see nothing but the inside of the kitchen hearth. The fire had been banked. I could just make out the glow of coals beneath the ashes. I waited while the kitchen servants finished up their chores, quenched the lamps, and went to bed.

When I was certain no one remained in the kitchen, I went back to work enlarging the hole. Now that I had the one stone out, it was easier to loosen those around it. The mortar was old and crumbly, and when I pulled out a second stone, those next to it gave way, making a hole big enough for me to wriggle through. Once free of my prison, I fitted the stones back into place for no other reason than to baffle my jailers.

When I stood up I found myself inside the kitchen hearth. Covered in soot and ash, I was blacker than a demon's heart at midnight, invisible against the sooty fireback. The kitchen was almost as dark. I kicked the ashes from the coals, to make the fire flare up enough so that by its light I could find my way to the back door. A little lick of flame danced above the embers. I stepped through it.

My nemesis was sitting by the fire. Moments before he must have been asleep. The stout servant who had twice laid hands on me was now wide awake and staring at the apparition that had stepped from the flames. If he tried to take hold of me again, I resolved to run him through with a meat fork or whatever else might come to hand, but he only sat and stared at me as I walked past him and out the kitchen door.

I crossed the yard, keeping to the shadows, all the while expecting to hear him raise the alarm. Nothing happened. In the yard the guards slept on. The gate groaned on its hinges. They didn't wake. I pulled it shut behind me and turned my back on Elen's house.

81

DISENCHANTED

Dark and quiet, the village lay asleep. I walked through its empty streets, as bold as if I were an apparition. Too late I spied a watchman leaning against the corner of a shed, but he only wrapped his arms around his body and shivered as I went past.

Perhaps I was a disembodied wraith. Do the dead know when their bodies have been left behind? The thought amused me.

Wraith or not, I feared no one. I had nothing more to want. No one could prevent my having it or take it from me.

I had one more obligation, and I would fulfill it if I could. Others had put their lives at risk for me. I owed it to them to see them safely on their way.

When I rapped on the door of the armorer's house, no one answered. I rapped again, a little louder. At last it opened, and the armorer, grumpy in his nightshirt, stared at me.

"It's Tamras," I said, remembering what I looked like.

He let me in.

Someone poked the fire into flame, and by its light I saw the forms of many men sleeping on the floor. Several had begun to wake. I saw Bru among them. He stood up and came to greet me.

"We feared you had come to grief," he said. "What kept you?"

"They locked me up," I told him, "but I got away."

The sleeping forms began to wake. The warriors of Bru's band sat up and gazed at me. Their faces I remembered from another lifetime.

"Why are you all here?" I asked.

"We saw their preparations," said Bru. "We were curious. We thought it might have something to do with you."

"How did you get down into the valley?"

"The same way you did." Bru chuckled. "Bands of armed men were everywhere. We blended in."

The men laughed.

Bru led me to the fire, to get a better look at me. "Are you all right?"

I nodded.

"Why have they sent their warriors out? Is Elen's house in danger?"

"They think it is." I sighed. "It's a long story."

Finn had built up the fire and now made a place for me beside him on the hearth. "Sit down, then," he said, "and tell it. We have all night."

I began by telling them about the army I had seen on my way to Elen's house and what I believed were its intentions.

"I chanced to mention it to Elen," I said, "and she saw it as a threat, not to my people, but to her. I meant to go myself, to warn my people. Now there is no need. Elen's army will turn the northerners aside."

The men were silent, but I saw their admiration in their eyes. It shamed me.

"It was no cleverness of mine," I said. "To Elen, everything that happens has to do with her."

"Not clever?" said Finn. "Clever enough to shoot two birds with one arrow."

"What do you mean?"

"Why did you go there? Wasn't it to free your friend from Elen's house?"

"Oh." How could I tell them that I had risked their lives for nothing?

"We have wasted our time on a fool's errand," I said.

"Now, now," said Bru. "The worst is over. Don't lose heart. We have only to follow Elen's army and wait upon our chance."

Finn, who sat beside me, turned me to the firelight. Though my face must have been concealed by soot and dirt, he read my eyes. "You say you were locked up?"

I nodded.

He turned to Bru. "I think she doesn't know."

"Know what?" I asked.

"Your friend has gone with Elen's warriors."

"That may be," I said, "but she has no need of rescue. She is content where she is."

"How can she be content?" said Bru. "She is a prisoner."

"Not anymore."

Bru looked as if he couldn't comprehend what I was telling him. I saw that we were talking at cross-purposes, but I didn't know where the trouble was.

Finn touched my hand. "Someone has deceived you," he said. "Your friend was taken out of Elen's house in shackles. She left with Elen's guard this morning. I think they mean to use her as a hostage."

Now I was the one who couldn't comprehend what I was hearing. "It must be someone else."

Finn shook his head. "I made very sure. When we heard they were going to bring a prisoner out, I thought it might be you. It wasn't, but the gossip of the crowd told me what I had guessed already."

Finn saw that I was still confused. He gave me a lengthy explanation, while I gathered my wits together. Finn had waited every day in the kitchen yard for word of me. At first he worried, because I had been accused of theft, but punishments in Elen's house were swift and public, and when nothing happened, he believed that I had made the most of my opportunity.

The day before, word went out to gather Elen's army. The warriors of the mighty were gathered there already, as well as the king's brother's men-at-arms, because of the return of the assassin. To these were added many of the common folk, some who served Elen's house as warriors, and others who had come hoping to profit from the gathering and now saw a chance for plunder.

All day they were busy making preparations. An advance guard left late in the afternoon, with the main body to follow in the morning. They told none of the common folk what might be the cause. It was something everyone was used to. With one thing and another, Elen kept her warriors occupied.

All day the armorer had work to do. In the evening he and Finn, together with Bru and his band, talked things over. They decided to wait until the army had departed before they tried to find me. In the morning Bru and Finn joined the crowd outside Elen's gate. When they saw Maara brought out with Elen's guard, they thought it wisest to do nothing until they heard from me. They believed that I had planned it all.

They still believed it. I saw it in their eyes. Though I might not have known that I had succeeded, they never doubted, when they saw her, that

I had made it happen. It was the most difficult thing, the one thing they thought might be impossible — to bring a prisoner out of the fortress that was Elen's house. Yet it had been easily accomplished, not by force, but by stealth and trickery.

Even while I listened to Finn's account, my heart beat with the words. *They brought her out in shackles.* Maara was a prisoner. Elen told me she was free. It was a lie. So Elen was a liar, and nothing Elen said could be believed. By her own words, she had condemned herself. *You find the lie, you pull its thread, and the whole unravels.*

What a conjuror she was! I began to awaken from my enchantment.

When Finn had finished, the men were silent. I felt them wait for a response from me.

"Someone did deceive me," I said, "but I will not deceive you. Elen convinced me that Maara had come home."

Then I told the men the story of my sojourn in Elen's house.

I would soon have to come to terms with myself, with what I had done and left undone, with what I had believed, against the evidence of my own heart. Where was the flaw in me that Elen had sought out and used against me?

No time now to think of that. My feelings must be mastered, before they overwhelmed me. I used what Maara taught me. I faced them without indulging them. Anger and regret. Disappointment in myself. And shame. Shame most of all, that I had given in so easily, that I had been so willing to believe. Then I swept them up into a bundle and set it aside.

Now there were things to do. Now we must lay our plans. As Bru had said, we could follow Elen's army and await our opportunity. We resolved to set out before first light. With so few warriors left in Elen's house, we might make our way undiscovered to the falls. The leap into the Giant's Maw held no terror for me now.

I kept watch while the others slept. I had slept enough. I used the time to think, not about the past I couldn't change, but about what lay ahead. We would be a full day behind Elen's army. If we were quick, we might catch up to them before the battle. Then we could bide our time and wait for the fighting to begin. Once it did, the fog of war would cover our intentions.

I made only one mistake. I neglected my injury. Though its cause may have been a fabrication, the injury was real. I might have begun my healing by remembering Maara's love for me. As I had plundered my memory for evidence against her while I lay under an enchantment in Elen's house, I could have brought back, with clear vision, all the evidence of love, but the injury itself prevented me.

After the first time I took a life in battle, Maara said that I had stepped into the unknown, but that would not be so when I had to kill a second time. When my trust in her was shattered, I stepped again into the unknown, and now I knew the pain that breaks our hearts. I still guarded mine.

I hid my caution from myself. I believed that I believed. Maara in shackles could mean one thing only, that she was Elen's prisoner. But as the night wore on, doubts came to trouble me. As soon as I looked for them, other explanations offered themselves. It might have been a show, for the benefit of the common folk or the king's brother. It might even have been someone else. I tried to put my doubts away, but I would not believe again so quickly until I had the evidence of my own eyes. Until I heard the words from Maara, I would put my trust in neither one thing nor the other.

In the morning, we leapt, not into the Giant's Maw, but into the maw of Elen's army. A warrior band of half a hundred, latecomers, caught us on the road. Bru's quick thinking deflected their suspicions. We were latecomers too, he said. As we were all well armed, they chose to believe us.

With our new comrades in arms, we climbed the cliff, up the same trail we had descended. It took us half the morning. As we traveled through the forest, Elen's warriors stopped often, and we had no choice but to stop with them. Where we would have made up time, they dawdled along the trail. They were in no hurry to find the battlefield. They were hoping the battle would be over by the time they got there.

When we stopped to make camp for the night, Bru volunteered to keep the first watch. Still untrusting, our comrades appointed one of their own band to watch with him, but he soon nodded off, and we crept silently away.

The trail wasn't difficult to follow, even at nighttime. After all, we were following an army. At last we too had to stop for a few hours of sleep. At first light we continued on our way.

All that day we traveled through the forest. I saw no part of it that I remembered, but my companions knew it well. They told me that by the next afternoon we would be in the wilderness. It was, in fact, no later than midday when we reached the forest's edge. Before we set foot into the open, Bru gathered us together. He thought it wise to send a scout a little way ahead of us, and he asked for a volunteer.

"I'll go," I said, but he shook his head.

"We know this country," he told me. "My son will go."

It was the first I had heard of their relationship. The boy's name was Matha, and he was the youngest of us all. His beardless face revealed his pleasure, that his father trusted him with our safety.

We made a cautious camp that night. We dared not light a fire in the open, so we had a supper of cold barley cakes and smoked venison. Bru sent out no less than five men to watch, all at some distance from our camp, so that we would not be taken unawares.

Again I volunteered to stand a watch.

Again Bru shook his head. "Your time will come," he said.

We had an uneventful night, and then an uneventful day, but when we sat down to another cold meal that evening, the men seemed wary. They glanced out into the darkness, as if they expected trouble to come at any moment. Our watchmen notwithstanding, each man kept his own watch. No one had much to say, and when anyone did speak, it was hardly above a whisper.

Despite their nervousness, or perhaps because of it, I slept well the whole night through. I relied on my companions. I trusted myself to their skill and their experience, as well as to their good intentions.

The next day was as uneventful as the day before. While we paused at midday for a bite to eat, no one said a word. They were listening. All day we had traveled under a cloudy sky. All day we had heard nothing but the wind. Now I could no longer feel the wind, but I still heard it. At first I thought it must be my imagination, but the others were listening to something too.

Then Finn said, "The battle has been joined."

When we resumed our march, Bru sent out two more scouts to go with his son. As the afternoon wore on, the clouds descended, until we were surrounded by a swirling mist. Our scouts returned to us before they lost us altogether. It was still early, but the mist grew so thick that we had to stop, or we might have stumbled into danger without warning. We listened again for the sounds of battle, but all we heard was silence.

In the field an opportunity for sleep is never wasted. We hoarded it. We stored it up, against the time when sleep would be impossible.

In the morning we awoke among the dead. They lay all around us. Some appeared to be asleep, but most lay in some grotesque posture, as if death had taken them as they writhed in pain. Blinded by the mist, we had blundered in amongst them.

When morning came, the air was clear, to show me what I had done. The dead had come to haunt me, I who caused their death. It was a truth I had recognized already. I had used the lives of innocents to accomplish my own ends.

Finn saw me sitting up. He took my arm and helped me to my feet.

"Come away," he said.

I couldn't move.

"Don't be afraid," he said. "They can't harm us now."

Living men could have been no greater threat to me.

Finn led me away while Bru and his men scouted the battlefield. As we ate a cold breakfast, they each made their report. It had been only a skirmish, they said, a meeting of Elen's advance guard with scouts from the northern army. A score of northern dead had covered the retreat of the rest, who would have hastened back to bring warning of the advancing enemy.

"Was this what we heard yesterday?" I asked.

Bru shook his head. "Not many fought here."

If the death I had seen that morning was just the remnant of a skirmish, how many would remain, lifeless on the battlefield, after a clash of armies?

Bru studied me. "Have you lost heart?"

I shook my head.

"Nevertheless, I think this is not what you expected."

"No," I said. "This is just what I expected. When I foresaw it, I didn't care, but now I do."

My mind turned inward, trying to remember who it was that counted these deaths as nothing. Her words echoed hollow in my heart. *Death is our destiny, and nothing matters.* I remembered her and understood her, but I had left her back in Elen's house.

Bru frowned at me. "Will you turn back?"

Would these lives too, these innocents, Finn and Bru, the armorer, the men whose lives I had saved in Merin's house, would they too be sacrificed?

"This is my undertaking," I told him. "I have not words enough to thank you for the help you've given me. I never meant to risk your lives along with mine. You've done enough. My turn has come. Go home."

Bru smiled. "I'm glad we understand each other."

I nodded and started to stand up. I had no heart for long good-byes.

"Let us now meet in council, you and I," said Bru. "We have an undertaking of our own, and we will need your help."

I sat back down.

"For the mighty we care nothing," he went on, "but many of my kinsmen fight beside them. So they keep their pride as fighting men, as I keep mine by keeping to myself. Now they are in peril. If I can help them, I must do it."

The men all nodded. No one accused me. They had no need to. I was quick to accuse myself.

"If I can help you," I said, "I will. This evil is my doing, and I will try to make amends for it."

Bru shook his head. "It is true that a little nudge from you has moved the world, but when that happens, the world was already inclined to move. I feel a great change coming. Whatever has been set in motion, let us ride it."

He reached his arm out to me and I took it. The men sat by, silent witnesses to our agreement. When we stood up to continue on our way, I saw on each man's face a light that came, not from the rising sun, but from within. They too felt change coming, and they transformed my guilt into a sense of hope and common cause, that we could bring some good out of the evil I had set afoot.

82

BATTLEFIELD

The sounds of battle that we had heard the day before could have come from quite a distance. A cloudy sky reflects sound as well as light, and in the wilderness there were neither trees nor hills high enough to form a barrier against it. All the same, caution was our watchword. We sent out no scouts. All of us together crept carefully to the top of each rise and peered over before descending the other side. From time to time one of my companions paused to sniff the air, but the wind blew from behind us and told us nothing.

At midday we reached a hill a little higher than the rest, and Bru and I ascended it while the others waited out of sight. From its top we had our first view of the battlefield. It was a landscape from a nightmare. No armies fought there now. Only the dead remained. At first they were all that I could see.

Though I knew better, my heart began to hope that these men were all asleep and that any moment they would wake and spring up again. I waited for these dead men to spring up.

Then someone did. It was a living man, plundering the dead. A mist blew by him, hid him for a moment. Not mist. Smoke. For no apparent reason, other living men had lit a bonfire, with logs stacked up into piles almost as tall as they were. In the distance I saw two more. Where they found so much wood to burn here in the wilderness I could not imagine, until I saw that they were not burning wood. They burned the dead.

The sight horrified me more than any I had yet seen on that dreadful day. At home we would have opened up the earth to place our dead within it, within the Mother's womb, so that she would take their bodies back into herself.

As living plants spring up from the dead seed, so their spirits would spring up again in time, clothed with living flesh. These dead would suffer a fate more cruel than they had met the day they died. Burning would release their spirits into the air, where they would wander, lost in a shadow world, longing for a house of flesh. Then they would seek out the living, and this battlefield would become a haunting.

I must have made a sound that told Bru of my dismay. I felt him watching me, and because he had before mistaken my regret for cowardice, I said, "My people would not dare to burn the dead."

"Nor mine," said Bru, "but the battlefield is a place unto itself. The mighty say the spirits of warriors killed in battle fly at once to the halls of their god of war, where they will be rewarded for their valor."

"Words are only air," I said, remembering an old saying whose ending was not spoken but understood, that it was one's deeds that mattered. Yet a deeper truth lay within it. How easy to speak such things to the innocent and gullible. How joyfully might a man go to his death if he believed such empty promises. This was a wickedness that baffled me.

"And how else could they dispose of them all?" said Bru.

If they wouldn't place them in the Mother's womb, they could at least leave them lying on her breast, I thought. And they did indeed leave many. When I asked Bru why some were burned and some were left, he said, "They only burn their own."

I would have preferred the mighty to treat me as the enemy, until I saw the ravens, plucking out their eyes.

I turned away, leaving Bru to read the battlefield. Elen had won the day, he told me. That was why her men now plundered the enemy dead and honored, according to their strange beliefs, their own. Bru reckoned that Elen had lost at least a hundred, and the northerners more than twice as many.

"Then it's over," I said. "Their hearts have been defeated. Now they will go home."

He shook his head. "Their chieftains will return for the negotiations."

"To make a treaty?"

Bru smiled at my ignorance. "No one treats with the defeated," he said. "They will come to negotiate a ransom for the prisoners."

Of course. Elen's army would have taken prisoners. But what did the northerners have to offer? Was I the only one who understood their poverty?

"How can they ransom them?" I asked. "Other than their arms, they have little of value."

Bru frowned. "Elen will take those first, before she takes their lives."

"What?"

"She won't leave any who might come back to threaten her again."

"Will she murder them all?"

"Some she will," he said. "The chieftains first, when they come to her tent under a banner of trust. Then she will pursue the remnant of their army until they scatter leaderless back into the hills they came from."

"Why would she do such a thing?"

"Because she can."

"Will she also kill the prisoners?"

"If they are troublesome, she may. If they behave themselves, she will enslave them."

He seemed so certain of Elen's plans that I wondered if he had some experience of her dealings with her foes. He answered my unspoken question.

"I have heard many stories of her ruthlessness," he said, "but I also have a story of my own. Many years ago, before Elen became a queen, her mother sent her to deal with a troublesome band of outlaws, bandits who robbed the caravans of her trade goods. When Elen learned from her spies that they were, as she called them, only a ragamuffin army, she disguised her band of warriors as a caravan and tricked the bandits into attacking them. Once defeated, they would not have been a threat to her again, but she murdered their chieftain and made the rest her prisoners. They were too fierce to serve as slaves, so she put them in cages and displayed them, as she would have displayed savage beasts, until they all died of shame and grief."

"Who were these men to you?" I asked him.

"My father's brother," he replied, "the man who fostered me."

There were scores to settle here, I thought to myself, and more to Bru than a man who saw his kinsmen in peril.

We had been on the hilltop for so long that the rest of the men came up to join us. We let them satisfy their curiosity. Then we went back down the hill, to take counsel together.

"When will the northern chieftains come to parley?" I asked Bru.

"Elen will have already sent an envoy," he replied. "They should return tonight, and the enemy come in the morning."

"So Elen's army will remain encamped another night?"

He nodded.

"Now that they've had their victory, will the sentries be less watchful?"

"Do you mean to try to slip into her camp unseen?"

"How else can I discover where they're keeping Maara?"

"Well," he said, "we could just join the army."

"How can we do that?"

"You forget. We are latecomers. The men we traveled with will be there by now. They will know us, and greet us as comrades in arms. And I think we may find other friends of ours among them."

So we determined that we would hide ourselves until after dark. Then we would join Elen's camp as if that had been our intention all along.

We put a few hills between ourselves and the battlefield before we settled down to wait. Bru handed out all that remained of our rations, and we ate a good meal that filled our stomachs and cheered our hearts. He made certain that each of us slept for several hours. We had a long night before us.

I did sleep for an hour or two, but for most of that day I lay awake, pondering what might happen. If we were accepted as part of Elen's army, we would have the freedom of the camp, but getting Maara out of it would not be easy. Elen would keep Maara close to her. That meant I would have to deal with Elen's guard, men chosen for their loyalty. And once I had succeeded in freeing her from Elen, how would I take her from the camp?

I could not think past the difficulty of the task that I had set myself. To find Maara and bring her out of Elen's camp to safety was as far as I allowed my mind to go. I made no other plans and gave no thought to the time when we would find ourselves together. What I would say to her, what she would say to me, did not concern me then. I kept my attention in that day alone. That was my shield.

We waited through the twilight, until we could bear to wait no longer. I thought we might have trouble finding the encampment, but Bru knew exactly where it was. He knew this land so well that he hardly had to guess where an army the size of Elen's would choose to stop.

By the time we got there it was almost dark. I could just make out how the camp lay within the landscape, as we looked down upon it from the crest of a hill. In a large open space, sheltered on all sides by low hills and hidden from the battlefield, we saw the campfires. I lost count after reaching four score, and I had counted less than half. At least a dozen men gathered around each one. I could not begin to think how many men there might be.

Behind the army on a hillside I saw a few tents, pitched close together. A little below them were the baggage wagons, set in a line, as if to guard the approach to the tents, or to form a barrier between the tents and the army. The oxen had been taken from their yokes, hobbled, and set out to graze. Red cattle were scattered in among them, meat on the hoof for Elen's warriors.

The camp even had a source of water. On the far side a change in the color of the vegetation told me the land was wet there. Perhaps there was a spring, or perhaps a stream drained into it. In addition to providing water, the boggy ground would prevent an enemy from approaching Elen's army on that side.

"How many are there, do you think?" I asked Bru.

"Many hundreds," he replied. He took a few minutes more to make a better guess. "At least a score of hundreds."

We stayed where we were, hidden in a patch of gorse, until the darkness was complete. The smells of cooking drifted up to us, along with the murmur of many conversations.

At last Bru said, "I'll go first. Keep me in sight. If I'm not well received, you must each do as you think best, but if you see me set my shield down, come and join me."

We watched him stumble over the rough ground beyond the reach of firelight. Then a sentry challenged him, and we heard him even at a distance complaining loudly that a man had come all that way to fight and no one so much as offered him a crust of bread. The sentry escorted him into camp. Bru was looking all around, as if for his long-lost companions. He must have found them, because he waved at a group of men around a distant fire and held his shield up, so that they would recognize him. Its device was so faded that I had never been able to discover what it was, but these men knew it. They stood up to greet him, and the sentry let him go. When Bru reached their campfire, he set his shield down.

The rest of us now straggled into camp, trying to look as if we had come to the end of a long and exhausting march. No one challenged us. Bru must have told the sentry to expect us.

The men who had welcomed Bru were not the men we had traveled with. Before long I understood that these men were his kinsmen. Finn knew many of them too, as did some of the other men. For half an hour each man recited his lineage to the others, until they had worked out who was whose second cousin twice removed. Then the clansmen all sat down and had their dinner.

I sat close to Bru and a little bit behind him, shielded from the firelight. I wanted to hear the conversation without drawing attention to myself.

We heard first about the battle. The two armies were fairly matched, but Elen took the northerners by surprise. They had begun their march, and when their scouts alerted them, they had to hurry back. They took the field with no time to rest, no time to choose their ground or agree upon a strategy. It was Elen who chose the battlefield and by clever tricks and feints lured the northern army to its doom.

Bru's band of warriors delighted in the tale. They took satisfaction in hearing of the northerners' demise, as if they had some complaint against them and this victory was their revenge. Then I remembered. *Our faithless friends,* they called them. The northerners had once used these man and then abandoned them. I wondered if Bru might not disapprove of the way that Elen planned to deal with them. I set aside a passing thought, that someone should take them a warning.

"Ask them where the northern army came from," I whispered to Bru.

"They approached us from the south," came back the answer.

I thought it not the best time to point out that if the northern army had intended to march on Elen's house, they had been traveling in the wrong direction.

Finn excused himself to use the privy. He made his way through the camp in the direction of the tents. The privy would be located for the convenience of the mighty. I watched his progress, until the conversation distracted me. Bru's kinsmen were speaking of the king's brother.

"He is here with his men-at-arms," said one. "Not as many as he promised, though he insists that more were sent for." The man gestured toward the far side of the camp. "His banner is the eagle."

Not that we could have made it out. It was too dark. Then I noticed the other banners fluttering from their standards in the night breeze. No one had to explain to me their purpose. In an army of this size, how else could a warrior find his fellows? And in battle they would serve to keep the clans together.

Now that we had entered Elen's camp, I should have been more hopeful, but I could not imagine how we would achieve our ends. The half dozen tents where Elen and her captains sheltered lay within a double ring of campfires. The ground around them bristled with spears, set into the earth to form a palisade. The men who would wield them were the same men who had surrounded Elen in her great hall. Even if we might against all odds succeed in getting in, getting out would be something else again.

When Finn returned from the privy, he tugged at my sleeve and drew me away from the others. Then he sat down beside me and said in a low voice, "They hold the prisoners in a hollow in the hills, not far from the tents."

I looked, but the hillside was in darkness.

"They have no fires," said Finn. "No supper either."

"How many are there?"

"Many," he replied. "More than the dead they left lying on the battle-field. There may be twice as many." Before I could ask my next question, he answered it. "Your friend is not among them."

Though I had hoped, I did not expect that Maara would be with the other prisoners. "She will be close to Elen," I said.

"I fear so."

"Are the prisoners well guarded?"

"Well enough. Why?"

"If I can hide myself among them, perhaps I can approach the tents from behind."

"What good would that do? Are we invisible?"

"One way or another, I must get into Elen's tent."

"Then let's be a little clever," he replied, "and consider how we may make ourselves invisible."

How would I be able to walk into Elen's tent unchallenged? Who would be granted entrance there? Only her captains and her scouts, no one unknown to her. But in the morning the northerners would arrive.

"I will go in with the northern chieftains," I said, "when they come to bargain for their comrades' lives."

"How will you manage that?"

I'd had no time to think it through. I grasped for an excuse. "I will go out to meet them and warn them of Elen's treachery."

Bru had sidled away from the campfire to eavesdrop on our conversation. Now he turned and joined us. "They won't believe you," he said. "And if they do, they will turn back, and that would not serve your purposes at all."

Bru gave me a few minutes to wrestle with this new dilemma. Then he said, "You can't do this alone. I think we will all go with you. We will say nothing of Elen's treachery, but will present ourselves to the chieftains as their escort. We will disarm them and take them to Elen's tent at swordpoint."

It was a bold idea. In my mind's eye I saw the whole two dozen of us, an armed escort for the northern chieftains, bringing them to Elen's tent in plain view of the entire camp. Then I saw the flaw in Bru's plan.

"Elen's guard will stop us," I said. "They don't know us. They won't allow us to go armed before the queen."

For a time all three of us sat with deeply furrowed brows, trying to think of a way around this difficulty. Then I had the first glimmer of an inspiration.

"The king's brother," I whispered. "Do Elen's guard know all his men-at-arms?"

Bru shook his head. "How can they? Some have only just arrived."

"Then we will carry the eagle banner and insist on being granted entry in his name."

"It might work," Bru conceded, willing to leave aside for the moment the problem of obtaining the eagle banner.

"And once inside," I said, "we will refuse to surrender the northern chieftains until Elen gives up her hostage, so that the king's brother can at last have his revenge."

Bru leaned forward and his fingers brushed my brow. "A subtle mind," he said. "And once Elen gives her up, will we hand the chieftains over and depart?"

"No," I said. "We must tell the northern chieftains of our plans."

"Why would we do that?"

"Because their lives are not ours to use."

Bru scowled at me. "These armies were not yours to use, and yet you used them."

He meant to touch a point of weakness. I refused to let him find it.

"At the time I had no other weapon," I said. "It was a crude weapon and bought us little more than time. The next sword that comes into my hand I would hone a little sharper."

"Ah," said Bru. "You have a plan for them. You are too subtle for me. I cannot see it."

"I have no plan for them, but to allow them to make their own plans, and to do that they must know the truth, or at least as much of it as we do."

Bru put on his stubborn face.

"If we prepare them for the possibility that Elen will not deal with them honorably, they may be willing to give us their help in return for ours."

Still Bru did not relent.

"I know you have no reason to show them any kindness," I said. "They used you shamefully, and they deceived you, but alone how can we accomplish what we mean to do? Once out of Elen's tent, how will we get away, with Elen's army on our heels? If we can somehow help the chieftains to escape, along with all the prisoners, we will be lost among the multitudes."

Bru saw right away the advantage of loosing chaos on the army of the mighty, but still he was cautious.

"We can offer them our help without giving away our own designs," he said. "How much would you tell them?"

"Everything."

"Why?"

"Because they will suspect a trick, and honesty will earn their trust. And because I am a dismal liar. It is my greatest strength."

But Bru was not convinced. "Wiser men than I taught me never to reveal my plans, not even to my friends, much less my enemies. They lied to us. Why would we treat them as men of honor."

"Because we are men of honor," whispered Finn. "Tamras is right. They lied to us, and they will expect no better in return. A lie will always out, and they will be relentless in trying to uncover it, but it is said that all tongues witness to the truth."

When Finn spoke of tongues, I remembered something that might defeat our plans.

"How can we talk to them?" I asked Finn. "I've heard their language, and I can't make head or tail of it."

"They will bring a go-between," said Bru. "Someone who speaks the language of the mighty, for all the good that does us. None of us speaks it well enough for what you have in mind."

"I do," I said. "It is my mother tongue."

Then Bru had to accept defeat. If I was the only one who could make herself understood, it was my plan that would prevail.

83

Best Laid Plans

While I had been arguing with Bru, my plan was taking shape. "We will have to arm the prisoners," I said, "but not too soon, not until we've found Maara." I turned to Bru. "We watched Elen's warriors plunder the dead. Their weapons must be somewhere within the camp."

"Taken by her men as booty, I've no doubt," he said.

"But Elen will have had her share. Where would they put such a great quantity of arms?"

"The baggage wagons," said Finn, "and there's nothing between the prisoners and the wagons but a little hill and a few guards."

"Would the mighty be so careless?" I asked him.

"No," said Bru, "but they would be so arrogant."

"Is it possible to see the tents from where the prisoners are?" I asked Finn.

"I believe so," he replied.

"We'll devise a signal, then. When they see it, they must rush the wagons all at once and arm themselves. What shall our signal be?"

"Well," said Bru, "we will all leave Elen's tent one way or the other. If we leave it with our swords drawn, let them come to us quickly, armed with whatever they can lay their hands on."

"And then we must all run for our lives," said Finn. "Shall we decide now which way to go?"

"South," I said. "To the north is boggy ground, as well as the king's brother's men-at-arms. To the west is Elen's house and the possibility that we may encounter stragglers making their way to the battlefield."

"And to the east is the whole of Elen's army," said Bru, "so south is where we'll go."

Bru sounded almost cheerful. Once he had accepted the idea of an alliance with the northerners, I think he found some enthusiasm for this new adventure.

"Is there anyone among us who can speak to the prisoners?" I asked.

"My son has a clever tongue," Bru replied. "He will make them understand."

I worried about Bru's son. He was so young.

"Then let him stay behind, close by the prisoners," I said. "He can watch for our signal, and they will need someone to lead them, until they join their chieftains."

Bru frowned. "He'll be sorry to miss all the fun," he said.

"There will be fun enough for all of us," I told him. "Ask your son if he will help me steal the eagle banner."

I left Bru to talk our plan over with his men, while Matha and I conspired together. The evening's rations had been taken around in great baskets by boys who looked very much like us, so we each found ourselves a basket and thus disguised ourselves as servants.

As we made our way to the other side of the camp, where the king's brother had established his own separate encampment, I made a quick study of Elen's army. The men I saw around me appeared to be all of the common folk. From their dress and from their language, I guessed that these men were like Bru's kinsmen, keeping their self-respect while making something of a living by their service. Matha confirmed my guess.

"My father's clan has kept away from Elen's house," he told me. "Other clans have not been so fortunate. Some have lost their lands. Others have lost so many of their people that they can't survive unless they join a greater house. Elen's house is where the wealth is, so there they go."

"What of Elen's people?" I asked him. "Where are the warriors of the mighty?"

Matha pointed to the campfires closest to the tents. I adjusted our meandering path so that we would pass close by them. When I got a better look at the men there, I could easily see the difference. They were better armed and better dressed, and they moved and spoke with confidence and with a swagger, as men do who are aware of their own importance.

The king's brother's warriors were much the same. Matha and I were so far beneath their notice that we moved among them as freely as we could have wished. Our plan was to locate the eagle banner and come back for it when everyone was asleep, but Matha tripped and fell against the pole that held it, sending it fluttering down into a fire pit. He snatched it out, unburnt but covered with ash. One of the men-at-arms took hold of him and boxed his ears. Matha yelped and begged his pardon.

"I'll clean it, master," he said. "I'll clean it and bring it back before first light."

The man growled at him, but let him go. Matha turned away and winked at me. He took the banner from its standard, shook it out, folded it carefully, and tucked it into his belt.

Now we had only to find a way to get in among the prisoners. Our baskets held a few loaves of bread, left over from the evening meal. Scattered among the campfires were some half-eaten loaves. I started to gather them up and gestured to Matha to do the same. When our baskets were full, we carried them to the place where the prisoners were kept.

Their guards each had a fire against the chill of the spring evening. The fires made a ring around a circle of darkness. A guard stopped us and examined the contents of our baskets, then let us pass. The light of his fire dazzled our eyes, and we tripped over several people before we could see well enough to find our way.

The prisoners reminded me of the prisoners in Merin's house. Their warrior spirit had gone out of them. They hardly noticed us, until we began handing out the loaves. Then the hope of satisfying their hunger kindled a little flame of life within them.

I saw many women among them. It had been so long since I had seen a woman among warriors that the sight of them surprised me. This much they had in common with my people.

When our baskets were empty, Matha asked for their leader, and they took us to a woman old enough to have retired from the battlefield.

Matha asked me what to say.

"Tell her their chieftains are coming in the morning," I said.

Matha did have a few words of their strange tongue, but he made himself more clear by signs. The woman seemed to understand.

"Tell her Elen isn't to be trusted," I said.

Matha scratched his head. Then he said the name, "Elen," pointed to the tents, and made signs of swords falling on the prisoners and on their chieftains. For one who hardly spoke the language, he was doing very well. Too well. A murmur of alarm went through the crowd around us.

"Quickly," I said. "Tell them we will help them."

Matha gestured to me and to himself, then in the direction of the camp, and made the sign for many. He must have found the word for help or alliance or something similar, because the prisoners grew quiet.

"Tell them we are also enemies of Elen's house," I said. "Tell them we will warn their chieftains."

Again he gestured to me and to himself and to the rest of our companions, then made a sign of swords falling on the tents, presumably on Elen and her captains.

The woman looked puzzled. She said a few words to a man who sat beside her, and he got up and left us. When I would have said something else, she gestured to me to wait.

The man was back a moment later, bringing with him two young men who addressed us haltingly in the language of the mighty. Between the two of them, they had enough words to understand me and to make themselves understood. I wasted no time trying to explain who we were and what our purpose was. They believed me when I told them what Elen meant to do with them. I laid out our plan for them and asked them to repeat it back to me, to make sure they understood it.

"In the morning you will escort our chieftains to the queen's tent," they said. "If you leave it with drawn swords, we must come to help you."

I nodded. "Matha will stay close by you and watch for our signal. You must be careful not to alarm the guards. It will seem natural to them that you will be watching for your chieftains, as long as you look like you're only waiting patiently. Don't give them any reason to suspect that you're planning something."

The young men nodded.

"Did you tell them the swords are in the wagons?" Matha asked me.

I shook my head. "I'm afraid if they know that, they will act too soon."

"Tell them I'll lead them to the weapons, once we discover where they are," he said.

I did as he suggested. As I rose to go, the woman took hold of my arm. She asked me, through the two young men, why I would help them.

"Elen holds a hostage who is dear to me," I told her. "I intend to take her back, and your escape will cover mine."

She nodded that she understood.

After we left the prisoners, Matha and I carried our empty baskets in the direction of the wagons. No one took any notice of us. When we reached them, we set our baskets down, and, like curious boys, we peeked inside each wagon until we found the ones we wanted. There were swords and spears and axes, arms enough for at least half the prisoners.

By the time we rejoined Bru, most of his men had already gone.

"I'm sending them out a few at a time," he said, "so that we are not all seen to leave at once."

Over the next hour, the rest of them wandered off, as if they were looking for others they might know, and while no one watched but me, they slipped into the darkness. Bru and I were the last to leave. Bru whispered a few words to his son, who handed him the eagle banner and went to find himself a place closer to the prisoners.

When we were beyond the reach of firelight, I heard a night bird call. Bru led me toward it, and there we found our companions. To follow the trail left by the northerners' retreat, we had no choice but to pick our way through the battlefield. The moon, half-hidden by mist that drifted not far above our heads, cast an eerie light over the bodies of the fallen. The back of my neck began to prickle, and it was all I could do to control my imagination. The more I tried not to think of them, the more I saw their spirits taking shape in the mist. Then something moved at the edge of my vision, a shimmer of silver in the moonlight.

"Wolves," said Bru.

I didn't need anyone to tell me that they were feasting on the dead.

"We can't bring the northern chieftains back this way," I whispered.

"Why not?" asked Bru. "Are they afraid of ghosts?"

"These are their friends," I said.

Bru took my arm, a little roughly, and pulled me away from the others.

"Will your woman's heart endanger us?" he asked me. "Tell me now."

"What does my woman's heart have to do with anything? Does not Elen too have a woman's heart?"

"Elen has a demon's heart," he said. "I know your heart means well, but it holds too much compassion and too little anger for waging war."

Maara had once told me much the same thing, but I had begun to appreciate my gifts. Had not my compassion brought these very men to help me?

I knew what Bru wanted. He wanted his leadership undisputed. And I thought there might be something else.

"You have no cause to doubt me," I told him. "Use your own knowledge of the battlefield. Will the sight of their dead comrades leave the northerners unmoved? Might it not fill them with grief and so take the heart out of them?"

"More likely the sight will fill them with rage," said Bru. "If anything, it will put the heart into them."

"And that will suit us even less. When we take them before Elen, they must control themselves, and they must look defeated, not belligerent."

We had stopped walking, and now stood face to face. The others had stopped too. Though they were out of earshot, they knew what Bru and I were arguing about. They had expected this dispute, and they were waiting for the outcome.

"If you don't trust my leadership," I said, "then leave me here. Go back to Elen's camp, or go back home. I am in your debt already more than I can repay, and I will not think less of you because you mistrust my ability on the battlefield. No one will follow poor leadership for long, and if they do, it is their own responsibility."

Finn took several steps toward us. I believe he meant to help me, but I motioned him away. This was something Bru and I must settle between ourselves.

Bru would not go back. That much I knew. He would feel himself dishonored if he abandoned me now. I had to find a way for him to trust me. It was my leadership he doubted, not my intentions. If he found me wanting in ruthlessness, perhaps I could make up for it with insight.

"Bru," I said. "Have I not told you everything? Have I kept secrets from you?"

Slowly he shook his head.

"Yet there's a secret you've kept from me," I said. "Perhaps you have even kept it from yourself. I intend to rob Elen of her prisoner, but I think you mean to rob her of her place."

Bru's first instinct was to deny my accusation, but the words died before they crossed his lips.

"She is in my place," Bru whispered. "I am the son of kings."

This was more than I expected. I knew that his people were in exile, but I had not guessed that Totha's heir now stood before me.

"If the opportunity presents itself," I asked him, "will you challenge Elen on the battlefield?"

Abruptly Bru sat down. "I hadn't thought that far ahead. I hardly know what I intended. I'm afraid to hope that we might succeed."

I knelt down before him. "In Elen's camp, how many are there of the mighty, and how many of your clansmen and the common folk?"

"Without the king's brother, they are about equal in number, but he has brought hundreds more."

"If all happens as we planned," I said, "if we take Elen's prisoner from her in the king's name, Elen will confront him, and the mighty will be divided."

Bru stared at me. He hadn't thought of that.

"If they come into open conflict, will you challenge her? Tell me now, and I will do all I can to help you."

Bru motioned to the others to join us, and there on the battlefield, surrounded by the dead, we made our plans.

84

The Northern Chieftains

We chose Finn, who was more diplomat than warrior, to go back to Elen's camp, to take counsel with Bru's kinsmen. He was not to reveal our plan, but to sound their leaders out, to see if they would rally to Bru's cause if there were any hope of victory. I knew I could count on Finn to insinuate and to suggest, to prepare them for what might happen in the morning, to put the plan into their minds in such a way that they would believe they had thought of it themselves.

We stopped far enough beyond the battlefield so that none of Elen's army would find us if they came out searching for more dead to plunder. There we waited for the chieftains of the northern tribes. As the dawn drew near, the mist turned to a dense fog that lay close upon the ground. I worried that the chieftains would slip past us, but at last we heard the soft clink of arms and the murmur of voices. They came to us as shadows, insubstantial, appearing and disappearing as the fog swirled all around them. If I had not been expecting living men, I would have mistaken them for apparitions.

We went to meet them. As soon as they saw us, they drew their swords, and I feared they had come to fight, but when I saw how terrified they were, I guessed that they had mistaken us for ghosts of the battlefield.

First we disarmed them. They gave up their swords reluctantly, but they had no choice. We outnumbered them three to one. There were seven chieftains, all men, and a young woman who bore no arms. She must be the go-between.

The chieftains' shields bore the animal devices of their clans, a boar, a stag, a weasel, and a few more fanciful I had no names for. None bore a wolf shield, but one did wear a wolfskin, not in the way the forest people did, but with the head atop his helmet and the body trailing down his back. I saw his eyes rest on Bru for a moment. Then he looked surprised. Bru knew him too.

I stepped between them. "Who speaks for you?" I asked in the language of the mighty.

The young woman stepped forward. "I do," she said.

I had spent the night working out in my own mind what to say to them, but first I asked Bru not to look quite so threatening.

"That is the very man who came to me," he said.

"Good," I replied. "Now he will have the chance to make amends."

Bru stepped back, but neither man would be the first to look away. They stood glaring at each other, stiff-necked and bristling, like dogs about to fight.

I left them to their silent contest and invited the northerners to parley. Their go-between was skillful, though a little hard to understand.

"Who are you?" she asked, meaning not me, but all of us.

"We too are enemies of Elen's house," I said. "We know her well, and we have seen how she deals with those she has defeated. She has laid a trap for you, and here you all are walking into it. Your chieftains are going to their deaths, and your comrades into slavery."

Bru was right. They didn't believe me. Little by little I handed them the pieces and let them put the puzzle together for themselves. I told them what would happen when they were in Elen's power. I made a picture in their minds of their own helplessness once they entered Elen's camp. I reminded them, without insulting them, how little they had to bargain with. I told them what they already knew — that Elen had attacked them without cause, without provocation. Why would they believe she intended less than their destruction?

Then I asked them for their help. I told them about Maara, that she was Elen's hostage and I meant to set her free. I told them of the factions that made up Elen's army, and how we might succeed in setting them against each other. I told them about the king's brother and showed them his banner, which would allow us to go before the queen. I told them of our plan to arm their friends. I answered frankly every question they put to me, and at last I won them over.

Whether or not they believed everything I told them, they agreed to join forces with us. Two had sons among the prisoners. All had friends and kin among them. They would not turn back, not even to avoid a trap.

Bru and the wolfskin chieftain had evidently settled their dispute. Each had taken the measure of the other and, at least for the present moment, set their differences aside. Bru's men fastened the northerners' weapons to their own packs in such a way that the chieftains could easily rearm themselves. As I had done with the prisoners, I made their go-between say back to me our plan, to make sure they understood it.

They had an idea I hadn't thought of. They asked my permission to send one of their number back to their camp, to bring all who were still fit to fight to cover their retreat. I gave my consent, and we agreed on a gathering place, a high hilltop south of the battlefield.

Bru grumbled a little. It was a risk. He had been thinking of the northerners as a distraction, a few hundred prisoners and their chieftains, outnumbered, lightly armed, causing just enough consternation to let us get away. Instead they would become an army.

"An army that may side with us against a common enemy," I said. "And even if they don't, the mighty may believe they will."

Bru took my advice. He didn't lead the chieftains back the way we came. We skirted the edges of the battlefield, depending on the fog to hide the dead. The fog also hid our approach to Elen's army. We stopped outside the camp and waited for the fog to lift. The sun was rising.

While we waited, I asked Bru for my wolfskin. He still had my few belongings in his pack.

"Elen knows me," I reminded him. "I thought I might have to take a helmet from a dead man, but the wolfskin will do just as well."

Bru opened his pack and handed it to me. I settled it over my head and fastened it with a thong around my neck to hold it in place. I wore the body down my back, like the wolfskin chieftain, and pulled the face down to cover my eyes.

"Better you should wait outside," said Bru.

We had agreed that Bru would do the talking and that most of his men would remain outside, blocking the entrance to the tent. There wasn't room for all of them inside it anyway, and the men outside would watch for trouble while preventing Elen's men from going in.

I was determined to be at the center of whatever was about to happen. "I'll go in as if I'm with the chieftains," I said. "I'll stay well hidden among them."

"All right," he said, and glanced at my bow.

If I was going to pretend to be the enemy, I would have to go unarmed. One of Bru's men took my bow and quiver and fastened them to his pack.

The light grew and still we waited. The fog stubbornly refused to lift.

"Let's go," Bru said, "before they're all awake and fed and have their wits about them."

"The prisoners won't be able to see our signal," I said.

"Doesn't matter. The fog will hide us well enough. After we leave Elen's tent, we'll find them. Then their chieftains can take command of them."

I explained this change of plan to the northern chieftains. I drew on the ground a map of Elen's camp and showed them where they would find the prisoners and the wagons. Then we took up our positions, Bru's armed men surrounding the northerners, and started through the camp.

Though the sun had been up for half an hour, most of Elen's men were still asleep. The few who were awake huddled around their cooking fires and shivered in the damp. Our sudden appearance out of the mist startled them, but they had been expecting the arrival of the northern chieftains, and once they saw the eagle banner, they believed we were what we appeared to be, their escort.

We made our way through the encampment without causing alarm. I could not yet see the tents, but when we passed through the line of wagons, I felt the ground begin to rise as we ascended the hill. The fog thinned a little. Then I saw the palisade of spears and heard a voice issue a challenge.

A sentry emerged from the mist.

"My lord the king sends the queen a gift," said Bru, holding up the eagle banner.

The sentry waved the northern chieftains forward. The chieftains, reluctant to leave the circle of our protection, hung back. Bru took a few steps, as if to lead them to the tents, but the sentry blocked his way.

"We have a message for the queen," Bru said. "Let us pass."

"The queen is not prepared for visitors," replied the sentry. "Leave these men with us. When she's ready, she will summon them."

Bru shook his head. "I am instructed by my lord," he said. "I am to take them in to her with his greeting, and if we are prevented, I am to take them back to him. He will not be pleased to see them." Then he stepped closer and whispered, "The man has a lover's heart. Let him indulge it a little. He has prepared a surprise for her, a wedding gift."

The sentry hesitated.

"He will soon be your king too," said Bru, "and I will see to it that he remembers you."

Another sentry joined the first, to see what the trouble was, and Bru made his case again. I feared that our plan was about to fail. We should have thought of that and made another plan. We could still take them by surprise and rush the tents. Then the second sentry gestured to us to follow him. He took us to the tent at the center of the palisade.

"Wait here," he said, and turned to enter.

Bru went in right after him, followed by the rest of us. Before the sentry could object, Bru had a knife against his throat.

85

ELEN

I looked around for Maara. She wasn't there. Elen was alone, unattended by her servant and unguarded, sitting on a camp bed, as yet unmade but luxurious with featherbeds and comforters. She was fully dressed in warrior garb—trousers, boots, and leather armor, dyed a dull red and studded with bright metal cast in clever shapes, that looked as if it had been made more for show than battle duty. She bore no arms, but on her belt she wore the knife she had taken from me.

Bru disarmed the sentry and turned him over to one of his men. Then he approached the queen. He had the eagle banner draped across his shoulder.

"The king's patience has worn thin," said Bru. "Where is the assassin?"

Elen stood up. She gazed at Bru as if he were a serving boy who had interrupted the business of important people. She ignored completely the armed men and the northern chieftains who had crowded into her tent.

"Who are you?" she asked, in the language of the mighty.

"You will speak none of that outlandish talk to me," said Bru in his own tongue.

"Has my brother-in-law so few true men that he must employ the ground they walk upon?" said Elen.

In the language of the common folk, true men were simply those of one's own clan. I had heard the mighty refer to the common folk as men of the earth. Until those words passed Elen's lips, I hadn't considered it an insult.

Bru would not be baited. "My lord prefers to keep clean hands," he said. "As I am of the earth, I feel no reluctance to dirty mine."

Though Elen understood the implication, she held her temper.

"I will ask you once to leave my tent," she said. "If I must ask a second time, I will demand of your lord, in appeasement, your head on a pike."

Bru laughed. "It is not my head that my lord values, but without it he would find the rest of me unfit for service."

Elen stared at him, while her mind probed at his defenses. "Your lord and I have an agreement," she said. "Will he break his word?"

She was testing Bru, to see if he was truly who he said he was.

"My lord has heard your words," Bru replied. "He has also heard the words of someone in your household. He finds the two at odds."

Elen waited.

Using what I had told him, Bru crept out on a thin branch. "A curious tale made its way from your private chamber to his ear, that you would offer him your hand but refuse him compensation for his loss."

For the first time since the invasion of her tent, Elen was afraid, not of Bru nor of his men nor of the king's brother. She feared treachery within her own house.

Bru pressed his luck. "Worse than that, you would have him keep the assassin in his household, perhaps to relieve you of another unwanted husband."

Elen's face twisted with rage. She was so angry that she forgot herself, and all her cleverness deserted her.

"What traitor carries tales from my house to his?" she demanded. "Who is the spy I have made welcome?"

"The treachery began with you," said Bru. "My lord seeks no alliance. You have only one thing he wants, and it is not your — ."

Bru said a word I had never heard before, but there was no doubt what it meant. It was a rude word for a woman's private part.

If Bru meant by this exchange to inflame Elen's anger at the king's brother, he was overdoing it. Now Elen would have no reason to surrender Maara. I hoped Bru hadn't forgotten our purpose here. I hoped he knew what he was doing.

The northern chieftains hadn't understood a word, but they guessed that the negotiations were not going well. I felt their apprehension in their stillness.

If this had been a story told around the hearth on a winter evening, Elen would have burst into flame, consumed by rage and by her own evil cast back upon her. Instead another tale told itself in Elen's tent that misty morning. Elen grew calm, and I felt her summon up from deep within herself the power of an enchantress, gifted in her cradle by fairy folk come to celebrate her birth. Before my eyes she transformed herself into an image of beauty and delight. She smiled, and it seemed that sunlight shone through the fabric of her tent and cast a golden light around her.

Bru stepped back.

"There is only one thing I want of your lord," said Elen. The music of her voice sent a shiver down my spine. "I want him to leave my lands forever. He wants the assassin? He may have her. I have no further use for her, for I will never take another husband."

She took a step toward Bru, and he took another step back.

"Come," she said. "Together we will bring her to your king."

She glided past Bru, who made no move to stop her. She slipped through Bru's men. They stood aside for her. Even the northern chieftains stood aside for her. Though they hadn't understood her words, her charm enthralled them too. I half expected them to drop to one knee, to do her honor.

She had almost reached the entrance to the tent. Was I the only one who saw through her lies? Once outside she would be free of us. She would call her men-at-arms.

I stepped into her path. I seized her wrist and moved behind her, twisting her arm behind her back. Before she could resist me, I plucked the knife from her belt and held it to her throat.

"Bru," I said. "Go with your men and search the other tents. When you find Maara, take her to the meeting place. Send someone to let me know when she is safe."

My eyes found the young woman, the chieftains' go-between. "Tell the chieftains to arm themselves," I said. "Bru's men will find the hostage. Have your men wait with me, until word comes to us that she is free. Then let them go and find their own. We will meet you on the hill."

While the chieftains took back their weapons from Bru's men, Bru stood staring at me, uncomprehending, as if he had been turned to stone.

"Bru," I said. "Go now."

Slowly he began to move. I drew Elen away from the entrance to the tent. With Bru leading them, the men filed past me. Some shook their heads, as if they were awakening from sleep. For a moment I feared the northern chieftains would follow them, but they did as I had asked and stood quietly, waiting.

I still had hold of Elen, and I dared not release her. To my surprise she didn't resist me. The strength had gone out of her, or perhaps her strength had been all an illusion. The flaccid arm by which I held her felt like a dead man's. It made my flesh crawl.

The knife I still held against her throat. I saw that its edge had drawn a little blood. With only the slightest provocation, I would have plunged it into her heart, as she had plunged this very knife into the heart of the man for whose death she had intended that Maara pay the price. Whether or not Bru thought it through, his insult had torn the veil from my eyes, so that I could see what Maara, blinded by love and guilt, could not.

Bru seemed to think that Elen had used Maara, had either commanded her or manipulated her into doing murder for her. I knew better. I knew Maara's heart, and now I'd had a glimpse of Elen's heartlessness.

I saw what had happened as clearly as if I had been a witness. Who but his wife could come so close to him? And Maara had told me that she and Elen were both covered with his blood. Maara awakened with the knife in her hand. I knew who put it there.

Maara's escape must also have been part of Elen's plan. She convinced Maara of her guilt, then sent her from the house, making certain she had the weapon with her. She never meant for Maara to get away. She wanted her caught, in bloody clothing, in possession of the king's knife, her flight as good as a confession of her guilt. Elen wanted Maara caught and killed, so that she would escape suspicion.

Before I had time to wonder why no one had yet raised the alarm, Bru was back. He was smiling and seemed to have recovered himself.

"She's safe as houses," he told me. "It's so thick out there, no one saw a thing. We went into the tents and out of them again, making our apologies to the captains, when we woke them. She was in the last tent but one. I told her Tamras says hello."

"Thank you," I said, "with all my heart."

"Nothing to it. What's next?"

"Next we let the chieftains go."

Bru nodded. "No sign of the prisoners yet. Not that they could have seen us."

"Take the chieftains to them, then. Arm them if you can, but see if you can get them out of the camp without anyone noticing."

"What shall we do with her?" He gestured at Elen without looking at her.

"Leave her with me a while," I said.

"What for? We're done with her."

"I'm not."

"What do you have in mind?"

I wasn't sure I knew. "I'll keep her quiet until you're all well away."

Bru frowned. "Don't put yourself at risk. We'll bind and gag her. Half her men are still asleep, and I convinced the sentry to tell his captain that she left orders not to be disturbed. We'll be gone before she can make any trouble for us."

I didn't tell Bru that my mind was playing with the idea of seeing to it that Elen would never make trouble for anyone again. Instead I said, "Bru, trust me."

For a long moment, he looked at me. Then he said, "I do," and left the tent. The chieftains followed him. Elen and I were alone.

When I let go of her, she turned to face me. With one hand she rubbed her wrist, while the other rubbed her throat. When I had seized her, the head of my wolfskin fell back, and now, for the first time, she saw my face. She didn't seem surprised.

"You understand why you mustn't call out, don't you?" I said.

She nodded. She had felt my desire to spill her blood and chose not to give me an excuse.

"Sit down," I told her.

She sat down on the edge of her bed.

"Do you walk through walls," she asked, "or is there more than one spy in my house?"

"You killed him," I said.

She smiled at me. "So your lord believes."

"Do you deny it?"

She shrugged.

"It was a clever plan," I said, "but you made one mistake. You let Maara get away. If she hadn't come back, no one would have ever given the matter another thought."

"Yes," she said. "How did it happen that she came back? Was your lord behind it? Did he deliver her to me so that he would have an excuse to enter my house with his men-at-arms?"

She didn't expect an answer. She was thinking out loud, trying to understand the situation, and at the same time hoping to provoke in me some reaction that would tell her when she was getting near the truth.

She knit her brows, as if there were a stubborn knot she couldn't untangle. "Even if your lord suspected me of causing my husband's death, I'm surprised he was willing to surrender the instrument."

"She was not the instrument," I said. "She was the scapegoat."

"Did she persuade him of her innocence? No matter. Let him believe what he will. One thing I don't understand. He gave her up willingly enough. Why is he now so keen to have her back?"

Then she remembered our first encounter in the tower room.

"No," she said. "You are the one who is keen to have her back."

I wouldn't have denied it, even if I had been as accomplished a liar as she was.

"You will find her changed," Elen said.

After she dropped that bit of poison into my heart, she smiled and started in a new direction. "So. It was not your lord who sent you. Now you have given him away. What treachery has he devised, I wonder. He has too few men here to challenge me on the battlefield, but it seems there is a plan to turn my prisoners loose. If he expects them to join forces with him, he will be disappointed. They don't want another taste of what we have already served up to them. They will vanish into the mist."

I listened to her, fascinated, as I watched her entangle herself further in her web of lies.

"You had better take your prize and vanish with them," she said, "before your lord discovers what you've done."

When I made no move to leave her tent, she sighed. "I begin to find our conversation tiresome. Is there something else you want from me?"

"If it's possible for one true word to escape your lips, I want to hear the truth from you."

"You want me to admit I killed him? Of course I killed him. Are you satisfied?"

In that moment I knew what evil was—the shadow that falls over the human heart, the unnecessary suffering, the destruction of possibility. To Elen the death of innocents meant nothing. Maara's death meant nothing. The suffering she caused meant nothing. That she had crippled Maara's soul meant nothing. The harm she had done to Maara was incalculable, yet to her it carried not one feather's weight.

What Maara believed about herself, that she brought grief to those she loved, came from Elen's lie. Because of that lie, she had tried to shut herself away from love, and when love found her, the lie led her to her sacrifice, as if her death would buy my happiness. Evil spread out from Elen like a stain, tainting, not only Maara's life, but the lives of everyone who loved her, corrupting what should have been pure and perfect.

I felt open up within me the place I had discovered for the first time in Elen's house, the place deep within my heart where hatred dwells.

"Show me," I said. "Was he lying in his bed?" I pushed her down. I pushed her hard. She lay across the bed, and I knelt over her. "Was he awake, or did you kill him in his sleep? Did you slip the knife between his ribs? Like this?" I set the knife under her left breast, over her heart. I let her feel the point, but I didn't push it in. I wanted her to see her death coming for her.

Elen showed no fear. Perhaps she felt none, so certain of her power that she could stay my hand by her will alone. She looked up at me and met my eyes.

"What was he to you?" she asked me. "He was nothing to you. You never cared for him. She is the one you care for. Go ahead. Make sure of her. Leave her nothing to come back to."

I willed my hand to strike. My hand refused me. I didn't understand what stopped me. To me Elen's death meant nothing. Her rotting corpse belonged in the privy trench. But if I killed her, I would never know. I would never know for sure. I dropped the knife and fled.

86

REUNION

Outside Elen's tent half a dozen of Bru's men waited for me. One took my arm and drew me into the fog behind the tents. We passed through the palisade of spears without stumbling into anyone. Behind us I heard Elen's voice, summoning her men-at-arms.

Though we could see nothing but the ground a yard or two in front of us, Bru's men seemed to know where they were going. We followed a path newly made, the grass trodden down but not yet worn away. It must be the path from the tents to the place where the mighty kept the prisoners.

When we reached it, the hollow in the hills was empty. The prisoners were gone. They had left only flattened grass, some shreds of tattered clothing, broken bits of armor, and a few bloody bandages. We followed the path they had made into the hills.

Bru met us on the path. "I was worried," he said. "Are you all right? What's happening down there?"

"I don't know," I told him. "The camp is still quiet, though I heard Elen call her men to arms."

"I'm surprised," he said.

"Why? Isn't that what we expected?"

"I'm surprised she's still living. When I left you, I believed you were going to kill her."

"I was," I said.

"Not that I would blame you, but I'm glad you didn't. She will soon discover her prisoners are gone. Whether she comes after them or turns her fury on the king's brother is anybody's guess, but I know where I'll lay my wager down."

"She will send her men-at-arms against the king's brother," I said. "She believes I was his spy. She doesn't care about the prisoners. She is confident they will all run for home."

Bru was pleased. "Just as we hoped."

"Has the northern army come?"

"Yes, most of them. The prisoners are with them now, telling them how we saved their lives. I think their hatred for Elen, together with their sense of obligation, will keep them with us for a while."

"Is Maara there? Is she all right?"

"She's fine," he said. "We found her unguarded and unbound. All that kept her there was her fear for you — that you were still in Elen's power. We almost had to take her away by force, until I had the presence of mind to tell her that at that moment you were in the next tent over, holding a knife to Elen's throat."

I let my friends lead me through the gentle hills. Then we started up a steeper slope. The farther up the hill we went, the thinner the fog became, until we emerged at last into bright sunlight. Not a hundred paces from us was the northern army in battle array, covering the broad hilltop.

I heard Maara's voice call out my name. She came running down the hill to meet me. My first glimpse of her caught her in mid-air, an image I have kept vivid in my mind. When she reached me, she held me at arm's length and looked at me. Then she pulled me into her embrace.

Bru and his men left us alone.

We held each other for a long time. I hadn't thought about what it would be like, to touch her again, to feel her arms around me. It was an awakening and a return, an awakening from a nightmare world, a return to the world I had thought I understood, the world I lived in before we were parted.

Her touch took me back in time, to our embrace outside the tumbled cottage in the wilderness. As she had then, love turned again and showed me her bright face. The other face of love I would not forget so easily. Not this time.

My legs began to tremble. "I have to sit down," I whispered.

Maara let go of me and took my arm, settling me gently down on the grass. She sat down beside me and took my hand.

"What have you done?" she asked me.

"What do you mean?"

She gestured at the northern army, at Bru and his men, then out over Elen's camp, still lost in fog. "According to your friends, this is all your doing, but they didn't tell me how you accomplished it."

"That would take many days," I said. "I hardly know myself."

"Better tell me, then, how it happens that you have an army at your command, because I believe they're preparing to do battle."

"They are at Bru's command, not mine, though I have pledged him my help, if there's anything I can do."

"Who is Bru?"

"The man who came for you." I smiled. "Did you not know him?"

Puzzled, Maara shook her head.

"I wouldn't have known him either," I told her, "but he knew me. He and his men were once Merin's prisoners, until she set them free. They found me, lost in the forest, trying to find Elen's house. When they learned where I came from, they offered me their help, to make some return for Merin's kindness."

I gave Maara time to take it all in.

"They think Merin set them free?" she said at last. "You set them free."

"Hush," I said. "They don't know that. They have already repaid me many times over. I don't want them to feel they are still in my debt."

Maara nodded, but I don't think she agreed with me.

"With whom is this army preparing to do battle?" she asked.

"With the warriors of the mighty."

"I thought the warriors of the mighty had defeated them."

"They did," I said, "and took many of them prisoner. Their chieftains came this morning to negotiate for their release. We convinced them to help us. We made a plan, which went wrong almost from the beginning, but everything worked out all right in the end. We got you back, and the prisoners escaped."

Maara frowned. "Do they think fortune will favor them today when she deserted them before? They must now be greatly outnumbered."

"Not if Elen's army is divided," I said. "It soon will be. Elen is at this very moment preparing to take the field against the king's brother."

"Why?"

"When we went to Elen's tent, we went in under his banner, demanding your release in the king's name. Then, as if that weren't enough, Bru provoked her anger against him."

"How did he do that?"

"He convinced her that the king's brother had learned the truth about his brother's death."

"What truth is that?"

I hesitated. I wanted to take care how I answered her. I wanted to relieve her of her guilt, but at the same time I feared causing yet more harm. How would it feel to her to know that someone she once loved had used her with such cruelty?

"What truth?" she asked again.

"It wasn't you," I said.

"It wasn't."

"No," I said. "You didn't kill him. She did."

"Bru said that?"

"Yes."

"How would he know?"

"He didn't," I said. "He threw it at her as an insult, but once he said it, I knew what must have happened." I saw the doubt in Maara's eyes. "You don't believe me."

"Do you think I never thought of that myself? I can believe it's possible, but how can I be sure it's true?"

"Because I heard her confess it."

Maara closed her eyes. I understood what she was doing. She was watching the world rearrange itself. When she opened her eyes again, her gaze slipped past me, into the distance. She looked a little sad.

A cry floated up out of the fog, a distant cry, not quite human. Then a long silence. Another cry. Not a cry of pain. A long howl of grief, a keening. Then cries of alarm. Shouted orders. Battle cries.

The cries came from far away and muffled by the fog, but understandable, their meaning clear. Elen didn't challenge the king's men to take the field, nor did she surround them and demand their surrender. She sent her warriors into their camp, hidden by the fog, to murder them.

Maara stood up and drew me to my feet. Soon we heard the sounds of battle. The king's men were beginning to fight back. All of us, the northern

army and their chieftains, Bru and his men, Maara and I, stood on the hill
and watched, though we could see nothing but the fog. I reminded myself
that the men who were dying there below us had come to Elen's house to
watch Maara die.

I was so intent on the sounds coming from Elen's camp that I didn't notice
a man emerge from the fog on the hillside below me. Maara did. She took
my arm and started to draw me up the path toward Bru and his men.

"Wait," I said. "It's Finn."

Behind him others came. Some I recognized as Bru's kinsmen. All were
of the common folk. All were armed and ready to do battle. When they saw
the northern army, they stopped, fearing a trick. Bru's men went down to
meet them, to quiet their fears and explain the situation.

Finn saw me and came to greet me. He extended his arm to me, but his
eyes were on Maara. "So," he said, "this is the one."

"This is the one," I replied. "Maara, this is Finn, whose brother left me
his bow."

Maara took his arm. "I am in your debt," she said.

"Not at all," he said. "Rain falls where water flows."

I didn't know what he meant by that.

Bru came and joined us. "What news?" he asked Finn.

"Whispers have gone round the camp," said Finn. "Watch for something
unexpected." He grinned. "Late into the night they were telling stories of
the king's return, not the false king they had been expecting, but the king
lost to them of old. I heard songs sung last night I haven't heard since I
was a boy.

"They awoke this morning and remembered. Then they watched the
queen behave as if she had lost her wits. They expected signs, and they saw
them everywhere. They woke to the sounds of murder, the killing of the
king's men. The fog hid the horrors from the eye but not from the ear. They
wanted no part of it. Half of them have already left the camp. Some will go
home, but many more will join us."

Men were still coming out of the fog. Bru's men took charge of them,
assembling them around their leaders, keeping them away, as much as possible, from the warriors of the northern tribes.

"We must soon make our move," said Bru. "When the fog lifts, I want
everyone in place."

"What can I do?" I asked him.

"Stay here," he said. "Stay safe. I will have need of that subtle mind of yours when the fighting is over with."

Bru had already spoken with the chieftains of the northern tribes and the war leaders of the common folk. He had made his battle plan. He explained it to Finn and me, while his men made certain everyone was ready. Bru meant to leave half the northern army on the hilltop, spread out as much as possible, to look as threatening as possible. When the fog lifted, they would be clearly visible from the camp. Their main purpose was to intimidate, but if Bru needed them, they would be fresh, ready to join the battle where they were needed or, if things went badly, to cover a retreat.

The other half of the northern army would approach Elen's camp from behind the tents, while Bru would take his men by way of the battlefield, to approach the camp from the east. He meant to pass through the camp, through what men of the common folk remained. He doubted they would oppose him. He believed many would join him. The northerners were to wait for Bru to engage the warriors of the mighty. Then they would crush the enemy between them.

A Hero's Tale

B ru left me with Finn and Maara. Finn remarked on how tired I looked. I reminded him that he had been awake as long as I had. In the end I gave in to his insistence that I sit down and rest, since nothing would happen until the fog lifted. Maara found a protected spot for us to sit, on grass so soft it was all I could do not to lie down upon it. Finn had brought food from Elen's camp, enough to share with us a modest breakfast.

"I'm not sure I understand," said Maara. "Who is fighting here, and what are they fighting for? I know the northerners would like to seek revenge for their defeat, but what of those who have deserted Elen's camp? What do they hope for, if Elen is defeated?"

"They hope for the king to take her place," said Finn.

Maara looked puzzled. "Haven't we just heard Elen's warriors murdering the king's men, and perhaps also the king himself?"

"Not that king," I said. "In the years you spent in Elen's house, did you never hear anyone speak of Totha?"

Maara shook her head, then frowned. "I've heard the name whispered," she said. "No one dared speak it openly. I never knew why."

"Let Finn tell it," I said. "It's his tale to tell."

"Totha was once the king in Elen's house," said Finn. "That was a long time ago. Our people are descended from him and from those who remained loyal to him. We have never forgotten that we are in exile, nor have we lost our lineage. We can name each firstborn son of Totha's line, from Totha all the way down to Bru."

Finn told Maara a short version of the story he had told me. "There are as many tales of Totha the king as there are winter nights," he said. "They tell of his journeys to strange and distant lands. They tell of the hardships he endured. They tell of the hardships his descendants have endured, hardships that made us strong and clever.

"The stories tell also of the evil that befell those who betrayed him. His treacherous kinsmen quarreled among themselves. The story of their descendants is an endless cycle of betrayal and revenge. What they visited upon Totha they visited upon themselves down through the generations, until at last their power failed, and the mighty came and conquered them."

"So the common folk of Elen's house are descended from Totha's people too?" I asked Finn.

He nodded. "They would have lost hope, but in their darkest hour, when they had been humiliated by the mighty, Totha's heirs came back to them. The mighty didn't know the difference between us. They made us welcome. They found us useful. They employed our craftsmen. They traded with our travelers. They let our stories in. We taught them to the common folk, until they too learned to long for the king's return."

"I hope you will soon be telling new stories in Elen's great hall," said Maara.

"I hope so too," said Finn. "And she will be in all of them."

"Who? Elen?" I asked.

I had been watching Maara. I thought I had been listening too, but perhaps I had missed something.

"Not Elen," he said. "You."

"Me?"

"If not for you, would any of this have come about?"

"Oh," I said.

"How did this come about?" Maara asked. "That's a story I would like to hear."

Finn settled himself like the storyteller he was. "In the heart of the forest," he began, "a hunter came upon a wolf, lying curled up asleep on the forest floor. He drew his bow, but before he let the arrow fly, the wolf sprang up and changed into a girl. She was just a little scrap of a thing. Could she be a forest sprite? A fairy child? Whatever else she was, she was an archer too, and her bow had a familiar look about it."

So Finn told his tale, while Maara listened and I remembered. He told how the hunter came to him, bringing his brother's bow. From the hunter's description of the girl, Finn knew who it must be. Since Maara too was from the house of kindness, he dwelt upon his sojourn there, where he knew me as a healer. Then Finn spoke of his brother, a man betrayed first by a northern chieftain, a man who wore a wolfskin, then by Vintel.

As a storyteller myself, I saw what he was doing. Two threads, bright and dark, knit his tale together — the light thread of the merciful, the dark thread of the avenger. Signs and symbols, picked out by the clarity of hindsight, revealed the hidden meaning of the tale. The wolfskin, first a symbol of betrayal, then a sign of reconciliation. The bow, brought to Merin's land and left there for me to find and carry back to them. In Finn's story, his brother was a messenger, the bow the message. It was by the bow they knew me.

Then Finn wove in his tale of exile, of how it came about that Bru, the rightful king, had dared to take the field against the mighty. Elen, their queen, held a prisoner whom the wolf girl sought to rescue.

"To return kindness for kindness," said Finn, "those who had once been prisoners themselves offered her their help. The girl asked only for a guide, but Bru read the signs and saw that change was coming."

"Did he really?" I asked.

"Well," said Finn, "he did eventually, didn't he?"

Finn told of our journey to Elen's house, our meeting with his friend the armorer, and our supper in the kitchen yard, when I was taken into the house to serve at table. With half a wink to me, he skipped the part where I was kicked out of it. He said only that I had rejoined them to finish my meal.

"It was then that she produced the knife," he said.

Maara flinched. "I should have thrown the cursed thing away."

"No," I said. "That's what got me back inside. They thought I stole it. They dragged me into the great hall and accused me before the queen."

I stopped. I was not yet ready to revisit Elen's house, not even in memory.

"For three days," said Finn, "we waited for news. There was no sign of her. No word. We feared the house of wickedness had swallowed her up and we would never lay eyes on her again. But then things began to happen. The queen suddenly prepared for war, and when her army marched out to the battlefield, they brought the prisoner with them. Now we would have our chance at rescue, we thought, but where was Tamras?"

Finn leaned toward us and lowered his voice, though there was no one anywhere nearby to hear him. "That night," he said, "when we were all asleep, out of the queen's dungeon she walked, past the queen's servants, and out of the house, in plain sight down the empty street. So she came to us and told us what she'd done."

Finn paused for effect, while Maara and I both waited to hear what it was.

"It seems there was an army gathering in the east, intending to make war on the people Tamras came from."

Maara nodded. She had seen it too.

"Too late to take them a warning herself, Tamras sent an army out against their enemy."

"How did she do that?" Maara asked.

"Strange," said Finn, "how evil will turn back upon itself. All Tamras did was inform the queen of the presence of the army. She also told her its intentions, but the queen didn't believe her. She thought it was a trick. She led her army out and took her prisoner with her. The rest you know."

Maara looked at me. "Not quite, I think," she said.

She was asking me to tell her what had happened while I was in Elen's house. Did she know it was another story of betrayal? I took a breath, while I wondered where to start. Finn put his hand on my arm to stop me.

"This is your tale to tell," he said, "but I will begin it, because it is a hero's tale."

I shook my head and started to protest, but Finn spoke first.

"There is an old story of a hero, a younger son of Totha, who embarked on a quest to distant lands, where he was captured and held in thrall to an evil queen. For a time he succumbed to her enchantment, but at last, by his pure heart, he overcame her. I have now seen that story told again."

"I'm not a hero," I said. "I had no idea what I was doing. I blundered through it all."

Finn touched my brow lightly with his fingers. "You may not have known what you were doing or how you did it, but look at the result. You set this woman free. You saved the house of kindness from the malice of their enemies. You divided the mighty and so gave Bru his opportunity. If he fails, he is the king no more. But I think he will not fail."

Finn watched me, waiting for me to understand.

"Whatever you took with you," he said, "whatever you may wish to call it, purity of heart, strength of spirit, greatness of soul, you took that and nothing more into the house of wickedness, and you came out of it again, bringing fortune to your friends and ruin to your enemies. If that's not a hero's tale, I've never told one nor heard one told."

"It won't make the telling any easier," I whispered.

"Perhaps not," he said, "but it may make the listening less painful." He turned to Maara. "Listen, but don't judge, until you've heard it all. She is utterly truthful, and she will not spare herself."

Then he got up and left us.

"Finn is too kind," I said.

"What is he afraid that I will judge you for?" Maara asked me.

I opened my mouth to answer her, but I found I couldn't speak.

"What are you afraid that I will judge you for?"

"You saw it all yourself," I said. "You were there."

"I was," she said, "and I was proud of you."

"Proud? Why?"

"You kept your wits about you. You spoke so well. I have seen many stand before her, men and women of the highest rank and with their wisest counselors. None of them was a match for her."

"In the end, neither was I."

Maara grew still. "It was a vile trick she played on you."

"And I believed her."

"For a time." It was half a question. In her voice I heard the hope that I had soon after come to my senses. I had to disappoint her.

"For the whole time," I said. "I forgot you. I forgot everything but what would make me doubt you. I knew nothing else until I left Elen's house, when Bru told me you were still a prisoner."

Once the words were out, I felt a bit lightheaded. Perhaps lack of sleep had caught up with me, or perhaps I expected her to tell me what I most feared to hear, that I was no longer worthy of her.

"Do you doubt me now?" she asked.

I saw in my mind's eye the image I had fixed there, of Maara running down the hill to meet me. I shook my head. "Of course not," I told her. "No."

"Then why is it that you feel so far away from me?"

"Do I?"

I felt it then, the barrier between us, as I had felt it long before, when it was the walls around her heart I felt. Now it was the walls around my heart.

"What do you need to hear from me?" she asked.

Her voice had an edge. I didn't know what she meant.

"Do I need to tell you that I never touched her, that I would never have allowed her to touch me?"

That was the farthest thing from my mind.

"I hope you would have done whatever you had to do to save your life," I said. "Where you bestow your body may not be within your power to choose. I care only for who has your heart."

"Then you have nothing to reproach me for."

"Reproach you? I don't reproach you. I reproach myself."

"For what?"

The memory of my time in Elen's house came back to me all at once. I had to clasp my hands together, to stop their trembling.

"The abyss," I whispered. "Three days in the abyss, when I believed you had betrayed me. How did she do that? How did she kill me with a lie?"

I was too tired to think clearly or I would have seen it then, that Elen had seized on one small fault, a fault I had in common with all of humankind, a fault I had never taken seriously. Jealousy.

I wasn't thinking then. I knew only that some part of me remained lost in the abyss.

"Help me," I whispered. "I don't know how to come back to you."

Maara moved closer and took my hands between both of hers.

"You're exhausted," she said. "Sleep a while. When you wake, the world will change."

She slipped her arm around my shoulders and laid me down, so that my head rested in her lap. She caressed my back in a way she knew would calm me.

"Forgive me," I whispered.

"Hush," she said. "I understand."

How could she understand when I didn't understand myself?

As if she'd heard my thoughts she said, "Have you forgotten that I too was once in thrall?"

"But not this time."

"No," she said. "Not this time. This time I had a shield against her."

"A shield? What shield?"

"You."

Had I not had the same shield?

"Then I have no excuse for my defeat," I said.

"When this day is over," she replied, "we shall see who is defeated."

88

THE KING

I woke in the afternoon with no memory of having fallen asleep. I was lying on the soft grass with Finn sitting beside me. Maara was gone. I sat up and looked around, fearing for a moment that her presence had been just a dream, until Finn said, "She'll be back soon."

"Where did she go?"

He nodded toward Elen's camp. What could await her there but danger? Had I found her only to lose her again?

I started to get up, but Finn said, "Wait with me."

"I need to find her."

He shook his head. "She told me to keep you out of trouble." Then he saw my fear for her. "She hasn't gone down there to fight. They have need of an interpreter."

I sat back down and tried to clear my mind of the confusion of sleep.

"Tell me what's been happening," I said.

"Well," he said, "you slept through the entire battle, though it didn't amount to much. Once they saw they would be overwhelmed, most of the warriors of the mighty threw down their swords. A few are holding out, it seems. Elen's personal guard, and some others. They have taken a stand behind the wagons that barricade the tents, where Elen and her captains ought to be preparing to negotiate the terms of their surrender."

"Ought to be?"

"She's in no hurry. She may believe she can still maneuver."

Remembering Elen's power, I said, "She may well succeed."

He shrugged. "We'll see."

I got up and went to stand on the crest of the hill, to have a better look at Elen's camp. The fog had lifted. Men were sitting around their camp-fires, much as they had been the day before. The warriors of the common folk had returned to their places. This time they were not Elen's men, but Bru's. Behind the wagons, warriors in battle gear stood ready to fend off an attack, but no one threatened them. Bru had set out only a few pickets, to give the alarm if Elen's guard left their enclosure. He seemed prepared to wait them out.

I saw below me too the evidence of murder, the corpses of the men who still lay as they had fallen within the king's encampment. This was an easy battlefield to read. Believing themselves safe among friends, few wore any armor. Many were unarmed. Most were bunched where the boggy ground had hindered their retreat, where they had been trapped and slaughtered.

Behind me the warriors of the northern army commanded the hilltop, though they were no longer arrayed for battle. They sat in groups, talking quietly among themselves and sharing what rations they had, or lay in the grass asleep.

I turned back to Finn. "I'm going down there," I told him. "Will you come with me?"

"I suppose I can't persuade you to wait until you're sent for?"

I shook my head.

"Then let's take these folks down with us and give them something to eat. I imagine Bru has more to do right now than send someone up to fetch them."

With difficulty we woke the sleepers, but they all came gladly enough, once we pointed toward the encampment and made the signs for eating. Trailing half the northern army along behind us, Finn and I made our way down the hill. When we reached the camp, Finn saw to it that the north-ern warriors were welcomed properly and given what hospitality was to be had, while I went to find Bru.

Bru had established a meeting ground where the warriors of the mighty had been encamped. Around a central fire the northern chieftains sat, along with many of the men I had met the day before, Bru's kinsmen, and with them Bru himself, as well as several others I didn't know. They were engrossed in earnest conversation, and at first they didn't see me.

I knelt down behind Bru and tugged at his sleeve.

"Aha," he said. "I was about to send for you. We have a difficulty, and I don't know how to untangle it."

"Where is Maara?" I asked him.

He gestured at the wagons. I didn't see her there at first. I saw only three men who stood talking quietly together. One I recognized by his size and by his shield, which he had slung over his shoulder. On it was a black bear. Then I caught a glimpse of someone in their midst, and from her clothing I knew it must be Maara.

Bru saw my alarm. "Don't worry," he said. "She's perfectly safe."

"Safe? She's surrounded by the enemy!"

"Not quite," he said. "That big fellow there won't let her come to harm."

"But he's one of Elen's captains."

"Yes," said Bru, "and he's also a distant cousin of mine." Bru frowned. "He's in a difficult position. He took an oath to serve the queen, so he won't take up arms against her, but he won't serve her by opposing me. He thinks he can induce her to surrender. I doubt it, but what have we to lose by allowing him to try?"

The bear shield chieftain moved again between Maara and me, cutting off my sight of her. I turned back to Bru.

"What will you do with Elen if she surrenders?" I asked.

"Therein lies our difficulty," he said. "The king demands blood for blood."

"The king?"

Bru pointed at a small, light-haired man who sat not far from us staring into the fire. His left arm and shoulder were bandaged, but it was not the pain of his wounds I saw in his eyes. Although he appeared harmless enough, two of Bru's men sat behind him, charged with watching him. His beardless face looked very young.

"He demanded also Maara's blood," said Bru, "but that is, of course, out of the question. As he is a defeated man, he must accept our terms. But what to do with the queen is a question that concerns all of us."

I nodded.

"You have a strong voice in this," he said. "Perhaps the strongest voice of all."

"Me? Why?"

Bru smiled. "When will you understand? The world has changed, and you are the pivot point. I wield only the power of my sword and of my friends. You wield the power of the unseen hand, the hand that moves the destinies of men."

I laughed. "Finn must have been telling you his stories," I said.

But Bru was not about to make a joke of it.

"I have sense enough to understand a story that tells itself before my eyes," he said. "This day will change the course of many lives, and what we do here will echo down the generations. I must be as sure as I can be that I make no mistakes."

"No mistakes," I murmured. I felt as if I had done nothing but make mistakes from first to last.

Bru frowned and looked down at his sword, which lay unsheathed across his lap. It seemed that he held it there more as a symbol of his authority than as a weapon. Its blade was clean.

"The easy road is to let the lad have her," he said. "After all, he has a right. He has this day witnessed the slaughter by her order of men he loved." Bru scratched his beard and looked at me. "I don't know why, but I am reluctant."

I think he expected me to persuade him to surrender Elen to her enemies. It was indeed the easy road. The young king had just cause against her, and her guilt was not in doubt. Let him ease his heart with her blood, while we kept our own hands unbloodied. Yet I shared Bru's reluctance.

Did I not wish her dead? Had I not that very day nearly plunged a knife into her heart? But I hadn't done it, and once the sting of my defeat had faded, I was glad. Although I had killed before, I had never in my life done murder, but that day I had come close to it. Blinded by my anger, I had almost done a thing I could not now justify. For all the suffering she'd caused, Elen deserved to suffer. Did she deserve to die? That was a question I couldn't answer.

I turned my thoughts to a more practical consideration.

"Elen won't surrender if she believes we're going to kill her anyway," I said. "She will force us to shed more blood before we can lay hands on her and put her to the sword."

"Yes," said Bru, "and that's why I've let her be. By some amazing bit of luck I have lost not one man in this endeavor. A few are hurt, but all are still living. The queen's men will fight to the death, and they will make our victory as costly as they can."

"Surely she is not worth the risk of even one life."

"Surely she is not," said Bru. "Yet there is another way." He glanced over at the young king. "That lad would not hesitate to lead his own men against her. He hasn't many left that are fit to fight, but he has enough." Then Bru gave me a look that had a hint of a challenge in it. "Did I not say there was an easy road?"

I saw it too. We need not risk the life of anyone we cared for. We could leave to the young king the task of bringing Elen to justice. By every law and custom, he had the right to take her life for the lives she had taken, and I knew what he did not, that Elen had killed his brother too, and by her own hand. Who had a greater right than he to deliver Elen to her fate? We had only to stand by and do nothing to prevent it.

Bru's words whispered themselves in my head. *What we do here will echo down the generations.* Of all the things that would echo down the generations, vengeance would echo loudest of all.

"Let us stop it here," I said. "The endless cycle of murder and revenge. Let us stop it here, today."

Bru's brow furrowed with doubt. "What then are we to do with her? Can we in conscience let her go and so loose her evil upon the world?"

"The world is already full of evil," I told him. "Though evil she may be, she has lost her power. She has no army. She has no home. If she has not the means to do us harm, we can safely let her go. The rest of the world will have to look after itself."

"And if someday she should regain her power and return to trouble us? Will we regret allowing her the opportunity, when we could have prevented it?"

"There is reason in your argument," I said, "but we might take a lesson from the stories of people who tried to prevent some future evil, and in the course of trying, caused the very evil they were trying to prevent."

Suddenly I felt Maara behind me. I felt her there even before she knelt down and touched my shoulder.

"Elen's guard will take the bear in to speak with her," said Maara. "What message shall I give him?"

She must mean the man I thought of as the bear shield chieftain.

"I have given Bru my opinion," I told her. "Whatever he decides, I will abide by it."

"And I will abide by Tamras's advice," said Bru. "Have him tell her she is free to go. She may take any of her men who wish to follow her, but she is to go now, today. That will give her a little time to outdistance a pursuit. In the morning I will give the king leave to gather the remnants of his army and go home, but he may take it into his head to follow her. As he is a free man who has done me no harm, I will do nothing to prevent it. She must take her chances with the world, as do we all."

Maara nodded and stood up. My eyes followed her until she had rejoined the bear shield chieftain.

"She wasn't surprised," said Bru.

"She knows me well," I said.

Bru chuckled. "She didn't see your eyes this morning. Still, I should have known what counsel you would give me."

Before Bru could explain himself, the young king's face captured my attention. His eyes were fixed on Maara, and a hatred burned in them that frightened me.

"May I speak with the king?" I asked Bru.

"Of course," said Bru. "I don't know how much of the common speech he understands. You might let him know what we have just decided."

I stared at the young man until he felt my eyes and met them.

"Do you understand the way I speak?" I asked him in the language of the mighty.

He nodded.

"How much blood will it take to ease your heart?" I asked him.

He gave me a sullen look and didn't answer.

"I have never understood how heart's ease can be bought with murder."

"Not murder," he replied. "Justice."

"Justice, do you call it? You came to Elen's house to see justice done. Have you seen it?" I gestured at the ruins of his encampment, at the bodies of the dead in full view of where we sat. "Is this the justice you expected?"

He frowned and looked away.

"And if you had received what you call justice, you would have conspired in a murder, because Maara is innocent."

His eyes came back to me. It was clear he didn't believe me, but he waited to hear what else I had to say on her behalf.

Although I knew it would only increase his determination to take revenge on Elen, I cared more about convincing him of Maara's innocence
than about shielding Elen from his anger.

"On my word as on my life," I said, "this very day I heard the queen
confess to murder. It was she who killed your brother and used her servant
as a scapegoat."

A flicker of doubt came into his eyes.

"I have no other witness," I said. "If my sworn word does not convince
you, then think it through yourself. Who stood to gain? Who stood to lose?
Did Elen take a husband willingly, or did she do it to satisfy her own ambi-
tion? And once she had done it, was he not a hindrance to her?"

I watched him work it out in his own mind. I left it to him to take my
argument to its conclusion, that if he had become her husband, he would
have shared his brother's fate. If Elen had not betrayed him that very morning, he might not have given credit to my assertion of her guilt, but now he
was disposed to think the worst of her.

The young king's face grew hard, so that he resembled the older man he
would become. He started to stand up, but was prevented by a sword's tip
set firmly upon on his shoulder. The men who guarded him were attentive
to their duty.

"Her life belongs to me," he said. "Though somewhere among her clansmen you may find one willing to pay her ransom, I will pay you as much
or more."

"We don't intend to hold her for ransom," I said. "We intend to let her go."

The young king sat quiet for a moment, while he tried to comprehend
what I had told him. Then he looked at Bru. "What says your chieftain?
What reason has he given?"

The young king had taken me for an underling, a go-between. For reasons of my own, for the first time I asserted my authority.

"Bru is not my lord," I said. "Though I may not look it, I am by right a
chieftain in my own land. Bru is my friend, and my ally in this adventure,
and we count among our friends these chieftains of the northern tribes.
Today we are the mighty. Accept our terms, and we may begin to forge a
friendship that in days to come will benefit us all."

"What are your terms?" he asked.

"Let vengeance go. Let Elen face the world alone, as she deserves no
better. Let her discover the consequences of her failure."

He shook his head, but before he could refuse me, I said, "Accept this counsel from me as a gesture of my friendship."

"You take from me what is my right and call it friendship?" he replied. "Her deeds condemn her. You are her conqueror. What makes you now her champion?"

Had I become Elen's champion? I searched my own heart then for the anger I had felt toward her, for the desire to take revenge for the evil she had done. It was gone, not because I felt pity or compassion for her, but because Elen wasn't worth the trouble.

"For what she has done, I too condemn her," I said, "but I condemn her, not to the justice of humankind, which trails a host of new evils after it, but to the justice of the world."

"Then let the world beware," said the young king.

"Indeed," I said, "let us all beware. Let us take care not to yield to evil's power, because evil has no power but what we give it."

"I gave her nothing!"

"You believed her lie. How did I so easily convince you of her guilt? Was it not there to see by any who has eyes to see it? What blinded you? Was it not your anger, which too eagerly sought out a victim whose blood you hoped would ease your pain?"

"What do you know of my pain?" he asked me. "You would feel as I do, if she had taken someone dear to you."

"She very nearly did," I said, "and with your help and your consent. Do you believe I don't understand your heart? Let me assure you, that if my friends and I had not been able to save Maara's life, I would have taken Elen's life, and I would have hunted you and yours to death, heedless of the consequences." I stopped, to give him time to see in my eyes that if any harm should ever come to Maara, I would carry out my threat.

"If you have nothing else to live for," I said, "if you care nothing for this world or for any of the living, if you are willing to let a greater evil loose upon the earth, then take your revenge and waste your life and the lives of those you call upon to help you."

"You give me counsel you would not keep yourself," he said.

"That's true," I replied. "And I also give you your choice, and with your choice, the consequences. Elen will leave this camp today, as soon as we can be rid of her. You will have leave to go tomorrow morning. Follow her or not. It's up to you."

With nothing to lose but pride, Elen accepted our terms. When she emerged from her tent, I hoped to see a pathetic figure. Instead she was as defiant as ever. She saw me standing next to Bru and tossed a few insults at me, but I didn't feel the need to answer her, and they fell harmlessly away. Bru gave her a cart and oxen to draw it, so that she could travel in some comfort and seek refuge among her kinsmen as befits a queen.

Maara found other things to do until Elen and her guard, escorted by the bear shield chieftain, disappeared into the northern hills. Then she joined me at Bru's fire. I was glad to have her with me. Now that the decision had been made and carried out, I began to second-guess myself.

"What grief may come of this, I wonder," I whispered to her.

"What grief do you expect?" she asked.

"I don't know," I said. "I fear having done the wrong thing."

"Did it seem wrong to you when you did it?"

"No," I said. "It seemed the only road."

"Then trust yourself," she said.

Remembering that Maara too had cause against her, I said, "What would you have done with Elen?" Then, before she could remind me that neither life nor Bru nor I had asked her that question, I said, "What would you have felt if we had put her to the sword?"

"I would have been sorry," she replied.

"Why?"

"Because I remember her," she said. "I remember the young girl she once was. She had many faults, but she was not wicked then, or I would not have loved her."

Maara's words surprised me, but what surprised me more was that they aroused in me no jealousy. Not that I was cured of my besetting fault. I did not delude myself about that. I understood that Maara had loved the good in her, and loved it still, and that was as it should be.

89

THE DEAD

The young king no longer sat with us by Bru's fire. Still guarded by Bru's men, he had been given leave to attend to his wounded and to the disposal of his dead. Bru gave him the use of several carts, to bear the corpses to the battlefield, where they would be sent to their gods on the funeral pyres.

Bru had his own men attend to Elen's dead, and they too were taken to be burned upon the pyres. Bru's men were also charged with gathering the bodies of the northern dead, while the northern chieftains had their warriors open up the earth, so that they could lay their friends within it, together in a common grave, as was the custom of the northern tribes.

Many of the mighty who belonged to Elen's house had chosen to go with her, but some, appalled by Elen's betrayal of the young king, asked to join his household. As they had not taken part in the slaughter, he accepted them.

Bru wanted me where he could find me, so I stayed by the council fire. Because Maara was fluent in both the language of the common folk and the language of the mighty, and able to make herself understood in the language of the northern tribes, Bru sent for her often. When her help was not required, I wanted her beside me, and when she moved about the camp, my eyes followed her.

"What's the matter?" she asked me once, when she returned to me. "Are you afraid I'll disappear?"

"Yes," I admitted. "I can hardly believe you're here at all."

She took my hand and squeezed it. "I know," she said. "I can hardly believe I'm here at all." She smiled. "Don't worry. We'll get used to it."

⚬⌒⚬

All around us the encampment rearranged itself. The young king moved his men from the ground where their blood had so recently been shed to the place left by Elen's warriors. Another section of the camp was given over to the northern army. Room had been made for them by the departure of many of the common folk, who had left earlier that day for the place once known as Elen's house, to secure it from attack. Bru considered it unlikely that Elen would try to return there, but he took prudent measures anyway, just in case. Finn had the foresight to send a storyteller with them, to prepare the people for their king's return.

Bru ordered the tents taken down, all but one. He would sleep rough with his men, he said, as he had always done. He assigned the remaining tent to me.

"I may be the king," he told me, "but you are the angel of this enterprise. I want you where no one can get at you. If we still harbor a traitor in our midst, who may try to take revenge in Elen's name, or even in the king's, it will be easier to guard the tent than to guard you in the open."

I was about to protest that I didn't need protecting, until he said, "Maara too may still be in danger from someone loyal to the dead king, Elen's husband." Then I was willing to accept his precautions.

"We must see that everyone is told of Maara's innocence," I said, and remembering Bru's words in Elen's tent, I added, "How did you know that it was Elen who killed her husband?"

"I didn't." He looked surprised. "Did she?"

I nodded. "When you accused her, I saw at once what must have happened."

"When I accused her?"

"Yes."

"Did I? What did I say?"

"You accused her of intending to use Maara to rid herself of another unwanted husband."

"Oh," said Bru. "I suppose I did. I was trying to make her angry. I didn't think about it."

"But once you said it, I knew it must be true. Such things aren't plucked from thin air."

Bru looked puzzled. "Is it true then? Was the king murdered on her command?"

"More than command it," I said, "she did the deed herself. After you left me in her tent, I confronted her. I accused her, and I got her to admit it."

"I'm glad to hear of this," he said, "because if any of the common folk still feel some loyalty to the queen, her betrayal of her husband will cost her their sympathy. And I'll feel more at ease about Maara's safety, once Elen's guilt becomes common knowledge."

"Then let us send for Finn," I said. "If anyone can tell this tale in a way that will carry it to every campfire, he can."

Bru agreed with me, and Finn was sent for. Though it was Maara's story to tell, I asked her to let me tell it. It would be painful enough for her just to listen to.

I took the time to tell almost the whole story. I left out only Maara's love for Elen and the cruel way that Elen provoked Maara's jealousy, to convince others, as well as Maara herself, that she had reason to kill the king. I began with Maara's tendency to ghostwalk. Maara knew she did it, and Elen must have known. I told Finn the story as Maara had first told it to me, of Elen waking her in the middle of the night, of the sight of both of them covered with blood, of finding the knife in her hand.

As I told the part about Elen sending Maara from the house, in bloody clothing, in possession of the king's knife, Finn's thoughts were already running on ahead of me. I knew that when he told the story, his listeners too would see what must have happened before the words were out of his mouth, so that he would not have to persuade them of the truth. The telling would confirm what they had already understood.

Finn turned to Maara. "She meant you to be caught," he said.

"I suppose she did," Maara replied.

"Did you believe you killed the king?"

Maara hesitated before she answered him. "Yes and no," she said. "I believed it might be possible. That belief was painful, but it also was a shield."

"Less painful than believing Elen had betrayed you."

Maara nodded.

"Why did you keep the knife?" he asked her.

"When I was hiding in the forest, trying to stay alive, I found it useful. After all, it was just a knife."

"So you took it with you to the house of kindness?"

"Yes."

"And gave it to the wolf child." Finn's eyes sparkled. "Not even the most cunning storyteller could conjure such a thing. The queen sent forth the knife with which she had committed murder, and it came back to her, bearing witness to her guilt and bringing retribution."

As darkness fell, Finn went about among the common folk, telling the story I had just told him, along with several more, to bring home to them the greatness of the deeds they'd done that day.

The place already had a name. It was called Totha's field, and many who had taken part in the brief battle with the mighty swore they had seen the man himself, as he was described in song, but in ghostly form, so that a sword's thrust went through him as through a wisp of fog.

Finn was not fluent in the language of the mighty, so he found a few who were and sent them to carry the story of Elen's treachery and Maara's innocence to the young king's men. If it stirred their anger against Elen, I didn't care, if only it kept Maara safe.

Bru had several cattle slaughtered, to ensure that everyone in the encampment would be well fed and to provide rations for the journey home. The smell of roasting beef also masked the smell of the funeral pyres. When they returned from burying their dead, the northern chieftains joined us at the council fire. We served them a generous dinner, but they had little appetite. Their day's work had left them deep in mourning.

"Did they raise a cairn?" I asked their go-between.

"There was no time today. Perhaps in the morning, before we go."

I turned to Bru. "It would be a gesture of goodwill if you could have your men help the northerners raise a cairn over their dead."

"Of course," he said, "though few now keep such ancient customs."

"My people do," I said. "It's been many years since we fought on a distant battlefield, but when we pass the cairns raised long ago, we set new stones upon them. They keep the dead alive in memory."

"They also keep the wolves from digging up their bones," said Bru.

"That too," I said. I turned back to the go-between. "If we are welcome, Bru's men will help you in the morning."

She spoke with the northern chieftains, then nodded their assent to me.

"They will be grateful," she said.

They would be less grateful, I thought, if they knew the part I had played in their defeat. All afternoon, as I sat by the council fire with nothing else to think about, I had been defending myself against the knowledge that all these dead had died because of me. It was I who sent Elen's army out against the northern tribes, and with it the young king's men, and it was I who encouraged Bru to incite Elen's anger against the young king. Now it was late, and I was tired, and my defenses gave way.

Maara felt me change. "What?" she whispered.

"This is my fault."

I spoke in the language of the mighty, not wanting to remind Bru that I still had a woman's heart. Then I remembered that the northerner's go-between was within earshot.

"What are you talking about?" asked Maara. "What is your fault?"

This time I spoke in the language of Bru's people.

"The dead," I told her.

"Oh," she replied. "Which dead do you mean? Elen's dead? The king's?"

She sounded out of patience with me.

"Those too," I said, "but just now I was thinking of the northern dead." I turned to face her. "Did you see the battlefield?"

"No. I didn't need to. I've seen battlefields before."

"Hundreds died."

"Yes," she said. "Warriors died."

She meant to remind me of something she had told me long ago, that nothing done on the battlefield need be forgiven.

"They gave their consent," she said. "Better they should die killing the warriors of the mighty than the warriors of Merin's house."

"I know."

That didn't make me feel any better.

"At least, when they go to fight Merin's people now, their strength will be that much less."

"What?"

"Did you think they would go home? What have they to go home to? What drove them to gather an army in the first place, to take such a risk as this?"

Then I understood. She had been eavesdropping.

"What have you heard?" I asked her.

"Somehow Vintel has managed to raise an army. Before their encounter with Elen, the northerners were certain their army was greater than Vintel's. Now they're not so sure, but they feel they have little more to lose, and they believe the prize will be worth the sacrifice."

"Oh."

"I was going to speak to you about this later, in private," she said, "but I think it would be best to deal with it now."

I felt my shoulders sag, as if the weight of this new challenge was more than they could bear.

"I have no idea what to do," I told her.

"You could begin by telling Bru the truth."

Bru heard his name. "Tell me the truth about what?"

"About who she is," said Maara.

"Who is she then? Is she not Tamras, a daughter of the house of kindness?"

Maara looked at me, waiting for my permission to speak. I nodded my consent.

"She is that and more," said Maara. "She is the rightful heir of the house of kindness, which we call Merin's house. Vintel, Merin's war leader, betrayed her and drove her into exile."

"Vintel?" said Bru. "I've heard that name before."

"We believe it was Vintel who killed Finn's brother," she said. "It was certainly Vintel who struck off his hand."

"Ah yes," he said. "Of course I remember her. And now she has displaced the rightful heir? How do such things come about?"

"It's a tale too long to tell," she said. "We were hoping to return home this spring to find the situation changed or to join with any of Merin's people who would oppose Vintel, but today I learned from the northerners that Vintel still leads Merin's warriors, and Merin's allies must have joined her, because she has an army at her command."

"What do you intend to do?" Bru asked me.

"I must go home," I said.

Bru looked past me to Maara. "What are your plans?"

"We haven't any," she replied. "We have not yet had a chance to talk this over. The northerners still seem intent on challenging Vintel. They have little to go home to and much to gain by Vintel's defeat. If we go home now, we'll be in the middle of a war."

Bru's eyes came back to me. "If you're going to war, you'll need an army of your own. It's fortunate you have one."

"I do?"

"Every man who follows me, will follow you."

I didn't see what good an army would do me. "I can't fight my own people," I said.

"Who said anything about fighting them?" Bru replied. "If you are strong enough, no one will be eager to fight you. First we must persuade these chieftains of the northern tribes that we would take it ill if they made war upon our friends. Then perhaps we can persuade your people to hear your cause."

"With Bru's help," Maara said, "we can take you to confront Vintel and keep you safe. If we go back alone, we'll be in her power."

"Bru has done so much for me already. How can I ask him to do more?"

"Nonsense," said Bru. "You've brought me home from exile. I would consider it a privilege if you allow me to return the favor."

"You have a people waiting for their king," I reminded him.

"They have waited for generations," he said. "They can wait a few weeks more." He turned to Maara. "Will you make my offer understood to the northern chieftains?"

She nodded.

"Tell them that from Elen's wealth I will give them grain and cattle, some to take with them now and more after the harvest, to show my gratitude for their help this day."

While Maara conveyed his message, I watched their faces. They listened with interest and respect, but waited to hear his conditions.

"Tell them," said Bru, "that I wish to build upon our friendship, begun as an alliance against a common enemy. I ask that they also accept an alliance with our friends, the kind folk of Merin's house, once we have restored to power Merin's rightful heir."

Maara spoke again to the northern chieftains, and this time they looked more cautious. They talked among themselves for several minutes. Then their go-between addressed Maara directly in the language of the mighty.

"Who is this rightful heir?" she asked.

Maara looked at me.

"Tell your chieftains," I said, "that Vintel, who has treated them with such ruthlessness, took Merin's power for herself and forced me into exile. I am Merin's heir, and I intend, with Bru's help, to challenge Vintel."

The go-between repeated this to the northern chieftains. Then the wolf-skin chieftain spoke to me directly.

"He offers to join forces with you," said the go-between, "to help you defeat your enemy."

Maara leaned toward me and whispered, "This is not an offer made out of friendship. He means us to fight alongside them against Vintel, and if we prevail, your victory will put you under an obligation to them."

"In any case I can't take up arms against Vintel," I replied. "She may still have with her those I once counted as my friends."

"If Vintel has raised an army, our friends will be among them. Even those who oppose Vintel's leadership will have been compelled to join her. Your friends don't know if you're alive or dead. They have no choice but to follow anyone who can lead them against their enemies."

"It would be a poor beginning," I said to the go-between, "if I were to ally myself to the adversaries of my people with the intent to shed their blood. That I will not do, and if you attempt to harm them, I will oppose you with all the strength at my command."

This assertion was not well received by the northern chieftains.

"I don't intend to impose my leadership on anyone," I said. "All I seek is the opportunity to let my people choose whom they will follow. For that Bru's help is all I need. We have strength enough to force a parley with Vintel."

I hoped that was true.

"What would you have us do?" said the go-between.

My first thought was to ask the northerners to stay where they were, to await the outcome of my meeting with Vintel. Then I thought again. Whatever the result might be, the northern army would still have to be dealt with. It would be safer to keep them in my sight, and as much as possible under my control. If they joined us, we could confront Vintel with overwhelming strength, and perhaps also end the conflict between the northern tribes and the people of Merin's house.

"With your help," I said, "we may bring Vintel to parley that much sooner, but I must be certain that we will all act together. Tell your chieftains I would be grateful if they will place themselves under my command."

When the go-between related this to the northern chieftains, they spoke among themselves for a long time.

"I'm not sure it was the wisest thing to ask them to join us," I whispered to Maara. "It may appear to Merin's people that I have conspired with their enemy."

"Or it may appear to them that you have overcome their enemy," she said. "That would be a powerful demonstration of your ability. Never forget that we are on the battlefield. This is Vintel's ground. To defeat her here you must prove yourself the stronger."

The go-between turned back to me. "What will you offer for our help?"

"My friendship," I replied.

"That's all?"

"I will not buy the peace between us or pay you tribute, as though we were a conquered people. Bru feels an obligation to you. I do not. Yet what I offer may prove of greater value than any reward you could demand."

"What is that?"

"An end to bloodshed."

The young woman frowned. "You offer empty words."

"Are your people not yet weary of this endless warfare?"

"We are accustomed to it," she replied. "It's the way life is."

"Is it the way life must be? Once before in living memory our people thought otherwise and reached out in friendship to each other."

"We have not forgotten," she said. "Nor have we forgotten that it was your people who broke the peace."

"And my people swear that it was yours. Shall we debate who was at fault or shall we make a new start?"

"What advantage would we gain by making peace?" she asked me. "Are we then to sit quietly at home and comfort our children's hunger with stories of your friendship?"

She was right, yet if I gave them anything, I wanted to give it freely, as to friends, and not in payment, as to overlords or mercenaries.

"It's an odd sort of strife between us, isn't it?" I said. "Every year your raiding parties take a portion of our grain and cattle, and every year we let some of our goods go, because what we lose is not worth dying for. Yet we die anyway. My friends have never found me mean-spirited or careless of their welfare. A gift of friendship is not tribute."

She was wise enough not to ask me what they might expect. She understood my meaning. What we lost in grain and cattle hurt us little. It was the loss of life that broke our hearts, and they too paid in blood for what they took from us. If we would still lose grain and cattle, but save our lives, both sides would be the better for it, and if we could keep our hands innocent of blood, we would give them no new cause against us.

The go-between related my offer to the northern chieftains. This time they had little to say to each other. I had an idea that they had already made up their minds, but meant to keep us in suspense. The wolfskin chieftain got up and left the council fire, and the others soon followed him. At last only the go-between remained.

"They will speak with the others," she told me, "and give you their answer in the morning."

"Remind your chieftains," I said, "that a generation ago a few among our people made a careless choice, and their children have paid the price for it. I offer you that choice again. This is your day to choose."

90

Reasons

Once the northerners had left the council fire, Maara suggested that we go to bed, as we would have an early start in the morning. Although it had been two days since Bru had slept, he escorted us to our tent, so that he could talk with us privately.

Bru had left us Elen's tent. Her camp bed was gone, but her comforters and featherbeds were spread out on the floor. An oil lamp burned beside them. When we had all settled ourselves, Bru asked Maara to tell him everything that was said in our negotiation with the northern chieftains.

"What do you believe they'll do?" he asked, after he had heard her out.

"They know where their best interests lie," she said. "They'll be with us in the morning."

"I don't much trust that fellow in the wolfskin," said Bru. He turned to me. "And I'm surprised you trust any of them."

Maara had told him a little of the history of my people's dealings with the northerners, including the alliance that led to the last war.

"I trust neither the northern tribes nor those of Merin's people who may still hold a grudge," I said. "If I welcome any of the northerners into Merin's house, I will take care to guard each against the other."

Bru gave me a sidelong glance and scratched his beard. "Are the people of Merin's house not always kind?"

"No more kind than anyone else in a dangerous world," said Maara.

Bru waited to hear the rest of what he felt she was about to tell him.

Maara looked at me. "Nothing could make him more your friend than he is already," she said. "Let me tell him to whom he owes his life."

By asking my permission, she had told him already.

"Do what you think best," I said.

Maara turned back to Bru. "It was Tamras who persuaded Merin to let her prisoners go."

Bru didn't seem surprised. "Does Merin always consult her daughter in matters of state?" he asked.

"I'm not Merin's daughter," I said. "Merin has no children. I am the daughter of her shield friend."

"And at the time," said Maara, "she was hardly more than a child. She had just begun her apprenticeship in Merin's house, yet Merin had the sense to heed what she knew to be wise counsel, though it came from an unlikely source."

"Why did you keep this to yourself?" Bru asked me.

"I didn't want you and your men to risk your lives for me out of a feeling of indebtedness," I said. "What Merin did for you was not an act of selfless generosity. It was also to our benefit, and almost without risk."

"That's not quite how I remember it," said Maara. "As I recall, compassion had a lot to do with it."

"If it was compassion that first prompted me," I said, "I have been well rewarded for it."

"I hope your compassion has taught me a little wisdom," said Bru. He sighed. "I could almost wish that your people will be foolish enough to reject you. I'd prefer to take you home with me. I've been an outlaw all my life. How will I suddenly become a king?"

"You are a king," I told him. "You'll soon find your way. And I thank you for your offer of refuge. If Merin's people choose Vintel, I will certainly take you up on it."

"And all your friends are welcome too, of course," he said. He frowned. "Perhaps it's too soon to be thinking of this, but if you do go home, will you take my son with you? He will be a king himself someday. I can think of no better place to foster him than with you."

"It would be an honor to foster him," I said. "I only hope he can find a teacher who can keep up with him."

Then I thought of Kenit, whose energy never failed him and whom I hoped to find still among Merin's people. The memory of Kenit's face brought with it the images of many others. I felt their presence, as if the people of Merin's house had crowded into the tent with us. All winter they had lived in my memory as they had been in times past. Now they became real again.

When Bru left us alone, I turned to Maara.

"Why were you so eager to tell Bru all my secrets?" I asked her.

"Bru has a high regard for you already," she replied. "Knowing that you saved his life will not increase it or make him feel any more indebted to the one who brought him out of exile. The men who follow him are something else. They have no reason to believe they owe their good fortune to anyone but Bru. Before our confrontation with Vintel is over, they may have to risk their lives for you, and I want no man among them to hesitate."

"That's exactly what I didn't want," I said. "I don't want anyone to die for me."

"And I would put the whole world to death before I let death come for you."

She meant it, and there was nothing I could say to answer her.

"Are you going to scold me?" she asked.

"Yes," I said. "Next time don't stand at the head of the line."

And suddenly I was truly angry with her.

"I was wrong," I said. "This is not my fault. It's all your fault. If you hadn't left me, none of this would have happened."

Maara looked at me as if I'd struck her. "No," she said. "None of this would have happened. We would not be together, not now nor ever again. If we had been lucky, we might both be enslaved somewhere far away. More likely we would both be dead."

I knew she was right, but I was too angry with her to tell her so.

"And Bru would still be an outlaw," she went on. "The mighty would still be lording it over the common folk of Elen's house, and the northern army would be murdering our friends and overrunning Merin's land."

"We could have found another way."

"At the time I didn't see another way."

"You should have told me about your plan."

"There was no time. Anyway, you would have tried to talk me out of it."

That was true.

Maara said nothing more. She sat watching me, as she so often did, waiting for me to see what I was overlooking. I thought I knew what it was.

"I don't mean to sound ungrateful," I told her.

"I don't want your gratitude."

"What do you want then?"

"I want you to understand."

"What is there to understand?"

"Nothing is that simple. I had my own reasons for doing what I did, and I think they were not entirely unselfish."

Her gaze slipped past me, as her mind searched out a way to tell me what she barely understood herself.

"Don't you want your life to count for something?" she said at last.

"I never thought about it," I said.

"Of course not. You never doubted that your life was important."

"Everybody's life is important."

"Not mine."

"Of course it is."

Hadn't I just loosed chaos on the world to save her life?

She shook her head. "If you had known me before I came to Merin's house, you would not have thought so. It was all I could do then to get from one day to the next. I had nothing to offer anyone."

"That's not true."

"I know that now. When I became your teacher, I began to see that the life I had lived gave me things to pass on to you that none of the others would have known or thought of. And I saw things in you that none of the others knew how to value. More than anything, I wanted to watch you achieve the greatness I saw lying like a seed within you."

Then I knew what she had been getting at. If I failed to fulfill my destiny, it would be her failure too.

"I wanted it too much," she said. "I wanted it so much that I knew the gods would take it from me. So I gave it up."

"That was never what I wanted," I told her. "Greatness means nothing to me. If greatness is a dream of yours, you had better set about achieving it yourself."

"It isn't in me," she replied. "Nor did I ever want it for myself. To be the handmaid to greatness is enough."

"If you had died, it would all have been for nothing anyway."

"Why?"

Not without love, I'd told the gods. If gods there were.

"Whatever destiny you believe awaits me," I said, "I wouldn't want it, if you were not a part of it."

"Don't be silly," she said. "I'm not immortal."

I shrugged.

"What I if die of winter sickness?"

I smiled at her. "Life hasn't asked me that question yet."

"But I think life has asked you many others."

"Too many to talk about tonight."

I started to untie the thong that held my wolfskin, but I couldn't see it well enough to undo the knot. Maara reached out to help me with it. I caught her hand and kissed it.

"Does that mean you're not angry with me anymore?" she asked.

"It means that it doesn't matter if I'm angry with you or not."

"Oh."

She took the wolfskin from me and set it aside.

"I'm not," I said. And I lay down and opened my arms to her.

91

BATTLE

I t was still dark when Bru woke me.

"Get up!" he said. "Get up and arm yourself!"

"What?"

"She's almost here."

"Who?"

"Vintel."

I wished for a cup of nettle tea, to clear the confusion from my head. For a moment I wondered if I might still be dreaming.

"Hurry up!" he said. "If she's an hour's march away, I'd be surprised."

"How many are they?"

"Don't know," Bru replied. "It was too dark for my scouts to see them all, but they heard them from quite a distance."

Maara was out of bed already. She helped me up.

"I'll get your army on its feet," Bru said, and left the tent.

"How can Vintel be here?" I asked Maara. "How did she know where we were?"

"I imagine she followed the retreat of the northern army," said Maara. "When they turned back, she may have thought they were running away."

That was the only explanation that made sense to me.

❧

Outside the tent, Finn was waiting for me. He handed me my bow and quiver. The first light of dawn glowed on the eastern hills.

A band of warriors approached us. Three score of Bru's best men, including every man who had been Merin's prisoner, soon stood before me.

"Your guard," said Finn. He took my arm and whispered in my ear. "Last night Bru asked for volunteers. When they learned that it was you who spoke for them, each one insisted on a place beside you."

Maara had been right. Any of these men would give his life for me. It would be up to me to ensure that no one did.

My guard escorted me to the edge of the encampment, where Bru awaited us. It hadn't taken long for the army to make ready. The men stood in groups around their leaders, waiting for someone in authority to tell them what to do. Then I realized they were waiting for me.

"Where is Vintel?" I asked Bru.

He pointed to the southeast. It was the direction from which the northerners had come to meet Elen's army.

"The hill where we gathered yesterday," Maara whispered. "Set a strong anchor there, with the rest spread out in a line along the hilltops."

I knew the hills she meant. They extended from the highest hill, the same hill where we had met the northern army, away toward the northeast, in the direction of the battlefield. Another range of hills met them at an angle, leaving a narrow pass between. When I first saw the battlefield, I understood Elen's strategy. The two lines of hills had acted as a funnel, and she had enticed the northern army into it, giving her the advantage from the beginning.

"Call my captains," I said to Bru.

When they had gathered around me, I told them where to deploy their men. They were to separate into two groups, each one to form up on the high ground, along each range of hills. They too had read the battlefield, and they knew at once what I wanted.

I reminded them that we were not there to fight.

"No one is to show himself until I give the signal," I told them. "Stay out of sight, just behind the hill's crest, and keep your eyes on me."

I asked for someone to bring me a banner. Matha stepped forward at once, holding high a standard. From it hung a banner bearing a wolf's head. I didn't have an opportunity then to ask him how he came by it, but I had an idea that he had taken some trouble to find it for me.

"My guard and I will bait the trap," I said. "When you see us raise this banner, have your men show themselves. Don't look as if you're about to charge down on them. I don't want to frighten them to death or make them run away. Just stand there easily, leaning on your swords. Remember, though they appear to be the enemy, they still belong to me."

"What about the northerners?" Bru asked me.

"Are they with us?"

He nodded.

"Good," I said. "I want their chieftains to come with me. Have them bring their go-between along. Let them bring a few hundred of their warriors too, and send the rest to the hilltop where they waited yesterday. Make sure they understand that they must stay hidden until they see the others show themselves."

"Why bring so many of them with us?" Bru asked. "We don't know them. There's no telling what they'll do."

"They're the enemy Vintel expects to fight," I said. "They're what she expects to see."

"Will they obey you?"

"We'll soon find out," I said. "They have pledged themselves to follow me. I might as well discover now how well they keep their promises."

Bru told the captains to prepare their men. They ran to carry out their orders, and soon everyone in the camp began to move.

"Wait here a moment," Maara told me.

"Why?" I asked.

But she had left me already and was running back to the tent. She went into it and came out again at once, holding my wolfskin. A young man with a bandaged arm and shoulder stepped into her path. In less time than it takes to tell, I nocked an arrow and drew my bow. I set the arrow's tip in the center of the young king's back.

Maara saw me. The young king glanced over his shoulder, to see what she was looking at. He met my eyes. Slowly he turned around and showed me his empty hands. I lowered the bow.

"What did you think you were doing?" Maara asked me, when she returned to my side.

"Better safe than sorry," I replied.

"Not to worry," Maara said. "He begged my pardon for believing Elen's lie. And he offered you his help. He is unfit to fight himself, but he has a hundred men still able to bear arms." She moved closer and said in a low voice, "I think you should accept his offer."

I nodded, and Bru went to speak with him.

Maara draped my wolfskin around my shoulders and tied the thong that held it in place. Before I could ask her why she wanted me to wear it, she put the wolf's head up over mine and said, "If you pull this thing down to cover your face, can you still see out?"

"Yes."

"Good. I don't want Vintel to know it's you until she comes to parley."

"Why not?"

Maara grinned. "Let's surprise her," she said.

The march to the hills took more time than I thought it would, and it took even longer for our warriors to reach the hilltops. I was afraid that Vintel would appear before we were ready for her, but at last everyone was in place.

All told I had almost four hundred with me, including my guard, the northern warriors and their chieftains, and the young king and his men. I hoped it was enough to convince Vintel that she had found the enemy, but not enough to make her cautious. I had them form up in a line blocking the narrow pass.

The place we had chosen was well suited to our purpose. Even if Vintel hadn't been following the trail of the northern army, she would have come this way, because it offered an easy path. She would see us as soon as she crested the hill, and then she would have a long gentle slope before her. It would appear to her that we, being a smaller force, had chosen to defend the pass, though we would stand little chance against her greater numbers. The temptation to charge down upon us would be irresistible.

We hadn't long to wait. Bru tapped my shoulder and pointed to a hilltop to our right, where one of his men was signaling to us.

"Get the banner ready," I told him, "but keep it out of sight. I don't want the men to show themselves too soon."

Vintel's army seemed to take forever. We heard them before we saw them, the tramp of feet as they trudged up the hill, the thumping of shields on armor, the murmur of complaint. I remembered that these were the folk of Merin's house, and for just a moment my heart warmed with anticipation, as if I were expecting, not the army of an enemy, but a visit from dear friends.

As soon as they crested the hill they saw us and stopped. Someone gave the order to prepare for battle. They unslung their shields from their shoulders and drew their swords. The light of the rising sun glinted on their blades. Slowly at first, they walked in a battle line down the hill. As they drew closer, the first ranks broke into a trot, and before they had covered half the distance they were coming at us at a run.

Vintel's army made my four hundred seem very small. The noise they made was dreadful, even at a distance. The thunder of their running feet, the roar of their battle cries, grew loud as they drew near. It seemed that the earth trembled under them.

I glanced at the men beside me. Though they knew I had no intention of allowing Vintel's army to reach us, they had all braced themselves to receive the charge.

I gave the order to raise the banner. The warriors on the hillsides stood up and showed themselves. They did just as I had told them. With shields still slung over their shoulders, they leaned on their swords. I had an idea that behind the helmets that hid their faces, they were smiling.

The front ranks of Vintel's army saw them first. They tried to slow their charge, but the warriors behind them pushed them forward. In a moment all was chaos. They were well within the funnel now, and the front ranks were prevented from retreating by those at the rear who had not yet seen their peril. Soon they were tightly bunched together, with hardly enough room to wield their swords. If we had chosen to, we could have trapped them there and slaughtered them. They stood where they were and waited for a charge that didn't come.

I beckoned to the northerners' go-between.

"Invite Vintel to parley," I said.

I sent enough of my guard with her to keep her safe. She stopped well short of Vintel's army and waited. Then I saw Vintel. A few words were shouted back and forth, and the go-between returned.

"They are yours," she said.

I pulled the wolf's head down over my face and stepped forward twenty paces. Vintel set down her sword and shield and came to meet me. I could never have imagined the look I saw on Vintel's face. It was her own death she was looking at. She stopped ten paces from me and fell to her knees. Believing that I wouldn't understand her words, she held out her open hands, to beg for mercy.

I pulled the wolf's head up to show her my face, and said, "Stand up, Vintel."

For a moment she didn't recognize me. Then her eyes changed. If at first she'd had a hope that she could negotiate a surrender, she let it go.

"Whose ghost is this?" she whispered.

"If I were a ghost come back to haunt the wicked, you would have seen me long before today."

"They told me you were dead."

"It would appear they lied. Did they also tell you they killed Maara?"

Her eyes admitted it was so. She got slowly to her feet.

"Did you murder Merin too?"

"You may think the worst of me," she said, "but I would not betray my oath. Merin is alive and well and living safely in her own house, and your mother with her."

As relieved as I was to hear that both Merin and my mother were still among the living, I was dismayed to think that they had stayed in the same house with Vintel, who they must believe had either driven me away or murdered me. Perhaps they'd had no choice about it. Someone else would have to satisfy my curiosity. I did not intend to ask Vintel for news.

"You have much to answer for," I said.

Vintel shrugged. "You are the victor here. Do what you will."

Vintel understood her position very well. If I chose to take it, her life was mine. I would never have to ask forgiveness. We were on the battlefield.

I knew what Vintel was feeling. I had faced my own death too. With no choice but to wait upon the will of the powerful, she had abandoned herself. She knew she was powerless. She didn't care. I wanted her to care.

"Do you believe I intend to treat you as you would have treated me?"

"Why would you not?"

"Because you and I are not alike."

"I dispose of my enemies before they can dispose of me," she said. "If you are too stupid to do the same, then Merin's house has been well rid of you."

"Merin's people had a right to choose."

A light came into Vintel's eyes, as she caught her first glimpse of a way out of her predicament. "Which of us would they choose now, I wonder?"

"Will you put them to the test? Will you abide by their decision?"

"You little fool," she said. "I have no doubt of their decision. What will you do when they turn their backs on you?" She gestured at the warriors of my army, looking down upon us from the hillsides. "More to the point, what will they do?"

"I can't speak for the warriors of the northern tribes," I said, "though I think they are too few now to trouble you. If Merin's warriors choose to follow you, I will take any of my friends who wish to join me and leave you in peace. If they choose me, I will expect you to do the same."

Vintel scowled at me. "What kind of trick is this?"

"Whether it's a trick or not, I hardly see how it could put you in a worse position."

Vintel hesitated, while she thought it over, but she soon saw the sense in what I'd said.

"All right," she said. "Let's get this over with."

92

Excuses

Vintel's warriors stood behind their shield wall, swords in their hands, in case our negotiation failed. Together Vintel and I approached them.

The moment I took my first step toward Vintel's army, my guard, prompted no doubt by Maara, rushed forward to surround me. I agreed to be accompanied by no more than half a dozen. The rest insisted on following not far behind.

As I approached Vintel's army, I looked for the shields of people I knew. Many I had never seen before, but I did recognize a few of them. When I came close enough for the warriors of Merin's house to see my face, a murmur began among them. Those who knew me passed the word along to those behind them who couldn't see. I doubted I could find my friends in all that multitude. I hoped that my friends, if I had any friends here, would come forward on their own to greet me.

When at last I stood before them, a few in the front rank set down their shields. The rest waited, uncertain and suspicious, to see what I would do. Before I could address them, I heard a cry and a commotion from within their ranks. Someone jostled her way to the front and pushed roughly through the shield wall. It was Sparrow.

I believe she too thought I was a ghost, but she didn't seem to care. Before any of my guard could stop her, she rushed at me and threw her arms around me.

"You're real," she said into my ear. "You're flesh and blood and bones. I can't believe it." She let me go and held me at arm's length. Tears started in her eyes. "Where have you been?"

"I've been in exile," I replied.

Anger kindled in Sparrow's eyes. It was not meant for me. She rounded on Vintel.

"Liar!" she said.

Vintel lifted her chin against the accusation but made no reply.

"Liar!" Sparrow said again. "How could you tell me such a dreadful thing if it wasn't true? Did my grief mean nothing to you?"

"If Vintel told you I was dead," I said to Sparrow, "it was because she herself believed it. It seems her loyal band of warriors couldn't face her with the truth — that we escaped them."

Sparrow turned on me. "How can you defend her!"

"I don't defend her," I said. "I've come to accuse her. It was Vintel's treachery that set all of this in motion. It's time the folk of Merin's house learned the truth about her."

There was another commotion in the ranks of Vintel's army. Several warriors emerged from the shield wall with Laris at their head. She extended her arm to me, and when I took it, she grasped me firmly, as if she didn't doubt that I was as alive as I appeared to be. She grinned at me and gestured to my army, and said, with a twinkle in her eye, "May I assume you're not going to put us to the sword?"

I smiled back at her. "I doubt that will be necessary. We can, I think, settle our dispute without too much bloodshed. I've challenged Vintel to single combat."

Laris looked alarmed. "With swords?" she asked.

"With words."

"Oh," she said, relieved. "In that case, Vintel had best admit defeat now and retire from the field."

"Mind your tongue, Laris," said Vintel, "if you expect a welcome next time you come to Merin's house."

"A welcome?" Laris spat back. "Who came to me, begging me to bring warriors to her aid?"

I stepped between them, before they could come to blows.

"Laris," I said. "You know the warriors of Merin's house. Will you gather their captains together and ask them to hear my cause against Vintel?"

"So," she said. "You do have cause against her. I'm not surprised." She glanced at Vintel over my shoulder. "I suspected she was responsible for your disappearance. I only found out this spring, when I arrived in Merin's house, that you and Maara had been gone since harvest time. Vintel claimed that you ran off. I didn't believe her."

Vintel made a sound to let Laris know that she didn't care if Laris believed her or not, but Sparrow shot a glance at her that made her take a few steps back.

"Vintel would have had us murdered," I told Laris. "We escaped her and took refuge in the north. Now I've come back, to accuse her of treachery and to give her warriors an opportunity to choose again whom they will follow."

Laris frowned. "You should come home to Merin's house, to plead your cause before Merin and the elders."

"No," I said. "It was these warriors who disregarded both the counsel of the elders and Merin's leadership and instead followed Vintel to war. I believe I can persuade them that they chose badly."

"And if you don't succeed?"

"As you can see, I have made a few friends in the wider world. They will be glad to make a place for me."

Laris took me by the arm and drew me away from Vintel. Sparrow followed us.

"You don't know the situation here," Laris whispered. "In Merin's house Vintel is the power now. Half the warriors there are hers alone, with no loyalty to Merin. Merin is permitted to remain in her own house as a courtesy and to give Vintel the appearance of legitimacy, but she is no longer in authority."

"Then she can hardly help my cause," I said.

"She may remind her warriors to whom they made their oath."

"Laris," I said. "I won't go where I'm not wanted. If Merin's people trust Vintel's leadership, let them bear the consequences. Only tell my mother that I am living, that I am well and happy and with people who value and respect me. I know you have your own house to return to, but I will welcome any of Merin's people who wish to come with me."

Sparrow slipped her hand into mine. I squeezed it, to let her know that wherever I made my home, she would have a place there.

"Vintel's warriors deserve to bear the consequences of their choices," said Laris. "What about the innocents who will also have to bear them? Will you abandon them?"

"What would you have me do? Shall I impose my will on Vintel's warriors at swordpoint? Can I win their loyalty with force? If I can't persuade them now of my fitness for leadership, how will I ever persuade them of anything else?"

Laris sighed. "I will call Merin's warriors to council," she said.

More warriors had come forward out of Vintel's army, some because they knew me, some out of curiosity. A few went to speak with Vintel, but most of them would have approached me if they had not been kept at a distance by my guard. Behind their shields, swords drawn and ready, Bru's men formed a strong circle around me.

Maara appeared at my side. A look passed between her and Sparrow, and Sparrow let go of my hand.

"Come away a bit while we wait," said Maara.

"Why? I'm safe enough."

"You and Vintel have nothing more to say to each other, and there's no point in trying to explain yourself to the curious. Save your words for the time when they will count."

It was wise advice.

After we had withdrawn a little distance, Maara turned to Sparrow. "What does Tamras need to know?"

Sparrow didn't understand what she was asking.

"What has Vintel told people about our disappearance? What excuses has she made? What has she accused us of?"

"She told everyone you ran away, back to whatever home you always intended to return to, and took Tamras with you. But that's not what she told me. She told me both of you were dead, and she said it was my fault."

"Your fault?" I said. "How could it be your fault?"

"Because I let you out of the armory. Vintel claimed she only meant to drive Maara away, so she locked you up, to keep you from interfering."

"Would she have let me go, to accuse her before the household?"

"She said she had a way to keep you quiet. She said she never meant for you to come to harm."

"And you believed her?"

"I didn't know what to believe. She said you attacked the warriors who were holding Maara. They had no choice but to fight back, and one of them was killed. That much I knew was true. They buried her in secret, but Vintel took me to see her body. It was your arrow in her chest."

"She told you they killed both of us?" asked Maara.

Sparrow nodded.

"But she didn't tell that to the others."

"No."

"Why not?"

"She was afraid they would blame her for Tamras's death."

"They would have," Maara said. "And Namet would have had something to say about what Vintel had planned for me."

"Namet knew Vintel was lying," said Sparrow. "She came to me and demanded to hear the truth. I told her everything. I told her about finding Tamras in the armory, and I told her what Vintel told me. She wouldn't believe that you were dead. She said that if she were twenty years younger she would go to look for you herself."

"How is she?" asked Maara. "Is she well?"

"I don't know," Sparrow replied. "She went home to Arnet's house before the snow fell. She refused to stay in the same house with Vintel."

"Is Merin well?" I asked.

"Merin is very well," said Sparrow, "and it's your mother we have to thank for that. The day you left, Merin fell ill. I couldn't convince her that Tamnet was alive. I'm not surprised she didn't believe me. I was deep in grief myself. Tamar came back just in time, and Tamnet grappled Merin back from the brink."

"How did Vintel explain her lie to Merin?" I asked.

"I don't know what she said to Merin," Sparrow replied. "By then Vintel was afraid that she would be found out. She said nothing publicly, and no one dared confront her about it. Instead she put the word around quietly that it must have been Maara who started the rumor of Tamnet's death, to explain your disappearance and to ensure that that no one would think to search for you until it was too late. Vintel implied that it was she who guessed the truth and sent for Tamnet."

In my mind I compared Elen and Vintel. Next to Elen, Vintel appeared to be no more than a simpleminded blunderer, yet the grief she had caused, the harm she'd done, were as hideous as Elen's wicked deeds. Perhaps stupidity is as dangerous as evil.

"I should have said something," Sparrow whispered. "I should have told everyone what Vintel told me."

"Why didn't you?" Maara asked her.

"I thought you both were dead," she replied. "I didn't see what good could come of tearing the rest of Merin's house apart. I spoke to Namet about it, and she agreed with me. She said if you were dead, Merin's house would need Vintel. If you were not, you would return and bring about Vintel's defeat."

"Namet was right," said Maara.

"Not yet," I said.

93

YOU AND WHAT ARMY?

Laris soon assembled a council of half a hundred. Each of them had made her oath to Merin, not Vintel, and each of them led a band of warriors loyal to her. If I could win these few, the rest would follow.

I stood silent for a time before them. One by one I met their eyes. I made them look at me. I knew them all.

"Didn't any of you wonder where I was?"

It was not what I had meant to say, but as I looked into the faces of these people with whom I had once shared a place, with whom I had once shared a life, I asked myself why I had believed I could come home. Why should I try to win over the very people who betrayed me? Their loyalty came, not from the oath they took nor from their sense of honor nor from their respect for the wisdom of Merin and the elders, but from fear. All Vintel had had to do was frighten them.

For a moment I was tempted to frighten them myself. A signal from me would bring my army down upon them. They saw my anger in my eyes and shrank away from it.

"Cowards!" I said to them. "Was it easier to shelter from your fears behind Vintel? Was it easier than thinking for yourselves?"

Out of the corner of my eye, I saw Maara approaching me.

"Tell them why you disappeared," she said.

"I disappeared because Vintel tried to kill me."

I heard among them not a murmur. No one believed me.

"You believed rumors put about in whispers," I said. "You believed scandal and idle gossip. You believed things so absurd that if you had dared speak them aloud, you would have seen they were ridiculous. I'm not surprised you don't recognize the truth when you hear it."

Maara moved closer and would have spoken again, but I gestured to her to back away. I knew that I was speaking from my anger, that my heart had overruled my head. I didn't care. I didn't care whether they accepted me or not. I almost hoped they wouldn't. I almost hoped they would set me free.

That thought calmed me enough to enable me to speak to them without emotion. I told them how Vintel lured Maara out of Merin's house, how she locked me in the armory, how Sparrow found me there and let me go. I told them what Vintel said to me, that she threatened Maara's life to make me promise to go home.

"You said I tried to kill you."

Vintel's voice came from close beside me. I turned to face her.

"Sending you home is not the same as killing you," she said. "I wanted you out of Merin's house for a while, that's all."

Vintel thought she was being clever. With Sparrow as a witness, she had no choice but to admit that she had caused our disappearance. Now she had to justify what she had done. But she had also shown herself to be a liar.

"You told me that if I agreed to leave Merin's house, you would let Maara take refuge with Laris," I said, "yet I found your warriors taking Maara to our northern border. What would they have done with her there? Did they plan to let her go? Do you claim that you didn't intend for them to kill her?"

Vintel shrugged, as if Maara's fate could be of no interest to anyone but me.

"Will you now deny what you just told me, that your warriors lied to you, that they told you they had killed us both? If they lied to escape your anger, they knew that was what you wanted. Why would I believe you would not have killed me too?"

Murmurs began among the assembled warriors. Vintel sensed that she was losing their trust and their good will.

"Maara was a danger to us," she said. "You were not."

"Maara was never a danger to us. Maara was one of us."

"Maara fooled you. She fooled Namet too. You were too young to know better, and Namet had been fooled before. I knew that Maara was just waiting for her chance."

"Her chance? What chance?"

"To betray us to our enemies."

"Was she?" I turned to Maara. "Your chance has come. Give the word, and I will call down upon them every warrior at my command."

Maara shook her head at me. Her eyes were angry. "Don't even think it." She wasn't speaking for the benefit of Merin's warriors. She was scolding me. "Don't even think it, much less say it. Was it only yesterday that you complained of the burden of responsibility for the northern dead? What will you feel if you conspire in the murder of your own."

I smiled at her and turned back to Merin's warriors. They were terrified.

"Maara has just saved your lives," I told them. "Who among you will accuse her of intending to bring harm to Merin's house?"

No one spoke. I waited, until they grew calm enough to hear me.

"Vintel was wrong," I said. "She was wrong about Maara, as she has been wrong about a great many other things. You followed her because you depended on her strength, but strength is not enough. Without wisdom strength is a bull blundering among the lilies."

"I hardly think Tamras can lay claim to wisdom," Vintel said. "She's just a child."

"This child has defeated you upon the battlefield," I replied. "But I was not claiming wisdom for myself. Merin is wise, yet you set her will aside. The elders are wise, yet you don't avail yourself of their counsel. If you had listened to their wisdom, you would not now be at the mercy of your enemies."

"Are you speaking of the northern tribes," Vintel asked me, "or are you speaking of yourself?"

Without waiting for an answer, she turned to the assembled warriors.

"Don't you see what is before your eyes? Don't you see that Tamras has joined forces with your enemies? Why would you believe that Tamras bears you no ill will? Was it not Tamras who just threatened to destroy you?"

Maara stepped forward. "If Tamras wanted to destroy you, you would be lying in your blood here on this ground." Then she turned to me. "They are at your mercy. It's time to stop toying with them and state your terms."

"My terms?" I said. "Here are my terms. If you are pleased with Vintel's leadership, then release me from any obligation to the folk of Merin's house and let me go my own way in peace with any who wish to join me. But if you recall a better time, when you trusted Merin's wisdom to keep you safe and free from fear, follow me back to Merin's house and let Vintel and all who belong to her go where they will, as long as it's somewhere else."

Merin's warriors turned to Vintel, perhaps to see if she had agreed to this bargain.

"I told her what answer you would give her," Vintel said to them.

She was trying to appear confident, but I sensed that she had begun to worry. I think she expected them to acclaim her right away. Instead they looked undecided, as they waited to hear what she would say on her own behalf.

"If I leave Merin's house," she said, "half your strength in warriors will go with me. Then who will protect you from the northern tribes?"

"As you can see," said Maara, "it is Tamras who now stands between you and the northern tribes."

Vintel would have ignored her, but the warriors had all turned their eyes to Maara and listened with respect.

"Oh, yes," Vintel said. "We can see that you have struck a bargain with the northern tribes. How much of our goods have you promised them and how long will you be able to appease them? When they tire of bribes and empty promises, you will regret the loss of the strength you now think so little of."

"I have promised them nothing but my friendship," I replied.

Vintel snorted. "How long will they be satisfied with that?"

"You misunderstand the situation here," said Maara. "The northern-ers you see are the remnant of an army so vast that they would have easily defeated you. They would have slaughtered every one of you here in the wilderness before marching south to murder everyone at home. Then they would have taken everything—your goods, your homes, your lands. All would be theirs, but for Tamras, who defeated them before they could do you harm. But for Tamras, the northern tribes would even now be feasting in Merin's great hall."

Vintel was so astonished she could think of nothing to say.

"The story is too long to tell you now," Maara went on. "You knew they had raised an army, but you could have had no idea how strong they were, or you would have stayed at home behind the walls of Merin's house and hoped you could withstand a siege. Instead Vintel brought you out to meet them, and when their army turned around, in her arrogance she thought they were retreating and pursued them. They were not running away from you. They were running back to defend themselves against the army that Tamras sent against them."

"Where is this army now?" Vintel asked. "Are you telling me the northern tribes have joined the army that defeated them?"

"As I said," Maara replied, "it is a tale too long to tell, though I think it will make next winter pass all the quicker when it is told by the hearth in Merin's hall." Maara turned back to the assembled warriors. "A short distance to the north you will find the battlefield. There you will see, still smoldering, the funeral pyres of the victors and the earth freshly heaped over the northern dead."

"Where are these victors now?" Vintel asked.

Maara smiled at her. "They were defeated in their turn by Tamras and her allies, more by cleverness than by force of arms. Some have joined us, but most have gone back into the north, to seek refuge where they can."

"I knew Tamras was fond of storytelling," said Vintel, "but this is beyond even her imagination. Who would believe such a preposterous tale?"

But when she turned to see the faces of the warriors, she saw that they did believe it. They would, of course, make haste to inspect the battlefield themselves, not because they were incredulous, but because they were eager to bear witness to such a great event.

"Now you must decide," Maara said to them. "Will you follow Vintel, who provoked the northern tribes into raising such an army, who then led you into peril, who would have led you to your death and the folk of Merin's house to their doom. Or will you follow Tamras, who saved you?"

"Tamras!" The cry went up so suddenly and with such energy it startled me. "Tamras! Tamras! Tamras!"

94

Victory

Never in my life had I been so popular. Merin's captains all surged forward. If my guard had not prevented them, they would have hoisted me onto their shoulders. Many of the warriors of Vintel's army rushed forward too and took up the cry, even though no one had yet told them what had happened.

Only the warriors belonging to Vintel kept silent. They withdrew from the others and gathered around her, waiting for an explanation. Vintel had to lead them away a little distance before she could make herself heard over the commotion. I watched as they put their heads together.

"Best put a stop to that," said Maara. "Let's see if Bru can spare us some of his men to escort them home. We can't risk letting them reach Merin's house before us."

A chill ran down my spine. "Would Vintel resist us?"

"She might try," Maara replied. "She has warriors enough to hold the fortress. And she would have hostages."

"Merin and my mother."

Maara nodded.

First I had to free myself from Merin's captains. I raised my arms, to ask for silence.

When they were quiet, I said, "Go now, and tell your people what has been decided here. Then I will welcome all of you to our encampment, where you can rest and have a bite to eat before we prepare for our journey home."

They looked disappointed.

"On the way we will pass by the battlefield," I added.

Then they grew more cheerful and went at once to speak with their warriors. As soon as they had gone, I looked around for Bru. I hadn't far to look. He had been waiting to congratulate me.

"I hope some of your men can remain with us a little longer," I said. "We will need a small army just to escort Vintel and her warriors home."

"I'd be glad to see to that myself," he said. "I wouldn't mind visiting the house of kindness again under different circumstances."

I almost asked him if he wasn't eager to go home himself, but I thought I knew what he was feeling. Bru was accustomed to the battlefield. He felt at home here. Today he was a warrior. When he returned from exile, he would become a king. I understood his reluctance.

"Shall we disarm them?" Bru asked me.

I looked to Maara for the answer.

"Let's not humiliate her," Maara said. "Vintel doesn't handle humiliation well. Let's talk to her instead."

"Talk to her? What more have we to talk to her about?"

"Her warriors are from her sister's house. Where else will Vintel find a welcome? Vintel's sister is one of Merin's strongest allies. It would be foolish to befriend our enemies in the north only to create new ones in the south."

I saw reason in what Maara said, but I didn't much like the idea.

"Let it go," Maara whispered.

"What? Let what go?"

"Your anger. Your resentment. Your sense of injury. You act now for every soul you have just taken into your care. You can no longer afford to indulge your petty grievances."

"Vintel would have murdered us," I said. "I hardly consider that a petty grievance."

"You have counted out to her the price of treachery. Let that be punishment enough."

Maara saw in my face what I would not say, that I didn't consider going to her sister's house a punishment.

Maara smiled at me. "You're not a younger sister," she said.

I thought of Tamar, who all our lives had resented my place as firstborn— older, taller, stronger—even as she followed me like a puppy at my heels.

"She will not be content to remain in her sister's house, in her sister's shadow," Maara said.

Was she speaking of Tamar or Vintel?

"What shall I say to her?" I asked.

"Offer her your friendship. She may not think that such a small thing now."

While Bru gathered an escort for Vintel's warriors, Maara and I went to speak with Vintel. I began by asking her where she planned to go.

"What difference does it make to you?" Vintel replied.

"Vintel," I said, "we need not part as enemies."

"We have been enemies from the beginning. Why would we part as friends?"

"If we can't part as friends, then let us at least part as allies."

"Why? So that you can call on strength when wisdom is not enough?"

I felt a distant echo of my humiliation when Vintel tried to steal my brooch, and I resented Maara for putting me in this position, asking favors of an enemy of such longstanding, an enemy I had at last defeated. Before I could reply, Maara touched my arm, to keep me silent, and addressed Vintel herself.

"If you insist on enmity," she said, "you and your warriors will return to Merin's house, disarmed and dishonored, as our prisoners. Tamras would spare you that, just as she would spare Merin's house the loss of a faithful ally."

Vintel gazed at Maara, as if seeing her for the first time.

"I have no quarrel with Merin," she said. "I will always be her friend and an ally of her house."

"With that we are content," said Maara.

Bru rounded up enough of his kinsmen to keep an eye on Vintel and her warriors. I was glad now of the men who made up my guard. Their duty to me would keep them occupied and away from the temptation to join the escort of those who had once escorted them. Of Merin's prisoners, only Finn was not accounted for, and though he had more cause than any, to seek revenge was not in his nature.

There was hardly time to make all the decisions required of me, and I had to rely on others to act upon them. Laris took charge of the warriors of Vintel's army who belonged neither to Merin nor Vintel, but to Merin's allies, to let them know that the people of Merin's house now followed me. I trusted her to present it to them as a thing accomplished, not as a choice for them to make between Vintel and me. If any of them wished to alter their allegiance, they would have to wait for our return to Merin's house.

Bru sent messengers to the men who were still waiting on the hillsides, to tell them to stand down. Those who were not needed for Vintel's escort he sent back to the encampment, to prepare a welcome for yet another army.

Then Merin's captains returned, followed by their bands of warriors, all eager to tour the battlefield. I asked the young king to lead them there. His language resembled ours closely enough that with a little effort Merin's people could understand him, and his people had never been our enemies. He could convey to Merin's warriors what had happened without opening old wounds.

"They seem to believe that it was you, not Elen, who defeated us."

The voice came from close behind me. When I turned, I found myself confronted by the northern chieftains' go-between.

It was inevitable that the northerners would discover who had sent Elen's army out against them. The stories were everywhere. Sooner or later the go-between was bound to hear them told in a language she understood, and stories have a way of traveling easily even through the barrier of language.

"This evening," I said, "the story will be told and told again around the campfires. As stories do, it will serve the present purpose, to bind Merin's warriors to me by admiration and by gratitude. I would prefer that you hear the whole and simple truth from me."

She waited.

"I have no time now to tell it properly. Join me this evening at the council fire. There I will gather my friends from Merin's house, and I will tell you all, as best I can, as much of the truth as I remember."

Soon the armies were once again in motion, making their way north. It occurred to me that I hadn't seen Sparrow since before my confrontation with Vintel.

"Don't worry," Maara said. "She'll turn up. Perhaps we'll find her at the encampment."

But at the encampment I had too much to do to think about finding anybody. There was hardly room enough to accommodate so many, and I worried that the crowding and the jostling might strike a spark that would ignite the tinder of their grievances, both old and new. After all, many of these people had not long ago been at each other's throats.

To my relief, the northerners, already set apart by their inability to understand any language but their own, preferred to keep to themselves. We settled them in the part of the encampment left vacant by the young king.

They soon made use of the water so close by. They got to work digging out a bathing pool, and many of them shed their armor and their clothing to bathe away the last remnants of the battlefield. It would not be so easy to cleanse their memories, but I hoped their hearts would have had time to heal a little before they learned that I was responsible for their defeat.

I kept open a place for Merin's warriors and her allies as far from the northerners as possible and with Bru's men as a buffer between them. Merin's captains and their warriors didn't arrive at the encampment until late in the afternoon. They had lingered long upon the battlefield. They had walked every inch of it, seeing for themselves how fierce the battle, and how costly.

They wondered at the funeral pyres, as much at the strange custom of burning the dead as at the number of the fallen. They marveled at the grave of the northern warriors and from its size reckoned up their losses. Each brought a stone for the cairn that would cover it, out of respect for such valiant fighters, and also out of gratitude, that they themselves had not been their adversaries.

Bru led Vintel's warriors to the hollow in the hills, to keep them from starting any mischief among those who had been their comrades in arms. So that they would not regard their isolation as a punishment, he treated them as honored guests. He took care to provide them with everything they needed, water for bathing, fuel for their fires, meat and bread, every necessity and every comfort he could think of.

All day I kept an eye out for Sparrow. I didn't see her.

⟜

When at last my work was done, I sat down beside the council fire. The last rays of the setting sun cast a golden light over the wilderness.

The encampment was unusually silent. Their bellies full, their arms and armor laid aside, the warriors dozed in the soft grass or spoke in quiet voices to their friends who sat beside them. Later, when the dark had fallen and the fires had been lit, the camp would wake again, and the storytelling would begin. Now, in the hush of evening, we rested in the balance between light and darkness.

I felt myself drift up into the golden air. I floated there as down floats upon the slightest breath. Below me lay the armies of the peoples of the world, at last at peace with one another.

Someone touched my shoulder. With a sudden thump I came back down to earth to find Maara kneeling beside me.

"Come with me," she said.

"Where are we going?"

"I thought we might try to make you more presentable." She brushed my cheek with the backs of her fingers and smiled. "When was the last time you washed your face?"

She stood up and held out her hand to me, to help me up. When I was on my feet, she let me go, but she didn't turn away. She was held there by something in my eyes. She touched my face again, then lifted my chin a little as she bent and kissed me.

I forgot that I was standing in the midst of armies. I forgot that my guard was watching over me. I gave myself to Maara in that kiss, as if we had never been parted from each other.

In the tent a bucket of warm water was waiting for me. Somewhere in Elen's stores Maara had found a cake of fragrant soap. She stripped me to the waist and bathed me. She even washed my hair. Then she shook out a clean linen shirt and dressed me in it.

"Where did you find this?" I asked her.

"In one of the wagons," she replied.

"Did they bring a change of clothing for the entire army?"

Maara chuckled. "Not likely."

The shirt must be one of Elen's. I was surprised how well it fit me.

Maara looked me up and down. "I suppose that will have to do," she said. She met my eyes. "Are you ready?"

"As ready as I'll ever be."

"Tonight," she said, "you must show them something new. You are no longer the child they remember. You are the leader they have chosen. Tonight you must show them Merin's heir."

"I must also convince them to accept the friendship of their enemies," I said. "I asked the northerners' go-between to join us."

"Good," said Maara. "That will be a start."

"She knows I've taken credit for the defeat of the northern tribes."

"I wondered how long we could keep that secret."

I laughed. "Hard to keep it secret when you shout it to the world."

"What will you tell her?" Maara asked.

"The truth," I said.

"Bear in mind that she may be more than an interpreter. Last night she spoke as much for herself as for the northern chieftains."

I heard Sparrow's voice outside the tent. Unable this time to get past my guard, she shouted her indignant protest. Maara lifted the tent flap and told the men to let her through.

"Your friends are waiting for you," Sparrow said, "but before we go, I need to tell you what I've done." She glanced at Maara. "I found our swiftest messenger and sent him back to Merin's house."

Sparrow turned back to me. "I would have consulted you, but in all the commotion I couldn't get anywhere near you, and I thought we should send word back as soon as possible."

"What message did you send?" Maara asked her.

"The news that you both have been found alive and well and will soon be coming home."

"That's all?"

"Not quite." Sparrow grinned at me. "I'm afraid I may have laid it on a little thick. I told him to say that Tamras is coming home at the head of a great army, that she has defeated her nemesis, Vintel, and sent her into exile, that she has also defeated our enemies, the northern tribes, and allied herself and Merin's house to the peoples of the northern wilderness."

"Sparrow will soon rival Finn as a conjuror of legends," said Maara.

☙

Around the council fire I found my friends. First to catch my eye was Taia's copper-colored hair. Beside her Kenit sat, and next to him was Laris with two of Merin's captains, people who, unlike the others, had always been friendly to Maara and me. It was fitting that they would now be rewarded.

When they saw me, they all stood up and gathered around me. I embraced each one and told them how glad I was to see them. I meant every word. For the first time since I left Merin's house, I was with my own.

We sat down around the council fire, all but Sparrow, who stood on her tiptoes and craned her neck, looking for someone.

"Who's missing?" I asked her.

I thought it might be Donal she was looking for.

"Maybe she got lost," said Sparrow. "I'll go find her."

And off she went.

I turned to Kenit. "Is Donal here?"

Kenit shook his head. "He took a slight wound in a skirmish with a raiding party. He would have come with the army anyway, but I told him someone had to mind the baby."

I was glad to hear Kenit speak of his child. I had hesitated to ask after him. This past winter was his first, and winter is not kind to children.

"How is your son?" I asked him.

"He is well," said Kenit. "Well and strong."

"I am very glad to hear it."

Taia turned to face me. "Are you going to tell us what you've been doing all this time?"

"I hardly know where to start," I replied.

A voice behind me said, "Start with why these northerners have been such a trouble to us. Was it you who put them up to it?"

I knew her by her voice before I turned around.

"Fodla!"

Sparrow was with her. It was Fodla she'd been looking for.

"Aren't you going to ask an old woman to sit down?"

Instead I stood up. "What old woman? I see no old woman here."

Fodla couldn't keep herself from smiling, and while her guard was down, I embraced her. She soon had her guard back up again. She shrugged me off and went to take a seat across the fire from me.

There were now nine of us from Merin's house gathered around the council fire. It was an auspicious number.

Taia again urged me to recount my adventures, but I said we were still waiting for one more, so they passed the time by telling me a little of what had happened in Merin's land since I left it. While the last harvest wasn't the bounty we were used to, there had been enough to last the winter, though they all had to pull their belts a little tighter. This year looked to be much better.

The northerners must have had another meager harvest. The raids began while snow still lay on the ground, and Vintel asked Merin's allies to send help before the usual time. Beset by troubles of their own, they were slow to fulfill their obligation. Then our scouts reported the gathering of the northern army. This news was enough to frighten Merin's allies into sending every warrior they could spare. Merin's house was their bulwark in the north. If Merin was defeated, their own houses would be the next to fall.

Bru stopped by the council fire long enough to be introduced to everyone. I invited him to join us, but he didn't stay. He had things to do, he said, and besides he couldn't understand a word of our peculiar tongue.

The young king too came by, but before long he excused himself, as his wounds were troubling him. The healer who had tended him left with Elen's army, and he had no healer of his own. He looked a little feverish.

"Is there a healer among you?" I asked Sparrow.

She nodded. "Shall I take him to her?"

Without waiting for my answer, she got to her feet and held out her arm to him, to help him up.

"Let the healer know that she is tending a king," I said to Sparrow.

"A king," she echoed.

It was a word seldom heard in Merin's house, except in stories.

At last the northerners' go-between arrived. She begged my pardon for her lateness, saying that she'd had matters to talk over with the northern chieftains. I invited her to take a place part way round the circle from me, so that we could each have a clear view of the other. Because I trusted Maara's intuition that she was more than she appeared to be, I offered her the opportunity to reveal herself.

"Will your chieftains join us or will you speak on their behalf?" I asked.

"I will speak on my own behalf," she replied. "War is their business. Peace is my business."

Another good sign.

"Then it's time we knew your name," I said.

"I am called Ru."

I turned to the others. "Ru speaks for the northern tribes."

Fodla bristled. "Let her speak somewhere else then. There's nothing she might say that I care to hear."

"Fodla," I said, as gently as I could, "I hope I can prevail upon you to change your mind. I think she has much to say that it would be well for us to listen to, but tonight I asked her to join us to hear with all of you the story of how the northern army was defeated."

Fodla glared at me. I refused to glare back at her. I held her eyes until she looked away. Though at home she was an elder, here on the battlefield she was a warrior, and I was her commander.

Sparrow returned in time to witness our silent battle.

"Is Fodla making trouble already?" she said as she sat down.

"Fodla is concerned that we not make the same mistake again that we made last time," I said. "I share her concern, and I'm counting on her to help me learn to do things differently."

Fodla's angry scowl relaxed a little.

"So," said Ru. "They say you defeated us though you were nowhere near the battlefield. How do you explain this mystery?"

Maara put her hand on my arm. "Begin at the beginning," she said. "Let Ru hear it all. Begin with the night Vintel drove us out of Merin's house."

95

A Very Long Story

B ear with me," I said to Ru, "while I tell my friends why I disappeared from Merin's house and what happened to me while I've been away."

"It promises to be a fascinating tale," she said.

I turned back to the others. "As you know, it was half a year ago, not long before the first snowfall."

Was it only half a year? It felt like another lifetime.

"Late one night, my sister Tamar brought us a message, given to her by someone she didn't know. She said Laris had returned and was waiting for Maara by the river. It was a lie. It was Vintel who sent the message, and when Maara left the house, Vintel's warriors took her prisoner."

"I don't understand," said Kenit. "Why would Vintel do such a thing? I know she wasn't fond of Maara, but that seems a bit much even for Vintel."

"Vintel wanted to be rid of both of us," I told him. "You must have heard the rumors that Merin intended to name me her heir. Once that happened, Vintel knew there would be no place for her in Merin's house."

"But that makes her actions even more difficult to understand," he said. "That she would kill a stranger I can well believe, but how could she dare to murder the Lady's heir?"

The image came into my mind of Vintel's face as I had seen it then, lit by a flare of firelight. At the time I called that look the pain of wounded love.

It was Vintel's pain that had driven her that night, or she would never have done anything so foolish. And that secret pain belonged only to Vintel.

"Have you never known Vintel to do something without thinking?" I said.

Kenit chuckled, and I went on with my story before anyone else could question the reason for Vintel's treachery.

"When Maara failed to return, I went downstairs to look for her. Vintel was waiting for me. She dragged me into the armory and told me that if I would promise to leave Merin's house, she would let Maara go to Laris. I had no choice but to agree. To explain my absence, Vintel told Merin my mother had died."

Fodla made a growling noise in her throat. "Damn near killed the woman with that lie," she said.

"That's why Sparrow sent Tamar to bring my mother to her."

Fodla nodded her approval.

"Sparrow found me locked in the armory. When I told her what Vintel had done, she let me out, and I followed Vintel's warriors north."

"How did you know where they had gone?" asked Laris.

"If they were taking Maara south to you," I replied, "I knew she would be safe enough. But if, as I suspected, Vintel meant to kill her, where else would they go?"

Laris understood my reasoning.

"I soon found their trail," I said. "I followed it for quite a distance, until I had the misfortune to turn a corner and stumble suddenly into the midst of Vintel's warriors."

Maara stirred beside me. She knew what I was about to say, and I half expected her to stop me, but she kept her silence.

"I killed their captain, and no one else had the heart to challenge my bow. Maara disarmed them and sent them back to Merin's house with their dead comrade."

"We heard nothing of the death of one of Vintel's captains," said Fodla.

"Sparrow tells me that Vintel buried her secretly," I replied. "She was afraid that if people knew of it, they would discover what she had done. But she cannot now accuse me of the murder."

"It was not murder," Maara said.

I turned to face her. "Why did we run away then?"

"Who would have believed us?"

"Harrumph," said Fodla. "Did you doubt that Merin and the council would have seen justice done?"

Fodla's words had an edge, as if she thought us cowardly because we ran away. I reminded myself that it was just Fodla's way of speaking, and I decided not to take offense, but Maara took offense on my behalf.

"Perhaps you have forgotten Vintel's power," Maara said. "She would have told the council the same thing she told Sparrow, that she only intended to drive me out of Merin's house, that she meant no harm to Tamras. She would have insisted that Tamras killed her warrior unprovoked. She would have demanded blood for blood, and with or without the consent of Merin and the council, she would have taken it."

Fodla chose not to argue with her.

Maara nudged me. "Go on," she said.

"Vintel's warriors were afraid of Vintel's anger. They told her they had killed us both. If we had known that Vintel believed us dead, we might have stayed close to home and tried to send word to our friends. Instead, fearing pursuit, we traveled far into the north. When the snow began to fall, we sought refuge in the forest, where we could forage for food and shelter among the trees."

"You spent the winter in a forest?" Sparrow asked. She poked me in the ribs. "You don't look like you wanted for enough to eat."

"We had plenty," I assured her. "We fished the streams and set snares for small game. Because I had the bow, from time to time we enjoyed a feast of venison."

I had already decided, and Maara had agreed with me, that we would tell no one about the forest people. Their survival depended on their invisibility. Besides, said Maara, no one would believe us anyway.

"It's a wonder you didn't freeze to death," said Sparrow.

"We found shelter in a hollow tree."

Fodla snorted. "How could there be room for two people in a hollow tree? Did you sleep standing up?"

"They are ancient forests in the north," Maara told her. "The trees there are immense, larger even than the trees in your own oak grove. We had room enough."

I was glad for the darkness. It hid the blush that warmed my cheeks. The smile in Maara's voice told me that she too was remembering what we had shared in that hollow tree.

"All winter we thought over what we should do," I said. "In the end we agreed we had no choice but to come home. Perhaps Vintel's power had grown weaker. Perhaps her adversaries had grown stronger. We decided to trust to fortune and our friends."

"You did not then have an army at your back?" asked Fodla. She was more curious now than belligerent.

"We did not," said Maara. "We would have come back alone, if we hadn't been captured by a raiding party of the northern tribes."

Ru had been gazing into the fire, only half listening to the recounting of events that did not concern her. When she heard Maara mention the northern tribes, she looked up and said, "Do you know who it was that took you?"

"I didn't think to ask their names," said Maara.

"Where did this happen?"

"We were traveling with a caravan of traders. We set out in boats, down a stream that we hoped would take us into the river that flows through Merin's land. A band of your warriors stopped us, and the traders gave them one of the boats with all its goods to obtain safe passage for the others. It was our boat."

"Was their chieftain a large, red-headed woman?"

Maara nodded.

"I know her by reputation," said Ru. "She is like your Vintel. She does as she pleases and answers to no one. She deals in goods, not captives, but she will take advantage of any opportunity. She little thinks of consequences, though she could hardly have foreseen the grief she brought upon us."

It had never occurred to me that the northern tribes played a crucial part in their own defeat, but Ru saw it right away. If we had been allowed to go home unmolested, we would not have known about the northern army, nor gone to Elen's house, nor caused Elen to send out her army, to deal them such a dreadful blow.

"Well?" said Fodla. "What happened? What did they do with you?"

"They took me to their encampment," said Maara.

"And Tamras?"

"They let her go."

"Why would they do that?"

Maara said nothing. She couldn't answer Fodla without revealing what she would have preferred to keep to herself.

"Maara bought my life with hers," I said.

"Hush," said Maara.

"Nothing else we say will make any sense unless they know that," I told her. "And soon enough Finn's tale will find its way to our campfires."

Maara sighed. "All right," she said.

"I know you have all wondered where Maara came from and why she left her home," I said. "Before she came to us, she lived in a place called Elen's house. Elen married, but she soon found her husband an inconvenience. She murdered him and made it appear that Maara was the murderer."

"Wicked," Sparrow whispered.

"Elen helped Maara to escape, not to save her life, but so that when she was caught, her flight would witness to her guilt. But she wasn't caught. She found her way to us instead."

I took time to look at the faces around the circle. I had their complete attention, as I unraveled the mystery of Maara's past.

"Maara knew that Elen would have to reward anyone who brought her back," I said. "She told the northerners she would lead them to Elen's house, if they would let me go."

I saw with satisfaction that every person there felt the touch of shame. The woman they had thought so little of, if they had thought of her at all, would have died to send me home to them.

"Did you agree to this?" Fodla asked me.

"I knew nothing about it," I replied. "Maara spoke to the northerners in their own tongue. Then she told me to go home, that she had something of value to offer them. She told me she would follow me."

"But she didn't mean to, did she?"

"No," I said. I glanced at Maara, who sat motionless, silent as a stone beside me. "I'm still angry with her about that."

"You didn't go," said Sparrow.

"No. It took me longer than it should have, but at last I guessed what she had done. She had told me about her time in Elen's house and that she had been accused of killing Elen's husband. The price on her head was the only thing of value she had to offer."

"Would you have gone to your death unresisting?" Fodla asked her.

"I kept my word," Maara said. "I led the northerners to Elen's house, and they were well rewarded for their trouble. After that I would have done all I could to save my life."

Fodla nodded. "Well done," she said.

I couldn't make up my mind if she was speaking of Maara's sacrifice or her determination to survive or both.

"What did you do?" Sparrow asked me.

"I followed them," I said. "By the time I caught up to them, they had joined a large encampment. At first I thought it was a base camp, a place from which to send out raiding parties, a place to which they could return with their wounded and their spoils, but it was so vast. Once I thought it over, there was only one explanation. They were gathering an army."

"How many were there?" Fodla asked.

"More than I could count."

"More than we were this morning?"

"Many more."

While I wondered how to explain to them why I hadn't turned back at once to warn them, Maara said, "When I saw that encampment, I knew what they intended, and I knew why. Tamras saw them from a distance. I walked among them. It was not want that set their hearts against us. It was grief."

"Do you believe they meant to do more than plunder?" Fodla asked.

"They meant to conquer," Maara said. "They made no secret of it."

I glanced at Ru. The grim look on her face told me Maara was right. All of this was news to me. I wished for time enough to hear Maara tell me everything that had happened to her during the time we were apart.

"What did you do then?" Fodla asked me.

Was she asking why I didn't return to Merin's house with a warning?

"My heart chose for me," I told her. "I followed Maara."

"Of course," she said. "But how did you follow her once she was lost among so many?"

"I knew where she was going. I believed I could find Elen's house myself, but I was wrong. I got lost in the forest, and I would be wandering there to this day if a hunter hadn't found me."

I paused for a moment, remembering my extraordinary luck.

"The fates were kind to me that day," I said. "The hunter knew the bow I carried. It is the bow that killed Eramet. Maara and I found it on the body of the man who killed her, the man Vintel murdered."

"Vintel murdered him?" Fodla asked. "When was this?"

"When she escorted Merin's prisoners to our northern border."

"I didn't know that," Fodla said.

"I did," said Sparrow. "Vintel told me she had avenged Eramet. She thought I would be pleased."

"Were you?"

Sparrow shook her head. "I took no satisfaction from it."

"What happened when the hunter found you?" Fodla asked me.

"When he recognized the bow, he brought me the brother of the man to whom it once belonged. His name is Finn, and he remembered me, because I helped the healer tend his brother's wound. I told him someone dear to me was held hostage in Elen's house and asked if he would lead me there. He did more than that. He sent for the others who had been our prisoners. Bru, the man you met this evening, is their chieftain. They have stood by me ever since and done all they could to help me. They have never forgotten what we did for them. They call Merin's house the house of kindness. It is a name we might aspire to be worthy of."

I expected Fodla to object, but she only knit her brows and glanced at Ru out of the corner of her eye.

"The next morning," I said, "they escorted me to Elen's house."

I brought a picture of the place into my mind and described it as best I could. I tried to do it justice. Anyone would see it as a lovely place, prosperous and safe, though I would always think of it with bitterness and regret. I told them how Finn and I went down into the valley and how I gained admittance to Elen's great hall. Then I stopped.

Maara leaned her shoulder against mine. "Tamras will claim she has no idea how it all came about," she said. "Perhaps she was guided by the fates, or perhaps it was her own cleverness that saved us. Whichever it was, her plan freed me from captivity and sent an army to defeat your enemies."

Maara paused to enjoy the silence of anticipation, as her listeners waited to hear how it was done.

"It was the simplest of plans," she said. "Tamras told Elen that an army of the northern tribes had gathered on her eastern border. I know Elen, and I know how she heard that news. She wouldn't believe they intended to make war on anyone but her. Tamras saw what she believed and encouraged her to believe it. Because a band of northerners had brought me to her only a few days before, Elen assumed I must be involved in their plot, though what good I could have done them as Elen's prisoner I can't imagine. At any rate, when Elen led her warriors out against the northern army, she took me along with them as a hostage."

"And what of Tamras?" Fodla asked. "Did she take Tamras too?"

"Elen locked me up," I said, "but I escaped. I left Elen's house in the middle of the night and went to the place where Finn was waiting for me. Bru and his men were there too when I arrived. In the morning we followed Elen's army to the battlefield."

"Did you see the battle?" Sparrow asked me.

"We were a day too late," I replied. "We saw only the dead."

"Were you a witness to it?" Ru asked Maara.

"No," she said. "Elen kept me under guard in this encampment."

"So you were still Elen's prisoner," Fodla said.

"I was," said Maara. "I remained her prisoner until the next morning, when Tamras and her companions arrived with the northern chieftains."

Then I had to explain how we made the northerners our allies, and I took some time to describe all the different factions and why they were there—the young king and his men, the common folk, the prisoners and the remnant of the northern army—as well as a little about Bru's people and the story of their exile. Finally I told them how Bru provoked Elen's anger against the young king.

"Once the mighty were divided," I said, "Bru and the common folk, with the help of the northern army, dealt Elen her defeat."

"When did all this happen?" Fodla asked.

"Yesterday," I said.

"What became of Elen?"

"I imagine she is seeking refuge among her kinsmen in the north."

"And the fate of Elen's house?"

"It's Bru's house now."

"And Bru and his people are your allies?"

I nodded.

"So when you learned our army was approaching, you persuaded the northerners to join your alliance against us."

"Not against you," I said. "Against Vintel. And I would not have permitted them to harm any of you."

"She was most convincing on that point," said Ru.

Fodla scowled at me. "What would have happened if Merin's people had made a different choice this morning?"

"Bru would have welcomed me," I said, "and I would have been glad to join his household."

"And the northerners?"

"They would have been free to choose."

Fodla turned to Ru. "And now?" she asked. "What will your people choose to do?"

Ru gazed at me for a moment before she turned to Fodla with her answer.

"Tamras offered us the friendship of Merin's house if we would help her to regain her place there," she said. "We will expect her to keep her promise."

Nothing more was said about the part I had played in the defeat of the northern army. One by one my friends, their curiosity satisfied, excused themselves and went to bed. When Ru got up to leave us, Fodla joined her, and the two of them wandered off together into the night. At last only Maara and Sparrow remained with me by the council fire.

"Is it possible that Ru isn't angry?" I asked Maara.

"Why would she be angry?" Sparrow said. "You did what anyone would do. You defended your own."

"Then perhaps she understands," I said.

Maara chuckled. "I think she understands that it's dangerous to be your enemy."

"And advantageous to be your friend," said Sparrow.

I smiled at her, but my smile turned into a yawn.

"It's past your bedtime," Sparrow said.

"You're welcome to join us in our tent," I told her.

But Sparrow shook her head. "If you two were reunited only yesterday, you must have a lot to talk about."

She started to get up, then stopped. "Oh," she said. "I almost forgot."

She took something from the pocket of her tunic and handed it to Maara. Maara held it in the palm of her open hand and gazed at it. It was the token Namet gave her on midsummer's day.

"Thank you," she whispered.

I had last seen it in Vintel's hands.

"How did you persuade Vintel to give it up?" I asked Sparrow.

"I didn't," she replied. "I found it hidden among her things."

"Does she know?" asked Maara.

"Oh, yes," Sparrow told her. "I ran across it not long after you left us. I told Vintel I meant to keep it, so that she could never deny her responsibility for what happened to you. I don't know what prompted me to bring it with me, but this morning I was glad to have it. If Merin's people had doubted Tamras when she accused Vintel, I would have used it."

Sparrow turned to me.

"I make no excuses for Vintel, but I want you to know that she regretted what she did. If she acted without thinking, she thought better of it in the morning. She went north to find you and bring you back, and met her own warriors coming home. When they told her you were dead, she had to make the best of it."

"Did you stay with Vintel as her apprentice?"

Sparrow shook her head. "I told her my apprenticeship was over, and she saw it was no use to argue with me. She let me go and awarded me my shield."

Sparrow answered my unspoken question. "We have not been again what we once were to each other," she said. "I could never have forgiven her."

96

HOME

I woke early, before first light. Maara was awake already. When I tried to slip back into sleep, she wouldn't let me.

"We need to make our plans," she said.

I snuggled closer and whispered in her ear, "I'd prefer to be doing something else."

"There will be time for that," she said, "but not now."

Still I refused to let her go. "Can't we make our plans in bed?"

"All right," she said.

Though she sounded reluctant, her arms tightened around me.

"I think we should let Fodla choose which of the northerners to bring home with us," said Maara. "She will insist on giving us the benefit of her experience anyway, so she might as well take the responsibility."

"Bru made a promise to them too," I reminded her.

"Let them take what remains of Elen's supplies. There is still beef on the hoof and oil and flour in the wagons. After we take what we'll need for our journey, the northerners can have what's left."

"And the young king?"

"Let's be generous with him too. He is in want of no more cattle, but a cart to bear him home would be a kindness. If you were to offer him the friendship of Merin's house, I think he would be glad to accept it."

"Is that why he joined us yesterday?"

"Partly," she replied. "He also meant to show you that he had taken your advice to heart."

"My advice?"

"Not to seek revenge."

It took half the morning, but at last we had everyone sorted out and ready to travel. After consulting with Ru, Fodla chose three of the northern chieftains, who, with the warriors of their households, would accompany us to Merin's house. Altogether they would be about three hundred, enough to allow them to feel safe but not enough to cause trouble. Fodla invited the wolfskin chieftain, despite Ru's warning that his had been the loudest voice opposing our alliance.

"That's why I want him," Fodla told her. "If we can win his trust, he will persuade the others who are reluctant."

The young king gratefully accepted the offer of several carts and the oxen to draw them, so that he and all his wounded could be taken home in some comfort. He and Bru, though lacking a common language, had by signs and gestures each extended the offer of friendship to the other. If Elen or her kin someday posed a threat to either of them, it would be wise of them to stand together. Whether Bru had thought of it or not, fostering his son with me would enable the boy to learn our language, so that when he returned home, he could serve as an interpreter with both the people of my household and the people of the young king's.

Before the young king left us, Maara and I went to bid him farewell. I told him he would always find a welcome in Merin's house, and though such offers are usually politely accepted, then soon forgotten, I had an idea that someday he would appear on Merin's doorstep. He asked Maara if she remembered the way to his house, and she assured him that she did, and that if we ever came north again, perhaps to visit Bru, we would be honored to accept his hospitality.

I hadn't seen Finn since early the day before. When Bru came to tell me that Vintel's warriors and their escort were ready to march, I asked him if Finn would be coming with us.

"He wouldn't miss it," Bru replied. "When he comes home again, he will have tales enough to last him all his life."

We agreed that Vintel and her warriors should follow behind us and keep a little distance from us, even when we camped for the night. Many of Merin's people had friends among them, and I wanted no one to be tempted to offer any of them a welcome. In my eyes, they were all as guilty of treachery as Vintel. They had come to Merin's house, not just as allies, but as guests, and they had betrayed Merin's hospitality.

Sparrow asked me if she should have the tent taken down and brought home with us. I told her to leave it where it was. I wanted to bring nothing with me that reminded me of Elen.

At last we got the multitudes moving in more or less the right direction. Maara insisted that we lead the way, though she sent scouts ahead of us so that we wouldn't stumble into trouble. My guard, of course, was never far away from me. Sparrow and Taia walked with us.

"How many days are we from Merin's land, do you think?" I asked Sparrow.

She and Taia consulted with each other. Sparrow thought a week, but Taia believed five days would be enough to bring us there.

"The way is always shorter going home," she said.

It didn't seem all that short to me. Even with friends to talk to, to pass the time, the days seemed endless. Soon all my friends had heard several times over every one of my adventures that I chose to tell, and I had heard every scrap of news of Merin's land that they could think of. When I could manage to ignore the army following along behind us, it almost seemed as if we were just a band of Merin's warriors, traveling the frontier in search of cattle raiders. And as the time went by, I felt more and more at home with them.

One night we camped in a place that I remembered. We had camped there once before, on our first day in the wilderness, when we went to the frontier with Vintel.

"If we start early," I said to Maara, "we might be home tomorrow night."

"Day after tomorrow will be soon enough," she said. "We'll need time to set up an encampment, and to greet the people of Merin's house. You will have this homecoming only once. Let's do it properly."

"I don't care about properly," I told her. "I want to go home."

"You'll care later," was all she said.

Without seeming to exercise her own authority, Maara imposed some order on what might have been unmanageable chaos. To those of Merin's captains she considered most friendly to us, she assigned some important task or appointed them to a position of responsibility. They took their duties seriously. They knew that if they did well, they would be asked to join the new leadership in Merin's house.

Fodla took upon herself all dealings with the northerners. She traveled and camped with Ru and the three chieftains, and used the time to become better acquainted with them. She was the last person I would have chosen for a mission of diplomacy, but she seemed to be having some success. I believe her frank manner met with their approval. She managed to wrap her tongue around a few simple words of their language. Once or twice I heard laughter coming from their campfire, inspired by Fodla's misadventures of interpretation.

Laris and Kenit were busy keeping track of the warriors belonging to Merin's allies. Whether they would remain loyal to Merin was still uncertain, but I hoped they would stay on in Merin's house until midsummer, so that I would have a chance to get to know them, and they to know me. Laris agreed to stay, to show them that, even without Vintel, Merin had the loyalty of other houses just as strong. Kenit too volunteered to stay until his son was a year older, and Taia thought her family could spare her for another year.

The next day we stopped early in the afternoon.

"How long will Vintel stay in Merin's house?" Sparrow asked Maara.

"No longer than can be helped," Maara replied. "She will be given time to take her leave of Merin. Then I want her gone. It will be difficult enough to keep the peace between Merin's people and the northerners."

Sparrow looked a little sad, but she understood. Nothing would suit Vintel better than a breaking of the fragile peace.

"If you want to spend tonight in Vintel's encampment," I said, "I understand."

Sparrow shook her head. "I'll walk with her tomorrow."

Then she leaned toward me and whispered something in my ear.

Later that night Maara asked me what Sparrow had said.

"It's a secret," I told her. "You'll find out in the morning."

Maara had me up before first light.

"We're going on ahead," she said. "Just you and me."

I wasn't unwilling, but I wanted to know why.

"So that you can have a few quiet moments with Merin and your mother."

Now that we were within the boundaries of Merin's land, Maara was willing to leave my guard behind. The night before, she had left instructions for them to stay with Laris and Taia, who would lead the army in my absence. We had a start of half an hour, and anticipation lightened my step. We could hope for at least an hour of peace and quiet before we had to deal with their arrival.

The rising sun revealed the beauty of Merin's land in springtime. After the darkness of the forest and the drab shades of the wilderness, the tender green of leaf and grass, the sparkle of sunlight on the river, the open sky, the blooming earth, made this place the loveliest of any I had ever seen. This was home.

I had taken for granted that I would always find a welcome here until my exile taught me otherwise. It made my homecoming all the sweeter, to have back again what I had lost. I wondered how I could have been so willing to remain with the forest people or to join Bru's household. This was the place I belonged to, as it belonged to me.

By midmorning we were within sight of Merin's house. The countryside was deserted. On such a beautiful spring day, people should have been out of doors, working on the practice ground or bathing in the river.

"Where is everyone?" I asked Maara.

"Behind us. Every able body would have gone with Vintel's army."

Then I caught sight of someone on the trail. A moment later she caught sight of us, and she lifted the long skirt of her gown as she hurried toward us. I wouldn't have known who it was if not for what Sparrow had told me the night before, but Maara knew her right away.

"It's Namet," she said, and before I could reply, she ran to meet her.

I dawdled a little, to give them a few moments alone together. When I reached them, Namet let go of Maara long enough to embrace me.

"Your mother is beside herself," Namet told me. "She refused to believe the worst had happened, but I know she was as terrified as I was. Even if you were living, we didn't know if we would ever see either of you again."

Namet wiped a few tears from her eyes with her sleeve.

"Is this Sparrow's surprise?" Maara asked me, while Namet composed herself.

"Yes," I said. "She told me last night that when she sent the messenger, she told him to be sure Namet was sent for, so that she would be here in time to welcome her daughter home."

"That was kind of her," said Maara.

"Yes," murmured Namet. "Very kind."

Namet knit her brows, as if she found it difficult to credit Sparrow with such an act of kindness. I hoped she might now be willing to reconsider her opinion of someone she had misjudged.

But Namet had no time to think of Sparrow. She was busy looking Maara over.

"How did you survive the winter?" she asked. "Were you hungry? Were you cold?"

Maara assured her that we had been comfortable and well fed. She answered Namet's doubtful look with the revelation that we had spent the winter among the forest people.

Both Namet and I let out exclamations of surprise.

Maara looked at me. "I think we can trust Namet with this news," she said. "Don't you?"

"Of course," I said.

"And Merin and your mother."

I smiled at her. "I'm glad to hear you say so. I've never been able to keep a secret from my mother."

"I can hardly wait to hear this wonderful tale," Namet said, "but first we must bring Tamras home."

Where the trail was wide enough, Namet walked between us, and where it narrowed, she gestured to Maara to go ahead, so that she wouldn't lose sight of her. From time to time I saw her reach out and touch Maara's arm, as if to reassure herself that she was real, and not a wraith conjured by grief and wishful thinking.

When we grew near to Merin's house, I saw that the place wasn't quite deserted. Two young women were sunning themselves in a meadow by the river. As lovers do, they saw nothing but each other. One was sitting up, gazing down upon her beloved, who lay with her head in her lover's lap. The sight of the two of them together, content in the warmth of springtime and in each other's company, made me long for the time when I was as innocent as they.

When I would have turned aside onto the path that led up the hill to Merin's house, Namet stopped me.

"Where are you going?" she asked.

"To find my mother," I replied.

"Do you not see her there, waiting for you?"

I looked up, thinking she might be keeping watch from atop the embankments.

"Not there," said Namet. "There." And she pointed to the two young lovers. They were both sitting up now. It was Merin and my mother.

This time Maara and Namet stayed behind while I ran on ahead. By the time I reached them, they were both on their feet. My mother seized me and held me at arm's length and scowled at me, as if she suspected that I might be an imposter. Then she drew me into an embrace that nearly squeezed the life out of me. When she finally let go, I gasped for breath.

Merin had hung back while my mother greeted me. Now my mother drew her into our embrace, a gentler one this time, and we stood like that, with our arms around each other, until Maara and Namet joined us.

While my mother wiped her tears away, Merin turned to Maara and embraced her with a warmth I would not have thought her capable of. I didn't know whether Maara or I was more surprised.

Then Merin turned to Namet. "You were right, Mother," she said. "I should have trusted your far-seeing eye."

"It was not my far-seeing eye that gave me hope," Namet replied. "I have always been unwilling to believe bad news." She turned to me. "And Tamras promised that she would bring my daughter back to me. I've never known her not to keep her word." She stood beaming at me until I felt myself blush.

"Perhaps we should sit down here a while," Maara said, "so that we can tell you what has happened."

There was a moment of confusion, while our mothers decided whether they would rather sit beside us so that they could hold on to us, or across from us so that they could get a good look at us. They finally did a bit of both. We sat down in a circle. Merin and my mother settled me between them, and my mother invited Maara to sit at her other side. Namet took the place between Maara and Merin.

I looked across the circle at Maara, hoping she would begin. I had told the story so often I was tired of it, but every time she told it, I heard something new.

Maara began with the night Vintel took her captive. Most of it they knew already, because Sparrow had held nothing back from them. They knew that I had killed one of Vintel's warriors and that Vintel's warriors claimed they had killed us.

"I never believed it," Namet said. "It could have been Vintel's lie, to cause us to lose hope. Or it could have been her warriors' lie. They would have said anything to keep on the right side of Vintel." She turned to Maara and took her hand. "I was afraid, because I knew you were in danger, but I never believed you dead. By a sense I can't explain, I felt the world still held you in it. I felt you in this world alive."

Something in her voice made me wonder if she had felt Eramet leave this world, even before word reached us.

Our mothers were anxious to learn how we had survived the winter. Maara made it into an amusing tale. They listened, enchanted, to our stories of the forest people. Namet asked question after question, wanting to know everything about them, and I suspected she would have liked to make a second journey beyond the wilderness, to see them for herself.

Maara said nothing of my illness that winter. There was enough in the story of our adventures to alarm them without relating troubles they didn't need to know about. As she told of our capture by the northerners, our dealings with Elen, the gathering of the armies and their encounter on the battlefield, they all grew very quiet. No one interrupted or exclaimed out loud. They held their breaths as they held their tongues, so that Maara would leave nothing out.

It took Maara so long to explain about all the armies and their factions—about Bru and the others who had once been Merin's prisoners, about Elen and her army, about the young king and his men, about the common folk and the mighty—that I heard the faint tramp of feet before she got to the part about our alliance with the northern tribes and Vintel's defeat. Maara heard them too.

"We should go now," she said, "and prepare to greet the army."

Merin looked puzzled. "Is Vintel returning already?" she asked.

"Vintel and all the others," Maara replied. "I thought Sparrow sent a messenger with the news."

My mother put her arm around my shoulders and pulled me close against her side. "He told us they had found you both alive and that you would soon be coming home," she said. "Then he went on and on about armies and battles and alliances with folk we'd never heard of. He counted even the northern tribes among our allies, and then we knew he must be talking through his hat."

The tramp of feet grew louder. All of us stood up and turned to face the north, as the first ranks of the army came into view. They were too many to keep to the narrow trail. They flowed like a river through the hills, filling the clefts between, where the slopes were gentle, surging over the crests of the lowest hills and spilling down the hillsides.

"What the messenger told you was true," said Maara. "Every warrior you see, and many more to come, have pledged their loyalty to Tamras. Among them you will find three chieftains of the northern tribes with the warriors of their households, who have come to court the friendship of Merin's house."

Namet shaded her eyes and watched as more and more of my army revealed itself. She didn't seem surprised. She smiled a little secret smile, as if this was something her far-seeing eye had already witnessed.

Merin and my mother stared at the army in astonishment. Then my mother turned to me. On her face was an expression of surprise that quickly turned to pride.

Merin's expression had more amusement in it. "So," she said. "I see there is no question now of your adoption. If you have come to conquer, I will gladly offer you my sword."

Merin was teasing me, but her voice had a solemn note in it, and I believe she would have offered me her sword before the entire household, if I had asked for it.

"I always intended to return authority to you," I told her.

"Do you believe I will accept it?"

Merin still had a teasing twinkle in her eye, but behind her words I heard her wish that she could settle the burden of her authority on someone else's shoulders.

"You had better decide which one of you it will be," said Maara, "because very soon someone will have to take charge of them."

"You are my right hand," I told her. "You can take charge of them. You've done a splendid job of it so far."

"Then let us go to meet them," she said, taking charge of us as well. "You and Merin will welcome them together."

97

The Battle of the Wilderness

W hile we climbed the hill, Maara related the rest of the story. She hurried through it, because already the people of Merin's house, alerted by watchers on the ramparts, were gathering outside the earthworks to witness the arrival of the army. They had expected to see Vintel's warriors coming home. Instead they beheld an army twice the size of the one that had set out. Some stared in wonder, while others grew fearful that Vintel had been defeated and these were our enemies, come to conquer.

Everyone was so intent upon the sight of the approaching warriors that they didn't notice Maara and me until we had almost reached them. Then they surrounded us and assailed us with questions. Servants and elders, companions too young and inexperienced to accompany their warriors to the battlefield, even country people who had taken refuge in the fortress, demanded to hear the news. The Lady raised her arms to ask for silence. When they were quiet she addressed them.

"As you can see," she said, "our lost children have come home. There is a lot to tell you, but it will have to wait, because we have much to do. All I have time to say is this. My daughter Tamras has won the victory in the north, and to her we owe our great good fortune. Go now and prepare a welcome for our guests."

Reluctantly they obeyed her, though they lingered long enough to eye me with doubtful curiosity. The elders went back inside with the servants to oversee the preparations, all but Fet. She stood apart, her eyes searching for one among the multitudes. I went to stand beside her and pointed to the northerners.

"There," I said. "Do you see the warriors of the northern tribes?"

Fet nodded. "I see them."

"She walks beside their chieftains."

Fet knit her brows, then smiled when she found Fodla. Without another word to me, she started down the hill to meet her.

I had not yet seen my sister Tamar. I asked my mother if she was still in Merin's house.

"She must be inside," my mother replied. "She has been caring for old Gnith."

I felt the icy breath of fear. "Is Gnith unwell?"

"A touch of winter sickness. Only a touch, but at her age, a touch of anything is dangerous."

Maara was already consulting with Merin about where the army would establish its encampment. I told her I was going into the house, to find my sister and to pay my respects to Gnith.

I found Gnith alone, sleeping soundly on the hearthstone in the kitchen. I sat down beside her. The silence of the empty kitchen was a relief after the commotion out of doors. I leaned back against the oven, still warm from the morning's baking. I closed my eyes.

At once Gnith joined me, as if we had both stepped through the veil of sleep into the same dream. *It's never what you expect,* she whispered into my ear.

She touched my brow, and I was in the dark. Deeper than the dark of the cave of running animals where I joined the hunters of the forest people, deeper than the dark of Elen's dungeon where I gazed into the abyss where love is powerless, deep in the dark there is a secret.

"Worn out, poor thing," said Gnith.

Someone touched my arm. I opened my eyes and saw my sister and several of the kitchen servants hovering over me. Gnith was wide awake and sitting up.

"Get her a bite to eat," said Gnith, and Tamar went at once to bring me a bowl of barley soup. When I took it from her hands, I saw the question in her eyes, as well as her reluctance to ask it.

"You will find Sparrow with Vintel," I said. "They will be the last to arrive."

Tamar still looked uneasy.

"She's fine," I said. "Everyone is fine."

"Are you fine too?"

"Fine as frog's hair," I told her.

She laughed, remembering, and sat down to watch me eat.

While I ate, Gnith looked me over. She plucked at my strange clothing, my deerskin trousers and Elen's fine linen shirt.

"Been gone far away," she murmured. "We went too."

The kitchen began to fill with busy people. Gnith lay back down, to take another nice long nap, she said. Tamar went outside to welcome Sparrow, and I went with her, because with Sparrow would come Vintel.

The army, accustomed to living in the field, had set about establishing an encampment outside the earthworks. Merin's captains, who could have sought the comfort of their own quarters indoors, remained with our guests, to see that they were well cared for, and no doubt to impress upon Maara their fitness for leadership. Though they had acclaimed me, it was Maara they looked to for direction, as they had once looked to Merin's right hand, Vintel.

The Lady, with my mother beside her, was overseeing the activity from a vantage point just outside the earthworks. She still looked frail. She leaned on my mother's arm, as much for support as from affection, yet she looked happier than I had ever seen her, with color in her cheeks and a smile for all who approached her. My mother too had changed—strong as ever, cheerful as ever, but not as restless, content to stand still right where she was, as if she had settled at last into a deep contentment.

While my eyes were on Merin and my mother, Tamar's eyes had been searching Vintel's army.

"I see Vintel," she said. "Sparrow isn't with her."

Vintel's warriors, surrounded by Bru's men, waited at the foot of the hill. Bru was standing in Vintel's way, his hand on his sword's hilt, his feet firmly planted, while Vintel berated him and gestured in our general direction. Though neither spoke the other's language, they understood each other perfectly.

Maara saw them too and started down the hill.

"What's he doing?" Tamar asked me. "What's going on?"

"Vintel is leaving," I told her.

"When?"

"Today."

"What for?"

"Vintel is no longer welcome here," I said. "Didn't Sparrow tell you? It was Vintel who drove me out of Merin's house."

Tamar looked puzzled. "Do you mean to tell me that Vintel agreed to go just because you came home?"

"She agreed to go because I defeated her," I said.

Tamar laughed.

I had no time to explain. I watched as Maara approached Vintel. She spoke a few quiet words to Bru, then gestured to Vintel to come with her, and together they started up the hill.

I wanted no more to do with Vintel. Another confrontation would accomplish nothing and might prove dangerous. I took Tamar's arm and drew her aside, so that we were a little distance from the footpath and hidden by the crowd. I kept my eyes on Vintel, to see if she would speak to anyone in passing, but she walked quietly beside Maara until they stood before the Lady.

My mother had vanished. I looked around for her, but she was nowhere to be seen.

"Where did she go?" I murmured.

Though I spoke more to myself than to my sister, Tamar knew who I meant and answered me anyway.

"Our mother won't have Vintel near her," she said. "Whenever Vintel speaks with the Lady, our mother keeps her distance."

I was glad to hear it. I thought I understood why Merin had stayed under the same roof with Vintel. This was her house, after all. And I couldn't fault my mother for staying with her, but it reassured me that my mother and Vintel hadn't been on speaking terms.

"She'll say the right thing," said Maara, who appeared at my side so suddenly that I gave a start.

"Who?" I asked her. "The Lady or Vintel?"

"The Lady," Maara replied. "She's very angry with Vintel, but she knows better than to squander an alliance."

"Will someone explain to me what's going on?" said Tamar.

Maara turned to her. "Your sister has given Vintel leave to go to any other house that will accept her. She intends to return to her sister's house, and it would be a shame if Merin were to lose that alliance."

"My sister gave her leave?"

Maara smiled.

Vintel spoke to the Lady for quite a while. I couldn't tell whether she was making an excuse or an apology, but Vintel did all the talking, while Merin listened with distance in her eyes.

Maara stayed with us and watched. Though she was often interrupted by people asking for instructions, in between her other conversations she told Tamar that I had defeated Vintel's army and that every warrior who would remain in Merin's house had sworn loyalty to me.

Tamar, ordinarily so full of questions, was rendered speechless.

At last Vintel had said all she had to say. She stood silent before the Lady and waited. Merin gazed at Vintel for so long that I knew something unexpected was about to happen. Then Merin placed her hands on Vintel's shoulders, leaned toward her, and kissed her cheek.

"What in the world?" I whispered.

"What indeed?" Maara replied. "Unless. . ."

"Unless what?"

"When Vintel claimed she would never betray her oath to Merin, I think she meant it."

"But Vintel did betray her."

"Let's think about it," Maara said. "Merin and Vintel have known each other almost all their lives. When Merin was a young woman, Vintel was a child here, a child who showed great promise. After her mother died, who would she have looked to for protection, even for love."

I slipped back through time and saw Merin and Vintel as they must have been after the war with the northern tribes. Each had suffered an unbearable loss. Their shared experience explained so much — their mistrust of strangers, their attitude toward Namet, the way they kept her at a distance, because she had suffered so little from what she had helped to bring about. Merin and Vintel had many things in common then, and each had needed someone. Merin's need was to be needed, but Vintel had needed so much more, and a mother most of all.

Now I understood. When Merin chose me to be her heir, Vintel had been disinherited, but it was never Merin's power that she wanted.

Vintel took Merin's hand and kissed it. Then she turned away and started back down the hill. On her face I saw the pain of that parting, and my heart ached with what she must be feeling — the humiliation of defeat, the loneliness of exile, and the loss of everything she loved. So keenly did I feel it that I was tempted to offer her a place with me.

Maara stepped between me and Vintel and took me firmly by the shoulders. "Don't let her see a look like that," she said.

I nodded, but I couldn't speak. Maara stayed where she was until I no longer needed a shield between myself and Vintel's pain. Then she stood aside, and we watched as Vintel made her way down the hill alone.

Vintel's warriors were impatient to continue their journey. Their companions had been taken into Merin's house, to gather up all their belongings, and Maara had offered a cart to carry them, along with supplies enough to last for several days. After that they would have to rely on the hospitality of others.

Many of Merin's warriors went down to see them off, and Vintel spoke a few words with each of them before she took her place at the head of the column. The companions shouldered their packs, and the warriors took up their shields. Before Vintel took up her shield, she turned to take a last look back. At once her eyes found what she was looking for, a lone figure standing on a knoll halfway down the hill. Beside me Tamar made a soft sound, a catch of breath, as if she feared that Sparrow would answer the invitation in Vintel's eyes. But Sparrow stayed where she was, and at last Vintel turned away and led her warriors down the river road.

Tamar would have run to Sparrow then, but Maara caught her arm.

"Not yet," she said.

Sparrow watched Vintel out of sight. When she turned to come up the hill, Maara let Tamar go.

Their embrace told me what I already suspected. Nor did it surprise me to discover that Tamar had become Sparrow's apprentice.

"She wouldn't take no for an answer," Sparrow told me.

I wasn't sure which thing she meant until I saw Tamar blush. I remembered with some bitterness the little girl who would make off with one of my treasures, not because she wanted it, but because it amused her to deprive me of it. But Sparrow wasn't mine.

Bru and his men, relieved of their responsibility for Vintel, came up the hill and set up their camp. I offered them more comfortable accommodation in the men's house, but they said they preferred to be out of doors. I think none of our former prisoners wished to return to the place of their captivity.

Fodla took charge of settling the warriors of the northern tribes. With Fet at her side, she issued orders to folk who couldn't understand them while at the same time telling Fet all about her great adventure.

After taking a meander through the crowd to say a few words of welcome, Merin went inside to rest a while, and my mother went with her. Sparrow and Tamar slipped off by themselves. Maara seemed to be everywhere at once, but whenever I arrived at the place where someone had last seen her, she had already left for someplace else.

The first excitement of the army's arrival was over. Now everyone had work to do. No one paid any attention to me. That was nothing new. Before I left Merin's house, I was only an apprentice, beneath their notice. Now they ignored me for a different reason. Six months before, I would have been scurrying about with the others, bringing food and drink to our returning warriors and seeing to the comfort of our guests. Several times I tried to help, but whenever I took something up—a breadbasket or a tankard of ale or a stick of firewood—someone would stop me and gently take it from my hands. Though no one was unkind, they made me feel set apart.

I went indoors, thinking I might lend a hand among people who had not yet heard the story of Vintel's defeat, but news traveled in that household more swiftly than the plague, and it seemed there was no one left in Merin's house who hadn't heard in some detail everything that had happened on the frontier.

The battle already had a name. They called it the battle of the wilderness. At first I thought they meant the battle in which Elen destroyed the army of our enemies, the northern tribes, but it was Vintel's defeat they meant, and my victory.

At last, feeling in the way, I went outside again and wandered down the hill. I intended to go sit by the river, to enjoy a little peace and quiet, to try to feel at home again. As I passed the footpath leading to the oak grove, my feet took me there.

Alone in the circle of the ancient trees, I waited. Nothing happened. I don't know what I expected. In the oak grove I had always felt protected, sheltered, safe from harm within the strong embrace of love that needs no human heart, no human hand. Now I felt nothing. It was a stand of trees spared by the ax of a credulous folk who once worshipped there. It was a stand of ancient trees. That's all.

I trudged back up the hill again. Maara was waiting for me.

"Where have you been?" she said. "Go make yourself presentable. Wash your face and change your clothes. You will sit at Merin's right hand tonight."

She stopped when she saw a tear trickle down my cheek.

"What's wrong?" she asked.

I opened my mouth to answer her. No sound came out of it.

Maara took me gently by the hand and led me inside the earthworks. The front door of Merin's house stood open, but we avoided it and instead made our way around the back and through the kitchen yard into the laundry room. A few servants were heating water there. A look from Maara was enough to clear the tiny room.

"What's wrong?" she asked again.

I shrugged. I couldn't put what I was feeling into words.

"Are you tired?"

I shook my head.

"What is it then?"

"Lonely," I whispered. And she put her arms around me.

No time to talk about it. No time to do more than take refuge in the arms of love again.

"I know it's not the homecoming you wanted," she said. "You have come home to a strange place."

That wasn't it, I thought, but I had no words, and no time. I let her go.

"As long as we're here," she said, "we might as well have a bath."

She handed me a tub and took another for herself. Then we went outside. I would have gone back in to fetch the water, if I hadn't been immediately surrounded. Two of the servants undressed us, while others filled the tubs. By the time they had us well scrubbed, someone else arrived with an armload of clean clothes.

Where they found my few scraps of clothing I could not imagine, but the trousers were certainly mine. I knew them by the mended places, the puckers and uneven stitches made by my clumsy needle. To my surprise they no longer fit me. Too big around the middle, too short to cover my ankles, they gave me the gawky look of a boy growing too quickly into manhood. Maara sent someone to borrow another pair that fit me better.

We entered Merin's house by the back door and elbowed our way through the uproar in the kitchen. Even in the great hall we were in the way. Maara started up the stairs. I thought she might be taking me to our old room, assuming no one else had occupied it, but she stopped at Merin's room and knocked. My mother opened the door and beckoned us inside.

Merin was sitting in a chair by the hearth, her dark hair lying loose over her shoulders. My mother resumed combing it while Maara and I sat down on the hearthstone. As if I had never been away, we talked of little things. I should say the others talked. I listened, while their voices and their laughter wove all around me, like the fabric of a warm cloak, a web of hearts. I snuggled into it and closed my eyes.

98

A Time of Peace

I awoke in Merin's bed. The room was dark. I was alone. A few coals glowed upon the hearth. I got up and blew them into a flame bright enough to see by. Someone had undressed me. My clean clothes hung unrumpled over the footboard of the bed. I put them on, ran my fingers through my hair, and peered out the door.

"There you are!" said Sparrow. "Maara said not to wake you, but they're about to start."

"Start what?"

"Come on!" she said.

The great hall was filled with tables and benches packed so tightly together that, once everyone was seated, I doubted the servants could squeeze between. More benches stood against the walls, to accommodate folk for whom there was no room at table.

Around Merin's high table, at the far end of the hall, was a bit more open space. Two tables were set crossways at either end of it, so that altogether it would seat about two score. Merin and Fodla stood beside it, engaged in lively argument. Sparrow and I joined them.

Merin smiled at me. "I'm glad you're here, as we are at an impasse. Perhaps you will advise us. Where shall we seat everyone?"

"The northern chieftains are our honored guests," said Fodla. "They must have pride of place."

"None of my plans would have succeeded without Bru," I told her. "Those who helped us win the victory should be honored over those who were made to yield."

"That may be so," she replied. "Yet are we not assured of the friendship of Bru and his people? The goodwill of the northern tribes is still in doubt."

"There are three hundred of them," I reminded her. "We could hardly fit all of them into the great hall even if we invited no one else."

"Each of their chieftains has chosen a dozen of his followers. Room for two score is all we need."

"And Bru will bring two dozen," I said.

Fodla scratched her head. "Let's make the table bigger," she suggested.

In the end everyone was satisfied. Two more tables were added to the ones set crossways, so there would be room enough for the northerners at one end and Bru's men at the other. Maara would sit with Bru, to serve as translator. Ru, who was both peace chieftain and go-between, would sit at the other end and translate for the northerners.

Bru and his men were brought in first. That much I insisted on. I hoped the Lady's welcome would assuage any bad feelings that might still linger from their captivity in Merin's house. She did all I could have wished, speaking to each one, taking each one by the hand, and in her simple elegant way, called each one friend and thanked them for everything they'd done for me. So charmed were they that none but Bru could find his tongue. Bru spoke for all of them, assuring her that they had done no more than repay a debt long overdue.

Next came the northern chieftains and their followers, and Merin spoke to each of them, took each one by the hand, until they were as charmed as Bru's men had been. Only the wolfskin chieftain failed to come forward to receive her welcome. He didn't see her gesture. He was staring at the wall over Merin's head. Too late I remembered the shield I had taken, the wolf shield, the spoils of war.

"Ask him if he knew the man who bore that shield," I said to Ru.

She didn't need to ask. She answered for him.

"It is his brother's shield," she said.

The wolfskin chieftain turned to me and asked a question.

"He asks who took it," said Ru.

"I did."

He understood me. I watched his eyes, while he felt again his loss and weighed his grief against the good we were trying to accomplish.

I made the only gesture I could think of. I went to take it down. I had some trouble reaching it, and Maara had to help me wrest it from the wall. Then I offered it to the wolfskin chieftain.

He made no move to take it. He met my eyes. His eyes were fierce, and he was close enough to do me harm.

"Let's not do this anymore," I said.

I waited a long time for his answer. Then he took the shield from my hands.

I don't know how anyone could have made themselves understood over the racket that echoed off the rafters of Merin's great hall. Everyone spoke at once, so perhaps no one felt the need to listen. I didn't even try to carry on a conversation. I smiled politely whenever anyone spoke in my direction while enjoying the best meal I'd had in ages — beef roasted to a turn, bread warm from the ovens, salted cabbage baked with apples, the ale just strong enough.

After the meal the people grew a bit more quiet. They must have been at last too full to talk. Some nodded over empty plates. When the fruit and honey had gone round, Merin stood up and waited for the silence that quickly fell.

"Tonight we welcome friends," she said. "Old friends." She gestured in Bru's direction. "And new friends." She bowed in the direction of the northern chieftains.

"And we have said good-bye to others, who have left us by mutual consent and with no ill will."

She meant Vintel.

"Tonight we stand in enmity to no one. Not even the oldest among us can remember stories of a time when that was so."

She paused and looked around her, at the warriors of her household and then at the elders.

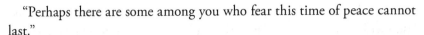

"Perhaps there are some among you who fear this time of peace cannot last."

She waited again. No one answered.

"While it does last, let us enjoy it, and let us learn what it can teach us."

She turned to me and held out her hand, to raise me to my feet.

"And let us learn what Tamras has to teach us, because she is the one who brought it about. Shall we all agree tonight that she has earned the place she was destined for?"

A murmur of assent went round the hall. No one objected.

"Good," she said, and she sat down.

Our visitors stayed for the three days ordained by custom. To my great relief, everyone behaved themselves. No matter what their private thoughts may have been, Merin's people extended to the northern warriors every courtesy. No one questioned my authority as Merin's heir. No one treated Maara with disrespect, and even those who once had snubbed her now sought her good opinion. We heard a few complaints from some of the warriors old enough to remember the war, but Fodla managed to persuade them, if not to trust, at least to tolerance.

The Lady tithed every farm for friendship gifts, and the country people didn't hesitate to offer our former enemies the fruits of their labor if it would guarantee a time of peace. Bru, as heir to the wealth of Elen's house, needed no more than provision for the journey home. To the northerners, I offered a little something over what they usually managed to make off with and told them we would welcome them again at harvest time.

They proved to be a proud people, and as they could no longer exchange their blood for spoils, they offered us instead the few things of value they had with them and pledged to bring more on their return. Some of them wore golden trinkets, finely wrought. These they were pleased to offer to the Lady. Others gave well-crafted knives, belts of tooled leather, ornaments of bone and amber, until I began to think we might be on the better end of the bargain.

One evening Finn persuaded Maara, with Ru's help, to translate for him some of the stories of the northern tribes. I listened, enraptured, to tales of creatures none of us had seen or heard of, to tales of heroes not unlike our own, to tales of adventure and discovery, each one more amazing than the last. I wished we had time to hear them all, and I determined to have Maara teach us what she knew of their language so that when they came to visit us again, we could learn more about them.

As sorry as I was to say good-bye to Bru and Finn and the others, I felt more relief than sorrow when our guests had left us. I wanted time to think and time to feel and time to grow accustomed to being safe at home. After a week or two, the routines of ordinary life began to soothe me into again taking for granted the life I'd lived before my journey into the wilderness.

One morning my mother took me down to the river, for a little private talk, she said. The day was unseasonably warm, and I pulled off my boots, rolled up my trouser legs, and dangled my bare feet in the water.

"Tamar will go home on midsummer's day," she said.

"What?"

"Someone has to go."

I stared at her.

"You can't," she said. "I can't."

"But Tamar is too young. She still has so much to learn."

"Her teacher will go with her."

"Sparrow?"

"Yes," she said. "Sparrow will exercise my authority until Tamar is old enough—and wise enough—to take the place of leadership."

The plan made so much sense that I could think of no way to object to it. My mother was right. We couldn't leave our people leaderless. One of us would have to go home.

"It's best, I think, for everyone," my mother said. "And Tamar will do better there."

I knew what she was getting at. Already Tamar showed signs of resenting my new position. It was one thing to be only an apprentice in a house where your sister was a warrior. It was something else altogether to be subject to her authority. Not even the reflected glory she had once imagined for herself could make up for it.

"And I think it will be good for Sparrow," said my mother.

She was right about that too. For Sparrow it would be an opportunity. Though she was now a warrior, no one in Merin's house would forget that she'd been born a slave. In my little village in the hills, she would be accorded all the respect that was her due.

I had one last hope.

"Has Sparrow given her consent?" I asked.

"Yes," she said.

Because she would soon be leaving, I tried to spend as much time with Sparrow as I could. She had asked me to teach her how to use a bow, and every afternoon we spent an hour practicing.

One day I couldn't keep from making an attempt to change her mind.

"I used to think you were ambitious," I said.

Sparrow turned to look at me. "What are you talking about?"

"Didn't it occur to you that I would have offered you any place you wanted?"

"That has nothing to do with it," she said.

"I don't understand why you want to leave us."

"Tamar can't go home alone," she said.

"That doesn't mean you're the one that must go with her."

"I chose to go with her," she replied. "I want to go."

"Won't you miss Merin's house?"

"Of course."

"And all your friends here?"

"Of course."

"And me?"

Sparrow set her bow down and approached me, and there, on the open hillside, she cradled my cheek in her hand and kissed me. I didn't resist her, but afterwards I glanced around, to see if anyone was watching.

"Even if I stayed," she said, "I would miss you anyway."

And then I understood that I was missing her already, and even if she remained in Merin's house I would miss her as much as if she left it, because I was missing what we could no longer be to each other.

99

THE DANCE

On the morning of the spring festival, I woke in Maara's arms. We had our old room back. Namet claimed her old room too, the one next door. She first asked us if we minded, then assured us that she was growing a little deaf.

It was my favorite time of day, when we would wake before the household and have a few minutes to ourselves before duty called us out of bed. This morning, though, Maara was still sleeping soundly because she had stayed up late the night before, preparing for the holiday. I leaned up on one elbow, to gaze down upon her sleeping face.

A shaft of sunlight slipped over the windowsill and crept inch by inch across the bed. Fairy dust danced in the sunbeam, and everything it touched it turned to gold — the worn wooden bedstead, the faded coverlet, the bronze of Maara's cheek. Before the sunbeam reached her eyes, I turned her face toward me and kissed her awake.

The moment we appeared downstairs the servants whisked Maara away to oversee yet another round of preparations. I wandered into the kitchen and made old Gnith a bowl of tea. She didn't remember that it was a festival day, but she enjoyed the tea. I held the bowl for her while she drank.

"Who are you?" she asked.

"Someone who cares for you," I answered.

I didn't ask a blessing. I already had everything I wanted.

I ate a little breakfast, then settled into a quiet corner in the great hall. Sparrow pestered me to join her and Tamar in the meadow by the river where the young people were gathering, but I sent them on without me. I had not forgotten how free I felt when I kept the holiday with the maidens of Merin's house. We enjoyed our freedom all the more because the people in authority left us to our own devices. Now I was one of the people in authority.

At midday I went out and joined them for the feast. Tamar mumbled something about a question she meant to ask our mother and went inside. Sparrow and I helped ourselves to dinner and sat down to picnic on the hillside.

"Where's Maara?" Sparrow asked me.

"Still indoors," I said. "It seems she always has too much to do."

Sparrow gave me a sidelong look. "Will she come out this evening for the dancing?"

"She will," I said, "if I have to drag her out of the house."

Sparrow laughed. "You suit each other."

I blushed.

"When did you know?" she asked me.

I looked back on the moment when I first beheld my heart's desire.

"It was the night I left Merin's house," I said.

Sparrow had been about to take a bite out of a joint of meat. Instead she set it down and stared at me.

"When did you know?" I asked her.

"Didn't I watch you mooning after her all summer?"

"You didn't say anything to me."

"Of course not," she said. "It wasn't my place to say anything to anybody."

"To anybody? Was it that obvious?"

"To everyone but you," she said.

"And Maara."

"She didn't know?"

I shook my head.

Sparrow knit her brows. "That's odd," she said. "I could have sworn Maara was angry with me."

"When?"

"Last summer. The way she looked at me sometimes, as if she wanted to accuse me."

"Of what?"

"Of holding on to you."

Sparrow took my hand between both of hers and squeezed it.

"Maara was right," she said. "I was holding on to you. I held on to you too long."

I was beginning to wonder what else I might have missed that was right before my eyes.

"I want both of you to know I'm sorry," Sparrow said. "If I had let you go, everything that happened might not have happened."

"Like what?" I asked her.

"Well," she said, "like Vintel's jealousy."

For the first time I thought about what would have happened if Vintel hadn't turned us out of Merin's house.

"If not for Vintel's jealousy," I said, "we would be at war. Or worse."

"Oh," said Sparrow. "I never thought of that."

"It would seem that everything happened for the best," I said.

Had everything happened for the best? It had certainly been best for Merin's house, for everyone in it and everyone protected by it. And how could I regret my time among the forest people or the friendship of Finn and Bru? Nor, I thought, would I give back a moment of the time I spent with Maara in the wilderness—until before my mind's eye came the unwelcome image of Maara in Elen's bed. Of all the days of my exile I regretted only three, three days that had saved the lives of everyone I cared for, three days that had taken from me something I could hardly put a name to.

What I had lost in Elen's house I despaired of ever getting back. I found no one in Merin's house to heal me. My mother advised me to be grateful that Maara and I had been so quickly reunited, and I had before me her example, that she and Merin could set aside twenty years of hurt and misunderstanding.

I had a little better luck with Namet. She understood that it was not my love for Maara that had changed, but something deep within myself. She saw that I had lost the credulity of youth, which we all must lose, so that we can see the world as it is. And she saw that there was something more. When she asked me what else it was that troubled me, the only answer I could give her was that I feared to go again into the oak grove.

So it was there I went.

Under the trees it was cool and quiet. In the distance I heard the shouts and splashes of young people playing in the river, and from time to time a strain of music drifted by. I sat down in the center of the grove. This time I had no expectations.

The oak grove was a pleasant place. Dappled light filtered through the canopy of green above my head, and I lay back on the mossy ground to watch the patterns change. A squirrel scampered along a branch, then stopped for a moment to peer down at me. I watched as it leapt from limb to limb as easily as I would cross a creek on stepping stones.

A sudden gust of wind rattled the leaves. I overheard them whisper their secrets to one another. I couldn't make them out at all.

Perhaps I closed my eyes.

The sky grew dark, as though a thundercloud had swallowed up the sun. Under one tree, a deeper darkness gathered, where Maara had left behind a shadow that dared me to occupy the place where she had felt herself abandoned. I went to sit there. I heard no distant music, no shouts or laughter, no whisper of the breeze, but only the hollow echo of her loneliness.

On that night two years before, I came into a place where I felt love all around me. Maara had felt it not at all. At the time I could not imagine what she was feeling. Now I knew, as if I could inhabit the shade of her, feel the world from inside her skin, behold the world from behind her eyes. It was a feeling not unfamiliar. I had fallen into it before, in Elen's house.

For my beloved I felt a new compassion. How had she reconciled herself to such a feeling?

I knew well the lessons her life had taught her. Hadn't she taught them all to me, so that I could profit from what she had suffered? No wonder she was so determined that I achieve my destiny, because my success gave meaning to her suffering, which would otherwise be wasted, an unproductive labor, that brought forth nothing.

And I also knew what her life had caused her to believe about the world, that we are all alone here, and that though there may be unseen forces at work in it, they are at worst malicious and at best indifferent, oblivious to our joys and sorrows, unconcerned with the strivings of humankind.

My life had taught me just the opposite. Sheltered and comforted from birth by loving hearts and loving hands, I never doubted that the world itself has love at its center, and that in spite of adverse situations and events, ultimately all life is moved by love.

Then I understood. There was not something gone from myself. Something was gone from the world, and to find it I would have to return to where I lost it. I would have to return to the abyss.

I fell, and there were no arms to catch me. I was alone in the power of the deep. Where once I felt the Mother's arms around me, I felt now only the cold, the dark, the lonely place where there are no answered prayers, no hopes fulfilled, no dreams come true.

Yet this is where the hunters of the forest people find their power. They know they are alone, and they accept it. I could not accept it. It seemed too cruel. Were we made to no purpose, destined to wander through our lifetime in search of something we may never find?

What is it that we search for? Every child knows the answer. We search for love. Love is our shelter. Love is our purpose. Love is why we are here.

In the depths of the abyss I stood my ground, ready to do battle, only to find myself abandoned by my adversary. In this lonely place, I had no one to complain to, no one to blame. Instead my own heart became the battlefield, and the adversaries were within me. Within my human heart, hope and fear fought each other to a standstill, and I was caught between, between the hope that someone cares and the fear that no one does.

Someone touched me, took me up from where I lay on the cold ground, and held me fast against her heart.

"I searched for you everywhere," she said.

While I gathered my wits together, Maara let go of me and peered at me in the dim light. She didn't question me. She sat beside me, held my hands, and waited for me.

"When I found you here," I whispered, "what were you feeling?"

"That was long ago," she said.

"Don't you remember?"

"I remember."

"Tell me."

"I felt alone," she said. "I was alone."

"How did you bear it?"

"Not very well," she said.

"I used to feel love here," I told her. "I can't feel it anymore. Love never comes into the oak grove anymore. Just as it never came to you that night."

Maara took my hand in hers, turned it over, caressed my palm, then kissed it.

"No," she said. "That night love did come into the oak grove. That night you came into the oak grove."

She had given me the answer. Sometimes even now I entertain the hope that Love lives in the world independently of us, but when I am most courageous, I believe that love was born within the human heart, and that the survival of love in the world, as well as its ultimate triumph, is entirely our responsibility.

Under the trees it was growing dark. Through the branches I glimpsed the deep red glow of sunset, already fading into night. Music drifted from the meeting ground, where the bonfires had been lit.

Maara stood up and lifted me to my feet.

"Dance with me," she said.

THE END

Ebooks!

The trilogy, *When Women Were Warriors*, is available in multiple ebook formats from Amazon, Barnes & Noble, Kobo, Smashwords, the iBookstore, and other online ebookstores.

Book I of the trilogy is available for FREE in multiple ebook formats from many of these ebookstores and also from the Shield Maiden Press website, shieldmaidenpress.com, and the author's website, catherine-m-wilson.com.

Autographs!

Autographed paperbacks and/or free autographed bookplates can be ordered from the author's website, catherine-m-wilson.com.

ABOUT THE AUTHOR

This picture was taken in 1968, more than 40 years ago, so if you should happen to run across me in real life, don't be disappointed that I no longer resemble the young woman you see here. I have grown old, and although not so cute on the outside, I am much lovelier on the inside.

I chose this photo because in it I am standing by the entrance stone at Newgrange, a megalithic passage tomb in Ireland, built over five thousand years ago. If mysterious portals exist in the world, this is one of them. Many authors will tell you that their stories come from a mysterious place, and when I began to write my trilogy, *When Women Were Warriors*, I suspected that perhaps I had once stepped into another world without knowing it and brought back some ancient long-forgotten tale. Wherever the story came from, it came more through me than from me. I made it from my own life and from my own experience, but I also heard a voice whispering within me that was not quite mine.

Catherine M Wilson
December, 2008
catherine-m-wilson.com